Napoleon's
Drop

Napoleon's Drop

By
Michael Fass

First published in Great Britain in 2020
by Michael Fass, The Coach House, Old Gore, Ross on Wye,
Herefordshire, HR9 7QT

Author's website
www.napoleon-on-st-helena.co.uk

Printed by Biddles Books
www.biddles.co.uk

Cover design by John Fass

Maps by Ian Ward
www.ianrward.co.uk

ISBN printed book 978-1-912804-69-6

Contents

Author's Note

IT IS A MATTER of historical record that there were many attempts by Napoleon's liberal supporters throughout Europe and the Americas to set him free from his remote island jail on St Helena so that he could resume his former life as the head of an elective *Junta* in South America or as a retired country gentleman in England.

Belmullet
Cork
Falmouth
London

Halifax
New York
Baltimore
Washington

Lisbon

Madeira

Freetown

Ascension Island

Potosi

Salvador
de Bahia

St Helena

Buenos Aires
Montevideo

Cape Town

The Atlantic
—World—

Cape Horn

N
W E
S

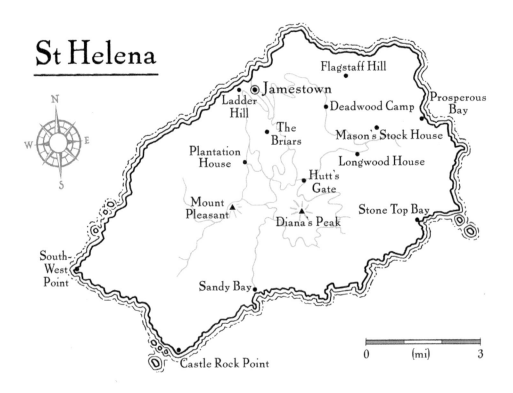

St Helena

Flagstaff Hill

◉ Jamestown

Ladder
Hill

Deadwood Camp

Prosperous
Bay

The
Briars

Mason's Stock House

Plantation
House

Longwood House

Hutt's
Gate

Mount
Pleasant ▲

Diana's Peak ▲

Stone Top Bay

South-
West
Point

Sandy Bay

0   (mi)   3

Castle Rock Point

The River Thames

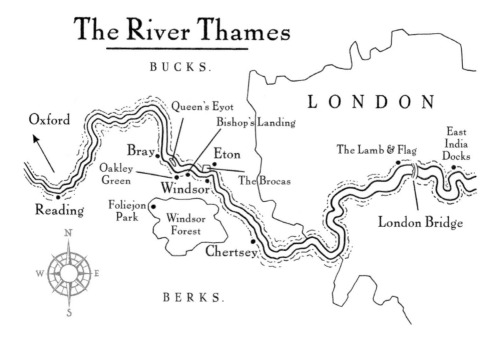

BUCKS.

LONDON

Oxford

Queen's Eyot

Bishop's Landing

Bray

Eton

East India Docks

The Lamb & Flag

Oakley Green

The Brocas

Windsor

Reading

Foliejon Park

Windsor Forest

London Bridge

N

W E

S

Chertsey

BERKS.

Chronology

Cast of Characters

Amherst, Lord, Under-Secretary at the Foreign Office
Balcombe, William, Agent to the East India Company
Birmingham, Alan, Lieutentant, 66th Foot
Bunbury, Sir Henry, Permanent Secretary at the Home Office
Cochrane, Lord Thomas, High Admiral of the Chilean Navy
Crauford, Robert, Director of the Alien Office
Dance, Nathaniel, Captain, the East Indiaman *Ganges*
Dunne, James, Lieutenant, 44th Foot
Du Plessis, Jan, Secret Agent, Simonstown, South Africa
Fielding, John, Chief Magistrate, Bow Street
Fulton, Robert, Inventor of the *Nautilus*
Goldie, George, *Dandy*, Lieutenant, 66th Foot
Goode, Julia, fiancé to Edward Hazell
Hazell, Edward, Assistant-Secretary at the Alien Office
Holland, Lord Henry, leading Whig, House of Lords
Kennedy, Patrick, Irishman of Ballymullen & Buenos Aires
Lowe, Sir Hudson, Governor of St Helena
Marryat, Frederick, Captain, RN, HMS *Beaver*
Napoleon, Bonaparte, ex-emperor of France
Piontkowski, Captain, Aide-de-Camp to Napoleon Bonaparte
Reardon, Rodolphus, *Dolf,* Captain, 66th Foot
Sayer, John, Bow Street runner
Skinner, John, Prisoner Exchange Agent, Baltimore, USA
Townsend, John, Bow Street runner

1 Off St Helena

THE MAN CLOSED the cabin door behind him. He was hurled immediately forward by the wind that caught the tails of his travelling coat and threatened to topple him over the side of the ship.

He grasped the taffrail with both hands and clung onto it as he regained his balance.

It was still pitch dark on the stern deck with only the efflorescence of the wake of the ship providing a dim light.

At five in the morning the *Alnwick Castle's* cabin passengers were still asleep but the sound of the ship in passage was continuous. She was an East Indiaman of 1,400 tons out of Calcutta and homeward-bound for London. Triple-masted and able to deploy a total of up to sixty sails, she had a crew of more than one hundred and thirty. She carried a mixed cargo of tea, cotton and spices for the auction houses of London.

The ship was eleven days out of Cape Town sailing in a north-north westerly direction. At table last night Captain Maxwell had indicated that they would reach landfall on the island of St Helena in the remote South Atlantic at mid morning on the following day.

The man on deck had enjoyed little rest all night as he struggled to decide what he should do when they landed.

His mission to China on behalf of the British Government had ended not just in failure but in ridicule. He was supposed to have made a treaty with the Emperor that would secure exclusive British

1

rights for its trade in the Far East. Instead, because of his refusal to *kow-tow* to his hosts, he was returning to London in disgrace. How his Cabinet colleagues would laugh! The man who had refused to bend his neck for England.

There was movement in the shadow of the deck as an officer of the watch, a midshipman of the Company's Marine, came forward and stood beside him.

"Good morning, your Lordship. I trust you slept well?"

Lord Amherst turned his head to acknowledge the young man's presence, but did not appreciate the intrusion.

"Damned cold morning is what I think. Now good day to you, Sir."

The midshipman saluted and withdrew, leaving Amherst to his thoughts.

The decision he had to take was now a pressing matter if he intended to keep the promises that he had made to certain friends before he had left London eight months earlier. The ship would be at anchor in Jamestown Roads, the island's capital, for a day or two only. If he was to act on their behalf, he would need to do so in the next thirty-six hours.

These *friends* were not of his party and formed the opposition to Liverpool's Cabinet of which he was only a junior member.

The present government vehemently opposed those revolutionary ideas that had finally been destroyed two years ago by Wellington's victory at Waterloo and had adopted a policy of vigorous repression at all attempts to introduce them into Britain.

However, these friends were of the opposite persuasion and believed passionately that, without democratic reform, the level of civil unrest would grow. They thought that this would end in nationwide insurrection of the kind that had recently occurred in the city of Carlisle. Up there, an angry mob had attacked the city's Corn

Exchange, stoned the magistrates and had only been dispersed by the Yeomanry which had been obliged to run the crowd down to restore order.

The friends believed that the symbol of this repression - and its opposite, freedom - was the incarceration of Napoleon on St Helena. They were determined that he should be rescued from his South Atlantic prison.

On his arrival London-bound into Cape Town, Amherst had left the *Alnwick Castle* to dine on board an out-going vessel, the *Ganges*, one of the East India Company's fastest brigs. The vessel was used as a guard ship to protect the slower cargo-carrying East Indiamen from pirates on the high seas. Its captain, Nathaniel Dance, was the senior master of the Company's annual China fleet. Dance was a well-known figure amongst the coffee-house brokerages of Lloyds and the Company's Court of Directors at its head offices in Leadenhall Street in the City of London.

Dance was also connected to a group of wealthy bankers and merchants who had trading interests in both Britain and overseas. A number of these were of Quaker origin and had become increasingly worried that the government's harsh regime would not only lead to further unrest in their cotton mills in the North Country but also damage their foreign trade.

The *Ganges* was twenty-six days out of London and its captain had the latest news of both discussions in Cabinet and of those who opposed its policy in the country.

As Amherst had been rowed across the harbour from the *Alnwick Castle* to the *Ganges* he had wondered at the reason that Dance had asked him over.

Later, as they sat alone together at dinner, he found out.

Dance opened the conversation:

"It won't do your Lordship. The Government is going at this business of the franchise in exactly the wrong way. The more the people are repressed, the greater the danger of insurrection. More and more right-thinking folk look around them for an alternative. They see in Napoleon an icon for their liberty. They want him back either as their king or for an example."

"Good God", surely they don't want Boney back?", Amherst replied.

"Indeed they do", replied Dance, "and a number of your friends wish for your help in achieving it."

"I know I gave undertakings before I left London but what on earth can I do from here?", Amherst exclaimed.

"They have asked me to convey to you a proposal for your part in arranging Napoleon's escape from St Helena, where you will shortly be calling at on your passage home"

"What is it that they want – that is if I agree to such a mad idea?"

Dance leaned forward in his chair and picked up a small hinged box that lay on the table in front of him. Amherst noted that it was made of walnut veneer and was obviously designed to contain something of value.

Dance continued: "Before I set sail from London three weeks ago, I met with your brother-in-law Lord Holland and his colleagues at supper in London. They instructed me to acquire this object on their behalf."

Dance passed Amherst the box and, opening it, he saw that it contained a finely made chess set carved in ivory; each piece mounted in its own dark blue, silk-lined mould.

Dance went on: "The base of one of its pieces – I will not tell you which one so as not to compromise you further than necessary - has been hollowed out. A message addressed to Napoleon has been inserted into it.

All your friends ask you to do is to request the Governor for an audience with Napoleon - which he will not deny as you are a high representative of the Government - and present the chess set to the Emperor. The details of the escape plan are not your concern."

Amherst bit his lip: so, this was what he had promised to his friends all those months ago. He had almost forgotten his last evening in London.

It had been a glamorous and politically charged occasion.

Lord Holland and his friends formed an unofficial opposition to the Government in London. In particular, Holland's wife, Amherst's sister, was in the habit of expressing vehement views in public about Napoleon and his heroic character. He was being treated abdominably, she said, and every right-thinking Englishman should support her husband's petition to Parliament. Napoleon should be released and returned to Europe or wherever else he might wish to go.

Amherst was seated next to her at table as the candlelight flickered in the light of the ornate mirrors that lined the walls of the panelled dining room.

"My Lord", she whispered into Amherst's ear, "surely the Government can see that they are inviting revolution and harming the very cause that they claim to support, which is peace throughout Europe."

"And how could I possibly be of assistance?", Amherst replied. "I am of the party of government, I sit in Cabinet and I am about to go on a year-long journey to the East on its behalf. I have to subordinate any personal feelings that I might have about its position or else I should be considered to be thinking or acting treasonably".

"Oh, William, don't be such a pompous ass", his sister responded. "You know quite well what I am talking about. The Prime Minister holds you in low regard or he would not be sending you on this farcical mission as far away as he can. Look around this dinner table and tell me that your fellow guests are not those who you would call your closest friends and allies. Think of your future and that of your country. We need every individual of feeling to join us in this campaign."

Amherst raised his head and, looking around the table, saw that she was right: these were indeed his dear friends, both personally and politically. The odd man out was William Wickham, the retired spymaster from the Alien Office, who sat at the far end of the table. Presumably he had been invited to dine because he was an old Oxford friend of their host, but he seemed out of place in this company. So far as Amherst was aware Wickham was no friend to any new-fangled ideas about liberty. He had spent much of his professional life opposing such ideas as the Government's chief spy.

"Dear sister, your proposal is potentially treasonable but if I can render a service to you and to our mutual friends I shall of course do so - but within reason."

Now this assurance – given months ago in London - was being called in as Amherst listened to Dance's proposal in Cape Town.

It was true that, as one of His Majesty's ambassadors, if he requested a courtesy visit to the great man, his request would be granted when he arrived at St Helena.

However, there would be risks involved in doing this and hell to pay if what Dance proposed that he should do was discovered by the authorities on the island. It was widely known that its Governor, Sir Hudson Lowe, had imposed the strictest conditions on Napoleon's household and their movements. If anything of this got back to London, his political career would be finished and he would be lucky to escape the rope.

At the recent treason trials in Maidstone, the Government had shown its utter determination to stamp out dissent. On dubious evidence produced by the Alien Office's spies, three Irish conspirators had been hanged. After the trial the Opposition's favourite newspaper, the *Daily Courier*, had made the most of what it described as a political trial and had widened its attack on the Government. This included severe criticism of Napoleon's imprisonment as yet another example of its repression of English liberties.

As dawn broke on the stern deck, Amherst turned back into his cabin. Within the next five hours they would reach the island.

2. *Jamestown Roads*

GOVERNOR SIR HUDSON LOWE and his party arrived early on the quayside at Jamestown as they wished to inspect the jetty before the arrival of the *Alnwick Castle*. Lowe wanted to ensure that the proper arrangements were in place for receiving an important visitor and member of the Government – the first to visit the island under his regime.

As the Governor and Thomas Reade, his deputy, waited, Lowe remarked:

"This jetty can be dangerous, Sir Thomas. The harbour is unprotected and the rollers you can see coming in from the South Atlantic make it notoriously unstable. One of the reasons that the Home Secretary recommended St Helena for Napoleon's prison - quite apart from it being one of the remotest places on earth - is that when the Duke of Wellington visited the island on his way home from India in 1805, the wooden jetty collapsed. The Duke was thrown into the water from which he had to be rescued by a sailor. He loathes the place."

Lord Bathhurst, Secretary of State for the Colonies - and a key member of the Cabinet to whom Lowe was responsible - made clear in all his correspondence that Lowe had absolute discretion in the way he managed Napoleon, the ex-emperor's household, and the island's population.

Napoleon himself, although supposedly kept in the strictest isolation, had found ways to engage in secret communication with his supporters. These included democrats in Britain; those who opposed the restoration of the Bourbon monarchy in France and members of a number of liberation movements in the Americas.

These breaches had occurred in spite of Lowe's security measures. He had introduced a lessee-pass system that only the Governor and his deputy could counter-sign and all correspondence and packages arriving and leaving Napoleon's residence were checked.

However, Lowe remained deeply suspicious of Napoleon's companions in exile. These included his personal servants and a number of key personalities on the island, both military and civil, whose motivations – the Governor believed – were treasonable.

Napoleon's household, whilst riddled with rivalry both above and below stairs, was nevertheless fanatically devoted to its leader. No matter how hard Lowe pressed for information about Napoleon's daily routine, indoor activities, discussions with his staff and all his other domestic arrangements, including the state of his health, the Governor was continually fobbed-off with half-truths, disinformation and downright lies.

It was as if Napoleon was taunting Lowe to do his worst by his captive. There had even been a rumour that the Governor was planning his prisoner's death by poisoning. The Alien Office in London had reported to Lowe that this had probably been put about by Napoleon himself.

"As you know, Sir Thomas, I have intercepted letters to and from Napoleon that have referred to plans for his escape on a number of occasions. I now have my own officer posted as Orderly at Longwood House and I have instructed that he should have direct sight of the prisoner at least twice each day. It's not working, and we now have a farcical game of hide and seek being played between this officer and Napoleon. It just won't do."

Lowe's investigation of letter-smuggling had led to his suspicion of Barry O'Meara as the conduit. O'Meara had been appointed as Napoleon's physician and had travelled with him on the *Northumberland* down to St Helena. The Governor had insisted on O'Meara's court martial and the doctor had been found guilty; dismissed from the Service and forcibly returned to England.

Lowe continued. "Since his return to London in disgrace, O'Meara and other sympathisers have been making trouble for Bathurst and the Government. Of the civilian personalities the most troublesome, in my opinion, is the East India Company's agent on the island, William Balcombe. He is well connected in London and on St Helena and is close to Lord Holland, who leads the opposition to Napoleon's imprisonment in the House of Lords."

Balcombe had served in the Royal Navy before being appointed the East India Company's agent on St Helena which he managed alongside his family-owned business on the island.

Every outward and in-bound vessel sailing to and from the East put in at St Helena for fresh supplies of food and water where they were obliged to purchase what they needed from the Company's stores which were under Balcombe's control.

The Balcombe family lived at *The Briars,* a comfortable house on the island, and had become acquainted with Napoleon on his arrival in October 1816 when the ex-emperor had lived there before his own residence at Longwood House had been made ready by the British for his occupation.

Balcombe's attractive fourteen year-old daughter, Betsy, had befriended Napoleon and had become his particular favourite taking liberties with him allowed to no one else. It was reported that he called her his *bambina* and that they sang songs together as they played hide-and-seek in the garden at Longwood.

Balcombe also managed the Government's annual budget for the upkeep of its prisoner and his household which was another bone of contention between Lowe and the island's local community.

Lowe had a particular suspicion about the supply of wines and spirits made to Napoleon's household by Balcombe's firm that were being consumed at the rate of over two thousand bottles a month which represented over four dozen bottles per head above and below stairs.

Two months earlier this had led to a serious dispute between the Governor; the island's guard regiment, the 66th. and its commanding officer, Colonel Nichol. A soldier coming off duty at Longwood at 9pm, or *gunfire,* the start of the evening curfew, had been stopped at the first guard post beyond the house and was found to be drunk. This was not an uncommon occurrence amongst the troops on the island but, as ill-luck would have it, Reade, the Governor's right-hand man - or crony, as many on the island believed - was going through the same checkpoint after dining with one of his friends and witnessed the incident. The soldier – a corporal – had not only been intoxicated but was also staggering under the weight of an ammunition sack. On inspection, the sack contained nine bottles of good claret that Reade knew had been supplied by Balcombe's firm to Longwood House.

The soldier was placed under close arrest with Sir Thomas threatening a full enquiry the following morning.

The relationship between the Regiment and the Governor had not been good for some time as Lowe believed that both its officers and men had become too close to the household at Longwood. This had led to frequent breaches of security around the house and its environs that could encourage an escape attempt.

In its turn the Regiment had little respect for Governor Lowe who they thought was over-bearing and small-minded. Whilst Lowe had been commanding a locally-raised regiment of militia recruited by the Allies on Corsica to keep the peace on the island of Napoleon's birthplace, the *Diehards* of the old 66th had distinguished themselves at the crossing of the Douro. The Regiment had then fought for over six years under Wellington's command in the Peninsular and had lost over two-thirds of their number at the battle of Albufera in 1811, the campaign's bloodiest battle.

Whilst Reade was in theory Nichol's superior officer, no one was going to tell the colonel his regimental business. At the enquiry that was held a few days later, whilst it was clear that an offence had been committed contrary to Army Regulations, and that the culprit should be flogged and demoted, a much more serious conspiracy had been uncovered.

This threatened both the Colonel and Balcombe, which while not displeasing the Governor, could also compromise him. It suited Lowe and Reade if this was a way to reduce the power of one of the most senior British officers on the island and its most influential civilian, but it would be a serious embarrassment to the Governor if news of any scandal reached Bathhurst and the British Cabinet in London.

It appeared that a profitable but illegal trade had developed in the buying and selling of the wines and spirits allocated by the British Government for consumption by Napoleon's household. Balcombe's firm purchased the goods on instruction from London via suppliers to the East India Company in Cape Town and delivered them from its warehouse in Jamestown to Longwood House after adding a handsome profit margin for the firm.

The monthly order from Longwood had been increasing for some time and the Government was being put under pressure by Napoleon's supporters in London to make even more generous supplies available. The Governor was strongly resisting this idea which, for him, was further evidence that seditious messages were being passed from Napoleon's supporters on the island to London. These were being carried by sympathetic passengers and crew in returning ships.

In addition, the inhabitants on the island, both civil and military were seen to be *in drink* with increasing frequency and recorded incidents of drunkenness had risen alarmingly. It was certainly the case that wherever Lowe and Reade dined out, the quality and quantity of alcohol consumed was of substantial proportions and nowhere more so than in the Officers Mess of the 66th.

It turned out in the course of the enquiry that while the origins of the scandal lay in London and in Balcombe's offices in Jamestown, the distribution end of the business lay closer to the 66th's camp on Deadwood Plain.

A Quartermaster Sergeant, one Joseph Lacey, who had served in the Regiment throughout the late war and was well known for his exceptional foraging skills - he could produce supplies off the land in the most trying circumstances when all other sources had failed - had made a connection while on duty with Cipriani, the Maitre de Hotel at Longwood. Together they had organised a racket at the back door of the kitchen in which a quantity of the household's monthly wines and spirits allocation was exchanged either for cash or for choice ingredients that Cipriani could then use to prepare Napoleon's favourite dishes.

Although strictly forbidden, the soldiers of the daily Guard had also become used to going to the back door and asking for a drink of tea or a piece of seedcake. During such transactions it was easy for them to take bottles away in their haversacks which they passed on to their popular Quartermaster. In the course of his duties he, in turn, was able to visit a number of other military camps and civilian houses where he found ready buyers for his product.

While Lowe was delighted to have *stopped up* this gross breach of discipline and Lacey was arrested and removed from the island to Cape Town for sentencing, neither the 66th. nor the islanders were best pleased to have had their access to this supply of good liquor ended.

On the 16th May, a week after Lacey's departure, the officers of the 66th organised their usual annual dinner to mark their victory at Albufera and to drink to the immortal memory of their dead comrades. It was a glittering occasion and the Regiment had invited a number of senior officers and prominent civilians from throughout the island's military and civilian elite to join the evening's festivities. These did not, however, include Lowe or Reade.

The evening began with the band's side-drummers beating the officers and their guests into the candle-lit dining room whilst the band played *The Farmer's Boy*, the regimental march. The dinner that followed was the best that could be had on the island - as were the last of the bartered wines.

It was the tradition, when dinner had ended, that the Commanding Officer would call for silence and the officers and their guests would rise as he proposed the health of the King followed by a toast to the Regiment and all who served in her.

On this occasion, when the Colonel had resumed his seat, a tall young man rose to his feet. It was Ensign George Goldie, who was known by everyone in the Mess as *Dandy*. His father was a wealthy land-owning Nabob who lived at Stanlake in East Berkshire and the allowance that he gave to his son enabled young Goldie to be turned out by the best tailors in London.

"Colonel", he began, "I am aware that the traditions of the Regiment require two toasts only on such occasions but I would like to propose a third".

The Colonel was not best pleased by this intervention but Goldie was a popular young officer and his bearing on parade brought credit to the Regiment.

"Very well, young man, but make it brief.".

Goldie reached for his glass and said:

"Gentlemen, please raise your glasses and drink a toast to *Napoleon's Drop*"

A great cheer went up from the assembled officers and their guests as Goldie sat down again. The toast could be interpreted in a number of different ways. The dislike of the Regiment for what it considered as interference in its internal affairs. Criticism of Governor Lowe's harsh regime on the island. The personal dislike of him and his deputy Reade that was felt by many present. Sympathy for the island's illustrious prisoner and, finally, hostility towards the British Government in London.

General conversation was renewed around the table and the convivial evening ended in the usual way with the senior officers retiring to their quarters and their juniors ripping the Mess apart as young swags will do.

Long after the bugle notes of Lights Out had echoed across the camp, festivities continued in the Sergeants Mess including the raucous rendering of the popular soldiers' ditty:

> *O'er the hills and o'er the Main*
> *Through Flanders, Portugal and Spain*
> *King George commands and we obey*
> *Over the hills and far away.*

Two days later Colonel Nichol was summoned to Plantation House, the Governor's residence; summarily dismissed from his command by Lowe for gross insubordination and ordered to return to London on the next available ship, *The William Pitt*, which was due to leave Jamestown on the following day.

The Governor would not tolerate such insults from one of his officers.

However, the affair did not go unremarked in other quarters. The generous allowance that Goldie received from his father was not his only source of income. His oldest friend, who he had known since childhood, worked in the Alien Office in London and was one of those responsible for ensuring the security of Napoleon on St Helena.

Before leaving home Goldie had met Edward Hazell at the East India Club. Hazell had proposed to him that he should act as an agent-provocateur for the Government in return for a secret income.

Goldie's mission would be to report to Hazell in London anyone who he might meet during his posting in the South Atlantic who showed disloyalty to the Crown or any other signs that he could uncover of potential plots on the island involving Napoleon and escape.

After he had made the *Napoleon's Drop* Toast and sat down again Goldie had looked around him at a group of officers sitting at the far end of the table. They were continueing to enjoy the joke at the Governor's expense. The ring-leaders were a slightly older pair than their fellows and with somewhat different backgrounds to the others. Captain Rodolphus Reardon had an unusual record of service.

He had originally joined the 71st Highlanders as a volunteer whilst the regiment was serving in Ireland and it was understood that he had been involved in security operations in the West during the 1798 Rebellion. He had sailed to the Cape with the 71st in 1806 and had been taken prisoner after the first disastrous British invasion of Buenos Aires. On his release, Reardon had returned to England before fighting in Portugal and receiving immediate promotion to the rank of captain and a transfer to the 66th for his brave conduct at the Battle of Vimiera.

Late one evening, when Goldie and Reardon had found themselves alone in the Mess, and Reardon had been on the cusp of being the worse for drink, he had told Goldie the whole sorry story.

"I embarked with the 71st from Cork in Ireland bound for the Cape in early February 1806", Reardon started. "By the time we left our station in Ireland, we had added many Irish recruits to our number. They made up the majority of the Regiment. They were landless, homeless and penniless mercenaries.

Our fleet took its time sailing down the coast of West Africa. We crossed over to Bahia in Brazil before re-crossing the Atlantic at Ascension Island. We arrived off the Cape at the beginning of January 1806. The plan was to land the invasion force across the open beaches of Table Bay before taking on the Dutch forces inland. After a brief encounter at Blaauwberg, the Dutch commander, General Janssens, aware that he could expect no re-enforcements from Europe, surrendered to our forces.

And that should have been that.

The majority of our troops who had sailed for the Cape", Reardon continued, "had already been ear-marked to continue their voyage on to India to act as re-enforcements. Only a token force would remain in South Africa as occupation troops.

However, the force's naval commander, Sir Home Popham, had other ideas.

Before he left for the South Atlantic Popham had entered into discussions with his City friends. He had agreed with them, that South America - and specifically La Plata and the Spanish province of Argentina - could provide rich pickings for the expansion of British trade.

Without waiting for fresh orders from the Government in London, and knowing well the time it would take for permission to be considered and granted, Popham persuaded General Baird, his Army counter-part - who had by now been appointed governor and commander in chief of the newly acquired Cape Colony - to delay the forwarding of the troops to India, as previously arranged by the Government. Instead Baird should *lend* them to Popham for an amphibious expedition to the Americas.

We could only speculate about how Baird was persuaded of this course of action but he was probably swayed by Popham's reputation as a *buccaneer* and what they both saw as the opportunity for booty."

Reardon paused. "Popham's case may have been strengthened by the arrival in his headquarters at Simonstown of a Scotsman named Russell who had just arrived from Buenos Aires via St Helena.

Russell reported that before he had left Buenos Aires he had heard that the Spanish Government's annual consignment of gold bound for Spain had arrived in the city from the state mines further west at Potosi. The gold would be stored in the city's arsenal before being shipped to the Spanish Treasury in Madrid. However, the Spanish fleet would not arrive until the Spring and, meanwhile, the gold was poorly protected and the city was defended by a single Spanish regiment and its local militia, who were nothing more than a rabble.

The idea of plunder made Popham's nose twitch and he and Russell went to see Baird together.

Baird was still against the idea as being completely contrary to his orders but eventually he agreed to lend Popham the sixteen hundred men that the naval commander said he needed for the escapade. Baird too was seduced by the dream of riches."

Reardon went on: "Our small force now sailed back across the Atlantic and on its way put in at St Helena for re-victualling where its governor was persuaded to part with an additional three hundred infantry and gunners from the garrison. They would be added to the force sailing towards La Plata.

I remember seeing the island for the first time and thinking that it was the last place on earth that I would ever want to be stationed. And here we are now in this God-forsaken spot."

Reardon continued: "On the 25th June 1816, we entered the city with our pipers leading the way playing *Hey Johnnie Cope,* witnessed by the whole of the city's population of some fifty-five thousand. We made a brave sight.

The Scotsman, Russell, had been as good as his word. When the treasury had been ransacked a total of £1,860,208 was dispatched to London on HMS *Narcissus.* Before she sailed the leaders of our expedition took their share of the spoils. Baird, back in Cape Town, was sent £23,000 to salve his conscience; the two commanders on the spot, Popham and Beresford, took £12,000 each and as a lieutenant I received £1,500. Every private soldier got £18.

I am told that when the loot arrived in Portsmouth at the beginning of September there were demonstrations and loyal speeches all along its route into London before it was lodged at the Bank of England.

The Government came under pressure to take more action and demands were made for the permanent settlement of the entire Viceroyalty that included Peru, Uruguay and Venezuela.

It was decided that immediate re-enforcements would be sent out from England to make the invasion of the Argentine permanent. This second force numbered more than three thousand men."

Reardon went on: "In addition, when the news of Popham's triumph reached the Cape, Baird, now in receipt of his pay-off, sent a further two thousand men. When all of these re-inforcements reached La Plata there would be almost seven thousand troops available for the occupation of the whole Province.

However, before they had arrived the situation of our small force had changed dramatically. Within six weeks the local troops had been re-organised and in August they re-took the city. We were all taken prisoner.

Officers were separated from their men and I was taken to a filthy warehouse on the docks where I was incarcerated. The conditions were appalling and many of my friends died of starvation and neglect.

Two weeks later a soldier and I, a man from my platoon named Birmingham, who had been kept with us to act as an officer's orderly, managed to escape. We disguised ourselves as stevedores and lived hand-to-mouth on the docks eating stolen food and hiding ourselves amongst ships cargoes at night.

Meanwhile, transports carrying the fresh troops from England had anchored two miles off Montevideo. A direct landing at Buenos Aires was no longer practical as the city bristled with defence works, but an attack on the undefended city of Portuguese Montevideo across the bay would do just as well.

News of the first British defeat had now reached London. Public opinion was outraged and a third force was assembled - this time out of Falmouth – and another five and a half thousand men sailed towards us.

The fresh troops arrived and easily took Montevideo on 28th June 1807, almost a year to the day after we had first landed. Two weeks later, the newly constituted British force crossed over to Buenos Aires and entered the city once again. This time its defenders were ready with over ten thousand local men available. They had been well trained by their officers and the militia was now organised by the municipal authority, the *Cabildo,* who vowed to resist the British to the end.

Whitelocke, the newly-arrived British commander, had never seen action before in his career. He had been appointed by the Cabinet not to fight but to administrate a new colony. He summoned his staff and told them of his plan of attack.

As you may not know, Goldie, the streets of Buenos Aires are laid out in a perfect grid-square pattern. The troops were to be divided into six columns each one to be assigned one of the main thoroughfares. They would march in column straight down these towards the seafront.

It was as ineffective a plan as had ever been devised by a British Army. I found out afterwards, that it was opposed by all of the senior officers involved with the exception of its commander, whose idea it was.

The attack was an unmitigated disaster. Many of the city's houses, have balconies on their flat roof tops with apertures cut into them that are designed to capture the breeze in hot weather. These made ideal cover for the defenders to fire directly down onto the soldiers making them easy targets.

By nightime over three thousand had been killed and the remainder found themselves trapped in buildings along their routes-of-march.

The only serious resistance came from a column of the 88th commanded by Major Richard Vandeleur who held out inside the church of La Merced where his men had found shelter and were refusing to surrender." Reardon paused.

"Birmingham and I left our hiding place when we heard the sound of gunfire and managed to join a group of British soldiers who had somehow fought their way down to the docks. At nightfall, General Whitelocke, sought terms, and the whole force, including our group, surrendered to the *Cabildo*.

The city leaders just wanted to get rid of us and to be left alone so two weeks later we were put back on board our own transports and sailed for England. *Soutie* invaders - salty sailors - the Dutch at the Cape had called us - one foot in the Atlantic Ocean and the other in South Africa. We had been utterly humiliated"

Reardon had obviously been deeply affected by his experience in South America. This would explain his views not only of the incompetence and venality of the British military, and its administration, but also his sympathy with the prisoner on the island.

Whilst Goldie had nothing specific to report about Reardon to Hazell at present, the fact that Reardon had taken up with a number of young Naval officers of the Island Naval Squadron, known for their liberal views and Christian evangelical tendencies, was now more understandable. It was also more suspicious. Reardon's story also explained his close friendship with Lieutenant Birmingham who had come to Goldie's attention before and, in particular, in the Mess on the night of the ceremonial dinner.

During the late war it had become the Great Duke's habit to leaven the lump of the often aristocratic young men - sometimes mere boys - who had obtained their commissions into the Army by purchase, with a number of those who he promoted from the Rank and File on the field of battle for their particular service.

Birmingham was one of these and, in consequence, enjoyed a unique position in the Regiment, and amongst its men. This gave him liberties not available to others. Goldie now knew that Birmingham, like Reardon, had served in the *Soutie* invasions and, before that, very probably with Reardon in Ireland. Goldie also had his suspicions that Birmingham had been involved in the recent drinks scandal. It was well known that he organised late night drinking sessions in both the Officer and Sergeant messes and at other locations on the island. Neither Reardon or Birmingham made any secret of where their sympathies lay.

Now, instead of living with the 66th's officers in Deadwood Camp, Reardon had been given permission to lodge with this odd Navy group out at Mason's Stock House, a cottage that overlooked Longwood. The Governor had ordered an observation post to be established at the house with a permanent look-out on duty. This had given Reardon intimate knowledge of the prisoner's daily movements.

Later, back in his room, at the end of the evening, Goldie jotted down Reardon's and Birmingham's names into his notebook as potential troublemakers on whom he should keep an eye.

At the end of the week, and just before the *Alnwick Castle* left for London, Goldie visited the ship to say goodbye to a departing brother officer. He handed a dispatch about the *Napoleon's Drop* incident to a clerk of the Company's marine service, who doubled as an agent for the Alien Office in London. The dispatch also described the actions of a number of other individuals who had lately aroused his suspicions and, in particular, recorded Lord Amherst's visit to Longwood to meet Napoleon whilst on the island and his own discussion with Reardon.

3   *Longwood House*

AT THREE BELLS there was a knock on Amherst's inner cabin door.

"Enter".

The captain's steward looked in and announced:

"Compliments of the Captain, your Lordship, St Helena is now in sight and we will be laying anchor in the Roads in thirty minutes."

Amherst wrapped himself again in his travelling coat and picked up the box containing the chess set, now folded in a piece of oilcloth that Dance had given him for the purpose. He tucked the set under his arm and stepped out onto the main deck. He had difficulty holding his balance as the ship listed into a vicious wind that blew directly from the distant Antarctic. He shuffled forwards and stood amidships on the starboard side holding onto a yard and looking out to sea.

Some minutes later, between heavy gusts of wind and rain, the faintest outline appeared of a dark and rock-like eruption that was more than the horizon – like the drawing of a pencil-thin eyebrow on a blank page.

He drew in his breath and, as the ship grew closer through the heavy swell, he could now see from the top of the island's black-faced mountains to its green sea's edge. He had never seen such a forbidding view. At the island's top, dark clouds scudded over the black mountains and at the bottom of its cliffs the strong wind whipped the rocks with sea spray that rose into the air before being hurled onto the hostile shore.

There was no sign of habitation or cultivation to be seen on the steep mountain sides or of the V shaped gap where the entrance to the island's only town and port was supposed to lie.

The island appeared to be utterly barren, deserted and forsaken.

The idea of organising an escape from this inhospitable place was pure fantasy and it would be absolute folly for him to risk his career - and possibly his very life - by joining in with such a conspiracy.

As the ship drew closer, Amherst could see a number of vessels anchored left and right of the gap in the mountains that pulled at their moorings in the strong wind. On the left-hand side of the landing he counted up to twenty East Indiamen and other assorted vessels either on their way out to - or returning from - the East and on the right-hand side an orderly line of eight warships recognisable from their ensigns as the frigates and sloops of the Royal Navy's island guard squadron.

The thin streak of a wooden jetty reached out from the shoreline into Jamestown's exposed bay and he could just make out a number of figures already moving about on it behind which stood a scarlet-coated guard of soldiers drawn up in three ranks.

He turned around with the intention of returning with the chess set to his cabin and abandoning any idea of attempting to pass it to Napoleon when the Captain appeared at his side.

"Good morning your Lordship, not a favourable prospect I think?"

"Indeed not, Sir", Amherst replied. "A God-forsaken place I should say."

"My Lord, as soon as we drop anchor and have secured the ship, I will order the tender lowered and you will be rowed ashore. I have arranged for my steward to accompany you and to act as your servant while ashore."

"Why, thank you, Sir, that is much appreciated", Amherst replied.

Thirty minutes later when this manoeuvre had been completed, Amherst stepped down the ship's ladder and was handed into the tender. At the same time a puff of smoke followed by a hollow boom came from the nearest Naval vessel. It sounded the beginning of a twelve-gun salute marking the island's formal welcome in honour of the arrival of one of His Majesty's ambassadors.

When the *Alnwick Castle's* tender had reached the jetty and been tied up, Amherst passed the chess set wrapped in its oilcloth to his servant. He had some difficulty clambering out in the swell and would have lost his footing without the help of a white-gloved hand that was proffered to him from above.

As he straightened up, he looked into the eyes of a thin-lipped, narrow-faced individual wearing the full dress of the General Staff. The man touched his cocked hat with his raised hand and said: "Welcome to the St Helena, your Lordship, my name is Lowe and I command here".

They walked to the end of the jetty and stood together for a moment in front of a line of dignitaries as Lowe said: "May I have the honour to introduce my personal staff and some others, Sir?"

Amherst stepped to the head of the line and was introduced to Lowe's staff starting with Sir Thomas Reade, deputy commander – but most probably the Foreign Secretary's spy on the island; Major Gorrequer, his military secretary and Major Hodson, the island's Judge Advocate. Lowe then introduced Amherst to Admiral Plampin, the senior Naval officer on the island, who in turn presented one of his captains, Frederick Marryat commanding HMS *Beaver*. At the end of the line stood William Balcombe, the East India Company's agent who, much to Lowe's intense annoyance, was greeted by Amherst with: "Hello, old fellow, how good to see you again."

Behind the line of officials stood three ranks of the 66th commanded by none other than Lieutenant Goldie dressed in his finest.

When Amherst had completed his inspection, Lowe invited him to mount the Governor's carriage for the ride to Plantation House, Lowe's residence, where Amherst would be staying the night.

Amherst was surprised to find Goldie joining them for the journey in the carriage but Lowe advised him that the young officer would act as his ADC while on the island and when he visited the prisoner, which, Lowe said, he assumed his Lordship would wish to do the following day.

It was now past two o'clock and raining hard. As they drove along the only paved road on the island, Amherst was impressed by the many patches of cultivation that they passed – it appeared that the island was more fertile than he had first imagined.

After meeting Lady Lowe and the Governor's two step-daughters on the steps of the house he was shown to his room. He placed the chess set at the bottom of his valise under a fresh shirt reversing the shirt's cuffs so that he would know if the had been disturbed in his absence and went downstairs.

Dinner followed at five in the afternoon and was not a lively affair. A number of guests had been invited but the conversation was dominated by the Governor's complaints about his allowances and Lady Lowe's about the laziness of the islanders. Goldie, who would also be staying at the house for the night, did his best to amuse the two girls.

Before he retired Amherst checked that his valise had not been touched before getting into bed. He lay in the darkness and began to worry about tomorrow's meeting. What tiresome people they seemed to be! How was he going to pass the chess set to Napoleon without arousing suspicion? What if it was inspected and he was caught red-handed? How would be explain himself to Lowe? He slept fitfully and woke early.

After breakfast the next morning Lowe summoned Amherst to his study.

"The British Government does not recognise any royal status", Lowe started. "The man is an ex-general only and should be addressed as such by all visitors. I would be grateful, my Lord, if you would observe the rules that I have set and address him only as General Bonaparte."

Amherst nodded but made no further response, He had already decided that he would address Napoleon as "Your Grace" whatever Lowe might have to say.

Lowe continued: "As you will be aware, Bonaparte is a notoriously spiteful character and he has not permitted me to meet him face-to-face for over four months as I refuse to use the title by which he likes to be known. You will therefore be escorted in my carriage to Longwood by my Adjutant, Gorrequer, and your ADC young Goldie. You will be met at the gates of Longwood by the Orderly Officer who will lead you to the house where you will be introduced to Bonaparte's Chief of Staff, Count Bertrand. He will take you inside where you will be received by the General.

I don't expect that you will have much to say to each other and I would be obliged if you would not engage with Bonaparte in any discussion about his conditions of imprisonment here or any other matters of that sort. These should be referred by him to me for my attention. I have arranged your carriage for twelve Midday."

"One other thing, my Lord", Lowe continued, "I permit no items of any kind, letters, books, newspapers and so on to be taken into the house or removed from it without I or my staff inspecting them. There have been too many leaks recently - let alone rumours of escape plots - for us to take any risks. I am sure you will oblige me on this point."

Amherst made no response to these instructions. Lowe had confirmed all that he had heard in London about the harsh regime on the island and he was heartened to think that what he was about to do was the right course of action. However, he would have to find a plausible reason for his gift.

He went upstairs to his room, put on his travelling coat, collected the chess set from its hiding place and, putting it under his arm, went back downstairs.

The journey to Longwood took over an hour and the landscape through which the party passed became more and more bleak. They had climbed out of what could almost be described as a fertile valley and up into the dark mountains that Amherst had first seen from the *Alnwick Castle*. By the time they reached a barren plateau, on which stood three tall Scots pines planted beside a small brick-built lodge, his thoughts had turned darker as he contemplated what he had to do.

By now he was actually afraid. He was a fool to have ever agreed to this. As they approached the lodge he saw that a British flag hung limply from an upstairs window and a number of red-coated soldiers stood outside.

As the carriage approached, the soldiers sprang to attention forming a ragged quarter-guard and out of the door a sun-burned officer appeared who Amherst assumed was the Orderly Officer sent up from the house to meet them.

The carriage halted and the man saluted Amherst with the words: "Good morning, my Lord, Captain Blakeney of the 66th at your service.

If you would care to dismount I will escort you and young Goldie here into the house and introduce you to the General's Chief of Staff who will be waiting for you. I will stay by the door and be ready to escort you back to the lodge once your audience is over."

Amherst dismounted from the carriage and shook Blakeney's hand.

Blakeney went on: "Before we proceed, I am instructed by the Governor to ask you on your honour if you are carrying any messages, newspapers or books for the General that would be injurious to the British interest and, if so, to hand over any such items to me now."

Amherst was so nervous that he could barely get the words out of his mouth.

"When I left England six months ago I was asked by the Cabinet to think of a suitable gift for Napoleon that would be a token of the goodwill that now exists between France and Great Britain. I purchased this chess set in Cape Town when we landed to replenish our supplies and I shall be presenting it to General Bonaparte during my meeting with him."

"I understand, my Lord, but I am obliged to examine its contents to satisfy the Governor's instructions?"

"Please go ahead", replied Amherst, thinking it was infernal cheek but not wishing Blakeney to get into any kind of trouble with the Governor or to arouse any suspicion on himself.

He held his breath as Blakeney took hold of the box, opened it and picked up one or two of the pieces in turn rolling each one between his fingers as he did so. He placed them back in the box and, closing the lid, gave it back to Amherst.

"I shall have to report this gift to Colonel Reade who will record it in his ledger of gifts made and received but I am sure the Governor would want London's wishes to be observed."

Amherst, now holding the box tightly, breathed again and they began to walk up the drive.

The house came into view.

Amherst was aware of the controversy that the choice of lodgings for Napoleon had caused. There were many in London who felt that it was a deliberate insult that Longwood House had been selected as his dwelling place. It was a mean house. It had been built fifty years before for a deputy governor of little importance when the island had been acquired by the East India Company and had merited only minimum investment since. It consisted of a central block and two wings. The latter appeared to be no more than a range of livestock and storage sheds.

The house had now been repaired with an assortment of ill-matched building materials and the overall affect was one of dilapidation and neglect. Amherst knew that there was a proposal for a new house to be erected in the grounds made from pre-fabricated units brought out from England, but there was no sign of their arrival.

They approached the front door and stood crowded together in a small porch. The door opened and a man in the full dress uniform of a general of the Imperial Guard stood before them. Bowing low in front of Amherst, he announced himself as "General Bertrand, Grand Marshall of the Imperial Household to His majesty the Emperor of the French." No wonder the Governor was at his wits end having to put up with this kind of nonsense.

Not to be outdone, Amherst bowed and replied: "William, Second Viscount Amherst, Plenipotentiary to the Sublime Court and Under-Secretary to His Majesty King George the Third at the British Foreign Office in London". That would show the man.

"Please follow me. I will enquire if the Emperor is willing to receive you". Willing, indeed!

Amherst and Goldie followed Bertrand into the house, along a dim passage and into a larger and lighter room that was furnished with a billiard table at one end and a chaise-longue at the other. The walls were covered with pale green wall-paper printed with a Chinese pattern.

Bertrand knocked on a door at the far end of the room and, after a minute, Napoleon, ex-emperor of France, entered. Behind him stood his personal bodyguard, a glowering giant of a man in the well-worn uniform of a Polish Lancer.

Here was the man who had alternatively terrorised, dominated and reformed the European continent for over twenty-five years.

It should have been an inspiring sight, but it was not. The emperor was greatly diminished and looked small and puny. At a little over five foot eight inches he barely came up to Amherst's shoulder even though, Amherst noticed, he had heels built into his scuffed buckled shoes that made him appear taller. He had a stout figure, a protruding belly, short neck and a sallow complexion. His lank, thinning hair reached below his collar at the back of the neck and was brushed forward across his temples at the front to hide his baldness.

He was shabbily dressed in a pair of wrinkled stockings with off-white calf breeches on his short legs; a cream waistcoat to his knees and a cut-away dark green satin top-coat with deep lapels at collar and cuff edged in worn red and gold thread. From the marks on his waistcoat it was possible to see what Napoleon had breakfasted on that morning. His face was pale and blotched. Amherst's first thought was: is this really the bogey man of Europe?

Napoleon's rise had been astronomic following the horrors of the earlier reigns of terror. By sheer determination and talent, he had transformed France that had become one of the greatest powers the world had ever seen. He may have had a tendency towards megalomania but he combined a unique combination of qualities. As an administrator he had been meticulous with an extraordinary capacity for hard work; as a soldier he had been efficient with an acute eye for detail; as a lover he had been romantic and dreamy to the point of indulgence and as a strategist an absolute genius.

He had his faults. He was pompous and conceited but with good reason to be so but, like Wellington, he always thought of his men and their welfare first. His reward had been that they had followed him to the very end.

He was now greatly diminished. The exception was his piercing eyes which he now turned on Amherst with a mixture of pride, inquisitiveness and contempt.

Amherst bowed and, speaking in French - the universal language of diplomacy - said: "Your Grace, I am delighted to make your acquaintance. It is a privilege to meet you. May I present my ADC, Captain Goldie of His Majesty's 66th Regiment of Foot"

Napoleon acknowledged Amherst but looked at Goldie with a barely perceptible nod of his head and replied: "Ah, Wellington's scum of the earth. The treachery of my Spanish allies cost me that campaign. How is my great adversary the Sepoy general?"

This was a snide reference to Wellington's early victories in India won against numerous but inferior forces.

"He was passing well when I left London, Sir", Amherst replied, "and continues in government as Home Secretary. Most of our troops are now back from France and have been re-deployed into Canada, Ireland and the West Indies. There is, of course, a great reduction in their numbers since our victory at Waterloo."

Napoleon ignored the remark and replied: "I understand that you are lately returned from China. Tell me of the situation there."

Amherst replird: "The Chinese emperor rules over four million people in a land so vast that it would take more than a year to travel from one end to the other. As a result, government is sporadic and partial. Most of the country is rural but with a small number of cities. The capital, Peking, is magnificent and the Chinese emperor's palace is undoubtedly one of the wonders of the world."

"I have heard about your mission and the way that your typical British arrogance led to its failure."

Amherst now began to understand the Governor's anxieties about breaches of security. Napoleon had obviously received news of the outcome of his mission from a returning East Indiaman that must have come through before his own arrival on the island.

"Not at all, your Grace", Amherst continued, "the Chinese Emperor greeted me graciously and agreed that trade between ourselves, China and India should commence with the establishment of a joint customs post at Shanghai. We expect this will promote trade links and help to open up the rest of the country."

Napoleon now changed tack. "How long do you think this farce of my captivity will last?"

Amherst was aware from Cabinet papers that this was a recurring theme of Napoleon's correspondence with the British Government and with his supporters in England and France.

"Your Grace, the Government's policy of exile was agreed by the Allied powers of which Britain is only one and as a result it cannot easily be overturned. However, it should not be understood as a punishment but as a precaution which will allow the nations of Europe both old and new to heal themselves without further disruption.

However, I am sure His Majesty the King would not wish you to be unduly discomforted and as a token of the goodwill of his Prime Minister and the Cabinet, I should like to present to you this chess set on their behalf."

Amherst now handed over the box containing the chess pieces as Napoleon gave him a look that said 'an insulting recompense for my miserable life here'. Passing it to Bertrand, he replied: "I thank you for this gesture and on your return to London I would be obliged if you would re-assure the British Cabinet that I have no further designs on Europe. I only desire to be allowed to retire either in Great Britain or

North America, where, as you know, my brother Lucien now resides with his family."

As Bertrand placed the walnut box on the edge of the billiard table, Amherst wondered, first, if its secret contents were already known to Napoleon and, second, if what he had just done would lead to the end of his career.

"When does your ship leave the island?", asked Napoleon, indicating that the audience was now over.

"Tomorrow", replied Amherst.

"Very well, you may take your leave",

Amhust bowed and said: "Thank you for agreeing to meet with me, your Grace, and I wish you well for the future."

He and Goldie stepped back as Napoleon turned around and left the room through the door by which he had entered, accompanied by his bodyguard.

Blakeney was waiting in the porch and, after their return to the Governor's house, Amherst was relieved to have fulfilled his secret task without discovery.

The following day he took his leave of Governor Lowe and was driven back down to Jamestown where he embarked for London on the *Alnwick Castle*. It was an uneventful voyage and three weeks later he landed at the Company's East India Dock in the Thames's Lower Pool.

Goldie returned to barracks and wrote up the final entry of his dispatch for Hazell at the Alien Office in London describing Amherst's visit to Napoleon. He recorded the gift of the chess set that Amherst had handed over. He also reported that Amherst had appeared unduly nervous as he did so and speculated that Amherst might have had something to hide.

Later that day, Bertrand removed the chess set from the billiard table and handed it to Piontkowski, ex-Polish lancer and Napoleon's faithful ADC and bodyguard.

"Here, you play chess, don't you?"

Piontkowski took the set back to his quarters where it lay for some days unopened until one day he asked Noverraz, Napoleon's third valet, if he would care for a game.

They set the board up and began playing. Half way through the game, Piontkowski won the Queen and, as he removed it from the board, rolled it between his fingers. It was a beautifully carved piece. He felt a very slight ridge on its trunk and examined it more closely. He could see a definite line running around it. He twisted its top and bottom in opposite directions and it came unscrewed in his fingers. Its inside was hollow and he could see that it contained a furled-up piece of paper.

He took it at once to General Bertrand who told him to check all the other pieces and return the set to him.

Bertrand read the note - which was in English - and went straight through to the Emperor's quarters. He knocked on the door and received an abrupt: "Enter".

Napoleon was lying in his bath reading a book. He spent many hours in this way. It was relief from his campaign aches and pains and the damp conditions at Longwood.

"Your Grace, I am sorry to disturb you but you will recall the gift that Ambassador Amherst left for you."

"No, I do not wish to remember his visit, the toady. What was it?", Napoleon replied.

"It was a carved chess set."

"Oh, yes, how stupid. Anyone who knows me also knows that I loathe the game. It was a deliberate insult to me."

35

"That may be so but it turns out that it meant more than met the eye. Pointkowski was playing a game and this was hidden in one of the pieces."

Bertrand handed the note to the Emperor who read it and huffed.

Your Grace,

We write to advise you that our plans for your rescue are well advanced and we expect you to be delivered into freedom in the next 8 months and not later than May next. Our emissary will use the word "Angouleme" to identify himself and we ask you to follow his instructions precisely. In the meantime, we are working daily for your release.

I am, Sire, your servant, etc.

H.H.

Liberté, Fraternité, Equalité

London, September 1817

"About time too. Those Hollands are generous with their gifts of books but they have taken their time to come up with this."

"I believe that they will have been under great pressure and even surveillance, as we are", replied Bertrand. "We know of Wellington and his obsessions. If Governor Lowe's behaviour is anything to go by, the British Government will be turning the screws on any opposition to your imprisonment here. Lord Holland has done well to get this message through and Lord Amherst took some risks too."

"That is all very well but I have made clear from the very beginning. I have no intention whatsoever of being party to some ignominious escape attempt dressed as a washerwoman. I shall only leave this house in the full-dress uniform of a Marshall of France – which, may I remind you - remains my rank. You may inform *Angouleme* of this if and when he makes contact, whoever he is and whatever he proposes."

With that the Emperor indicated that Bertrand should withdraw and resumed his reading.

The Alien Office

EDWARD HAZELL, WHOSE official title was Assistant Secretary at the Home Office, glanced up from his desk. He checked his pocket watch as he did every evening when he heard the sound outside his window of a Guards band coming up Horse Guards. Since the Gordon riots, a picquet marched through London every evening before being posted at the Bank of England overnight. It should be precisely five minutes to five.

He glanced again at the paperwork in front of him and wondered how he was going to explain its contents to his superior.

His private secretary, Francis Nicholson, who had joined a month earlier, entered his office with a bundle of papers.

"Good evening, Nicholson. I think we've done enough for one day. How about a drink at the club on your way home?"

They left the building together and walked across the parade ground towards Pall Mall.

Nicholson, like Edward, was also a Cambridge graduate but he had won his place by merit rather than preferment. He was ambitious; had a keen mind and was not afraid of hard work. If he had a fault it was his habit of asking too many questions too early in the morning but he had already shown himself capable of holding Edward's coat when trouble came.

When they were settled with their drinks Edward asked:

"You're relatively new here, aren't you Nicholson, so you won't remember what the Office was like during the war. Since Napoleon's defeat our resources have been much reduced and I am one of the few left here with experience of both American and continental affairs that stretch across the Atlantic."

"When did you join, Sir?", Nicholson said.

"I joined the Home Office after Cambridge through a connection of my father's", Edward replied, "but I was seconded immediately to this office and have been here for the past eight years.

As you know, an Aliens Act - which included the setting up of this office - was passed in 1797 at the time of the Irish Rebellion and the French revolutionary wars. The Government believed that its supporters and their ideas would cross the English Channel and cause unrest here."

"And, what was the Act's purpose?", Nicholson asked.

"The Act authorised the Government to keep a watch on all Ports of Entry, both on the coast and inland", Edward continued. "Its secret purpose was to identify anyone planning to disrupt the King's peace and its work was soon extended to include both domestic and foreign intelligence and espionage.

We work closely with other government departments including the Post Office which handles the Mail and the Foreign Office which receives reports from our ambassadors and agents overseas.

Whilst we employ our own agents, mainly in London and the South Coast ports, we also work with London's stipendiary magistrates, and their foot-soldiers, the Bow Street runners, who are responsible for maintaining order in the capital.

When I joined in 1809 our sole concern was to defeat Napoleon. Our first director, William Wickham, waged a secret war against the French. His base of operations was in Switzerland which provided easy access to France. He also ran agents in Antwerp, Genoa and Hamburg to keep watch on enemy shipping.

Just after I had joined, we lost our precarious foothold in Europe when the Army was evacuated from Corunna and we had to run our agents out of Jersey onto the French coast.

My chance came three years later in 1812 when the United States took the opportunity to declare war on our military and commercial interests as our backs were turned fighting the French.

My role was to gather intelligence that would enable us to help the Navy plot the movement of American privateers. These ships - carrying so-called *letters of marque and plunder*, issued to their captains by the American government to legalise their piracy - came out of American east coast ports with the intention of breaking our blockade and supplying American goods, including armaments, to Bonaparte's forces in Spain.

I helped to create and manage a network of agents in American ports who reported on shipping movements that enabled me - if I was lucky - to predict the location and likely direction of the enemy's attacks.

As you know, it took two years to bring the Americans to the negotiating table. I stood down my spy network at the end of those hostilities but now I think that with General Bonaparte making trouble on St Helena, we are going to need it again. I suspect that it's where any rescue attempt will come from."

"I hear some bad stories about our present Master, is there any truth in them?", Nicholson asked.

"Ah, you mean General Crauford", Edward replied. "His seat is at Newark in Ayrshire. He worked as an *exploring officer*, or spy, for Wickham before he was appointed to Wellington's army in the Peninsular. There, he commanded the Light Division throughout that long and bloody campaign. He was known as *Black Bob* by his soldiers for his foul temper, dark moods and reputation for brutality.

He hanged looters after the raising of the siege of Cuidad Rodrigo, but he was also known to care for his riflemen's welfare and he never lost a battle.

You had better be warned that Crauford harbours a particular hatred of the Americas and of all things on both of those continents. He served in the second disastrous expedition to La Plata in the Argentine and later in the campaign on the Chesapeake and in Washington where his closest friend Willam Ross was killed at the battle of Bladenburg.

This turned our Master into an implacable enemy and dangerous opponent of the United States.

It has also prejudiced him violently against any possible interference from the Americans that might now affect British interests in the South Atlantic."

"And, how did you come to be doing this job?", Nicholson asked.

"When it was decided that Napoleon should be imprisoned on St Helena, I was the obvious choice to be responsible for the prisoner's security because of my previous experience and knowledge of operations at sea.

You've seen the map. Any rescuers would have to sail great distances to reach the island. Both Ascension Island in the North and Tristan de Cunha in the South have been reinforced with our troops and artillery to repel a rescue.

The most convenient point of departure for an attempt would be from Buenos Aires but this would still be some two weeks sailing time from St Helena through seas that can become very violent. There are only a few opportunities each year during which wind, tides and weather might permit a landing on the island.

Even then it would be almost impossible to land undetected", Edward continued.

"Sheer cliffs rise vertically above all of the island's beaches. General Bonaparte is watched twenty-four hours a day by a guard force of more than 3,000 troops. The shore is observed from the island's headlands and artillery is positioned on every beach. The island's naval guard squadron of eight vessels circle the island continuously. Any ships approaching the island are stopped and searched before being allowed to enter the Roads at Jamestown where their crews are not allowed to land. Only officers with the written permission of the governor can come ashore.

Longwood House, where Napoleon lives with his personal staff and domestic household, is kept under constant observation. Sentries are posted at twenty-yard intervals and a curfew is imposed at eight each evening.

The British Aide de Camp attached to Bonapartes's household is instructed to have a clear sighting of him at least twice every day. Each observation has to be reported directly to Governor Lowe or Reade his deputy using a system of coloured flags that are linked to the Governor's residence.

The chances of escape are minimal but we can take no chances. I spend all of my waking hours on the business. I have a close friend stationed on the island who keeps me informed of the situation there. Nevertheless, this may not be sufficient to frustrate a serious rescue attempt carried out by determined opponents with ample resources that could come from any one of a number of directions. We have to be on our guard at all times.

Now off you go home. I need to get some sleep", Edward finished.

The following morning, after greeting Nicholson, Edward rose from his desk and leaving his office, crossed the corridor, before knocking on Crauford's door.

"Come."

He opened the door and entered the room. Crauford looked up from his papers.

"Good morning, Sir. I'm sorry to disturb you but I should like to show you a dispatch that I have just received from St Helena."

"Very well, sit down. This had better be important. I have a meeting with the Treasury at noon to discuss our annual budget."

"I think that it merits your attention," Edward replied.

The two men's relationship was professional but not warm. Whereas Wickham had encouraged his staff to speculate wildly on alternative interpretations of conflicting reports as a way to find a path to the truth, Crauford demanded immediate solutions preceded by little discussion.

Edward relied on the co-operation of his colleagues at the Post Office to do his work. At a meeting with them last month Crauford, whose irascibility was notorious, had exploded over the trivial matter of a missing reference number on a Post Office intelligence document. As a result of his outburst the meeting had ended prematurely and the Post Office's *Secret Department* team had advised Hazell that their participation in the Alien Office's work could not be guaranteed unless his master curbed his tongue.

"Well, what is it about?", Crauford said.

Edward held a folded paper in his hand.

"This dispatch has just come off the *Alnwick Castle*. She docked at the Company's quay in-bound from Cape Town and St Helena on the morning tide. As you know, my informant on the island is an ex-school friend of mine, Lieutenant Goldie of the 66th, who serves in the garrison. In his letter he describes a visit made by Lord Amherst to Longwood House where General Bonaparte is lodged. His Lordship is not a member of the Cabinet but has close connections with a number of its key members. He is the brother-in-law of Lord Holland, who as you are aware, leads the country's opposition to the

Bonaparte's captivity. As a result, Amherst could well have divided loyalties and I wonder what he was doing at Longwood anyway"

"That infernal man, Holland!", Crauford responded, "he is nothing but a trouble maker with his talk of the liberties of man. If we could find a way to discredit him - and that loathsome wife of his - I know of more than one person in the Government who would be delighted.

I know about Holland and his trouble-making but do we have any evidence of Amherst's treachery?"

"He seems to be a fairly blameless type personally", Edward replied. "He originally stood for Parliament in the Liberal interest but his recent ministerial career has been unspectacular and the failure of his mission to secure our trade with China may well end it.

We have not followed him closely but we do keep a file on him".

"How so?", asked Crauford, "I thought it was forbidden to hold files on serving ministers".

"It was and is, Sir, but the rule can be, let us say, *adjusted* if a minister comes under suspicion and with the special permission of the Prime Minister, which was given in this case."

"Do we have actual evidence against Amherst?", Crauford asked.

"We have a note to the Office written by Wickham", Ewdward replied, "that describes a dinner at which he was a guest. Wickham lists the diners, of which Amherst was one, and records the highlights of the conversation which was all of the Emperor Napoleon; the iniquities of his imprisonment and the means of attaining his liberty, etc., etc. This is to be achieved both through action in Parliament and by other, unspecified, means. Wickham had the impression that these *other means* could include a rescue attempt. He ends his note with the comment that he was surprised to find a minister of the Crown in such company."

"Disgraceful. And what do you propose that we should do about it?"

"There is more, Sir", Edward continued. "Although Governor Lowe has forbidden visitors to and from Longwood House to carry any kind of communication with them, we know that letters and messages have been getting through to and from Boanaparte's supporters in London. How else could he and they be so well informed and so up to date with the views of others?

Amherst was advised of these conditions by Lowe before he made his visit to Longwood but he claimed that he had been asked by the Cabinet - he probably referred to the Secretary to the Colonies, Lord Bathurst, to whom he is closest - to provide a gift for the prisoner on their behalf."

"What was it?", Crauford asked.

"I am told by Goldie", Edward went on, "that it was a chess set made of ivory in a presentation box that His Lordship said he had purchased in Cape Town where he had broken his journey home,"

"Not much to see there. What's your point, Hazell?"

"It is this", Edward said. "I have searched all known references to Napoleon's leisure preferences and past-times but I can find nothing anywhere that suggests that he – or any member of his immediate family or entourage – have ever had any interest whatsoever in the game of chess."

"That's possible, but the gift could also have been intended for the general use of his household", remarked Crauford.

"I agree, but I still think there is something odd about it."

"Well, what do you propose we should do?"

"With your permission", Edward went on, "I should like to instruct my agent in the Cape to carry out enquiries about Lord Amherst's purchase of the chess set: where it came from, who made it, what it cost, whether he collected it personally, and so on.

In addition, I would like the Post Office to intercept his mail and check that there are no coded messages or references in it to Bonaparte or his supporters either here; in the Americas or on St Helena.

I should also like Bow Street to keep a check on his movements; where he goes outside official business; who he meets and what they talk about. If there is anything going on, we need to know about it."

"Very well, but you are to obtain the necessary Warrants from the Home Office and keep me informed of your enquiries and of any other matter that I should know about related to the prisoner on St Helena."

"I will and thank you, Sir, for your time."

Edwaed felt that he had done better than he might have expected with Crauford.

He returned to his office and began to put in place the arrangements that he had proposed.

His first task was to obtain the Warrant that would authorise the Post Office to intercept and open Amherst's mail.

This would be easier said than done. Whilst Hazell knew that the Prime Minister would support the idea, it was not with Lord Liverpool that he would have to negotiate. It was not only politicians who were divided about Bonaparte's imprisonment and there were many in the Government service whose loyalties were ambiguous at best and downright treasonable at worst.

One of those who was known to be ambivalent was Home Office Under-Secretary Sir Henry Bunbury, its professional head and formerly at the War Office. He would have to be persuaded to place the Warrant for signature before the Home Secretary. Bunbury had enjoyed an unusual career as a soldier, diplomat and artist and had met Bonaparte at the time of his surrender to the British on board HMS *Bellepheron* in Portsmouth.

Whilst Bunbury might have been expected to align himself with the party in power, he was a complex individual who not only enjoyed the game of politics played at the highest level and amongst the elite of fashion - including the Court - but also held some unconventional views on social policy that he promoted amongst colleagues. For example, he expressed strong views about the efficacy of capital punishment and the way that the London mob made sport of it.

At present, as a former military commander, he was particularly concerned with the plight of soldiers lately discharged from the Army many of whom had become unemployed in the economic slump that had occurred in consequence of the peace. This was also contributing to the rapid rise in crime in London although Bunbury sneeringly discounted the way that Ministers and their mistresses complained that it was no longer safe to walk the streets after dark.

From previous encounters with Bunbury, Edward was aware that in order to get what he wanted he would need to be at least subtle - if not downright deceitful. He decided that he would deploy two main tactics at the meeting to be arranged later in the day at the Home Office. Bunbury was a very great snob. First, he was a social snob, so that the liberal use of the right names dropped into his ear would have a good effect and, second, he was an intellectual snob and would relish a dual with a worthy opponent.

In case of urgent need, Hazell kept a number of blank Warrants in the safe in his office and he now took one of these out for completion. As a precaution, he would not sign it himself but would ask Crauford to do so. This would not only indicate to Bunbury its importance but would also appeal to his snobbish instincts: Crauford was very close to the Great Duke who also happened to be Home Secretary and Bunbury's ministerial superior.

After obtaining Crauford's signature, Edward sent a messenger to the Home Office requesting a meeting with Bunbury late the same afternoon.

Bunbury greeted him with: "Ah, young Hazell. What can I do for you that requires such haste? I hope you are not going to involve me in another of your squalid schemes? You will recall that the last time that I agreed to help you, three men were hung at Maidstone gaol. I know that you Alien Office ruffians invent plots where none exist and fabricate evidence to obtain false convictions. I am having none of it, d'you hear."

Edward kept his peace.

"I am most grateful to you for seeing me so late in the afternoon, Sir Henry, but I hope that you will agree it is on a matter of national importance."

"National importance, my arse", replied Bunbury. "You're in a hole and I am the only person who can get you out of it."

"That's partly correct, Sir, we have let our eyes off the ball. It's about Napoleon, Napoleon Bonaparte, on St Helena."

"What's that got to do with your lot, Bunbury replied. "That's a matter for Lord Bathhurst at Colonies, the Foreign Office or my good friend Governor Lowe on the island. It's not a matter for us at the Home Office and especially not for you at Aliens."

"I know, Sir", Edward went on, "that this would usually be so, but General Crauford feels that it is the Home Secretary who would be best placed to take overall control of the secret operation that we propose. It involves the security of the State both at home and abroad of which, as we are all aware, the Duke has very great experience."

Edward knew that this would appeal to Bunbury's self-importance as he would be able to take any credit going if things went according to plan but would be able to blame the Alien Office if they came off badly.

"Very well. What is it that you want?"

"I should be obliged if you would obtain His Lordship's signature to this Warrant."

Bunbury took the draft from Edward and sat down at his desk to read it.

"Wh-a-a-at", he almost screamed, "You are asking me to recommend that we should spy on a member of our own Government?"

Edward remained calm.

"Yes, I am, Sir. We have reason to believe that Lord Amherst is potentially willing to do great harm to our country with grave implications for the safety of the Realm. I have no proof as yet of his treachery. It will take another six weeks to have some more definitive evidence out of the Cape, but there is something about his stay on St Helena that doesn't add up. If there is a conspiracy to organise Bonaparte's escape, we need to be ahead of it and this Warrant can help us to be so."

"That's all very well", Bunbury retorted, "but I will need more than mere tittle-tattle about a second-rank minister to convince the Duke. Bonaparte is imprisoned more than four thousand miles away and it's your job to make sure he stays there. It would be more than bad luck if he was to escape and it would cost you more than your job. You would be strung up."

"I appreciate that this is a most sensitive business, Sir Henry. As it happens, General Crauford may well be dining with the Duke at Apsley House this evening. I could suggest to my Master that it might be helpful if he mentioned the matter to the Duke in more detail. He could advise the Duke that you will be placing the Warrant in front of His Grace tomorrow morning."

Edward did not know if Crauford was going out that evening or not, but he knew that Crauford's wife Lucy was up in town and the Duke usually entertained on Wednesdays. Nor had he actually said that Crauford would be seeing His Lordship that evening; he had said that he *might well be*.

At this point Bunbury knew that Hazell had outflanked him and that he was not able to compete with these high connections.

"Very well", he replied, "I will place the Warrant in front of the Home Secretary tomorrow as you have proposed. Call in again at around mid-day and I will return it to you and make sure that you keep me informed of any developments. Now remove yourself and your dirty business from my office."

Bunbury said this at the same time as giving Edward a theatrical wink of the eye. Edward knew Bunbury enjoyed the power that he gained from having inside information about any of the Government's secret activities.

"Many thanks for your time, Sir, and I will convey your best wishes to the General."

Mission accomplished.

When he had returned to his office, Edward carried out his next task: a letter to his agent in Cape Town.

This would be a straightforward instruction to a trusted agent who lived just outside the dockyard at Simonstown.

Du Plessis was a man of simple pleasures who Edward had met on a secret mission in South Africa during the American war of 1812. American privateers had found it convenient to put into Simonstown for re-victualling on their way out to the Indies where they had attacked the East India Company's shipping and sold the plundered goods to Dutch traders in the Philippines.

The Royal Navy had fought an engagement against these privateers in the Straits of Malacca whilst defending a Company fleet on its way back from China. Heavy losses had been suffered on both sides. It had been Edward's job to cut off this source of irritation to the Government - with its easy pickings for the Americans. He had done this by providing the Navy with advance notice of the arrival of the privateers out of the North Atlantic. Du Plessis had been a vital source of information.

Du Plessis hated everyone but particularly American privateers. During the American war one of them had captured his ship off the Falklands before stealing his cargo; burning his ship and leaving him and his crew stranded on the islands.

His pleasure took two forms that were ideal for Hazell's purposes: revenge and money. Du Plessis had volunteered his services to the British as a way to revenge himself and Edward had rewarded him well for the information he provided. It had added significantly to his stock of intelligence at a critical time.

Edward had been obliged to stand Du Plessis down at the end of the war but had since kept in touch with him from time to time. Now Edward could to re-activate his spy.

He explained to Du Plessis that he should find out all he could about the visit of the *Ganges* to the Cape and anything about Captain Dance's time in port, particularly his shopping habits.

Edward needed to know if Dance had purchased any gifts while in port. He was to conduct the assignment as quickly as possible and report back to London by the fastest route.

In a final twist he reminded Du Plessis that this was an operation that he, Edward, was running against the hated Americans who were once again meddling in Britain's affairs.

He called Nicholson to fetch his hat. They would take the letter to the *Secret Office* at Post Office headquarters in Lombard Street at the same time as delivering the Warrant signed by the Home Secretary that authorised the interception of Amherst's mail.

Edward left his third and final task - briefing the *Runners* - until after he had been informed that his letter to Du Plessis had been safely encoded at the Secret Office and dispatched to Cape Town in the Foreign Mail.

5 *Lombard Street*

EDWARD APPRECIATED THAT he would not be able to manage this operation alone. It was time that Nicholson should be indoctrinated into further secret aspects of the Alien Office's work.

They travelled by hansom cab to the first of their appointments. As they moved through Westminster and up Fleet Street, Edward described the background to the work of their associates at the Post Office.

"How much do you know about the Post Office's work?"

"Not much," Nicholson replied.

"You need to know the basic facts. It was founded by Protector Cromwell in 1637. Its first Postmaster-General, John Thurloe, was also his chief spymaster. Opening the Post remains one of its key activities.

The Office pays high salaries to a small group of talented staff numbering never more than twelve. They are all well-educated men - graduates of Oxford or Cambridge – who are justly proud of their enciphering and decoding skills."

"What did the Secret Office do in the war?", Nicholson asked. "My father told me that it was vital."

"Yes it was," Edward replied. Napoleon's forces in Spain were twice the size of the Allied army so knowing the enemy's intentions in a war of rapid movement was critical for victory.

When Wellington's code-master, George Scovell, failed to de-code French messages in the field, he forwarded copies of the originals by fast packet from Lisbon to the Post Office in London. There were a number of occasions when French ciphers were successfully de-coded and returned by the Secret Office to Wellington's headquarters in Spain within ten days of their original receipt in London.

Since the end of the war, the main work of the Secret Office has been the interception and de-ciphering of letters to and from Ireland where the conspiracy between Irish insurrectionists and like-minded supporters in England is the current greatest threat to national security."

"When did you first work with them?", Nicholson asked.

"I got to know the staff at the start of my career when I acted as personal assistant to Director Wickham", Edward went on. "In the American war there were many occasions when I used the services of the Secret Office. My opposite number in America is a man called John Skinner. He is the Postmaster- General in Baltimore and a lawyer who holds violently anti-British opinions after our troops burned down his house during the campaign on the Chesapeake. He is also their chief spymaster.

I got to know more about Skinner last year when Crauford introduced me to a cousin of his, a young army officer named James Dunne, with whom he had served in the American war. Dunne told me his story as we dined together at my Club."

"As you know, Mr. Hazell, the war against the United States of America that started in 1812 could not have come at a worse time for Britain", Dunne began.

"At the very time when all of Britain's resources were stretched to the limit and beyond, our American cousins on the other side of the Atlantic decided to strike.

Ever since the end of the War of Independence, the United States had been looking at Canada through envious eyes. For America's growing and land-hungry population - and for its political leaders - it was both obvious and inevitable that Canada would soon become an American dominion. 'Oh! Canada' sighed the members of the United States Senate whenever its name was mentioned in debate.

Our Government was finally forced into action as a result of a petition that had arrived in Parliament signed by more than four hundred Glasgow merchants and their MPs. Their petition complained at the loss of trade that they were suffering as a result of the actions of American privateers.

They claimed", Dunne continued, "that the privateers had been boarding British registered merchant ships and sailing them into American ports where their cargoes were being sold and their ships either auctioned off or destroyed. As further proof, they said, the cost of insurance at Lloyds stood at an intolerable sixteen percent of the value of each cargo shipped. They demanded that the Government should act.

The most notorious of the American privateers, *The Damned Yankee* - Captain Henry Deacon commanding - came out of Baltimore, which was the home port of many of these seagoing bandits.

She was a sleek, three-masted schooner, one of the fastest afloat on the world's oceans with a crew of over 140 seamen. By this time, she had already plundered more than two hundred and fifty British vessels and taken over 450,000 tons of cargo worth £2.6 million.

HM ships of the North Atlantic Squadron were ordered to rendezvous off the New England coast at Hampton Roads - the mouth of Chesapeake Bay - where the Navy's C-in-C summoned his naval and army commanders on board his flagship.

I have been told", Dunne went on, "that he advised them that their job would be to organise a series of punitive hit and run raids on the towns and villages in the Bay. The objective would be to make life so uncomfortable for the local population that the American government would be obliged to sue for peace.

There would be only one rule of engagement on which he would insist: any persons, households, settlements or villages that submitted themselves to the invaders, would be respected and left in peace. However, if anyone resisted - if so much as a single round was fired towards British soldiers - all their supplies, including their livestock, grain and fodder would be confiscated or destroyed. Their houses would be burned to the ground and their inhabitants taken into protective custody. It was my bad luck", Dunne said, "that I was at the forefront of this policy.

I was told that Cockburn, the naval landings chief, had spoken first and had said that it was about time the British stopped pussy-footing around and taught the *Jonathans* a lesson. Cockburn had 1,700 Royal Marines on board his ships who were itching to see some action."

Dunne went on: "General Robert Ross, the Army commander, with long experience of bitter fighting in the harsh conditions of the Iberian Peninsular, was more circumspect. Apparently Ross replied that he also had troops on the same ships but wanted to know how he was going to get them off and re-supply them once they were ashore.

We began practising disembarking our men on board the Navy's ships as they lay at anchor on the coast.

Three days later, our men were ready and we were authorised to make the initial assault. We were to launch our attack towards the settlement on St Leonard's Creek at the mouth of the Potomac River. A joint raiding party of twelve hundred soldiers and marines would be landed by thirty barges from three warships, HM ships *Diadem*, *Marlborough* and *Plantagenet* that were standing off-shore.

On the following morning it was still pitch dark as my men began to assemble on the ship's decks", Dunne continued.

"A silent *Reveille* had been ordered an hour before dawn and we maintained absolute quiet on board.

Each man had been issued with three days' rations and an extra 50 rounds of ball and powder.

I would be commanding the first troops ashore.

I peered over the side of the *Diadem* at the landing craft to which my platoon of thirty men had been assigned. Two sailors sat in the stern of the launch apparently oblivious to the dangers ahead.

My men had never participated in a sea landing before except for their brief training. To bring the soldiers and sailors ashore in small boats to face an unknown enemy, whose defensive preparations had been observed all the previous day, was going to be a highly risky undertaking.

I had celebrated my twentieth birthday whilst crossing the Atlantic. I had joined the 44th in the previous year at our depot at Warley. I am the eldest son of the Anglican Archdeacon of Wicklow in Ireland. My uncle sits as MP for the constituency in Dublin. He made the connection needed with our colonel, Colonel Brooke, a fellow-Irishman and this led to my father arranging to purchase a Commission on my behalf in the regiment.

I had wanted to be a soldier since childhood and I was thrilled to have joined such a distinguished body of men. As you know, Mr. Hazell, the 44th were the heroes of Salamanca. They captured a French Imperial eagle in that battle and had served with distinction in the earlier American Revolutionary wars. As a result, our veterans hated all things American - both human and animal – and spoke often of its perfidious settlers and blood-sucking insects.

I remember pacing backwards and forwards on the deck behind my men. It would the first time in action for a good many of them and I wanted them to distinguish themselves in whatever action was to come.

It was now four o'clock in the morning as we waited for the signal to embark. I calculated the tree-lined shore lay some six hundred yards away.

I saw the flag raised to mark the embarkation of the first wave of troops and we tumbled into the nets hanging down the landward side of the ship. A sailor in the stern directed the troops to man the oars as we set off, four to each side.

It had been a moonless night so that I could watch our progress towards the shore only by the effervescence in the water as the soldiers pulled on the muffled oars of the launch.

On the shoreline there were dozens of craft like ours beached on the grassy bank of the creek and hundreds of men were sitting on the narrow ground between the shore and the edge of the woods that fringed it.

There was no sign of yesterday's enemy who had watched the fleet's arrival closely", Dunne continued, "and my platoon were ordered into the woods in the direction of the settlement. One of my men pointed to a track and the platoon fell in along it. The woods were planted with a fine stand of oak. My sergeant came up beside me and whispered that the woods were thinning. There seemed to be some farm buildings, barns and sheds ahead. He thought there must also be a dwelling close by and proposed sending off a patrol to investigate.

I thought that this was a sensible idea. I ordered him to take four men and have a good look around. I said that he should make a sketch of the place before we decided on a plan of attack.

The Sergeant selected his men and disappeared into the woods ahead. The rest of us lay down beside the track.

Thirty minutes later the patrol re-emerged and Sergeant Mills reported that it was a big spread. He had counted eight farm buildings before coming across a fine three-storeyed house. The house had a

57

fine stone fronted exterior. The main door and all the windows had been barricaded up. Three farm carts had been turned over in the yard to make a defensive barrier outside the back door.

I said that we would wait until daybreak. I then ordered the platoon to move towards the farm buildings and inspect their contents. I reckoned that one of them would be the milking parlour and that a dairyman or maid would be the first in the household to come outside in the morning.

I decided that we would snatch him or her and have a quiet word that they should go back inside; tell the head of the house that we had surrounded the estate and that they should surrender. I didn't want any trouble.

It happened as I had predicted. At six o'clock the back door of the house was eased open and a man squeezed through it. He crawled under the up-turned carts, stood up and started towards the milking parlour opposite.

As soon as he was away from the house, two of my men grabbed him and I gave him his instructions.

My platoon watched anxiously as the man made his way back into the back of the house and disappeared inside.

I gave the man a good ten minutes before I ordered my men forward. A line of them led by a corporal broke cover and porting their arms approached the front door.

However, as my corporal reached the front step a window on the first floor was thrown open. A rifle barrel was poked through it, and a shot rang out. The round hit the corporal who dropped to the ground in a crumpled heap. The rest of my attacking party stood paralysed before racing back into the cover of the farm buildings.

I knew that I would now have to carry out a full assault."

Dunne, obviously able to recall every moment of the experience, went on: "The front of the house did not provide the approach cover we needed but the up-turned carts in the back yard would do so.

I deployed some of my men for a direct assault on the back door and ordered the remainder to provide them with covering fire from behind the up-turned carts.

I made a particular point that they should mark each window at the front and back. If an individual or firearm showed itself they were to open fire at once.

On the Sergeant's whistle, the men rushed forward onto the barricade. A rifle barrel appeared at an open window on the first floor. Immediately a shot rang out and a man slumped over its sill. There was no further fire.

My assault party reached the shelter of the back porch and broke down the door after shooting out its lock and hinges. They waited for me to join them before entering the house.

My sergeant and I went inside, and across what was obviously the kitchen, before stepping into a wide passage that led to the front of the house.

I heard voices and, reaching the end of the passage, we arrived at the front hall, where we found ourselves at the bottom of the main stairs.

Looking up I saw a white-haired man lying slumped on the landing halfway up below an open window facing the rear of the house. He had obviously taken his shot from there.

A young woman knelt beside him cradling him in her arms as the blood from a gaping wound in his chest - the marksman had taken his shot well - covered her dress and was spreading in a pool across the wooden floor.

Two children who looked to be between nine or ten years old, stood beside their mother. An older woman - presumably the dead man's wife - stood to one side, sobbing loudly as she watched her husband's life ebbing away.

'Oh! Papa. What have they done to you,' the young woman cried, looking downwards as Sergeant Mills and two of his soldiers mounted the stairs behind me.

'Murderers, you have killed an old man who was doing no more than defending us and our liberty.'

'Madam', I responded, 'your servant was fully briefed to advise you of my orders. If you had surrendered, no harm was either intended or would have come to you. However, he was instructed to tell you that if you offered any resistance, then you would be treated as an enemy, either killed or taken prisoner and your property destroyed. I assume he gave you our message? You chose the latter course and have paid the price for your resistance.'

I said that my men must now do our duty and I asked where she wished to bury the old man who, I presumed, was either her father or father in law.

The woman replied that he was neither. He was her step-father, Mr. Bland, and introduced her mother Mrs. Bland to me. She said her name was Elizabeth Skinner, the wife of a Mr. John Skinner of Baltimore. She said that her husband was a leading man in the city; that I had just made a lifelong enemy of him and that Mr Skinner was close to the President, Mr. Madison. The President would hear of this outrage, and would take his revenge on me and my murderous men.

I told Sergeant Mills to summon another two men and find a blanket or piece of carpet in which to carry the dead man downstairs.

I told the family to follow me outside where we would find a suitable spot to bury the woman's step-father at once.

I led the way downstairs and onto the drive where my men had gathered around their dead comrade. When they saw the contents of the blanket, they murmured angrily amongst themselves until quietened by the sergeant.

I looked around before turning to Elizabeth Skinner and inviting her to indicate a suitable resting-place where my men would dig a grave and bury the old man right away.

Mrs Skinner pointed towards a grove of trees at the edge of the property.

Sergeant Mills instructed four of his men to detach themselves and form a digging party whilst I gave out my orders for the burning of the house and farm buildings.

It was the most distasteful set of instructions that I had been called upon to issue since joining the Army."

Dunne went on. "A grisly scene was now played out on the property. One group of soldiers dispersed among the outbuildings and began to set fire to them. Dense black smoke rose from the thatch and timbers and sparks from the flames flew up into the sky.

Meanwhile my burial party dug frantically at the ground and a pile of spoil rose at the grave's edge.

We carried the dead man's body towards the spot and the family followed, stumbling, behind.

I moved between the graveside and the buildings supervising the awful work.

When an hour had passed Sergeant Mills declared that the grave was deep enough to take the body. By this time all the buildings were well alight and smoke had begun to drift across the burial site.

I turned to Elizabeth Skinner and asked her if she had a family Prayer Book from which she wished me to read the burial service.

Mrs Skinner did not respond but turning to the boy told him to fetch his father's prayer book from his study.

The boy ran off and a few minutes later returned with a prayer book which he handed to his mother.

'You killed him, so you can bury him', Elizabeth said, thrusting the book at me.

I ordered my men to form an orderly line behind the family and, recalling a morning's instruction at the Depot at Warley, I turned to the pages marked 'Funeral Rites' and began to recite the burial service.

We brought nothing into the world and we take nothing out. Dust to dust and ashes to ashes..............

Finally, the service was over and my men began to fill in the grave.

I turned to Elizabeth Skinner and explained that my instructions were that any prisoners should be embarked on HMS *Tonnant* on which General Ross flew his flag. The General would decide what would happen next to her and her family. I said that I would be submitting a full report of the all that had happened here today.

Thirty minutes later as smoke began to rise from its roof, I turned my back on the house and led my platoon with the family at its centre under close escort back up the track towards the shore.

The day's work had been the worst possible result that I could have imagined and I was anxious at the response that I would receive from my superiors. However, I believed that I had only done what I had been ordered to do. If there was blame to be apportioned, it lay with the Skinner family and their pointless resistance.

When I reached the shore, I looked for the launch from which we had landed and, hailing its crew, I loaded my prisoners and men into it.

Twenty minutes later I reached the ship and climbed aboard the gangway. I was met on deck by the Adjutant of the 44th.

He asked me what I had been up to and who my prisoners were.

I replied that they were called Skinner and that we had burned their property after one of my men had been fired on and killed.

The Adjutant told me to come below and tell my story. It was clear that I had invited the Skinner family to surrender; that they had resisted and that I had been following my orders, when we burned the house to the ground.

The Adjutant ordered me to write up my account of the incident and sign it before the prisoners were transferred.

Two hours later I escorted Elizabth Skinner, her mother and two chidren onto General Ross's flagship and presented myself to him.

Ross told me that it was unfortunate but that I had done as I had been ordered. I saluted and withdrew.

As I came back on deck I noticed a group of people standing at the ship's rail gazing to shore amongst whom was Elizabeth Skinner. I made a slight bow to her which went unacknowledged. She was talking to a man in a black frock-coat I did not recognise as a member of the British contingent.

Just before I went down the gangway to return to my ship, I asked a midshipman of the watch who the man was.

He told me it was Dr. William Beanes who had been taken prisoner earlier in the week. Apparently, he had refused to treat a number of our wounded ashore and was being held in custody on board. The midshipman thought that Beanes would come in useful if there were any casualties of the day's action.

I was rowed back to my ship and as the other parties returned I had to tell and re-tell the story of my day. That evening I was summoned to Colonel Brooke's cabin.

The Colonel said that it could not be helped; that such things happen in war and that he was sorry that I had lost a man. He had read my action report and that as far as he could see I had followed my orders to the letter. He concluded by saying that the *Jonathans* were the very limit and that as far as he was concerned they deserved everything that was coming to them. He told me to get some rest and that we would be ashore again in the morning."

Dunne ended his story. "I went below to my cabin and took off my uniform - it stank foully of the smoke from the burning farm buildings and I lay on my bunk sleeping fitfully until morning. I was disturbed by recurring images of pooling blood and burned timbers."

"Now you've heard the whole story," Edward said to Nicholson. "That was what Dunne told me of how the campaign on the Chesapeake started". Edward went on: "I pieced together the rest of the story from a variety of sources including from my friend Captain Wild previously of the *Butterfly* who was captured in the war. He was kept at Fort McHenry under unspeakable conditions by John Skinner, who I learned later is the head of the American spy service."

It had been a long morning in the law office that Elizabeth's husband, John Skinner occupied on Calvert Street, the centre of Baltimore's commercial district.

The task that the President had given him, whilst a considerable honour, was no sinecure. By the beginning of the year, some eight thousand American soldiers and sailors, most of them volunteers, had been taken prisoner.

Most of the soldiers had been captured by British troops in the frequent skirmishes that occurred all along the Canadian border. The American militia had developed an unfortunate habit of either turning tail or raising their hands above their heads at the slightest sign of trouble. Pressing back on the enemy was not a manoeuvre that they had practised much. As a result, American losses from surrender were mounting.

The mainly volunteer American army was now facing a much greater threat as the British launched their land campaign against the capital using regular troops. President Madison and his military advisors needed every man available.

If more troops surrendered - and if word got back that American prisoners were being mistreated by the British - it would be almost impossible to raise the numbers needed to defend either the capital, Washington, or Baltimore itself.

The original agreement for prisoner exchange had been made in Halifax, Nova Scotia between Britain's Attorney General in Canada and the United States Commissary General for prisoners of war.

Whilst this *Cartel* had laid down the basic rules of exchange much had been left to the discretion of local agents of which Skinner - selected for his legal background - was one.

Skinner's first run had been to bring back three hundred and seventy American soldiers from captivity in Canada. On the British side there were more seamen than soldiers in captivity. Skinner's next assignment had been to arrange the exchange on parole of one hundred and sixty sailors taken off British ships by American privateers who were now being held in the United States.

These prisoners had been brought into Baltimore over the previous six months and had been imprisoned in Fort McHenry outside the city. Skinner's job was to exchange them for American soldiers held in Halifax. A number of British and American vessels had been designated as exchange ships. Skinner would be travelling on an American vessel, the *Pelican*, taking British prisoners northwards.

American prisoners would travel in the opposite direction on a Royal Navy ship that would return them to Baltimore.

The first stage of the process would be to draw up a list of British prisoners - taken from both Royal Navy and commercial vessels - who would be exchanged. The list would be based on equivalent military ranks: flag captains for colonels; first officers for majors; deck officers for captains, midshipmen for lieutenants and finally - the great majority - deckhands for private soldiers.

On his desk Skinner had a list in two columns: one British and the other American topgether with a pile of draft Parole tickets which each exchanged prisoner must sign before they were released.

"Clay", he called to his clerk in the outer office, "At what time tomorrow have you ordered the trap to take us out to the Fort?"

"Ten o'clock Mr. Skinner and we should be there by eleven. The Governor is expecting us and has made an office available for our use."

"Very well. I will see you tomorrow at ten. You can close up the office and go home. I shall be fifteen minutes behind you."

John Skinner rose from his desk glancing at the framed water-colour painting on the wall opposite as he did at the end of every day.

It was a picture of his beloved home at St Leonard's Creek thirty miles outside the city. Built by his grandfather over seventy years ago it had been extended by both his father and himself. The front of the house now had a stylish façade in the manner of Adam surrounded by domestic buildings. The property included an arable and livestock farm of more than four hundred acres.

St Leonard's had become one of the most prestigious estates in the area. He went back there as frequently as he could - which was not often enough - but he had complete confidence in his beloved wife Elizabeth's management. She had the advice of his his father in law, Mr. Bland, when it was needed.

Skinner returned to his lodgings for the night and the following morning reached his office in good time.

An hour later he and his clerk arrived at the Fort and were admitted to the governor's office.

"Morning John, good to see you. I shall be relieved when this job is over. Guarding prisoners is no work for grown men. I have done my best to provide for them but conditions here have inevitably been harsh. There has been little to spare in the way of supplies and feelings have been running high amongst my men at the stories they have heard about the treatment by the British of our prisoners at Halifax."

"I understand", Skinner replied, "We will work as quickly as we can. I expect we will complete the lists in a couple of days. Then those eligible for parole will be taken down to the city and put aboard the *Pelican* which is waiting for them in the harbour. I will be escorting them on the journey north and returning to the city with our own prisoners in two weeks' time."

"Very well. I will show you to your office. Here, take these."

The governor handed Skinner and Clay a linen handkerchief each.

"You may find these useful. The prisoners stink to high heaven so I have soaked them in lavender oil."

Skinner followed the governor out of his office and down a passage that led to an iron door. Guards stood on each side of it and two others appeared beside them.

"These two men will accompany you and remain with you throughout the day. I am not expecting trouble but you never know. It's best to be careful."

Skinner and his clerk were let through the door and followed the two guards into the part of the Fort that was being used as a prison.

The guards stopped outside a studded door and unlocked it. A table and three chairs stood inside. A ragged line of men in filthy rags stood outside. Some were on crutches, others leaned on their fellow prisoners for support. Their faces were haggard and their bones stick-like. They gave off a foul stench of unwashed bodies and stinking breath.

The guards took up position at each end of the table. Skinner turned to Clay.

"The governor was right about the harsh conditions. I hope that our prisoners are not being held in the same way. If they are, there will be hell to pay on both sides."

Skinner instructed the guards to bring in the first prisoner.

"Your name, rank and vessel."

The man who sat in front of him had a ruined face with deep blotches under his eyes and bedraggled hair. As he scratched his scalp Skinner could see movement under his black nails.

"Wild, Captain, the Schooner *Butterfly*, captured off Madeira last July."

"Are you prepared to provide the United States with your Parole? That is, that you will be returned to Halifax and thence to England on condition that you undertake not to sail in any capacity whatsoever whilst this war continues?"

"I am willing to sign but not without recording that I protest most vehemently at the way that I and my crew have been treated since our capture."

"If this has been so, then I regret it, but you should be aware that we also have reports of our prisoners being mistreated by the British."

"Where should I sign?"

Clay pointed at a blank Parole form: "Sign here….. and here….."

'Whereas, John Skinner Esq. Agent for the care and custody of Prisoners of War at Baltimore has granted me the undersigned prisoner, described on the back hereof, permission to return to England upon condition that I give my parole of honour, I do hereby declare that I will not enter into any naval, military or other service whatever against the United States of America and will keep it inviolably.

Signed.......'

"Good day to you Captain Wild. I wish you a speedy return home. I shall be your escort into Halifax so we will meet again when you come on board."

And so the long day got under way. It was a depressing business as more and more complaints were made about the way that the British prisoners had been treated but finally it was over.

Skinner and Clay were escorted out of the Fort and made their way back into Baltimore.

Two days later the job was done and Skinner returned to the governor's office.

"It's not been a pretty business. I would be surprised if the prisoner's complaints did not end up in front of the Board of Exchange. Let's hope to God that our own prisoners are not in so poor a condition. The vessel in which they will be taken north is prepared. I would be obliged if you would bring the men down to the quay in batches of twenty-five for embarkation on tomorrow's tide."

On his return to the city Skinner sent a message down to the port advising the *Pelican* that loading would start the following day.

The next morning he packed a light valise and went on board accompanied by his clerk, Clay.

At eleven o'clock the first group of prisoners arrived at the quayside and staggered up the gangway.

By two in the afternoon all the prisoners had boarded and the ship was rowed out into the Bay before hoisting sail.

Three days later after an uneventful passage the captain raised the special signal flag that identified the ship as an exchange vessel and they entered the Port of Halifax under escort.

Skinner disembarked first and was met by William Miller, RN, his opposite number on the British side.

"Greetings, Sir, I trust that you have had an easy passage. If you would come with me to the Port Office we can check the Parole documents that you are carrying and begin the exchange. I have interviewed the men we have been holding and have made out their tickets."

Skinner returned to the *Pelican* and spoke to the captain.

"You may begin the exchange. The British prisoners are to be led one by one down the gangway where I will identify them and pass their Parole ticket to this officer. Our job will then be done and they will have been returned to British hands. When the exchange has been completed I will transfer to the British ship that will be carrying our boys back to Baltimore."

When all the British prisoners had left the ship, Skinner walked down the quay with Miller to where a Royal Navy vessel waited. On the quayside stood a table and chair at the head of a line of men who could only be described as skeletons.

If the British prisoners at Fort McHenry had been filthy, haggard and stinking, these were in a much worse state. Skinner drew in his breath; he needed that linen handkerchief now. The American prisoners were emaciated; their bones stuck out from their hanging flesh and their eyes were sunk deep into their skulls.

Miller held out the Parole forms and Skinner checked the men up the gangway one by one. Most were not strong enough to climb up on their own and had to be helped by sailors before being taken below.

By late afternoon loading was complete and the ship set sail south. Skinner went to his cabin and made out his report.

The President himself would hear of the harsh treatment the prisoners had suffered at the hands of their British captors but the news would have to be kept from the American public for as long possible.

One way to do this would be to remove the men to Baltimore's lazarette as soon as they landed and to restrict access to their families only. This might sound harsh but it would be vital to prevent further desertions from amongst the American volunteers.

John Skinner vowed that when the opportunity arose he would have his revenge for this outrage. His open hostility to the British had changed to a deadly hatred.

Two weeks later as he ate his supper in the chophouse on York Street, Clay appeared beside him holding a letter.

"This came for you just as I was shutting up the office. It's marked *Urgent*."

Skinner took the letter and slit it open with his knife.

Kinsale Farm
St Leonard's Settlement
Tuesday 21st
5pm

Dear John,
At 2pm this afternoon we saw smoke rising from the direction of your house.

We dared not approach as we knew that British forces had landed in the Creek..

However, at 4pm I sent Henry to find out what was going on.

He reached the house - or what remains of it — to find it burnt out along with all the buildings around it.

I understand from your man, that when the British arrived there was some resistance and I am very sorry to tell you that your father in law, Mr. Bland, was shot dead and Elizabeth, her mother and the children have been removed off-shore as prisoners.

I have taken all of your staff that I could find into the shelter of my house and I will keep them here until you arrive.

I am most deeply sorry at this course of events and will be ready to assist you in any way that I am able. Please do not hesitate to call upon me for anything you may need and you will, of course, be welcome to stay with us at Kinsale should you so wish.

I remain your good friend and neighbour,

James Wright

PS This letter may be delayed as the British have cut off all communications from the coast.'

Skinner bowed his head as he absorbed the dreadful news before looking up at his clerk.

"Read this, Clay and find me a horse to take me out to Kinsale at once. My father in law is dead; my wife and children have been taken prisoner and my house burned to the ground. Damned those Britishers, I will revenge this outrage"

He left thirty minutes later and arrived at Kinsale by evening. James Wright met him at the door of his house.

"I am most fearfully sorry about this John. Your servants are in the kitchen downstairs waiting for you. They have had their evening meal."

"Thank you, friend. I want to hear their story before I decide what to do next."

He went down and heard the story of the attack and its aftermath.

He decided to spend the night at Kinsale. He would visit his ruined house in the morning.

The next day he rode across to his home. The sight that met his eyes was one of devastation. The house had a large hole in its roof; the surrounding farm buildings were wrecked and his prize herd of milking cows crowded around the burned-out milking parlour lowing piteously.

He could do no good staying here.

He was back in the city by lunchtime and went around at once to see his lawyer friend and close colleague Francis Scott Key, the other prisoner exchange agent resident in Baltimore. Skinner needed his friend's advice urgently.

When he arrived at Scott Key's office he told him the dreadful story.

Scott Key listened to his news in silence.

"This is unspeakable. Your father in law dead and your wife and children prisoners of the British; but I have an idea. I am supposed to board the *Minden* this morning. I received a note from President Madison yesterday that the vessel would be placed at my disposal in order to affect the exchange of Dr. Beanes, an old friend and ally of the President.

I am to go on board Cochrane's flagship the *Tonnant* where Beanes is being held and open negotiations for his release.

The British took him on suspicion of allowing the execution of a number of wounded soldiers who had surrendered. I believe that there are also some other civilian prisoners who are being held on board. Elizabeth could be amongst them, At least we can find out where she is and will be able to speak with the British commanders."

"I have no evidence that Elizabeth is on the *Tonnent* but at least it would be a place to start", Skinner replied gloomily.

At two o'clock the two men went down to the town quay and located the *Minden*. Her captain welcomed them on board and an hour later they set sail out of the harbour into Chesapeake Bay at the mouth of which the captain believed the British fleet lay at anchor.

It was a fine day with a fair wind. Three hours later they reached Hampton Roads and saw the British fleet ahead. It was an awesome sight with over seventy ships of all shapes and sizes at anchor. The *Minden* raised her exchange pennant and began to sail between the ships looking for the *Tonnant*.

When they had located her, the captain drew alongside and stated their business. An officer of the watch responded and the party was allowed to board.

As Skinner reached the deck, a swirl and rush of petticoats flung itself at him as Elizabeth wrapped herself around him. She clung to him as she sobbed into his ear "Oh my darling, my darling."

Over the next thirty minutes, Elizabeth recounted the terrible events that had occurred at the farm.

"Yes, I know my dearest", Skinner responded, "I rode straight out there when I heard the news and stayed the night with James. He will look after the servants for as long as needed. We will, of course, rebuild the house as quickly as possible and return there together but first we need to get you and the children off this ship and out of captivity.

There has been some kind of trouble involving Dr. Beanes. Francis has also come on board to sort it out. I was lucky to be able to travel with him. You stay here while I go and find out what he is planning."

Skinner went back on deck and found Scott Key deep in conversation with Beanes.

Scott Key looked up at Skinner. "There has been a terrible mistake. The doctor here was trying to help the wounded not execute or imprison them. I shall have to go back ashore and get the full story before returning. Then I can place the proper evidence in front of General Ross who is in a rage about the doctor's alleged behaviour. It will not take me more than twenty-four hours. Then I shall return. I will insist that Elizabeth and your family are included in any parole that I arrange."

Scott Key was as good as his word. The following day he returned with six affidavits signed by British soldiers who had been wounded at Upper Marlborough. They all attested that Dr. Beanes had attended to their wounds and had treated them with respect.

The two lawyers asked for an audience with Ross and presented the evidence to him. Ross was somewhat mollified but not yet wholly convinced and raised the issue of the dead corporal of the 44th.

The two lawyers responded that they regretted the unnecessary deaths at St Leonard's and that, in return for the release of Dr. Beanes and the Skinner family, they would request that the President should authorise the parole of seventy-five British soldiers being held at Fort McHenry who would be returned to the Fleet.

"That will hardly be needed", replied Ross, "the Citadel will be in our hands within a week. You will be able to witness our victory from on board."

"Nevertheless", responded Scott Key, "I think that I will write that letter to Mr. Madison, just in case your plan of attack does not bring you the success you expect."

Scott Key, the Skinner family and Beanes were all held on board for another two days as all around them preparations were made for the final assault on Baltimore. This would start with a British naval bombardment and an attack on Fort McHenry.

At four o'clock on the following morning Skinner felt a sudden movement in the ship and, looking out of a porthole, saw that the whole fleet was raising sail and moving upstream.

Two hours later the ship was shaken by an enormous salvo of shells directed at the Fort. Hurrying on deck, Skinner could see the land of shot on and around the Fort which was covered in smoke.

At the same time a flotilla of small ships was moving in shore to start the assault.

The battle raged all day. It was impossible to calculate which side was winning. As evening drew on Skinner could still just see the tower at the top of the fortification. An enormous Stars and Stripes had been hung from it which must have been made by the defenders. It was now being displayed in defiance of the British.

The small group of Americans on the *Tonnant* clapped and cheered as they were hurried below deck by an officer.

The next day the prisoners were summoned to Ross's cabin

"The assault has not yet been successful. We have decided to call off the attack whilst we re-group. We will renew our attack later in the week. Meanwhile I want all supernumeraries off the ship. I have agreed with Scott Key here that you will be returned ashore in exchange for one hundred and fifty British prisoners to be delivered on board this ship. The exchange will be supervised by you", here Ross pointed at Key and Skinner, "acting as agents for the United States and as men of honour.

You are fortunate that my men gave you, Beanes, a good report or you would have paid the ultimate penalty. I have further agreed with Scott Key that you, Sir" - now pointing at Skinner - "will pay compensation of $100 for the death of the 44th's corporal.

Now, you are dismissed."

With that Ross turned his back on the two men and they were led out of his cabin.

The same afternoon the *Minden* was detached from the Fleet with Scott Key and Skinner on board to fetch the British soldiers out of Baltimore with whom the American prisoners on board would be exchanged.

Three days later Elizabeth was at the ship's side to watch the released British prisoners come on board. She too was appalled by their appearance. The party then went aboard the *Minden* for its journey back into Baltimore where they would be free at last.

The family spent its first night ashore with friends in the city but next day they set off for home. They would stay at Kinsale until their own house was habitable again.

John Skinner lay in bed in the principal guest room next to Elizabeth unable to sleep as he went over again in his mind the events of the last few days.

His loathing of the British which had first been one of hatred now became a vow of revenge for the wreckage of his home and the treatment of his family and nation.

As they moved through the London streets Edward continued his explanation of Crauford's attitude to the Americans.

"Crauford makes no secret of his feelings about the *Jonathans*. You know what we are up against and why I am anxious at the part they could play in the South Atlantic. That is why we must tread very softly in both London and on St Helena. Skinner will offer any support that he can to anyone planning an escape attempt on Napoleon's behalf.

Hazell and Nicholson arrived in Lombard Sreet and paid off the cabby. Getting through security at the locked door to the left of the

Post Office's main gate in Lombard Street was not just a formality. The two men had to show their personal passes signed jointly by Crauford and Postmaster General Anthony Todd before the door-keeper, an old soldier of the 95th, would open the door. He gave the pair a cheery greeting: "Still at it then, Mr. Hazell, Sir? Go straight up."

The Secret Office was located on the first floor of the building above which were a number of spacious apartments where the bachelor staff lived in considerable comfort. Hazell's friend James Longdon, greeted the two men.

"Hello, old boy, how are you. We have not seen you here for ages. What kind of trouble are you in?"

"This is Nicholson, my new private secretary", Edward replied, "who I am introducing into this operation. He has been cleared for top-secret intelligence.

I'm not in any trouble but I would be grateful if you would arrange for this letter to be en-coded in the Atlantic code before sealing it and sending it downstairs for dispatch."

"Good gracious", Longdon exclaimed, "Are we going to war with the Americans again?"

"No, it's not about America yet - although it may well become so if my suspicions are confirmed", Edward replied. "It's to Du Plessis at the Cape. You remember, that fellow who helped us with the privateers. Now I need to re-activate him to answer a question about General Bonaparte's imprisonment on St Helena."

"Glory, I thought we had heard the last of that ghastly little man."

"So did we all, but you know how things are in London with all this talk of his being released. The Government is determined that will not happen and it's my job to make certain that it doesn't."

"Well, good luck to you. I'll put it into the code and send you a receipt when the letter has been sent."

"Have you any plans for the weekend?", continued Longdon. "It's my birthday on Saturday. I'm having a few friends around. How about joining us? Come at about six and, by the way, Julia will be coming. I know you still fancy her and she likes you."

This was a continual topic of conversation between the two men. Longdon's sister Julia and Edward had known each other since Cambridge days. Longdon was determined that the two should become more than just friends. Edward was very fond of Julia. She was both attractive and intelligent, a thoroughly modern woman. But, whilst he was very much attracted to Julia, he was anxious about their relationship on both personal and professional grounds.

The spying game was all-consuming and left precious little space for a personal life, let alone a married one. More serious were his professional concerns about Julia.

Julia's step-father, Sir Thomas Goode - her father had died in India when she was a child - was a well-respected MP who sat in the Liberal interest and, whilst not a member of Lord Holland's inner circle, was known to share his views about Bonaparte and St Helena. Holland stirred up trouble in the Lords and Sir Thomas did the same in the Commons.

Edward could not tell Julia the nature of his work which he found frustrating. All he could tell her was that he worked at the Home Office on immigration matters. He could say nothing about his secret work against the Americans or the French.

On the last occasion when they had met, Julia had accused Edward of being a government stooge and involved with prosecutions at the Maidstone trials.

Edward had no idea how she knew about his involvement but suspected that her father had must have told her. If so, this was a gross breach of parliamentary privilege after MPs had been briefed in private by a team of Home Office officials of whom Edward had been one. Her step-father should certainly not have said anything to his daughter about Edward's role in the affair.

Edward knew that as an only child Julia was very close to her mother and step-father. They spoiled her. As a result, she usually got her own way and if she had asked Sir Thomas about Edward's prospects, he would have told her.

There was even a risk that she could compromise his present assignment if anything leaked about the counter-measures that he had planned against the Holland set in London and against Bonaparte on St Helena.

However, whilst he must be on his guard, perhaps Saturday evening would be an opportunity to think again about their situation.

"I would be delighted. Until Saturday then and don't delay with that letter to Du Plessis."

Edward and Nicholson made their farewells and left the Secret Office.

Walking out into the sunshine, they hailed a passing cab. Edward said: "As you have now been indoctrinated into one of my secrets, you might as well know the other. Get in."

"No. 20, Bow Street, please.", he told the cabby.

"You in trouble Guv? That's Mr. Fielding's gaff."

"Just take me there, if you please."

Edward had to make the last of his arrangements which could potentially be the most fraught.

Bow Street was as leaky as a sieve and it would be difficult to keep his operation against Amherst a secret.

Edward shuddered. Secrecy was in his blood. It was one of the reasons that his affair with Julia had not developed during these last few months. Of course, he had been busy but there was more to it than that.

Since childhood he had always found it difficult to share his thoughts with others and this had made him an effective spy. He would not speak unless he was spoken to and rarely offered an opinion. It was difficult to know how this had started. Edward was one of five children and ranked third in the family pecking order. Above him was his sister Lucy who never stopped talking. She always answered a question for him before he could open his mouth to reply even when it was addressed to him.

He had often found himself on his own at achool not because he was unpopular but simply because he actually enjoyed his own company. Later, he had made a number of close friends at Cambridge but they were individuals who were content to be silent in each other's company as they read in College or walked the Fen country at weekends.

It was on these expeditions that he had first developed his interest in birds and in closely observing their habits. Later he had studied maps and navigation, the details of which fascinated him.

On graduation, his father, who had already placed two sons into the legal profession, told Edward, his third son, that he would have to make his cateer in the army or navy and that, given his skills, the Navy would suit him better. However, Edward had been violently seasick on the packet from Newhaven on the only occasion on which the family had crossed over to France on holiday and was not attracted to the Service as a career.

It was shortly before he was to graduate that his tutor at Trinity asked him what he intended to do when he left and when Edward responded that his mind was not made up, had suggested the Civil Service. He put this to his father who remarked that he could do worse; it would lead to a secure job and that he could put Edward in touch with a former colleague at the Home Office.

So it was arranged that Edward would meet with William Wickham who appeared to be in charge of a department that was responsible for public order. They met at Crown Street in Whitehall two weeks later. However, after exchanging pleasantries about their shared experience of College, it became plain that Wickham's work involved a little more than maintaining public order in London and the provinces. He was Britain's top spymaster.

If Edward should decide to join Wickham he would become involved in secret work of the utmost importance for the defence of the realm. After an apprenticeship of three years, and if Edward was considered proficient at the work, there would be only one condition to his permanent employment. This would be that he would never be able to speak about it to anyone outside of the Office. This would include his wife and family, should he ever acquire one.

This was another reason that Edward had difficulties in his relationship with Julia: he would not be able to be honest with his wife. He would never be able tol tell Julia about his work from their wedding day onwards.

His first three years in the Office were traumatic. Following the brief truce of Amiens in 1803, all out war with France had already lasted for a further six years before Edward's recruitment in 1809. Three years later America decided to attack Britain.

The stated reason was the way that Britain was applying the *Press* to American merchant vessels as its own Navy ran out of sailors to man its warships. The real reason was the increasingly successful blockade that Britain had applied to Napoleon's continental empire, which prevented American trade with Europe.

One day Wickham called Edward into his office and informed him that in addition to his duties protecting merchant convoys in the North Atlantic he was to go down to South Africa on his first secret mission. American privateers were threatening Britain's trade in the Far East. Their ships were putting into Simonstown for supplies before proceeding into the Indian Ocean to harass Company vessels laden with goods on their way home from Asia. British ships were being boarded, ransacked, set on fire and sunk. If this continued Britain's overseas trade would suffer and the City of London would no longer be able to finance the war.

Wickham warned Edward that he would find the population of Simonstown hostile to British interests as many of the Dutch merchants remained loyal to Holland and resented the recent British take over. In addition, the docks would be full of American and French spies and their sympathisers whose aim was to destroy Britain. If they discovered what he was up to they would expose and murder him.

He would be using a false identity and would sail in three day's time. He was to use the alias John McCulloch, a merchant from Leeds, which would give him good reason to remain in Simonstown making connections with traders and shippers in the port.

Edward spent the next two days clearing his office. He wrote a note to his father saying that he had to go away unexpectedly for a few weeks on government business. He was uncertain if he should communicate with Julia about his absence. Wickham was emphatic that his staff should never imply that they would be away. Edward decided that he should not write to her directly but would leave it to his friend Longdon at the Post Office to inform her.

Edward's passage to the Cape was uneventful and five weeks later he landed at the Cape. He took a lease on a small office on the docks; set himself up in trade and took a room at the Neptune Hotel just outside the port. The hotel was frequented by passengers and, more importantly, by ships' captains and seafarers that would enable him to pick up gossip around-the-clock.

Wickham had issued Edward with a set of code books which he kept locked in his office safe. He made jottings in his pocket book that recorded the significant arrivals and departures of American and other vessels. At the end of each week he transferred these into code for dispatch to London.

The Navy's spy at the Cape was a grizzled old lieutenant of Marines who had not worn the King's uniform for six years. He posed as a gang-master recruiting replacement crew for merchant ships. He also lodged at the Neptune and he and Edward could meet privately in the evenings without arousing suspicion.

However, they were aware that the rival American espionage service led by its chief, John Skinner, also had agents in the port. They would need to take care if they were to remain undetected. Although Edward changed his daily routine as often as possible, he still felt exposed. The British presence was resented and he was often subjected to hostile comments.

One day when he had been living in Simonstown for four months he began to be aware of the same man walking down the street outside his office each morning. Edward became suspicious that he was being watched.

He and his Navy opposite number devised a plan. Edward would leave his hotel and walk to a notoriously low dive ouside the port called the *The Dublin Inn* about fiveteen minutes away. It was managed by a veteran of the 88th who preferred the sunshine of the Cape to the climate in Ireland.

The Navy's spy would follow Edward at a distance and check if he was being followed. Thirty minutes after Edward had arrived at the tavern, the Marine entered and, with a shake of his head, confirmed that Edward was free of *lice*. They sat companionably together at the back of the tavern with an eye on the door.

However, half way through the evening as the noise rose around them, two men, sailors, and clearly the worse for wear, lurched towards them.

"I know you's", the man nearest to Hazell said to his companion and made to place his hand on the Marine's shoulder. As the seaman's partner pretended to pull him back by the arm, the man suddenly drew a knife from his boots and plunged it into the Marine's stomach. Edward jumped up from his seat and tried to grab the killer at the same time as the landlord, seeing what was happening, took down a musket from above the bar and shot a ball into the ceiling.

As the shot rang the whole company froze allowing one of the men to escape through the crush but not before Edward had grabbed the other man by the throat almost throttling him. The Marine clutched his stomach, blood covering his fingers.

"I've seen these two before, they're Americans", said a man who came up to Hazell speaking with a strong Dutch accent. "My name is Du Plessis. I have medical training; let me see the wound."

The landlord appeared at their side. He took hold of the Marine's assailant saying: "I'll lock him up in the cellar for the night, Sir. We can interrogate him in the morning. This man needs the lazarette."

They put the Marine officer on a stretcher and took him to the Port surgery where his wound was stitched up. It wasn't certain if he would survive the night.

One thing that was certain was that Edward and the Navy man's cover had been blown. Somehow, the Americans had found out that they were British spies. Was it the Navy's man who had been in Simonstown for much longer than Edward or was it a leak from as far away as Baltimore or London?

No matter how it had happened, they had been compromised.

Du Plessis had accompanied the stretecher to the lazarette and asked Edward the reason he thought they had been attacked. Edward hinted at the culprits and Du Plessis told Edward that he hated the Americans for the way that they had treated him and his crew at sea.

He would be delighted to help Edward if thought he could make a difference.

For the next two months Edward kept to his office and Du Plessis roamed the docks. They only met in secret when there was intelligence to exchange. As the war moved in Britain's favour, fewer American raiders came down south and Wickham recalled Edward to England. The vessel in which he would travel would call in at St Helena for fresh supplies.

Twelve days later Edward went on deck to watch their arrival into Jamestown, the island's only landing place. St Helena appeared to be extremely hostile with high cliffs, strong winds and choppy seas. He wondered if he should stay on board or go ashore for the night. He decided that a night on land would be preferable. After a hazardous ride in the the ship's tender he clamberd onto a pontoon fastened to the dockside and took a room in Porteous's lodging house.

His ship would be in port for two days and on the following morning Edward hired a carriage to explore the island. It was as bleak and unhospitable as he had imagined and obviously quite impregnable. Even so, there seemed to be a significant number of troops in residence. When he asked the reason, he was told that both French and American men of war were often sighted out at sea.

He returned on board and six weeks later landed back in London. He reported his adventures to Wickham who remarked: "You did well as far as it went but the Americans caught onto you very quickly. How do you explain that?"

"I don't know, Sir. The cover you gave me was good but the Navy's liaison had been around for a long time. Perhaps, it was he who was blown."

"Well, at least we are beating the blasted *Jonathans* at last. Burning the White House certainly taught them no end of a lesson."

Before he left the office at the end of the week, Edward gave a messenger a note addressed to Julia saying that he was back in his office in King Street. Edward invited her to join him at the theatre on Saturday evening. He hoped that he would be able to explain himself without Julia asking too many questions about his recent absence.

The Bow Street Runners

IN THE EARLY nineteenth century London was a lawless city. In fact, it was two lawless cities. The first was the city of Westminster that included the Parliamentary Estate with its members of both houses; the seat of government in Downing Street with its Departments of State and the grand houses of the newly-rich. These were built cheek by jowl with the mean and crowded streets inhabited by the poor. The focus for lawlessness were the hundreds of *stews* concentrated around Covent Garden and Haymarket. These dens provided all manner of vice for the affluent classes and attracted every kind of criminal.

The second city was the City of London, the original city of the Romans and the merchants of the medieval craft Guilds. This city was becoming the richest place on earth through its trade with India and the Far East. This city jealously guarded its ancient privileges, making its own arrangements for the security of the offices and the warehouses that stretched up and down the banks of the Thames. Its main problem was the activity of large and well organised gangs operating along the riverside who robbed warehouses and attacked shipping at anchor.

"Ever been to Bow Street?", Edward asked Nicholson.

Edward was only half joking. If there had been anything on Nicholson's record that suggested felony, he would never have been appointed to his post in the Alien Office.

Edward went on: "You will know the name of Henry Fielding. He was the lawyer and playwright who campaigned for action by the

Government against London's criminals. He converted his house in Bow Street into a courtroom and recruited a small team of *Runners* to chase down suspects.

Fielding died of overwork in 1764 but his brother John took over his work. John was born blind at birth and affects a terrifying appearance in court. He wears a black silk scarf across his eyes tied by a bow at the back.

We will look in on him on our way to our appointment.

Although much of the crime in London is of the petty variety, there are occasions when we are obliged to call for help from Fielding on more serious matters. This has been when suspected spies have to be followed around London.

During the war these came mainly from France but since it ended our focus has been on Ireland. Members of the London Corresponding Society have been suspected of plotting insurrection and last year's trial at Maidstone was the result of the work of the *Runners*. I had a part in that operation and have had to watch my back ever since.

There have never been more than ten men on the Fielding brothers' books at any one time but there is an ad-hoc network that they can call upon if needed. The staff at Bow Street also turn a private profit by pursuing private vendettas on behalf of the rich and powerful. This often includes the provision of security to members of the Government and the Royal Court. One well-known Runner, who you are about to meet, saved the King's life when he was stabbed by a frenzied attacker outside St James's Palace three years ago," Edward concluded.

They had now reached No. 20. Edward and Nicholson stepped out of the cab. The house looked like an ordinary bow-windowed mansion from the outside but had been converted into a courtroom on the ground floor.

Quite apart from being able to convince John Fielding that his business was for the public good, and a suitable use of Bow Street resources, Edward would still have to steer a tricky path between the public and private work of the Runners's staff.

In particular, the two most senior and experienced runners would need careful handling if the game that Edward wanted to play was not going to be given away.

The first of these two individuals, John Townsend, a former coster-monger from the East End of London, was a larger than life character and well known in the city of Westminster as the King's saviour. He affected a white top hat, dark blue top-coat and highly polished black boots. He was allowed access in and out of St James's Palace and the smart London homes of the aristocracy.

He helped his rich patrons solve their petty difficulties that included the gambling debts of their young blades; the unwanted offspring of their teenage *molls* and the often already married - and invariably penniless - Irishmen seeking the hand in marriage of their only daughters who were the heirs to their huge fortunes.

Townsend was known to have a vicious temper; a large appetite for women and took offence easily. He was a terrible snob and an expert in the pedigrees of all the great families born on both sides of the blanket.

As a result, there was no way that he could be disguised as anyone other than who he was - but this could help Edward's present mission. Edward needed the access that Townsend could provide to target Amherst's social network. He needed to know who Amherst was meeting and what was being discussed in the fashionable drawing-rooms of Westminster.

The question was: how could Edward apply sufficient pressure on Townsend and how much money would he demand for his discretion?

As usual Bow Street was a scrum. The entrance hall was crowded with people trying desperately to get inside - hoping to gloat at an enemy before they were taken down from the dock. Moving in the opposite direction were who were desperately trying to get out - to catch their last glimpse of a loved one leaving under escort for transfer to *The Fleet* prison or to a hulk anchored in the Thames. The latter inevitably followed by an eight-month voyage to Britain's vicious prison colony on the fatal shore of New South Wales.

The two men elbowed their way forward and Edward asked at the desk if Townsend was in.

"He's in his office", the clerk replied without looking up. Edward and Nicholson walked down a narrow passage and came to a closed door outside of which stood the usual assortment of supplicants. A strange sound came from within.

He elbowed his way to the front of the queue and pushed open the door. The sight that met his eyes was not wholly unexpected. The first thing he saw was Townsend's breeches around his ankles followed by the sight of his bare arse pumping away at a girl lying on her back across the front of his desk whose legs waved in the air and whose hands gripped the edge of the desk beneath her. Her bright red dress was bunched at her waist. Ribbons of the same colour were woven into her hair, her bodice and her shoes. The ribbons floated in the fetid air of Townsend's office.

Townsend glanced over his shoulder as he shouted "Get out of here right now or I will cut your throat.". Then he saw the two men, turned around and, pulling up his breeches, said "Begging your pardon, Sirs, please come in and sit down". At the same time, he gave a sharp slap to the girl's backside and told her to scarper. "They are like wasps, Sir, I just can't keep them off me, always wanting some favour or another."

"I bet!", Edward thought – private favours in return for the dismissal of public charges - as he sat down wondering how to play the meeting.

He decided that an avuncular rather than a disdainful manner would work better on Townsend who would not take kindly to being thought vulgar or that Edward was patronising him. Townsend liked to think that his police work had equal status to the work of the Alien Office.

Edward also calculated that he had the advantage in his relationship with Townsend and Bow Street. He was familiar with Townsends's file at the Alien Office.

The file described the small matter of Townsend's profits from introductions he had made to a private members' club in Mayfair. The club turned out to have been heavily involved in male prostitution that included the entrapment and blackmail of a number of senior Government officials. The scandal had been covered up but it had enabled the Office to keep tabs on a number of important people when it required information about threats to national security. This had included the exposure of an official who had been passing intelligence about troop movements between England and Ireland that could have assisted Irish rebels.

If the Office had obtained more complete information, Townsend would have been in serious trouble. As it was, he was uncertain of just how much the Alien Office knew about him and this should make him willing to listen to what Edward had to say.

"How are you, John? Not short of company, I see. This is my assistant, Francis Nicholson. His father sits in the High Court."

Townsend shook Nicholson's hand.

"Delighted I'm sure. Sir. I've heard your father's name mentioned. Wasn't he involved in that Cheapside murder case last year? Now, what can I do for you?", replied Townsend, turning to Edward without hesitation or any hint of embarrassment.

"Well, the first thing you can do, John, is to tell the crowd outside your door that your office is closed for the rest of the day. When they've gone, close the door behind you and lock it."

Townsend did as Edward asked telling his petitioners to go home before sitting down again behind his desk.

"And, what brings young Hazell around at the end of a blistering afternoon?"

Now, who was being patronised?

"It's a highly delicate matter of national security that has been drawn to the attention of the Home Secretary who, I know, would appreciate your help."

Edward was aware that Townsend hero-worshipped the Great Duke. The mention of this connection would appeal to all his snobbish instincts.

Edward explained what he wanted.

"I have here a Warrant signed by the Home Secretary himself that authorises the Alien Office to organise a surveillance operation against Lord Amherst.

I want you to observe Amherst in plain sight in the course of his usual socialising. You are to report to me of any meetings that he holds with any member of the Opposition or any other individual who you consider might be hostile to the Government's interests."

"Well I never, Mr Hazell. Spying on a minister. You could get me sent to the Tower."

Edward laughed.

"You've done much more dangerous work than this in your time. You are to report to me on a weekly basis or at once and in person in the event of an emergency.

There will be nothing in writing."

"Very well, Mr. Hazell, and what will be my reward? More than the usual I assume?"

"You will escape the rope, that's for sure", Edward replied, making an oblique reference to Townsend's former troubles.

"And there is more than enough reward in knowing that you will be serving the Duke and your country. However, because of the need for your utmost discretion and because you will be appearing as a gentleman in public places such as the Theatre Royal, the Office will reimburse you generously. I will speak with General Crauford and obtain his agreement to the precise terms."

Edward also knew that the use of Crauford's name would send a particular shiver down Townsend's spine. The senior runner had once told him that, whilst campaigning in the Peninsular, Crauford had ordered Townsend's brother, a rifleman in the 43rd, to receive thirty lashes for insubordination as the Light Division had crossed the Duoro into Spain. On his return to London at the end of the war, his brother had sworn his revenge on *Black Bob* if they were ever to meet. This was highly unlikely, but would be another reason for Townsend's discretion.

"That will be quite acceptable, Sir. As it happens I am due at Lord and Lady de Lacey's this evening for a supper in honour of their newly married son and daughter-in-law. He sits for the Tory interest in the Lords but has friends in all parts of the House. I will keep my eyes and ears open for anything connected to Lord Amherst."

"Many thanks for your time, John. This assignment is to have priority over all your other work. I shall inform Mr. Fielding of this before I leave Bow Street. He will not, however, know the full details of our discussion except that you will be working most urgently in the public interest."

As Edward and Nicholson turned to leave Townsend rose from his chair to take their hands and remarked to the younger man: "By the way, Sir, if you are ever in need of company I have a very pretty young niece who I am sure would appreciate getting to know you better."

"Thank you but I am well suited", Nicholson replied, as Edward thought: "Cheeky bastard!" They left Townsend's office closing the door behind them and stepping into the now empty corridor.

Their next interview would test Edward's skills even more.

Townsend and his closest colleague, John Sayer, were as different as chalk and cheese, oil and water, sun and moon. Whereas Townsend was larger than life; Sayer was pencil-thin, spoke only sparingly and was always dressed from head to foot in black. Townsend loved gossip and was gregarious whereas Sayer was utterly private, never shared confidences with anyone and only spoke when absolutely necessary.

In their professional work, Townsend moved about in the full light of day whereas Sayer worked in the dark and seldom emerged from the shadows. However, when it came to espionage they made the perfect partnership, which was the reason that they were ideal for Edward's purpose.

Sayer's office could not be accessed directly from Bow Street. Typically, he had shut himself away in an annex that was only accessible from a door at the back of one of Bow Street's holding cells. Cell number seven was kept permanently empty for the purpose of gaining access to Sayer's office and Edward had to ask the duty jailor to unlock the cell's door to let him and Nicholson through it.

They crossed to the cell's back wall and knocked gently on the barely discernible outline of a door with a single ring set into it.

"Enter."

Edward and Nicholson stepped inside.

Sayer looked up from his desk where he had been reading a document, He covered it at once it with some loose papers.

Secretive as always, thought Edward.

"Ah, I heard that you were in the building, Sir. What can I do for you?"

Edward introduced Nicholson as his assistant and they sat down on the only two chairs in the room. Visitors were obviously not expected to stay long.

"Ah, John, the notorious Bow Street grapevine seems to be working well, but what I have to say to you must remain in this office and never be repeated outside of it."

"Very well, Mr. Hazell, you have some experience of my discretion."

"Indeed I do. I will always be grateful to you for your help in dealing with that conspiracy in Falmouth two years ago and for your silence about it since. The Office would have been severely embarrassed if anything about that operation had been made public. A Naval officer, son of a Marquis no less, involved in treasonable activity with the Americas; Buenos Aires, wasn't it?"

Edward had not been directly involved in the conspiracy but had heard about it from others. He feigned forgetfulness about an operation that had gone badly wrong which had led to the escape of the officer with the whole of his ship's crew to South America. It was rumoured that the stolen sloop, *HMS Peacock*, had first set into Baltimore, where it had been converted from two to three masts to change its appearance, before sailing on to La Plata. Its young commander was now most likely to be engaged in piracy up and down the Pacific coast or supporting local revolutions against the Spanish There was even rumour of the formation of a Chilean navy.

The only person who came well out of the affair was Sayer.

Sayer had a family connection in the dockyard at Chatham and had brought a strange story to the Alien Office.

The yard was home-depot to the Channel Fleet and a repair shop for ships coming out of the Line. Sayer's nephew was one of hundreds of dockyard workers who went on board to get ships ready for sail. In the course of his work – he was an apprentice shipwright – he had made friends with some of the younger crew of the *Peacock*.

She was a frigate that had been used for cutting-out work along the French coast as a part of Lord Cochrane's flotilla that had gained a reputation for extreme risk-taking. Like many of Cochrane's captains she was commanded by a young aristocrat with something to prove. A long predigree but empty pockets.

In the course of his work Sayer's nephew became suspicious about some of the alterations that were being made to the ship. On enquiry he was told that these had been ordered by its captain 'for the event of re-deployment to the West Indies'.

Sayer's nephew knew that the *Peacock* would never be suitable for service in such conditions and one evening when he visited his uncle in Bermondsey spoke of his concerns.

Sayer already knew that there had been trouble in the dockyard after the mass redundancies that followed the end of the war. He reported his nephew's suspicions to the Alien Office and was instructed to go into the yard in disguise to assess the mood. He should report any potentially subversive activity that he found there.

Sayer spent a week working as a porter before reporting back to the Alien Office that his nephew's suspicions were correct. It seemed that the ship was being made ready to sail but he could not find out her intended destination. Her crew had been told it was to be a top secret assignment.

So concerned was he that Sayer decided that he would take his chances and sign on to sail with her. His last message to London was that the ship would be sailing within the next two days.

The *Peacock* left the Medway and sailed down the Channel towards the Needles. However, a storm broke out on her second night which ripped the mainsail and brought down one of her masts. Her captain summoned the crew and told them that whilst they would be obliged to put into Flamouth for repairs, he could now tell them that they were bound for South America. They could all look forward to the prospect of a new and more profitable life. Loud cheers greeted this announcement. In the meantime, they were all confined to the ship and, on pain of death, no one could go ashore.

Sayer calculated that his chances of getting ashore would be reduced once they put into Port and that he would have more time to warn the authorities if he left the ship sooner rather than later. When they were still some way offshore he dived overboard and swam over a mile to land. He went straight to the Navy Office in Falmouth and reported what was happening on board ship.

The Port Admiral heard his story but refused to believe it as he knew the captain's family and could not imagine that such treachery could be intended. Sayer pleaded with the Admiral to no effect except that Sayer would be permitted to send a message about this improbable story to the Alien Office in London via the Admiralty's new telegraph system.

Peacock duly arrived in Falmouth and when her captrain visited the Port Office to pay his respects, he passed over forged sailing instructions for inspection and told some cock and bull story about reinforcing the Channel Fleet. The ship was allowed to sail. By the time the Alien Office had exerted sufficient pressure on the Admiralty to apprehend the ship and its crew, they were long gone. Sayer returned to Bow Street a week later and barely managed to hide his anger and frustration at the failure to arrest the deserters. He swore that he would never allow such treachery to happen again.

Now Sayer glanced out of the window giving Edward a moment to gather his thoughts. As a consequence of their working together previously, theirs was a more equal relationship in the secret war than was Edward's with John Townsend.

Edward decided that, unlike Townsend, he should brief Sayer fully on the situation in London and on St Helena. He knew that Sayer was a diehard Tory and Royalist. A cold fish he might be but Edward needed him to be fully engaged, not only with his head but also with his heart. This was potentially the most difficult and dangerous operation in which they had been involved together. There would need to be absolute trust and confidence between them.

"I have just briefed your colleague, who will be moving openly amongst those who should have knowledge of any plot - if there is one - to rescue General Bonaparte from St Helena.

He does not know the details of the reason that he is to watch Lord Amherst and his friends, but he will report to me anything suspicious he sees or hears about any one of them. If I think that an individual should be investigated more closely, I will call upon you and your own agents. I know that you keep these men apart from your usual Bow Street activities.

Your work must be carried out in absolute secrecy and, in particular, John Townsend must know nothing of the details of your activities.

The likely areas of potential trouble", Edward continued, "will come from the leaders of the Opposition in Westminster; from amongst the merchant houses of the City and from East India House. We have reason to believe that the Company is involved not least because we know that their captains are implicated in the carrying of letters to and from General Bonaparte that have not been censored by Governor Lowe. If threats to security do emerge, we will need to keep a close watch around the docks and wharves on the Thames especially those used by the Company - and on its ships.

There is a lot of sailing traffic to and from India via St Helena. We will akso be watching the South American trades to and from La

Plata. Buenos Aires is the nearest major population centre to the island. It's an obvious place from which to organise an escape attempt.

Shipping from the North American East Coast, especially Baltimore, will also be observed. I have already placed a man there. You will recall from the Falmouth debacle that Baltimore is the centre of their counter-espionage operations. If the Americans are involved in this, which I think they are, that will be the place where plans will be made and resources assembled. Attempts could also come out of Bahia or Rio de Janeiro which are both porential jumping-off points."

Sayer remained silent throughout Edward's briefing and for some moments afterwards.

"How long will this operation continue? Whilst I have the resources available for as long as you choose to pay for them, it is inevitable that the longer it goes on, the greater the risk of exposure. My agents can become stale and may lose concentration."

"I agree entirely", Edward replied, "but these are early days. We will know more of the potential threat when we receive some intelligence that I have sent for out of the Cape. This will take about seven weeks to arrive here. We will also begin to receive regular reports from Townsend's work as well as your preliminary surveillance at the docks. That's as much as I can tell you at present"

"How should we communicate with each other?"

"What do you suggest?"

Sayer was silent. Edward thought for a minute.

"Coded messages are too laborious and although they would be secure, either of us making regular visits to collect mail at the Post Office, here or anywhere else could arouse suspicion.

I suggest that we should meet face to face as and when required."

"Very well, Mr. Hazell, that seems workable to me", Sayer replied. "I suggest that we should also have a way to meet in an emergency. How about a flower seller comes to your door with a bunch of violets addressed to a Miss Jamieson? Then we will meet on the steps of the Lambeth ferry crossing on the Middlesex bank as soon as we are able?"

"Excellent idea", Edward said. "I think that's all for now. The next time you hear from me should be after I have received my first report from Townsend or if I receive further intelligence from any other sources. You may then be required to put your first *tail* on an individual.

Thank you for your time, John, and until we meet again."

Edward and Nicholson left Sayer's office and returned through cell number seven to the main Bow Street premises. John Sayer was a strange cove, there was no doubt about that, but in Edward's experience he was extremely effective. That was what was going to count in this operation.

It had been a long day but his initial plan – such as it was – was now in place. He would report to Crauford about the arrangements he had made, but that could wait until the morning. He would call in at his wine merchants, Justerini & Brooks in St James's Street, on his way home and order some claret for Saturday's party. It would be delivered to James Longdon's lodgings at the Post Office in Lombard Street. Nicholson could make his own way home.

Edward was looking forward to his dinner date at the weekend with James, Julia and their friends. His social life had suffered over the past two months as he had been on secret duties almost the whole time. He was looking forward to a convivial evening that would be in stark contrast to his time in the office.

On Saturday evening at dinner, the wine he had selected was considered to be of excellent quality and the conversation between old friends was lively. Julia, seated next to him, was looking lovely in a bronze silk dress with just the right amount of *décolletage*. She positively sparkled.

"Edward, where have you been? We have not seen anything of you for ages. What have you been up to?"

"I confess that I have been very busy at the office. I am sorry if I have neglected you all".

"It's not neglect, it's worse. You promised that we should spend time together this summer. I have hardly seen anything of you at all. Now a little bird has told me that you are involved with the Holland set. What's that all about? You do not even like them and their friends. I know you don't share their views."

"It's nothing. It's just something at work", Edward said. "The Department has some business with Lord Holland in which I am involved which I can't avoid. It's to do with his interests in Jamaica where he has substantial holdings. It's all over now and I'm back to my usual duties."

"Well, my father says it's a bit more than that. He says that you had something to do with that trial in Maidstone and that you have been promoted to Assistant Secretary. Is that true? Why didn't you tell me?"

"It's true; I have been promoted but only from one side of the office to the other."

Edward began to wonder where Julia was getting her information. He knew her father had good connections with the Holland set but Julia was getting uncomfortably close. He would have to change the conversation quickly.

"I may have to go away sometime in June but we should arrange a day out in the country together before I leave. How about a trip on the river? We could hire a skiff at Windsor and go upstream to Monkey Island."

Julia clapped her hands.

"What a lovely idea, Edward. I will bring a picnic and we can have the whole day alone together."

At that point the conversation became general again and Edward did not have to go into more detail about his work. He would have to be careful about what he told her. He might even have to place Sir Thomas under surveillence.

At the end of the evening Edward and Julia shared a carriage home together and he put his arm around Julia's shoulders in the darkness. Julia responded at once and placed her mouth against his ear. Edward felt her tongue tickling it as she murmured: "Mama will have gone to bed and Papa has gone down to the country for the weekend. Why don't you come in for a hot chocolate or something stronger? I'll send the servants to bed."

"Really, Julia, I should like that very much but I have to be at work early tomorrow to catch up with my paperwork. Another time, perhaps?"

"On a Sunday, surely not?"

Edward made no reply. When they reached Julia's house he handed her down from the carriage and escorted her up the steps to the front door. They leaned into one another and Edward put his arms around her waist and kissed her on the lips. She opened her mouth and he put his tongue inside it. They kissed passionately for a time working their tongues around each other until she broke off with a sigh.

"Oh! Edward. I like you so much. Do, please, come in"

He held her hands tightly for a few moments before kissing her once more on the lips and turning away.

He arrived back at his apartment in Eaton Square intending to go to bed but found that he had too much on his mind. It was not only his relationship with Julia that troubled him but also the increasingly problematic situation in London and on St Helena.

After nineteen years of war which had cost so much in blood and treasure, the extreme hostility of the Government in London to Napoleon was contradicted almost precisely by those who supported him and continued to hold him in the highest regard. It was becoming an impossible situation that was threatening to tear government and nation apart.

Of all the dramatic events of the nineteen-years war against the French, three in particular were coming back to haunt Edward.

Worse, some of the names that were now cropping up as opponents to the government's present policy had also been Britain's protagonists in earlier conflicts.

The first of these events took place only a year after the outbreak of the war against the French and had been provoked by Napoleon's intention to invade Great Britain via Ireland. This triggered a national insurrection on the island. One result was the large numbers of Irish who had left Ireland and gone overseas. These now did whatever they could to harm British interests.

The second was the result of Napoleon's conquest of the whole of the European mainland that prevented Britain's merchants from trading on the Continent and forced them to look elsewhere for business. This had led to the organisation of two disastrous military expeditions to South America in 1806 and 1807 that had caused great damage to Britain's reputation abroad and had prejudiced a number of potential allies in Napoleon's favour.

The third had been the petty war that had broken out between Britain and the United States in 1812 after complaints from Washington that its sailors had been forcibly pressed into the British Navy and its merchant ships banned from the Mediterreanean sea. This had led to the burning of the capital's newly-built White House. The Americans were now providing active support to conspirators.

Edward was also increasingly concerned at the way that certain individuals, amongst them Captain Rodolphus Reardon of the 66th on St Helena and John Skinner at the Post Office in Baltimore - each of whom had reason to hate the British - were moving against him. Even the captain and crew of his old adversary, the American schooner, *The Damned Yankee*, appeared to be involved.

Deadwood Camp

Meanwhile, at Deadwood Camp on St Helena, Colonel Nichol's departure left the Regiment unsettled. A replacement would be sent out from England but would not arrive for at least three months. In the meantime, the Second in Command, Major Lascelles, was appointed in command.

Lascelles was not a popular officer. He had not fought at Albufera and was no *diehard*. He was short in the leg and with a reputation for the strict application of Army Regulations. He was also on good terms with Lowe and Reade that meant the Regiment following their instructions to the letter. This would not be to the taste of many in the Officers Mess.

A week after Colonel Nichol had left for England all the Company officers were summoned to be addressed by Lascelles.

"Good morning, gentlemen, and thank you for your attendance. I think that I made it clear that *all* officers were to attend my orders. I see that Mr. Birmingham is absent."

Turning to the Adjutant, Captain James Baird, he growled:

"You understood my orders, Sir? I made no exceptions. Where is Mr. Birmingham?"

Baird looked embarrassed.

"I believe he is in Jamestown on regimental business, Sir."

"You believe...... you *believe* he is on business in town! It's your job to *know* where our officers are at any time of the day or night. This is typical of the slackness in the regiment which I have long observed. What if I was asked by Sir Hudson or Sir Thomas of the whereabouts of the prisoner General Bonaparte and I replied "I *believe* that he remains at Longwood House?

I would expect to be removed from command at once and so shall any of my officers who either do not know where their fellow officers can be found, or who wander off camp on unauthorised business or unspecified duties.

As from today", Lacelles went on, "all officers will sign themselves in and out of the Guardroom. If you are reluctant to behave as officers and gentlemen, I will oblige you to behave like the rank and file.

All officers are confined to camp until further notice. I expect to see you here at the same time tomorrow to receive further orders.

One other matter before you are dismissed. Whilst I am in command, the Governor has granted me the acting rank of Lt.-Colonel so you will address me as *Colonel* at all times."

Goldie and his fellow officers looked at each other in dismay as they filed out of the Mess. More trouble could be expected when Birmingham returned to camp.

The Regiment's base at Deadwood was situated in the hollow of a plain a mile from Longwood House where Napoleon was imprisoned although *imprisoned* was a harsh word to describe his conditions. On his arrival at the house a recreational area had been agreed within which the prisoner could take his exercise, walking or riding. This covered some 30 acres of gardens and shrub-land. Some of it was open ground with good views towards the south and east. Part of it, to the north, was tree-covered and provided poor visibility for watchers.

This had become an increasingly disputed aspect of Napoleon's daily routine. The Governor felt that his orders from London allowed his prisoner far too much freedom to roam about out of sight with its attendant risk that he might escape. Lowe argued that Napoleon should be visible to his guards at all times but this requirement caused great difficulty for the troops on duty.

The issue was: how close should the first line of picquets be placed around the prisoner's house and to what extent should they intrude on the day to day activities of its occupants? This question became the battlefield on which Napoleon fought his last campaign. The Regiment found itself pig-in-the-middle of the disputes that followed.

Both on and off the island the question of the positioning of the cordon of guards was a prime reason for disagreements between civilians and the military and, within the military, between those who took a more liberal view and those who had harsh opinions about Napoleon.

Napoleon ruthlessly exploited these disagreements and turned his daily routine into a game of hide and seek with his guards. He would set off on foot in plain view before disappearing behind a stand of trees. He would then miraculously re-appear on horse-back surrounded by his entourage similarly mounted. This made the Governor's instructions almost impossible to implement.

Colonel Nichol had taken a somewhat enlightened view of his responsibilities and had refused to allow the Governor or Sir Thomas Reade to interfere in his arrangements. Lascelles was less confident and inclined to accept the Governor's demands. If implemented, these would cause the Regiment serious inconvenience.

The camp had been constructed piecemeal around a derelict farmhouse. Accommodation for the men was initially under canvas but over time a number of wooden huts had been built to house administrative tasks such as the guardroom, armoury and ammunition stores.

Whilst the officers had made themselves relatively comfortable by improving the farmhouse and its outbuildings, the rank and file were less fortunate. Many of them lived under canvas and experienced extremes of heat and cold, depending on the season. In summer, hot winds came from the African continent in the east. In winter a cruel wind blew from the southern Arctic.

Overall conditions were poor and morale suffered as a result. Although much was done to alleviate the boredom of camp life with horse, mule and ox racing the most popular activities, tedium threatened to overcome initiative amongst both the officers and their men.

That evening in the Mess there was subdued discussion amongst the officers. A new regime was clearly anticipated and further restrictions could be expected. Goldie noticed that Reardon and Birmingham, who had now returned from Jamestown, were in close conversation and had attracted a following of juniors around them.

The next day back in the Mess - and addressed again by Lascelles - their worst fears were realised. Lascelles announced the introduction of a new set of Standing Orders.

Static posts were to be drawn in by a further 200 yards around Longwood House and stand-to at dawn and dusk would be extended by one hour each morning and evening. The number of mobile patrols would be doubled.

This would mean longer hours and more work for the Regiment. It would be very unpopular and, if a cause for unrest amongst the troops was needed, these new orders would do nicely.

What followed was entirely predictable: the officers went about their duties with long faces and the rank and file were openly mutinous. The troops now thoroughly disliked their posting on the island. Its remoteness made them feel isolated and forgotten. Their diet was monotonous and their recreation in camp limited to racing, ratting and gambling, all involving debt. There was a single inn in Jamestown from which they had been banned and grog was hard to come by.

These frustrations began to be focussed on the prisoner at Longwood House. If he was released they could move on to a more congenial station. As a result, Napoleon became either an object of pity as a victim who deserved immediate release or as a tyrant who deserved immediate death.

The next day Goldie was summoned to attend upon Colonel Lascelles and was appointed assistant to his friend, Captain Baird, the Adjutant. Although this would involve receiving orders directly from Lascelles it would give him a birds-eye view of the Regiment's activities. It would help him to write the reports he made to Edward Hazell back in London.

Trouble was not long in coming.

Three days later Lascelles again summoned the officers to review the implementation of his orders. At the end of the meeting Lascelles asked for questions and *Dolf* Reardon, responsible for the Regiment's Pioneers, in which the most battle-hardened soldiers served, raised his hand.

"Yes, *Major,* I have a question."

The whole Mess froze.

"Captain Reardon, I have indicated the way that I should be addressed. Please be so kind as to respect my rank. What is it?"

"My Pioneers have had no rest since your orders were issued three days ago. They have had to dismantle, remove and rebuild every static guard-house and piquet fence around the perimeter of Longwood House. They are demanding extra rations and time off in lieu for their effort. They will stop work unless they are rewarded."

These remarks were followed by an ominous silence before Lascelles spoke:

"Captain, if you are unable to keep your men under control, I will remove you from their command and have another officer ensure that my orders are obeyed. Come to my headquarters as soon as this meeting is ended. That is all, gentlemen. You are dismissed"

Reardon stood defiantly as Lascelles left the Mess before following him to his office. Lascelles sat down behind his bureau.

"Close the door and remain standing. You, Sir, will not speak to me without using my formal title. Nor will you question my orders in front of your fellow officers. I will have no insubordination in the Mess or among the ranks. If I hear another word about extra incentives the offenders will be court marshalled and will feel the lash. Remember that the Regiment is on active service. Under Standing Orders I have the power to sanction the hanging of those found guilty of mutiny.

As for you, your Commission is at my pleasure and if you give me any further trouble, I will have the Governor remove you from the island accompanied with a request to Horse Guards that your appointment should be cancelled without compensation. Have you any questions?"

"No, Sir."

Reardon gave a perfunctory salute, turned on his heel and left the room.

When he arrived back in the Mess he was surrounded by his friends who questioned him about his conversation with Lascelles. Goldie heard him remark loudly: "We'll see who has the loyalty of the men - and it's not that man."

Goldie noted in Orders that Reardon and Birmingham were due to share duties over the coming weeks. Reardon's Pioneers were ordered to construct a new fence around Longwood's gardens in which

Napoleon walked each morning and tended his vegetable garden in the afternoon.

Birmingham's company would be providing a rotating twenty-four-hour piquet whilst the work was in progress. Lascelles had made clear that this would be a critical duty as there would be gaps in the fencing during each night.

It was also likely that one or the other of these officers would be in direct contact with Napoleon as he liked to hold conversation with Regimental officers. This was to find out what was going on: who was up and who was down amongst the civil and military personalities on the island. Napoloen also took the opportunity to rile them about their turnout and quality: no one could match his Imperial Guard.

Lascelles had made it absolutely clear that there was to be no communication whatsoever between Napoleon and the troops.

A week later, on a wet April day with a chill wind blowing from Antarctica, Baird asked Goldie to go up to Longwood to see how the work was coming along and to assess the morale of the working parties and piquet men.

Reardon and Birmingham greeted him warmly and he spoke to a number of the men and inspected their work. If they were no longer mutinous they were certainly still surly although Lascelles had ordered extra rations to be distributed.

Goldie stood on the fence line with the two officers when there was the sound of a cough behind them.

They turned around.

It was Napoleon himself and he appeared to be alone.

The three officers stood to attention and saluted him smartly.

It was the first time that any of the three had seen him at close quarters. They were dismayed by his appearance in spite of what they had been told about him by Blakeney, the Orderly Officer at Longwood.

He was taller than they had expected but his shoes were covered in mud; his stockings were wrinkled and dirty and his face sallow, blotched and sweaty, as Blakeny had reported. Goldie's first thought was that Napoleon could not be in good health.

"Bonjour, messieurs and what exactly are you doing in my garden?" He spoke in broken English and Reardon recalled that Napoleon was taking lessons from one of his staff and held regular conversation with Betsy Balcombe.

"Sir, we have been ordered to reduce the boundary around the house and to increase its security", Reardon replied.

"Ha. And why might that be? Am I going to wriggle under the fence and get my knees filthy? You English. You never stop tormenting me. I suppose this is the Governor's idea?"

"We are only following orders, Sir. If I had my way you would have been back home long ago", Reardon replied.

"Really, and how would you do that?", Napoleon said.

"We would have you released on parole."

Birmingham nodded in agreement. It was obvious where the sympathies of these two officers lay.

In a sudden switch in the conversation - remarked on by many as being his habit – Napoleon pointed to one of Birmingham's sergeants, who was standing nearby watching the exchange, and said: "I recognise that man. He has been inside my house. Is he a spy or a thief?"

"Neither, Sir. I know of no reason that he should have been anywhere near the house," Birmingham replied; but he did so with a backwards jerk of his head that indicated that the sergeant should make himself scarce.

Goldie, witnessing the exchange, reckoned that the man must have been a part of the drinks racket with which - it had been suspected - Birmingham had been associated, and that Napoleon knew it.

"This new fence you're putting up. Do you think that it will prevent my escape if I decide to leave?", he asked.

Another switch in the conversation.

"I don't know about that, Sir, but it is one of many barriers on and off the island, including our Navy out at sea," Goldie replied.

Napoleon touched the corner of his hat with his finger.

"A pleasure to speak with you, as always, gentlemen" and with that he turned back towards the house.

Over the next few days Goldie returned to the fence line on a number of occasions but did not meet Napoleon again. He recorded in his diary the comments that Reardon and Birmingham had made but was not certain if they represented a serious threat to security or were just loose talk. He would report their words to Hazell in his next report and leave his friend to decide.

However, it became clear from their conversation in the Mess that Reardon and Birmingham had met with Napoleon on a number of occasions.

Birmingham's rhetoric about the iniquities of Napoleon's imprisonment became more frequent and vocal.

One Friday evening after supper, the juniors, including Goldie, took up their favourite places in easy chairs in front of a roaring fire at one end of the Anteroom. It had been another miserable day out in the open and, although baths had been taken, Goldie still felt the chill.

"It's deplorable, no, more than that - an outrage - that Napoleon is still a captive in this Godforsaken place", began Birmingham.

Goldie had noticed that the officer had been drinking quite heavily at table earlier.

"We are keeping captive the liberator of oppressed people throughout four continents and the leader of the most successful army in Europe since Julius Caesar. He is kept like a pig in a sty and I say that it is a damnable and ungentlemanly business in which we are engaged."

With this statement, Birmingham stood unsteadily to his feet and, lurching towards the mantle over the fire, placed an elbow on it before turning back to address his fellows.

"Now, will you all stand and join me in a toast to the prisoner?"

A number of his young colleagues stood up and faced the fireplace, Goldie not amongst them.

"Raise your glasses, my lads, and drink to the Emperor's safe return to his homeland and to freedom everywhere – Here's to *Napoleon's Drop!*"

At this precise moment Lascelles entered the Anteroom and stood glaring at Birmingham and those who were raising their glasses and repeating the toast: 'Napoleon's Drop.'

"Mr. Birmingham, Sir, pray be so kind as to join me in the dining room *immediately*."

Birmingham smashed his glass against the fireback in the Russian manner and slowly moved towards Lascelles who waited for him by the door.

The group of officers broke up and Goldie retired to his room for the night. He was now seriously alarmed. He needed to communicate his grave concerns to Hazell without delay.

Reardon and Birmingham's opposition to Napoleon's imprisonment was now an open secret. It was possible that other members of the Mess had become involved. There was no chance that what had happened that night would not be reported throughout the Regiment. Goldie would have to increase his surveillance on the two officers and be ready to resist any plans they might make for Napoleon's rescue.

The following morning was a sombre affair. Birmingham entered the Mess escorted by Baird, the Adjutant. They sat alone together at a small table in the corner. Goldie noticed that Birmingham was without his gorget, sash or sword – the symbols of his rank. No one spoke to either of the men during breakfast.

At Daily Orders Lascelles announced that Lieutenant Birmingham was under open arrest and that a report had been made to Sir Thomas and Judge Advocate Major Hodson, who were jointly responsible for the discipline of the troops on the island. The report, said Lascelles, detailed the offences of which the officer had been accused.

Later the same day a notice went up in the Mess:

Lieutenant A. Birmingham, 66th Foot.

That on 22nd May 1819, Lt. Birmingham did knowingly contravene Army Regulations and Regimental Standing Orders and will be tried by General Courts Martial on a date to be agreed.

Signed:
Sir Thomas Reade, CB

Signed:
CRG Hodson, Major

The Mess was shocked by the severity of Lascelles' reaction but was not altogether surprised. Birmingham had been taking liberties for some time. He had been fortunate to have escaped trial after the drinks scandal.

Worse was to come when Goldie received a summons to appear in front of Lascelles.

"Major Hodson will be prosecuting", Lascelles started, "and as a member of the Regimental staff you will appear as a witness for the

Governor. The Major will be taking a statement from you in the next few days."

Hodson arrived at Deadwood to take statements shortly afterwards.

"This is a bad business, Goldie. We are here to do our duty by the King and not to question our orders. I am acquainted with your father - he lives at Kintbury does he not? - and I know that he would not wish you to be mixed up in anything that might touch upon your honour or that of your Regiment. These things are hard come by.

Now, describe to me precisely what occurred in the Mess and Birmingham's part in it."

Goldie kept his account as brief as possible but he was aware that he would not be the only witness so that it would be pointless to deny what had happened.

He signed his statement. Hodson moved on to his next interview.

A week later, the notice of the date of the Court Martial was published. The mood in the Mess and throughout the Camp became darker. Birmingham's service in Spain and in the South American *Soutie* invasions was well known. There was a dangerous atmosphere amongst the men, especially the veterans with whom Birminghame had fought in the Peninsular.

That afternoon Goldie joined Reardon and his Pioneers on the fence line at Longwood. The guard company – without their former commander and now under Reardon's supervision - laboured all around them.

"Ah, Goldie, good of you to come up. It's slow progress here. Why the long face?"

Goldie told Reardon about his interview with Hodson.

"I'm damned if I am going to say a word against Alan. He is a brave man and the Regiment owes him much for his conduct at Albufera. And at any rate. I agree with him. It's a rotten business for both Napoleon and ourselves."

At that moment Reardon's sergeant, who had been listening to this exchange between the two officers, interrupted.

"Just tell us how we can help, Sir, and we'll have Mr. Birmingham out of harm's way in no time."

"Don't you dare speak like that again, Sergeant. It would be mutiny and we would all be for it. Now get back to your duties."

Goldie and Reardon looked at each other. There could be real trouble brewing. Should they inform Lascelles?

On the day of the trial, except for the outside working parties, all ranks were confined to the Camp. Goldie and Reardon rode across to the Governor's house together where they visited Birmingham who was being held in the Governor's study escorted by two officers.

The trial was a foregone conclusion. A series of witnesses – amongst whom was Goldie - were called to confirm that Birmingham had used the words of which he was accused.

He pleaded not guilty on the grounds that what he had said had been the truth but Major Hodson, in his final remarks, noted that the charge was one of insubordination. Birmingham's defence could not justify an acquittal.

The jury of officers who were drawn from other units on the island were not altogether sorry to see the 66th humiliated in this way. Birmingham was found guilty as charged.

The findings would be reported to the Governor, Sir Hudson Lowe, who had the authority to pass sentence. In the meantime, Birmingham would be held in the jail down at Jamestown. He would not be allowed back into Deadwood Camp under any circumstances. The sentence was confirmed with the Governor's recommendation to Horse Guards that Birmingham should be stripped of his Commission without compensation and sentenced to two years in a military prison.

A week later Reardon spoke with Goldie.

"I say, have you heard? Birmingham leaves under escort on the *Phaeton* sailing on Thursday. I am going into town this afternoon to bid him goodbye. Are you coming with me?"

Goldie agreed to accompany Reardon. They left camp together after an early lunch and rode down into Jamestown.

The town jail was on the seafront. Its cells were usually occupied by naval deserters. It was a squalid spot. Wind and spray blew incessantly across the anchorage and it was impossible to keep dry inside the building. Birmingham was being held in a small cell furnished with only a bed, table and chair. He was bitterly cold.

"How are you, old boy?", Reardon began.

"I am as you see me", Birmingham replied, "It's poor reward for my service but I will not change my mind about the Emperor Napoleon."

"The situation is not as we would wish, of course, and there are many who share your view", Reardon replied. "I will continue to do my best to make the case for Napoleon's release. I am sorry it has come to this. Is there anything we can get you?"

"There is nothing more", Birmingham responded, "except that I was not able to say goodbye to the men. As you know, a number of them fought with me in Portugal and Spain. They were my good companions and saved my life on more than a few occasions. Please pass onto them my salutations and tell them that I hope to see them again when this business has been settled."

With that, the two British officers shook the prisoner's hand and left his cell.

The following morning it happened to be the turn of the Regiment's Pioneers to collect the weekly rations from Jamestown. Goldie saw them set off down to the port following a number of wagons.

It was Goldie's intention to write a report for Edward about Birmingham's dismissal – and its implications - and dispatch it to London via the *Phaeton*.

He retired to his room and wrote of the Birmingham incident and of his meeting with Napoleon including the emperor's comments about escape. Goldie concluded by saying that it was difficult to judge if a rescue attempt would come from on or off the island, but that there was an ugly mood on St Helena at present.

He called for his horse at mid-day and rode down into the port. HMS *Phaeton* was preparing to sail but drawn up at the foot of the gangway was what looked very much like a detachment of the 66th. They were dressed in full review order. Goldie had read Daily Orders and there was no mention of a Guard required in Jamestown.

As he approached, he saw a closed carriage halt at the bottom of the steps and Birmingham, a sailor on either each side of him, start up the gangway.

There was a command of "Present Arms" from the 66th's sergeant and the file of men came to the present.

Birmingham paused and, turning around to face the men, gave them a smart salute as they burst into song. Astonished, Goldie could hear the words of the *Farmer's Boy* ringing across the dockside:

> The sun had set beyond yon hills,
> Across yon dreary moor,
> Weary and lame, a boy there came
> Up to a farmer's door
> 'Can you tell me if any there be
> That will give me employ,
> To plow and sow, and reap and mow,
> And be a Farmer's Boy?

When the singing had ended, Goldie approached the sergeant.

"What the hell are you lot doing down here and with whose permission?"

120

"No one, Sir", the sergeant replied. "As you know quite a few of us fought with Mr. Birmingham in Spain. He saved the lives of one or two of us. We wanted to pay our respects to him before he left."

"You had better make yourselves scarce smartish. I never saw this. Now go. Get back to barracks and return to your duties. This will never be mentioned again."

"No, Sir. Very good, Sir" and, with a quick salute, the sergeant ushered his men away.

Goldie returned to barracks and spoke to no one about what he had witnessed but wrote up the episode into his journal for Hazell.

The Regiment remained deeply unsettled following Birmingham's departure and Goldie was particularly anxious about the attitude of the Pioneers. Some days later he checked Orders and saw that they had been posted onto the fence line. Reardon would be in charge of them again.

He went up there on a fine May morning and found Reardon already in deep conversation with Napoleon across the demarcation line.

Napoleon was speaking as he arrived.

"I don't know what it is about you English. You are a vindictive race and will take it out on anyone who gets in your way. We French never intended to make trouble in Europe. My invasion barges were made of linen and our real enemies lay beyond the Elbe. My grand strategy was to make Europe safe for democracy. You wrecked that vision."

"That's as maybe", Reardon replied, "but you threatened us with your ideas of liberty although they are now widely accepted in Britain. It's just that we have a repressive government in London at present."

Still ignoring Goldie, Napoleon replied:

"Precisely. And that is why I am needed back in Europe. To lead the forces of reason against oppression" and, without pausing, said to Goldie: "Good morning, Lieutenant, and how are you?"

Goldie saluted.

"Passing well, Sir, although the Regiment has suffered a long winter and needs some new faces."

"Really", Napoleon replied, "I hear you have got rid of some old ones."

"No one is here by choice and we continue to do our duty as best as we can", Goldie remarked. "It is only your presence that keeps us here. I am sure we would all prefer to be somewhere else."

"Well, if I were released", retorted Napoleon, "and returned to civilisation, you could get on with your lives."

This was seditious language but before Goldie could reply, Reardon said "I heartily agree. That's very true. I should think we all look for better times and a more forgiving government in London."

"Indeed we do, indeed we do", Napoleon said, and with that withdrew towards the house.

"Really Reardon, you were sailing close to the wind. Remember, who this man is. He enslaved the whole of Europe"

The fencing party had crept closer during these exchanges and Goldie was anxious about what they might have heard.

The Regiment had to stay clear of politics and Reardon would do well to remember it.

Mr. Porteous's Boarding House

MARRYAT WAS BORED. St Helena was not London and the society in which he now moved had nothing like the excitement of the politics and gossip that he had enjoyed before he had left for St Helena.

Of course, he was fortunate to have been given a command at sea when so many of his brother officers were unemployed and living on half pay. However, acting as a guard ship captain in the South Atlantic was hardly the same as the glory days that he had spent cutting out French warships in the Mediterranean under the command of his hero Lord Cochrane, known throughout the British Navy as the *Sea Wolf.*

Before he had left London Marryat had even heard a strange rumour that Cochrane was planning a naval campaign somewhere in the southern hemisphere.

HMS Beaver, his command, was a tub: uncomfortable at all times and intolerable in bad weather. The ship's duties were to patrol the seas offshore, to be ready to repel intruders and to board all incoming vessels before inspecting their passenger lists and cargos. They were also to provide shore parties to strengthen the defence works on potential beach-landing sites.

The ship worked to a routine of two weeks on duty at sea and one week off. The crew were obliged to remain on board at all times in case of emergency but the officers could arrange to go ashore and stay in lodgings. The most congenial of these - or at any rate the least uncomfortable - was Mr. Porteous's.

The lodging was owned and managed by Henry Porteous who was responsible to Willaim Balcombe for the East India Company's *gardens* on the island. These produced all the fruit and vegetables that the Company supplied to both its own ships and others passing through.

As a consequence of Napoleon's presence on the island, the Company also held highly lucrative contracts with the army's local Commissariat from which both Balcombe, its Agent, and Porteous profited by supplying daily rations to over three thousand troops and five hundred sailors.

Marryat had the financial means to arrange for a more or less permanent room to be made available to him at the lodgings. He enjoyed the mixed company that stayed there; some for a short time only on their way to or from India and others who were resident on a more permanent basis.

They were a pretty rum bunch.

Henry Porteous affected a sunny disposition but in conversation with Marryat he revealed himself as a much more complicated personality. He had originally served as a supply officer in the Company's Madras Presidency and had made himself rich from military contracts during Clive's campaigns.

This experience had led him to seek an appointment in a more congenial climate and he had used his contacts within the Company to secure his appointment on St Helena. Mrs. Porteous, who was an attractive India-born woman with many admirers amongst the garrison's officers, looked after the needs of their guests. She was in charge of indoors whilst her husband was free to travel across the island on his horticultural duties.

Since its discovery by the Portuegese the island had long been a racial entrepot. Mr. and Mrs. Porteous were a prominent and popular couple who counted William and Jane Balcombe and their two children, Jane and Betsy, amongst their closest friends. As a result, Porteous was very well informed about what was going on throughout the civilian population, in the Governor's household and at Longwood, where Napoleon was held captive.

The strangest guest in the lodgings was the Marquis de Montchenu. He was one of the three international commissioners selected by the Allies at the Treaty of Vienna to oversee the administrative arrangements for the prisoner.

Montchenu was a die-hard French royalist in his seventies who had lived in exile in Switzerland during the revolutionary wars. He had been rewarded for his loyalty to the restored Bourbons through this appointment.

He claimed to have suffered horribly at the hands of the Republic - he put it about that he was the only one of his family to have escaped the guillotine - and had a single topic of conversation. This was that it was his job to see Napoleon rot in hell.

Marryat and Montchenu took an instant dislike to one another. The scene was set for a series of fierce arguments in the boarding house snug which, lit by a rare coal fire, was one of the few places on the island in which it was possible to keep warm in winter.

"Monsieur Marryat, it is the very least that the tyrant deserves. If it was my decision, he would be tried and executed by a military tribunal tomorrow", declared Montchenu.

Marryat sat in the snug with Montchenu and Porteous on a foul evening in late October. The autumn weather had come in early this year and the wind rattled the shutters and made the thick curtains shake. Each man nursed a glass of Madeira in his hands.

"I think that his punishment has gone too far", replied Porteous, "His health is not good. He spends much of each day in the bath and he is eating less and less. He cannot keep his food down. There must be something seriously wrong with him. Keeping him here can only be making it worse."

"Quite apart from the fact that he only has quack doctors available to him", said Marryat. "They come from off our ships or from the garrison. In my experience they are utterly useless, only charlatans sign up to our service. He needs a decent physician"

"He's lucky to have anyone", Montchenu replied, "If it was my decision I would ban all medical treatment. The sooner he's gone, the better and preferably in a coffin".

Porteous and Marryat glanced at each other. The man's views were intolerable.

A few days earlier Porteous and Marryat had shared a very different conversation.

"It's becoming impossible to remain neutral over this imprisonment", Porteous had said. "I saw Balcombe yesterday. He says that Napoleon is seriously ill and needs urgent medical attention. All Governor Lowe does is to send in another idiot doctor. This time it's Verling, that useless Dutchman. The doctor is so bad I'm told that they will not even have him near the medical wards in Jamestown and that's saying something.

Betsy Balcombe was up at Longwood the other day and for the first time Napoleon spoke to her about his death. He told her that the British are planning to have him murdered. He has completely lost his appetite and won't touch his food.

If he cannot be got off the island because of the attitude of bigots like Lowe and Montchenu, there is a grave risk he will die here. If that happens we will all be held responsible."

"I agree", Marryat replied, "It would have other even more serious repercussions. We are at an historic turning point. I believe that the forces of reform are stronger than those of conservatism. Although we have a Tory, right-leaning government in London – with Wellington at its centre whose motto is 'no change at any price' - it cannot last.

When I left London there was much sentiment in favour of setting Napoleon free and letting him live wherever he wishes.

There are many on the island", continued Marryat, "who share these views - I am one - but unless a move is made soon, it will be too late."

"There is a man who might help us", Porteous replied. "He is an officer in the 66th called Reardon. He has well known liberal sentiments. He also has access to the Emperor's household as his duties take him up there. I know that he has recently been in conversation with Napoleon over the garden fence, as one might say. He could be an ally. Shall I ask him to dine with us tomorrow?"

"Good idea", Marryat remarked, "We can hear his views and consider if there is anything that we can do to make Napoleon's life more tolerable,"

Then next evening Reardon joined Porteous and his lodger for supper.

The conversation had to remain general whilst Montchenu was with them but, even so, things almost got out of hand when the Marquis started his usual evening rant against Napoleon.

"I have had a letter from Paris that includes new instructions for Napoleon's welfare. His daily regime is to be restricted further by tightening the cordon around Longwood again and banning his daily ride. These new measures will, hopefully, frustrate him even more."

"For God's sake", cried Reardon, "are you trying to kill him?"

"With any luck", replied Montchenu, pushing his chair back from the table.

"Well, I'll be damned, Sir", Marryat replied, "Shame on you. Napoleon is a great man and should be treated with respect. I won't see him insulted like this".

Marryat and Montchenu squared up to each other at the door and, as he made to go, Montchenu paused to remark "He's a dead man walking".

Marryat turned around to Porteous and Reardon who were still seated at the table and said: "We'll see about that."

"Well, if we are serious about this, how would we get him off the island?", responded Reardon, "One thing is for sure, we would need a lot of help."

Porteous rose and fetched the decanter. "We would be committing treason and would hang for it. You two", he pointed at Marryat and Reardon, "are under military discipline. If you are discovered, you would both be shot by firing squad. I certainly don't trust Montchenu and we should be on our guard at all times. He could be listening at the door as we speak. I don't like his man-servant either, he's a creepy little man.

If we are going to embark on a rescue, the first thing to do is to bind ourselves to secrecy."

"I have no difficulty with that", Marryat said, "What about you, Reardon?"

"I'm ready for this. It's not the first time that I have thought about it. I think that we would get enough support here on the island and beyond to do it. It will take some organising though and it can't be hurried. What should be our first step?"

"I suppose that there would be three stages to any attempt", Porteous said. "We would need to persuade Napoleon that we have a viable plan; identify an escape route from Longwood to a pick-up point on the coast and arrange for his extraction from the island by sea. Each of these present serious obstacles. Let's take the most difficult one which is that we would need a vessel to reach an agreed landing place on St Helena. This would represent a major conspiracy throughout the Atlantic World.

"The first step is definitely the escape vessel", Marryat responded. "I will write to my former master Lord Cochrane on our behalf and seek his advice in very general terms - nothing too specific. If there is anyone in the world who could mount an operation like this, it's him."

"We are grateful to you, Marryat. This is potentially dangerous work but it is imperative if we are to save the Emperor's life."

With that, the three men raised their glasses in a silent toast.

The following morning Marryat wrote to Cochrane in London via his daughter Amanda using a private code that they had created in the glory days of *HMS Impérieuse.*

In his letter Marryat explained the situation on the island and that he had found support for an escape attempt should Cochrane share his sentiments. If not, would he please destroy the letter. It would not be spoken of again. Nor, for old times sake, should Cochrane contact the authorities about its contents.

In the meantime, Marryat would use his command to find out all that he could about possible landing sites and their access to Longwood House.

It would not be easy. Colonel Lyster, the Inspector of Coasts and Volunteers, had already carried out extensive defence works around the coast that included gun emplacements and look-out points.

These were manned on a twenty-four-hour basis so that reaching the beach from either the seaward or landward sides was almost impossible. As Marryat sat in his room with a map of the whole island on the table in front of him, he ran his finger around its contours. He was looking for the right spot for a landing from the sea.

However, he soon realised that the key to the success of any escape plan would be in the way that the garrison could be deceived into thinking that an escape was taking place somewhere else. A diversion would be a vital part of any plan.

The continuous naval patrols would also be a problem. Standing Orders were that at least two vessels should be at sea at all times circling the island from opposite directions. One idea would be that Marryat and the *Beaver* would need to be on duty at the time of the escape so that Marryat could turn a blind eye to any approaching vessel. Again, this would not be at all easy given that his officers and crew would be on the look-out for intruders.

Marryat intended to raise these issues with his fellow conspirators on the next occasion when they were alone together in the snug. It would have to be at a time when Montchenu was away.

Meanwhile his contribution would be to become even more familiar with every inch of the coastline in order to identify potential landing places.

He would avoid suspicion by having the permission of the Naval authorities to survey the coast for defensive purposes and particularly to help the Navy's crews appreciate the island's coastal features. A product of his work would be to provide each of the Navy's ships with a portfolio of accurate sketches for use on board to assist their recognition of the beaches from the seaward side.

As a well-known cartoonist this would be a credible reason for spending time on the coast and visiting the scattered shore parties guarding the headlands and beaches. Colonel Lyster's defensive arrangements might be considered comprehensive but Marryat's task was to find a gap.

He travelled on horseback in a clock-wise direction from Jamestown. He found that access to the beaches he surveyed at Flagstaff Point, Prosperous Bay and Stone Top were all very steep with each one having only a narrow, single track down to the water's edge. South-West Point had no access at all and had to be replenished by sea.

The place that had the most potential was Sandy Bay, the furthest away from Jamestown and least accessible on the island. Here, there was no headland from which troops could keep watch and only sheer cliffs down to a narrow strip of shingled beach. The nearest guard post was a quarter of a mile away with no direct sight of the Bay. The beach was not suitable for cannon and the authorities had obviously decided that escape from it would be impossible.

With this single exception, Lyster had constructed either a brick or wooden look-out point on the nearest headland that looked directly down onto every beach or a battery of cannons landed from the sea and positioned on the sand, facing seawards.

Marryat found no other embarkation point anywhere around the island that was not visible from land and he now understood how the three thousand men of the island's garrison were kept occupied keeping watch.

Small parties of men were rotated in and out of these locations with orders to maintain their vigilance in their area of responsibility. A complicated system of flag signals was designed to enable them to communicate with their neighbours on each side in the event of emergency.

However, he was also acutely aware of the loneliness and boredom of such remote postings. At several locations Marryat encountered men who had lost all sense of their duty and passed their time gaming and drinking. This indiscipline could provide the distraction that the escape party would need.

When he was off duty, Marryat spent all of his time surveying the coast in this way and no suspicions were raised about his real purpose. Indeed, when he had finished his work, Admiral Plampin was delighted to receive the twelve portfolios for the use of his captains and wrote to Marryat thanking him for 'his imaginative and helpful contribution to the prisoner's confinement'.

Meanwhile Porteous had also been busy.

His horticultural duties took him all over the island in all weathers as he inspected the state of his gardens. As Marryat surveyed the coast, Porteous started doing the same thing on land.

He placed Longwood at the centre of a map of the island that he kept locked in his study. When he returned home at the end of each day, he marked onto it each road, path and track to, from and around the house and estate that he had ridden.

However, his survey was not only physical but also social.

He began to record the regular movements of civilian and military individuals and groups to and from Longwood. In particular he noted those of Governor Lowe and his staff, including Reade, Gorrequer, the governor's ADC, and Hodson.

By day these movements were mostly predictable but in the evenings and at night they were less so.

By day, Lowe's weekly routine was set. On Mondays he worked in his office at Plantation House where he was joined by Reade and Gorrequer, who lived in, and Hodson who came out from Jamestown. On Tuesdays he went down into Jamestown with his wife and step-daughters in his carriage to shop. Lowe usually took the opportunity to look in on Hodson at the Court House on Shore Road. On Wednesdays and on Thursdays he visited military units accompanied by Reade anywhere across the island.

Lowe did this on horseback and the party often included the commanders of the various units he was inspecting. He seemed to favour units based on the north and east sides of the island including those at Sugar Loaf, Flagstaff Hill and Prosperous Bay. It was not clear if this was the direction from which he thought an attack might come or that this part of the island provided open country with scope for a good ride.

Lowe also frequently rode around the boundary of the Longwood estate that represented his prisoner's permitted area of mounted exercise and amongst the line of military picquets on duty around the house itself. At such times the Governor hoped to catch a rare glimpse of his prisoner, the elusive Napoleon.

On Fridays he remained at his headquarters. At weekends he made social visits with Lady Lowe throughout the island and went down to Jamestown for Sunday worship.

Of most interest to Porteous was the movement of military units throughout the island by day and night. Whilst Reardon should have an intimate knowledge of these, the 66th could not be everywhere at once. Parties of men from other regiments and corps were continually on the move.

In spite of the night curfew from dusk until dawn, Porteous, with Balcombe's approval, obtained the Governor's special permission to be out after dark to undertake a cull of the rats that plagued the island in their thousands.

With the excuse that rats favour darkness, and that his garden workers did their most productive eradication work at night, Porteous was able to travel wherever he wished. Amongst other things, was able to record the timings of the changing of the guard at key junctions around Longwood.

As the soldiers became more familiar with him - and he brought them the occasional bottle of rum to drink in the longest watch of the night - some even shared that night's password with him to facilitate his movements. In this way he could go unchallenged.

Using these excursions, he began to draw up a picture of the main social interactions of key individuals normally going about their business in the open by day but sometimes in secret by night.

There had been rumours ever since his arrival on the island that Napoleon was a ladies man. It was almost public knowledge that Albine, wife of the Comte de Montholon, a member of Napoleon's household living at Longwood, was often seen slipping across the landing between their family suite and Napoleon's bedroom. It was even rumoured that their second daughter, christened Josephine-Napoléone in his honour, was Napoleon's last child.

Napoleon's favours were not confined to those living with him at Longwood. He had, apparently, instructed his staff to procure the favours of the best looking women amongst the civilian population, including slaves.

This had led to a certain amount of clandestine activity between Longwood and the houses of eligible females, the most desirable of which was Elizabeth, the daughter of John Robinson, a local farmer. She lived at Hutts Gate and was known in Napoleon's household, and throughout the community, as the *Nymph* on account of her exceptional looks.

There certainly seemed to be regular night time traffic between Jamestown and Longwood, both official and illicit. This could pose a serious problem for any escape party moving north-eastwards. However, there was much less activity south and west of Longwood which would influence the choice of an escape route and extraction point.

Porteous took particular care to record the timing and movement of night time picquets in and around Longwood as these would cause the greatest difficulty. He expected Reardon to be familiar with their basic outline but Deadwood Camp, where the 66th was based, was not the only source of troops.

The barracks on Ladder Hill in Jamestown also provided men for picquet duty. These troops tended to be used for roving patrols whose routes were much less predictable than the static guards who were placed at twenty yard intervals around the perimeter of the house.

It was also rumoured that additional troops would soon be arriving on the island, drawn from amongst the 44th Foot who were on their way to India.

Porteous calculated, however, that human nature being what it is, a pattern to the roving patrols' routes would emerge if he observed them for long enough.

It was not risky work in itself but if he spent too long gathering the intelligence that he needed, suspicions were bound to be raised about the amount of time he was spending working at night.

He needed to disguise his intentions further. He decided to hold a competition each night amongst the picquet men who would have to guess the number of rats his workers had killed during the hours of curfew; the winners receiving another distribution of rum. This ruse worked well and his true intentions continued to remain secret.

Six weeks later Porteous reckoned that he had collected enough information to report back to the group. The three men met in the snug one cold Saturday night. Montchenu was dining out with the Russian commissioner, Balmain, so they could speak freely.

Marryat spoke first. "As you know, I have surveyed the whole island. It will not be at all easy to stage a break-out as every beach is guarded around the clock. However, I think that a beach to the south of Longwood, for example, at Sandy or Powell bays, would be marginally more viable. Each one is very slightly sheltered from the sea although the last time I sailed past them in the *Beaver* the sea spray was so high that we could not see their beaches. Of course, this makes it even more difficult for a landing at night but also for the watchers on the nearest headlands. Sandy Bay is the more difficult to access, as unlike Powell Bay, there is no way down on foot and no cannon actually on the beach.

The two nearest garrisons consist of eight men on duty at any one time. I have visited them on three separate occasions and each time have found them drunk. They are drawn from the locally recruited St Helena Regiment so are often either late for, or absent from, duty preferring to remain at home with their families, unlike the regular troops."

"What you have said confirms my own observations", replied Porteous.

"I have found both day and night time movement around Longwood to be much more frequent on the north side. The main garrisons are all stationed between Jamestown and Longwood. So too are the houses of the principal civilians and their social networks, with the exception of Farmer Robinson and the *Nymph* at Hutts Gate.

We will have to make certain that none of her current suitors are out and about on the night of the escape. I have had to hide from Lieutenant Goldie of the 66th on a number of occasions as he has ridden past in the dark. It is rumoured that they are lovers. I agree that a route that skirts Diane's Peak would be our best chance."

"Very well", replied Marryat, "Let's plan along these lines. An escape route from Longwood to the coast via Deep Valley and the beaches at either Sandy or Powell.

I also have news from England. I have had a response to my coded letter to Lord Cochrane that has been delivered to me by the captain of an East Indiaman, an ex-Navy comrade of mine, outward-bound for Calcutta. I was correct about the rumours that I heard about his movements before I left London.

Cochrane has been appointed C-in-C of a newly created Chilean Navy so he will have good reason to be in the South Atlantic. He informs me that his friend Lord Holland has agreed to sponsor a plan to rescue Napoleon and take him to South America.

Cochrane will sail from the Thames for La Plata in his new steamship *The Rising Star*", Marryat continued, "accompanied by a number of ex-officers from the Army and Navy who have volunteered to serve under him there. I understand, Reardon, that one of them, a Lieutenant Birmingham, served with you in the 66th before the Governor had him removed from the island for gross insubordination.

Birmingham could be particularly useful to us as he is familiar with the island from his time here. When Cochrane arrives in Baltimore he will rendezvous with an American schooner and load up an underwater craft that Lord Holland has hired from its owner to use for the rescue. I know such a craft exists, but I have never heard of it being used except onshore. The conditions off the island here will be a much more difficult, if not impossible, challenge."

Porteous and Reardon gasped. Porteous spoke for them both: "You are making this up. I have never heard of the existance of any such thing. How on earth do the crew breathe under water and how does it propel itself?"

"I have no idea about the details", Marryat replied, "except I do know that it was rumoured that the French were building something like it on the Seine at Rouen during the war. If it was actually built they never used it against us. Cochrane assures me in his letter that such a machine exists and that he has had assurances that it works.

Apparently, Holland has already informed Napoleon that his escape is being planned. When we are ready we are instructed to contact Napoleon with the details using the code word *Angouleme*. This will assure him that we are genuine.

That is all I have for you at present but I expect that we will receive more details from Cochrane in due course. I will contact him again - probably after he has arrived in the Argentine - when we have finalised our arrangements here.

I understand, Reardon, that you have opportunities from time to time to speak to Napoleon directly, so you will be our point man. It's dangerous work. Use the code word Cochrane has given me to introduce yourself to him."

"It's true, I do meet with Napoleon from time to time", Reardon replied. "Apart from my duties that include reporting on his movements to the governor on a daily basis, I also routinely inspect the fence line with my men. I've spoken to him several times in the past months. It won't be easy to be alone with him, but I will find a way."

"And remember", finished Marryat, "that what we are doing will be high treason and an early death by firing squad if we are found out. Take extreme care and speak to no one about any of this until we are ready."

With that the three conspirators retired. Porteous went to join his wife in their private quarters; Marryat returned to his damp lodging room and Reardon returned to his duties.

Mason's Stock House

THE CIRCUMSTANCES AT Mason's Stock House were certainly very strange.

It was situated on a small rise five hundred yards to the west of the fence that surrounded Longwood. Mason's front parlour looked directly at an extension to the house that included the veranda, billiard room and salon of Napoleon's residence. It was in the salon that Napoleon spent much of his time with his companions when he was not in his private quarters.

These rooms could also be seen by going to the very end of Mason's garden from which Napoleon's study, bedroom and bathroom could be overlooked. Governor Lowe had commandeered the house as an observation post immediately after Napoleon's arrival. He had ordered that an officer should have sight of the prisoner at least twice each day.

Although another officer was stationed inside Longwood on a permanent basis, this individual was not always in a position to report back that he had seen Napoleon and Governor Lowe had ordered a second officer to be stationed permanently at Mason's Stock House to make similar reports.

Major Lascelles ordered Reardon to move out of the Officers' Mess at Deadwood Camp and into the house. This may have been meant as a punishment for Reardon's close relationship with Lieutenant Birmingham as the quarters at Mason's were extremely primitive but it had also placed him in close proximity to Napoleon. This move had made Goldie even more suspicious about Reardon.

Mason's had originally been allocated to the Royal Navy Squadron as a place for the use of its officers on shore leave. There were five rooms, three upstairs and two down, one of which was used as a sitting room, the other as a Mess. Although these rooms were intended to be used for short periods only, two of the rooms were now occupied on an almost permanent basis.

A Midshipman serving on HMS *Vigo*, Robert Grant, who was dying of consumption, had been given special permission by his captain to live in the house. Grant was very ill and would not last the winter. He was of an evangelical persuasion and a small group of like-minded young men, including a number from the garrison in Jamestown, joined him each evening for earnest discussion and to pray for his recovery.

The first time that Reardon participated in this activity he was surprised to find that the group, in addition to praying for Grant, also prayed for the salvation of Napoleon's immortal soul. When Reardon challenged the group about this, their response was that he was the greatest man who had ever lived - not including Our Lord, of course - and that each one prayed silently for his liberty.

Reardon was astonished by this admission but it meant that his housemates provided excellent cover for his secret activities. They would be unlikely to report any suspicions they might have about him to the authorities - given their own treasonable thoughts.

His first few weeks at the house had been relatively uneventful. He was obliged to observe Longwood through a naval telescope and make a written report into the log on an hourly basis. He also had to raise a colour-coded flag up the flagpole outside that could be seen from the Governor's residence at Plantation House.

Blue meant that he had seen Napoleon in the last sixty minutes; green in the past three hours, etc. He was to hoist a red flag if there had been no sighting for more than twelve hours. If this occurred, troops would be called out of barracks from Deadwood and Jamestown and the Navy advised of a potential breach of security.

At curfew Reardon's daily duties ended and a long evening stretched ahead. After supper the party assembled for prayer which was held in Grant's room as he lay in bed coughing blood into a linen handkerchief. These sessions started with a reading of a passage from the Bible, usually tales of battles between good and evil from the Old Testament.

Then followed extempore prayer which could include a brief reference to saving Napoleon's soul and reclaiming it for Christ. The service ended with the rendering of one of Mr. Wesley's new-fangled hymns. Reardon took part in order to allay any suspicions of his true motives, but he found the whole thing extremely tedious.

However, after he had been in residence for four weeks his patience was rewarded.

One morning he was observing Longwood through his glass when he saw that Napoleon's carriage had been drawn up in front of the veranda surrounded by a number of mounted riders. It was already hot and the sun was shining out of a cloudless sky. At around mid-day Reardon watched as Napoleon emerged from the house and got into the carriage. A number of ladies joined him on the seat opposite whilst a servant passed up a number of large baskets.

The whole party set off and it was not long before that Reardon realised that it was heading straight up the track towards the Stock House. He rushed upstairs to fetch his dress jacket before going downstairs again and fastening his sword.

The party arrived at the front door five minutes later and one of the riders dismounted.

He bowed deeply. "Good morning, Sir, my name is Charles, Comte de Montholon. I am the Emperor's Chief of Staff. This morning His Excellency saw what a lovely day it was going to be and decided on a picnic. The Emperor has noticed that your house has a very fine lawn and he wishes to take lunch on it with his household. The Emperor has also sent a message to the Balcomes at The Briars to join him here if they are able – it will be a real *dejeuner sur l'herbe* - I hope that you won't object. Who do I have the honour of addressing?"

Reardon saluted and replied: "My name is Captain Rodolphus Reardon of the 66th and we should be pleased to entertain your Emperor. It is not the first time that I will have met his Excellency. I have had the honour of conversation with him whilst performing my duties on the perimeter at Longwood".

Turning towards the carriage and facing Napoleon and the ladies, Reardon bowed low and said, "You are most welcome, Excellency. Ladies, would you like to follow me?"

The whole party dismounted and Reardon led them to the well-kept lawn at the back of the house where Napoleon's servants began to lay out lunch. They had brought with them a wicker chair in which Napoleon was helped to sit down as the ladies and gentlemen of his household spread themselves around him.

Napoleon's appearance had deteriorated greatly since Reardon had seen him last – which must have been almost a month ago. His hair was now even more lank and his pasty face was covered with a sheen of sweat. The last time Reardon had seen him his skin had been uniformly grey, now it was blotched with red patches. The veins of his neck stood out in purple.

He had also put on more weight and took frequent shallow breaths while continually clearing his throat. He was not a healthy man. Reardon thought that if they were going to get him off the island alive it would have to be done soon.

Reardon was invited to join the party for the picnic lunch and Napoleon indicated that he should come and sit beside him.

Napoleon's chair faced Longwood directly and, easing himself further into it, he remarked: "Now I understand the reason you are here. This is the best place from which to spy on me. Typical of that loathsome man Lowe but I recognise you, do I not? I have seen you before, I think?"

Whilst Reardon should have been concerned that the British post had been uncovered and that Napoleon now knew of the full extent of Lowe's spying operation, he made no reference to it.

Instead he started: "Yes, Excellency, we have met before. Last month my men and I were working on the perimeter at Longwood strengthening the fence."

"Ah, yes, I thought I recognised you", Napoleon replied, "and where is your companion today, was it a Lieutenant Birmingham?"

"Yes, Excellency, it was", Reardon responded, "I regret that he is no longer on the island and has been removed to England."

Reardon had deliberately introduced the idea of Birmingham's enforced removal in his use of the words 'regret' and 'has been removed' that suggested that Birmingham had not left of his own accord.

"What a shame, I enjoyed my conversations with you both", Napoleon replied, "why has Lieutenant Birmingham gone?"

It looked as if Napoleon knew more than he was letting on and that he had heard something of the affair in the Mess of the 66th.

As a way to test this, Reardon decided that he would not speak of the real reasons for Birmingham's dismissal and see how Napoleon would react: "Lieutenant Birmingham", he said, "was obliged to return to England for family reasons, Excellency."

"Family is important", replied Napoleon, "but in my opinion duty has a higher call on our loyalty. Was not your colleague a notable hero of your Regiment?"

"Indeed he was, and so he was reluctant to leave his duties but found that he was placed in an impossible position by his superiors."

This should enable Napoleon to have his suspicions about Birmingham's departure confirmed without too many confidences being broken, Reardon thought.

"That's a pity, he was an interesting character - and when might you travel the same route?", Napoleon asked.

This seemed to be a further provocation.

Reardon decided to take another step.

"I am from Ireland originally and I shall return there one day."

"So, what are you doing in the hated British Army, the Irish loathe the English, do they not?"

"Indeed they do,", Reardon replied. "I joined up during the Rebellion twenty years ago. My father was a successful corn merchant in Dublin but he had close connections with England through trade. There were only two possibilities at that time: to join the English or the rebels and my father was very clear that his family should be on the winning side.

I was originally commissioned into a Highland regiment but I was transferred into the 66th by direct order of the Duke of Wellington after Vimiera. He must have seen me do something right during the battle."

"Ah, so you know something of your arch enemy the French", Napoleon exclaimed, "at least about our military skills?"

"I don't know about your skills", Reardon replied, "but before the war my father often did business in France. When I was growing up he sometimes took me over there with him."

"Ah, did he now. The advantages of the mercantile system. And what part of France did you and your father visit?"

"Our main agent lived just outside Angouleme, Excellency,"

Napoleon turned sharply towards him and Reardon felt the full force of those famous black eyes boring into him. There seemed to be an utter silence around them as if the air had been sucked out of the sky or like the moment of airlessness before the explosion of an artillery shell on the field of battle.

Napoleon's whole attention was fixed on Reardon. Did Napoleon suspect a plot designed to expose his own escape plans or had he realised the full significance of the word that Reardon had just used?

"Really, Monsieur, that's very interesting. One of my most loyal regiments - *Le Cent Sept*, the 107th Infantry Regiment - had its headquarters in that fine city. They fought alongside me at Austerlitz and Dresden and when I had to withdraw from Moscow - I will never call it a *retreat*, except from the clutches of winter.

They formed part of my rear guard. They were always the bravest of the brave. O my beloved Angoulemists! I have been writing about their service in the memoirs that Captain Piontkowski here has been helping me with", as he pointed towards a tall man in the uniform of the Polish Lancers sitting beside him. Napoloen gave a deep sigh.

Reardon was now certain that Napoleon had understood his message and that he would know whose side Reardon was on. The next step would be to convey to Napoleon how and when his escape would be organised.

A few minutes later there was a great commotion at the gate and the Balcombe party arrived. This was a dangerous development for Reardon. It was well known that William Balcombe was sympathetic towards Napoleon's situation and that he had access to those in power in London in a way that the Governor did not.

145

This was making Lowe increasingly suspicious of what Balcombe might be saying and who he might be meeting with on the island. Reardon did not want to be associated with Balcome if it raised the risk of Lowe linking him with Napoleon's sympathisers.

Reardon should take great care not to imply anything in his conversation with Napoleon about what he and his colleagues might be planning. Absolute secrecy had to be maintained until the very moment of escape.

"Good to see you Reardon", Balcombe opened, "I trust you are keeping well. Not the most comfortable lodgings on the island I daresay but I hope that my stores are keeping you well supplied?"

"Yes, thank you, Sir", Reardon replied, "we are well looked after but I fear that Mr. Grant will not be with us for much longer."

"No, a sad business. I knew his father when I served on HMS *Romney.* He is a good man who will be brought low by this news. It's a damnable climate aboard ship in these latitudes."

Meanwhile Betsy, dressed prettily in white buckskin shoes, white stockings and a pinafore dress was now engaging Napoleon in conversation. If the rumours were true, the girl took liberties with Napoleon that no one else dared. She flung her arms around his neck and whispered into his ear. She then plucked a buttercup from the lawn and, with a girlish giggle, held it under his chin saying: "Do you like butter, Sire?". Napoleon responded at once and administered her a good tickling in the ribs.

All seemed to be going well until Betsy decided that she would stand on his thighs and attempt to balance herself, arms outstretched, above his head like a bird. Napoleon swore loudly in French and she jumped down. "Leave me alone, tiresome girl. You hurt me" and with that he turned to Balcombe saying: "Keep Betsy away from me" and resumed his conversation with Reardon.

"Well, Monsieur, I fear this short idyll must end soon", Napoleon remarked, "I shall have to get back to camp or I shall be reported missing. Although it might give Governor Lowe a heart attack it is beneath my dignity to play such games with him. Thank you for entertaining us today and perhaps I shall have the honour to meet you in the future when we can resume out reminisces of Angouleme." With that his party gathered their things together and left for Longwood.

Twenty minutes later Reardon watched through his glass as Napoleon re-entered the veranda and soon disappeared inside, presumably to his private quarters.

It had been a tense but successful day for Reardon. He had made contact. It looked as if Napoleon had decided that Reardon was a genuine emissary from his friends in Europe and not an *agent provocateur* of Governor Lowe.

Reardon could not have known that the last time Napoleon had seen a French naval vessel was when the *Duchesse d'Angouleme*, a twenty-four gun frigate captured at Toulon, had been anchored next to HMS *Northumberland*. This had been shortly before he had left Europe and sailed down to St Helena. The name selected by the conspirators must surely be a good omen.

Marryat had mapped out the likely pick-up points on beaches around the island and Porteous now had the details of movements across the island by day and night. It would be Reardon's job to plan and execute Napoleon's actual extraction from Longwood.

This would be the most difficult part of the operation as Longwood was ringed day and night by sentries posted at every ten paces apart. There would be no way of breaking through this cordon without the knowledge and connivance of the guards.

The escape would have to be carried out on a night when Reardon was in a position to manage the piquets and their deployment. This would only be possible if it was soldiers of the 66th on duty who were also sympathetic to Napoleon's cause.

Reardon thought back to the episode on the quay at Jamestown on Birmingham's departure and earlier of the comments of the Regiment's Pioneers on the fence line. He decided that this would be the weak point in the Governor's defences. It would be highly risky for all those involved, both Napoleon and the piquet duty men.

The worst that could happen to Napoleon would be that he would be recaptured or, perhaps, shot whilst attempting escape. If the soldiers taking part in the plot were discovered, they would be court martialled and die by firing squad. Reardon appreciated that he would be asking a lot of them.

Two days later he met Marryat and Porteous for supper at the boarding house to share with them what he had learned.

"I met with Napoleon two days ago", Reardon Started. "He came for a picnic in the grounds at Mason's. We lunched on the lawn and he engaged me in conversation. He was interested in my service both here and in Spain and Ireland. He seemed to want to get to know me better and so I decided to take the risk. I introduced our code word quite naturally into the discussion. I was surprised how readily he absorbed it and understood what I was talking about.

Later, he repeated the word to me in another context. This confirmed to me that he had understood its implications. I think that when I approach him again he will be fully aware of our intentions and their implication."

"Very well done, Reardon", Marryat responded. "You seem to have exploited the situation brilliantly. I think that we should now move on to the next stage and make a detailed plan."

The other two nodded and drew their chairs closer.

"Of course, we cannot finalise anything until we hear more from Lord Cochrane", Marryat continued. "He will need to know our plans well in advance of the rescue and that means some detailed work at our end."

"There are three elements to consider", replied Porteous. "We have to think of Napoleon's escape from Longwood; the route from the house to the coast and his actual removal from the beach. There is a good division of labour between us if Reardon here takes responsibility for the exit from Longwood and you, Marryat, take care of selecting the beach we will be using and diverting attention from it. I will lead the way across the island. How about we plan it this way?"

"Excellent idea, Porteous", Marryat replied. "You in agreement with that Reardon?"

"Yes", Reardon responded, "but I'll need to find a way to approach my men and it can't be hurried."

"Very well then", Marryat replied, "I hear the toast favoured in your Mess is to *Napoleon's Drop*", as he raised the glass in his hand to drink. The three men touched their glasses together.

The following day Reardon went down to Deadwood Camp. The first thing he needed was to know the forward roster of the troops who would be guarding Longwood over the coming months. The Adjutant would be the person to ask and Reardon would have to find a good reason for doing so.

Captain Baird's office door was closed. Reardon knocked and entered.

Baird looked up. "Morning Dolf. What are you doing down here? I thought you were keeping out of trouble."

"I'm doing fine, thank you, which is more than I can say for poor old Grant and his pals. He is not a well man. I doubt that he will see through the coming winter. That's what I wanted to speak to you about. The weather's mild out at Mason's and I would like to get Grant outside into the open air.

At present the the doors are too narrow to get his bed into the garden. I was wondering if I could borrow some of the Pioneers for a couple of days to do some building work. We can move Grant outside without him having to get out of bed. He is very weak now."

"Of course, old man," Baird replied, "delighted to help. No need to tell the Colonel. We will call it a routine training exercise. When would you like them up?"

"Oh, anytime this week would be fine", Reardon replied. "Can you send Sergeant Flynn with them as he seems to be the only one who can keep them under control."

Flynn had commanded the informal sending-off party for Birmingham on Jamestown quay. The sergeant and Reardon were old friends from Peninsular days.

"Very well, expect them tomorrow."

"By the way", Reardon asked, "so I don't exhaust them too much, are they due on the fence line at Longwood any time later in the month?"

Baird turned around and consulted a chart on the wall behind him.

"This shows the Regiment's duties over the coming period. Let's have a look. No, nothing this month, but we take over from those deadbeats of the 20th for the whole of October. The Pioneers will have to take their turn. I have not yet worked out their precise routine but they will be on duty towards the end of the month. It will include some night guard."

This was the information about the piquet that Reardon wanted. For the rest, it would be between him; Sergeant Flynn and the Pioneers.

The following day he was back at Mason's for the arrival of the Pioneers.

They were a hardened looking bunch. Almost all had done time in the Regimental lock-up for one reason or another and many bore the scars of a lifetime of drunken brawling. When the Regiment needed to produce a boxing team for bouts against the other troops on the island, it never had to look further than to its Pioneers.

Flynn saluted smartly. "Top of the morning, Sir. Nice little spot you've got here. Room for us, is there?"

"Morning Sergeant", Reardon replied. "Now, don't get any funny ideas. Remember, I know you and your scoundrels, so no tricks. You have a job to do although I have laid on some entertainment for tonight. Come with me, and bring your blockheads and their gear with you."

"Oh, don't be like that, Sir, "Flynn said, "We're doing you a favour, so we are."

The Pioneers got to work and Reardon supplied them with cider at their lunch break which they drank outside. Flynn sat a little distance from the others and Reardon came and sat down beside him.

"I've met Boney again", Reardon opened. "He came up here for a picnic a few days ago. He didn't look too well and I am anxious he might die here on the island, like poor Grant upstairs."

"That would be a bad thing, Sir", replied Flynn "Such a great man brought so low. Imagine if that was to happen. There would be revolutions all over Europe, let alone in Ireland, so there would."

"What's it to you and your boys?"

"Well, Sir, as you know some of us fought on the Rebel side in '98 before we took the King's shilling. We were starving when we did it but we still have the love of liberty running in our veins."

If there was going to be an opportunity for Reardon to speak about escape, this was it.

"Before he left the island Lieutenant Birmingham told me that when he reached England he planned to meet with some individuals who want Napoleon back there."

"If there's any chance of that, Sir, count us in", Flynn replied.

151

"Well, as a matter of fact a number of us have been thinking about how it could be done."

"Go on, Sir."

"We have had a look around and have noted the routes to and from Longwood. We would have to persuade Napoleon that our plan would stand a chance of working. Contacts in America would be willing to help us to organise a rescue attempt."

There, it was out. Reardon held his breathe.

"And what would be our part, Sir?"

"If you and your men would be willing, I have found out the dates and times on which you will be on piquet duty over the next month. We would have to arrange Napoleon's escape at night during one of those watches."

"And, how would we do that?" Flynn said. "The guard surrounds the entire place. There are officers on duty throughout the night. We would be seen at once."

"Not necessarily," Reardon replied. "Night will fall early at that time of year. When you and your men take over your hundred-yard section of the fence, that should give us enough scope. My idea would be that Napoleon changes into a corporal's uniform when he leaves the house so he would be well disguised as he mingles amongst us. I would arrange that I would be the Officer of the Guard on the night"

"Then what?", Flynn asked.

"We have scouted out a route south westwards towards Sandy Bay. It is less frequented than other directions and has fewer dwellings along it. We are planning to take Napoleon off the beach there."

"But, what about us? If we are found on the island afterwards we will be shot."

"We all will be. We shall leave together and not come back. You will be Napoleon's escort. He is not in good condition and will need help.

He may even have to be carried. Our intention is to take Napoleon across the Atlantic to Buenos Aires. You will come with us. When we arrive you and your men will receive a reward of £2000 each. You can use it to make a new life. There is an active Irish community in the city. I have contacts there who will help you find work. You will never be able to return to Ireland but I guarantee you that the girls are just as pretty as on Grafton Street in Dublin."

"You think you've thought it all through, Sir, but it sounds like a lunatic plan to me", Flynn remarked. "How can you guarantee that we will be on duty on the night that the rescue vessel reaches the island? How do we know that we will be stationed on the fence in the right place and be together at the right time?"

"Leave that to me, Sergeant. We are short of officers and I am going to volunteer for duty. The Adjutant is an old friend of mine. He will not object if I offer to assist him with his Orders. There are others in the garrison who will be involved. By the time that the rescue party arrives at the rendezvous, we will be ready."

"What if the plot is uncovered beforehand or if we are caught on the night?"

"Then, we will all be for it and hope that our comrades can shoot straight. Now back to work. We will speak again when I have more news."

At that Sergeant Flynn stood up to return to his duties. Reardon felt the hair stand up on the back of his neck. Now the plot to rescue Napoleon had become real. He would be putting other people's lives at risk as well as his own. If he was found out he would pay with more than just his commission.

10   *The Cocoa Tree Club*

IT WAS THE most dazzling, and afterwards, the most discussed night of the year.

It was Midsummer evening, the 24th June, when the current year's crop of *debutantes* would be presented by their mothers to the Club's all-female Committee of Management. This would be in front of over two hundred of its members. They would be meeting in the Club's newly built ballroom and dining facilities in St James's - managed by the admirable Mr. Brook.

Brooks had started as an all-male drinking house in Pall Mall but five years ago it had been taken over by a group of society women and re-named the Cocoa Tree Club. It was the first of its kind in London and membership was highly sought-after. Women appointed all of its officers and had an absolute veto on all new members. It was unique.

There were two principal attractions in the room. First, there were the debutantes themselves who would be accepted into the society of the highest in the land and would thereafter represent the flower of its youth, breeding and wealth.

Second, there were the *beaux* who were inspecting this year's crop of young women. Here, they would make liaisons that would lead to marriages that could advance their political careers and increase their wealth.

The girls wore white gardenias in their hair or tiaras, if they possessed them. The young men wore either their military scarlets or cut-away coats with richly embroidered waistcoats.

The members of the Cocoa Tree Club's committee sat on gilt chairs on a raised dais at one end of the ballroom as each girl was led up by her mother and presented by name.

The Cocoa Tree's entry rules were very strict. One black ball could exclude an individual and his or her family from membership which removed at a stroke any hope of further social advancement.

This contradicted the fact that at least one of the club's founders, Lady Holland, was herself a runaway from a previously annulled marriage who, as a result, would never be received at Court.

An event that made the evening particularly memorable for long afterwards was when a footman whispered into Amelia Stewart, Lady Castlereagh's, ear to advise her that the Duke of Wellington sought admittance to the ball. Whilst as a high Tory he would never wish to be a member, it would be hard to refuse him entry on an occasion like this. Amelia went downstairs to speak with him.

It was a firm rule of the Club that evening dress should be worn, that is britches and white silk hose, as befitted a gentleman. Wellington stood at the door in trousers and frock coat.

Lady Castlereagh knew the Duke well. They had been neighbours in Ireland when they were children and in their teenage years had been to many county balls together. Amelia had followed Arthur's career from that day to this and they had always retained a soft spot for each other.

Of course, he had come a long way from his roots in the minor Irish aristocracy. He was now the greatest man in the Nation.

Arthur Wellesley had followed his elder brother to India to seek his fortune and had soon proved his worth in the Princely wars of conquest. He had also made himself rich by plunder. He was not known as the Sepoy General for nothing and had shown his exceptional ability in many ways. He was able to get inside the mind of his enemies and understand their intentions. He could *read* the ground on which he would fight and he paid very close attention to the administration of his army. It was reputed that he had not taken a day's leave in six years of war.

Amelia was also well aware that he was arrogant, snobbish and serially unfaithful to his wife. He was now at the height of his powers and it was rumoured that he would soon take over from Lord Liverpool as Prime Minister.

"Amelia, my dear", Wellington started, "How delightful to see you! I hope that you are keeping well. We have not enjoyed each other's company for far too long. I have become too busy with the country's affairs and have been neglecting my friends."

Without pause for breath, Amelia, knowing quite well that The Duke had only crossed the road from Boodles, the Tory stronghold, replied: "Arthur, it is a pleasure to see you, as always, but I regret that Your Grace is not dressed for the occasion and would not be permitted entry on such a grand night for the Club."

The Duke gave Amelia a broad smile: "Ah, My Amelia, you always were a feisty one" and bowing low turned away back up St James's.

Brooks club was dedicated to the Whig cause and on this occasion a number of its leading personalities were present including Lord Holland and his set, which included Lord Byron and his latest paramour, the mercurial Lady Caroline Lamb. She clung on to Lord Byron's arm but it was rumoured that he was tiring of her.

Amongst those also present was John Townsend of the Bow Street Runners. He was no dancer but it was a good opportunity to observe the Holland House set at their leisure. Townsend was a walking encyclopaedia of the aristocracy. As he circulated around the ballroom, he noted the names and pedigrees of many of those present.

There was one group of guests that he did not recognise but when he asked about them he was told that they were guests of Lord and Lady Holland who had come down from Scotland. One of them, in particular, caught his attention. Townsend had seen him somewhere before but could not recall where it had been. If the man was a visitor at Holland House, it was not there that he had encountered him.

No, he recognised him from somewhere else, but where was it?

He ran through his mind the usual haunts of the Holland set and recalled that a few weeks ago they had all attended Mr. Sheridan's new play *The Rivals* at the recently opened Drury Lane theatre. Now he had him. He had been sharing a box with the Hollands.

On enquiring of a fellow theatre-goer, Townsend had been told that he was a Dr. Blane, apparently well-known as a medical man in Scotland's capital. He claimed to have discovered a cure for consumption from which two of the Hollands' children had already died. Hence Blane's acquaintanceship with their circle as an insurance for the survival of their two remaining children.

At the end of the evening at the theatre, Townsend, with his insatiable curiosity, and wanting to know more about this stranger, had left his seat and followed the good doctor up Fleet Street and into a public house situated between Covent Garden and the river.

The Lamb & Flag, was one of London's oldest pubs and had become notorious seventy-five years earlier as a meeting place for Jabobites. Later it had been frequented by individuals sympathetic to the American cause. Townsend knew that Hazell at the Alien Office had kept a close eye on its patrons during the war of 1812.

Indeed, Townsend had been involved in the exposure of a conspiracy that had originated in the pub. The affair had ended with an American spy being *cut out* on the London docks, arrested and hung in the Tower for espionage. The pub had easy access to both the Upper and Lower Pools on the Thames.

Townsend had speculated about the reason that Blane should have had an interest in a pub on the river. He became even more suspicious when Blane held a long conversation with an individual who, Townsend later learned, was the captain of an East Indiaman whose home was in Rotherhithe.

The Runners had investigated this man a few years earlier. He was Captain Price of the *Hotspur*, which, at 1500 tons, was one of the Company's largest vessels.

Price had been implicated in the production of fraudulent cargo manifests but nothing had been proved. Was Blane now part of a conspiracy in the South Atlantic to rescue Napoleon? Captain Price had certainly come a long way up-river for a drink.

Dancing at the Cocoa Tree Club had now started and Townsend walked discreetly behind the line of debutantes and their parents lining the edge of the room. He moved towards the group of men and women around Lord and Lady Holland and shouldered his way into them as far as he could.

The Scotchman Blane was speaking: "It won't be long now, My Lord. I was up there last week and Johnson is putting the finishing touches to the craft. I think that we can meet your Lordship's deadline for the sailing date in three weeks' time. If you would like to visit the yard with me, you would be very welcome."

"I don't think that will necessary, my friend", Holland replied, "I don't want to give the game away. I have every confidence in your arrangements. I have communicated your progress to our friends."

Townsend retreated.

Something was afoot but what, where and how, he did not yet know. He would need to consult with Hazell and Sayer and see if they had any ideas.

The following day Hazell had a message from Townsend inviting him to look in on Bow Street as soon as he could.

When he arrived, Edward went straight to Townsend's office and found Sayer with him. He asked Townsend to give him a word by word account of the events of the previous night at which Townsend, from long experience, was an expert. The words that made any sense to the three men in the context of St Helena were the words 'craft', 'sailing date' and 'yard'.

Each of these suggested that something was being constructed; that it would be water-borne and that it was nearing completion. But what could it be?

"I don't know, Mr. Hazell", Sayer said. "I remember a strange man called Johnson who used to hang about the Lower Pool, now part of the East India Dock. He was a shipwright by trade who had lost his business in a fire that it was rumoured he had started himself for the insurance money. He claimed that he had designed an underwater craft that could be used to attack shipping or carry spies onto the French coast.

I know Johnson carried out a demonstration of his craft on the Thames in front of potential investors. The craft sank and the two men inside it drowned. Their widows sued Johnson. When he refused to pay out he was declared bankrupt and spent time in Newgate. The last that I heard he had got into a dispute with some tea merchants down at Rotherhithe and had dynamited a barge of theirs.

"Wait a minute", Townsend interjected, "Now I come to think of it, that Captain Price who I saw with Dr. Blane at the *Lamb & Flag* is connected with Johnson. As well as his captaincy with the Company, Price has always traded in his own right. He was a co-owner of a barge that was destroyed with all of its cargo. The goods that were lost were rumoured to be worth more than £2,000. Perhaps the two men are closer than meets the eye. Price could be blackmailing Johnson with promises of freedom from his debt in return for his help with building a 'craft'."

"We need to know a lot more about Price and this Scotchman, Blane", Edward said. "Does Price have any connection with the Holland House set? Has he ever visited St Helena? And about Blane: where does he live; what does he do with his time when he is not at Holland House? What is his connection with either Price or Johnson?"

"When I get back to the office, I will check our files," Edward continued, "and see if we have anything on either man."

"I think someone told me that Blane served in the Company as a surgeon in India and recently purchased a house outside London", Townsend replied, "but I don't know where."

"Good. If it's on or near a river, canal or port that might give us a clue about the location of a 'yard'. Could you go back to your informant and ask them to refresh their memory. If they cannot remember, lock them up until they do. We need to know quickly. We will meet here again as soon as any of us has more information", Edward replied.

The meeting broke up.

Edward returned to the Alien Office and summoned Nicholson to his office,

"Afternoon Francis. What are you up to?"

"Oh, routine stuff. You remember you asked for a summary of our current intelligence about the prisoner on St Helena. I think you said that you needed it for Crauford and the Colonies Sub-Committee next week. I've drawn up a draft report with schedules. Would you like to see it?"

"Drat", Edward exclaimed, "I had forgotten about that. Crauford's worried about our expenses. Bow Street's services don't come cheap but I see no alternative to their use. They have eyes on the street that we do not and Townsend has expensive tastes. He's a rich man apparently. That's what I want to speak to you about. During the Atlantic war we found that our own side was not above some profiteering.

The Company claimed that what they did was only a part of their legitimate 'carrying trade', but we know better. Some of their captains colluded with the enemy. They diverted cargoes from their intended destinations in the East and made a tidy profit in Baltimore instead.

This would also have meant calling in at St Helena en route so some captains may have acquaintances on the island. We need to know which Company employees were involved and who their contacts might have been. This is urgent. Can you stop what you are doing and get onto to it at once."

"Check our Registry files", Edward continued, "and see if we have anything on a Captain William Price, resident of Rotherhithe. He is a senior sailing officer in the Company but is also suspected of trading on his own behalf. We know he has powerful friends on the Company's Court. He has been investigated for illegal activities in the past."

Edward sighed as Nicholson left his office. He would have to speak with Crauford. He would advise him that the Committee meeting might have to be postponed because of urgent business. He was now worried that he would have to cancel his date with Julia.

He had not seen her since the evening of the supper party but she had not been far from his thoughts. Julia, although educated entirely at home, was well informed and interested in current affairs. She had already made clear to Edward her strongly held - and liberal - opinions.

He had obviously not mentioned to her his own involvement with Napoleon's imprisonment when they had met at supper but he judged that she would be vehemently opposed to his mission if she knew about it.

He was keen, however, that this difference of opinion should not cloud their relationship. He risked the security of his operation by arranging the date that he had made with her for a day on the river, but he needed the cover that their day together would provide if he was going to do some snooping.

161

The following morning Edward had hardly sat down at his desk when Nicholson knocked and entered.

"I have the information you asked for".

Edward saw that his assistant had a thick file under his arm.

"Sit down, sit down. You've been quick. Up all night?"

"Yes, as a matter of fact I have", Nicholson replied. "By the time I had all the information that I needed it was too late to go back to Wandsworth so I dozed on and off in the Duty Officer's room. I couldn't sleep as my mind was turning over what I have uncovered."

"Good", replied Edward, "let's have it then."

"Well, it's clear that this Price has been implicated in a number of unsavoury deals", Nicholson went on. "He began his career in Liverpool as the mate on an Irish packet. He soon gravitated to London where he served with the London and Rochester Line on their short sea route between Shoreham and Bilbao. He was appointed a captain in 1796 but was dismissed on the grounds of insubordination three years later.

Price returned to Liverpool and used his master's ticket to contract with investors in Cumberland and Westmorland to manage a number of triangular trade voyages on their behalf. He narrowly escaped prison when they accused him of the theft of a cargo in West Africa. By this time he had amassed a considerable fortune. He used his wealth to return to London where he found himself a young wife, daughter of a Company captain, and it must have been this connection that enabled him to join its marine.

The couple purchased a house in Rotherhithe where many of the Company's captains live. They tend to congregate at the *Mayflower Inn* in the evening. A captain can enjoy an extra night in bed when the tide is out and be rowed out to his ship from the *Mayflower* when the morning tide comes in as his ship passes by on its way downstream."

162

"Well, I'll be damned", Edward exclaimed, "I know the *Mayflower*. I once met an agent there. The privileges of rank."

Nicholson continued: "He definitely has form regarding the South Atlantic. I found entries in your hand recording that he landed a cargo on the American coast during the war. Your spies reported that he had set out from St Helena on a course for India but instead turned up in Baltimore three weeks later. He said that a violent storm had driven him westwards but there was no evidence of it.

"Ah, I remember him now", Edward said. "He pretended that the weather had driven him onto the American coast but it was obvious that he had been breaking our embargo. Unfortunately for us he had powerful friends in the City and we were not able to prosecute him for trading with the enemy.

I daresay Townsend is also right about his suspicion of cargo manifest fraud but the majority of captains indulge in private trade. No action was taken against Price on that score either."

Nicholson went on: "Since the war ended he has been sailing the *Hotspur* to and from the Indies and has made himself even richer. I have no doubt that he has the means to become involved with Holland. His wife is known to want to improve her social position. A connection with the Holland set would be a good way for he and his wife to achieve this."

"Thank you, Francis", Edward replied. "Very thorough and more than sufficient to justify our putting a tail on Price. I will speak to Sayer and ask him to find Johnson and follow Price. I have no doubt that something will come up. Price is a nasty piece of work."

Edward took a cab to Bow Street first thing the following morning and briefed Sayer on this latest piece of intelligence. Sayer was to find out where Johnson was hiding and, if possible, search his lodgings for any evidence of this so-called 'craft'.

He should inform Edward at once if he found anything.

Townsend was also in his office at Bow Street at the time and Edward advised him that he should watch out for Captain Price who could be expected to contact Dr. Blane and the Hollands at any time. He did not give him the whole story as Townsend was incurably inquisitive. It would be unwise to give him too much background information.

Three days later the first news came from Sayer who reported that Johnson had simply vanished from London. He and his men had visited every place where Johnson was known and no one had seen or heard of him for at least the past four weeks.

It was rumoured that he had left town to visit a sick relative in Sussex but, again, Sayer had found no evidence that he had been seen anywhere on the road. They would keep up their search but at present his whereabouts were a complete mystery.

They had had better luck with Price.

"I put one of my teams onto watching the house in Rotherhithe, Mr Hazell", Townsend reported, "and yesterday evening Price left the house after dark and, after a short walk to the *Mayflower*, took a carriage to the West End. We lost him in Covent Garden – he may have been onto my men – but on the off chance that he would reappear, they checked the snug at the *Lamb and Flag* and there he was in deep conversation once again with the man Blane. My men could not get close enough to hear what was being said but reported that the two men looked conspiratorial."

"Excellent, good work both of you", Edward said, "I want you to keep up your observation of Price and continue your search for Johnson. There is definitely something going on here. If we can just link Price, Johnson and Blane together I think that I could get arrest warrants for all three of them. Then we could question them at our leisure."

The following day Edward received a message from Townsend saying that he required an urgent meeting.

When Edward reached the Runners office, Townsend said that he had two important pieces of information. "I was at a soiree arranged by Lord Holland to welcome home Sir Pulteney and Lady Malcolm who have just returned to London from St Helena. He was in command of the Naval squadron on the island. It was a congenial evening with the hosts circulating amongst their guests.

I spotted Dr. Blane and the Scotch contingent quite early on and kept my eye on them as the evening went by. After a time, I didn't think that anything more to our advantage could be learned and was about to leave when your Captain Price turned up. It was well after eleven and the party was beginning to break up. He went up to Blane, whispered something to him and they left in a hansom cab together shortly afterwards."

"I caught a cab", Townsend continued, "and followed them down Kensington and into Park Lane. They reached Piccadilly and finally drew up outside the *Lamb & Flag* in Covent Garden. I followed them inside and after a short time they were joined by two other men. These men obviously knew Price and he introduced them to Blane. They had a conversation which I was unable to overhear.

After about an hour Blane left followed by Price and the two men. I decided to follow Price and the men. They went down onto the Embankment; past Parliament and the Tower and into the Lower Pool at the Company's dock. There are a number of East Indiamen in harbour and they went aboard one of them. I learned later was the *Hotspur*, Price's command. It looks as if the two men are members of his ship's company."

All Edward's suspicions were confirmed by this report. It linked Holland, Blane and Price together. Price regularly sailed his vessel to the South Atlantic. If the 'craft' did exist it would be Price who would carry it down.

The question that Edward now had to answer was whether the conspirators should be apprehended at once or if he should let them continue at liberty until he had located the craft.

"And what is your second piece of news?", Edward asked Townsend.

"I have found out more about Blane and his background", Townsend replied. "You were right, he worked as surgeon to the Nawab of Oudh so he already has close connections with the Company. He made a fortune in India and returned home to Scotland before moving down to England.

We have found out where he lives. Sayer and I believe we can locate the place where his vessel is under construction. Blane's house is outside Windsor on the edge of the forest. He purchased it recently from a bankrupt. He is running a sanatorium there at the same time as using it as his home."

Sayer had a set of maps of the Home Counties on Townsend's desk and pulled out the map for East Berkshire.

He placed his finger on the round tower of Windsor Castle and ran his finger up the Long Walk and across the royal forest towards Wokingham.

"There", he said, "there it is, Foliejon Park. Once part of the royal forest. Now a freehold dwelling. And, look, not four miles west of the Thames"

"We should find out more about the area at once", Edward said, "This could be the link we have been looking for.

It so happens that I have promised myself a day on the river on Saturday. I will combine the trip with a little spying. I intend to hire a skiff in Windsor and go upstream via Boveney Lock and Queen's Eyot towards Maidenhead. There are a number of boatyards on that stretch. I will have a look at each one as I row past.

You, Sayer, will take the land route and walk up the towpath on the Berkshire bank, also from Windsor. I suggest that we meet back here on Monday to compare notes. Thank you, gentlemen, for your efforts so far. I think we are now entering a new phase which will bring us closer to the conspirators."

Edward returned to his office and called Nicholson.

"We are making progress. We have now linked the Hollands with others. These include Captain Price whose record is, I suspect, about to get a lot worse."

Edward briefed Nicholson on their latest intelligence and asked him to arrange for the hire of a skiff on Saturday out of Mr. Parr's yard at Windsor.

Edward wrote a note to be delivered to Julia. He would collect her from her house on Saturday morning. He would be bringing a packed lunch with him. They would take the nine o'clock stage from Hyde Park Corner and reach Windsor by midday. He had hired a skiff and they would go upstream as far as Maidenhead. She should bring an umbrella in case of rain and a parasol in case of sun. He was expecting an exciting day. No, that would not do. Julia might get the wrong idea. He crossed out the words exciting and replaced it with enchanting. That would cover a number of eventualities.

He called a clerk and asked him to deliver the note to Julia's address.

He should now speak with Crauford and bring his master up to date with the situation. The involvement of Holland and the East India Company could be a serious embarrassment to the Government.

Whilst Lord Holland led those who opposed the Government's policy regarding Napoleon's imprisonment, it was unlikely that the Home Secretary, the Duke of Wellington, would sanction a charge of treason against a fellow peer and member of the House of Lords. Edward would need to tread carefully.

The East India Company's involvement was even more problematic. The wealth of many members of the Government was founded on their dividends from India. The idea of destabilising the Company's activities and Cabinet member's incomes would not be popular.

He arranged to meet with Crauford.

"Well, what have you got?", Crauford asked. "I am lunching with His Grace at two this afternoon. We are discussing some changes I am plannong to make to the uniform of the 95th. I want him in a good mood. Not bad news, I hope?"

"No, Sir. Not bad news, but important", Edward replied, "I will try not to spoil your lunch."

Edward spoke about what had been uncovered. It only remained for him to find this craft and they would be able to break up the plot.

Crauford listened to the story before he spoke.

"This will be a serious matter for the Cabinet, Hazell. Quite apart from Lord Holland, which will be a political matter, the involvement of the Company widens the scope for any scandal.

As you know, Holland leads the opposition to St Helena in the Lords. It may be possible to shut him up with the threat of treason but the Company has supporters in the Cabinet. My father was fond of saying 'nothing causes more trouble than disputes over money' and, as you say, we will need to tread very carefully. We can't go about impounding Company vessels in London or at the Cape.

I will speak to Wellington about Holland. I suggest you speak with Bunbury at the Home Office about the Company's part and the other conspirators."

"Very good, Sir, I will make an appointment with the Secretary. I also expect to have more news from the Thames within a few days. Both I and Sayer of the Runners will be searching its banks."

"Keep in touch and inform me of any developments", Crauford ended.

Edward left Crauford's office and made an appointment to meet with Bunbury as soon as possible.

Bunbury met him with his usual greetings.

"Morning, Hazell, got into another hole, have you? I suppose it's like that last scrap when you managed to mislay one of His Majesty's ships of the Line and all its crew. Where did they end up? Buenos Aires, wasn't it? That seems to be the destination of choice at present for all our rogues and renegades."

Sir Henry liked his little jokes at the Alien Office's expense.

"Nothing like that, Sir Henry", Edward replied, "it's rather closer to home."

Edward described the situation. He ended that General Crauford has spoken to Lord Wellington about the political aspects of the situation but that he, Edward, had been instructed to deal with the other conspirators. However, because of the Company's involvement his master had suggested that Bunbury could help.

"You see, Sir Henry, there are many investors in the Company who will not take kindly to reading in their newspaper that one of its ships has been impounded and its crew arrested. The Office would very much appreciate your advice."

"A matter of convenience, then, that you are obliged to come to me?", Sir Henry responded. "And what do you think I can do to influence these backswoodsmen of the Tory Party who are using their dividends to build grand new Adam fronts onto their very ordinary houses?"

"I don't know, Sir". It was always a good idea to plead helplessness in front of Sir Henry. He liked to be flattered that he was the only one who could get the Government out of trouble in this kind of situation.

"Leave it with me, boy, and I will see what I can do. Meanwhile, stay away from the Dock. If a Company ship is set alight, I will know who to come after and so will all of London."

With that Sir Henry gave a chuckle and turned back to his desk. This was as much as Edward was going to get out of him for now.

11 *Messum's Boatyard*

SAYER LEFT HIS office in Bow Street early on the following morning to follow up this new lead.

He took the first stage of the day from Westminster to Reading via Windsor and alighted at the White Hart. Standing on Windsor bridge, he glanced down at the river that was running fast below him and then up at the castle. A light breeze was moving the sovereign's standard that flew from the top of the Round Tower which confirmed that the King was in residence.

The sun was out and it was going to be a hot day. Sayer took off his black serge topcoat and folded it over his arm. He wanted to look as casual as possible to anyone who might be watching the river. He crossed over onto the Berkshire bank and walked fifty yards up the towpath opposite the Brocas heath. He found the ferry that would take him upstream through Boveney Lock and towards Maidenhead.

He asked to be put ashore at Bishop's Landing where the Bone Water joined the Thames main river. The landing place was marked by the ruins of an ancient friary lying beside the riverbank that had once been owned by the monks of Reading Abbey.

The area in which Sayer was interested was a rectangular strip of land about three miles wide and six miles deep. Ir was bounded in the west by the Royal Forest and in the east by the Thames. Foliejon Park, Dr. Blane's residence, lay close to the forest on the landward side. The village of Bray lay opposite, situated on the waters-edge some four miles below the town of Maidenhead.

Sayer stepped off the ferry onto the dilapidated landing stage. He began to walk upstream along the towpath beside the river. From time to time he saw the thatched roofs of the nearby farm dwellings at Oakley Green that lay between the village's fields, orchards and scrubland. Brown and white spotted cattle grazed the fields. Groups of cows watered themselves on the muddy riverbank in groups.

The day became very hot. Sayer regretted his black suit. He took off his waistcoat and carried it over his arm along with his coat. He had bought a pie and a small flask of cider in Windsor. He found a fallen oak trunk on which to sit and have his lunch. The river snaked past him. There was some traffic moving on it, mainly barges carrying bricks down to London that had been manufactured in the clay pits at Reading.

There was no sign yet of a boatyard along the river's bank.

After lunch he dozed fitfully in the afternoon sunshine. It was very pleasant to be outside of London for a change and away from the city with its perpetual crowds, stench and noise.

He awoke with a start in the late afternoon. He had better get a move on. At around six he reached the outskirts of a village that must be Bray and saw its square Church tower in the distance.

It was very quiet except for the sound of the water eddying along the riverbank and the occasional call of a moorhen.

He was startled by a sudden noise and halted in mid-stride. It was the sound of the hammering of rivets on metal with which he was familiar from his days working in the dockyard. It was completely out of place in these rural surroundings.

Sayer bent himself double and backed away as quietly as he could. He found a large tree and sat down behind it.

As the light began to fade he got up and crept forward. A few yards further on he came to a wicket fence that stretched left and right in front of him: to its left into the fields and to its right down to the water's edge.

Sayer moved gingerly along the fence looking for any gap through which he could climb. After a few minutes searching he came across some loose planking and squeezed himsdelf through the fence. He found himself at the back of a boatyard. A number of ruined river craft lay strewn about, some propped up on wooden struts and others surrounded by tangled piles of old rope, timbers and broken spars.

It would be an extraordinary piece of luck if he had stumbled on what he was looking for at the first boatyard he had come across. However, this place was the nearest to Foliejon Park as the crow flies. Its location would fit.

Work had obviously ended for the day. The yard was now silent.

Sayer stood upright and, keeping to the shadows, moved towards the black bulk of the yard's boatshed. He went around its side to the front. A slipway and rafts led to the water. He looked up and read above its door the words *Messum's Boatyard Est. 1782.*

He returned to the shadows and waited for nightfall when a half-moon would emerge. He moved around the clapboard shed looking for a way inside. He found a door secured by a heavy padlock. He looked for another way in. At the very back of the shed he found a piece of board that had split. He took out the knife that he always carried with him and started to enlarge the damage to make a hole through which he could squint.

What he saw made him gasp. He ripped away more of the board and squeezed inside.

Standing on a wheeled trolley was an extraordinary object. It was balloon shaped; about ten feet in diameter and twelve feet high. It was hinged down one side and looked like an orange that had been peeled and halved. Each segment was made of leather stretched over curved bamboo struts.

Across the object's width was a seat at each side of which was a handle attached to a paddle on its outside. This was obviously the way it was propelled. A metal rod positioned in front of the seat was joined to an external rudder at the stern; this was its steering mechanism.

A hatch was let into the top of the craft with a ladder let into the interior. A set of cane pipes provided air for a snorkel when submerged. Sayer could not see how ballast would be pumped in and out of the craft but a pair of bellows let into its base could serve that purpose.

Sayer reckoned there would be space for a maximum of three crew. He stared at it in shock for some time before taking a piece of paper and a pencil out of his pocket. He drew a rough sketch of the object's main features. Tools lay all around on the floor of the shed. He reckoned that it would be finished in a week or so.

It could then be run down the slipway on its trolley and launched into the water at the riverbank. Alternatively, it could be loaded onto a barge or floated downstream as far as the tideway and into the docks. However, the machine looked very flimsy. Sayer doubted if it would be sufficiently seaworthy to undertake a rescue at sea.

Sayer had almost finished the sketch and was about to put it back in his pocket and return through the hole in the shed when he heard a sound behind him.

He half turned around but not quickly enough to avoid a violent punch to the side of his face followed by a vicious kick in the groin. As Sayer dropped to his knees in agony his assailant kicked him hard on the shin. His attacker fell on him immediately, crushing him on the ground as he seized Sayer by the throat with one hand and punched him again in the face with the other.

The man was more heavily built than Sayer. Sayer could feel the life being squeezed out of him. He could smell gin on the man's fetid breath and just managed to knead his attacker hard between the legs before losing consciousness.

The man loosened his grip around Sayer's neck momentarily. Sayer threw himself to one side with his last breath and took the man's arm in a lock. He twisted the man's arm behind his back until he heard a distinct cracking sound as it came out of its socket. The man screamed in agony.

Sayer didn't dare use his knife because of the mess it would make and, reaching around the man's neck instead, pulled it violently to one side. He felt it break and the man's head went limp.

Sayer sat winded on the ground holding his head in his hands.

After a few minutes he recovered a little and searched the man's pockets. He found a half empty flask of brandy some of which he drank to ease the pain in his ankle. His first thought was that it would be vital that there should be no signs of struggle. The man could not be found in the yard in the morning. At least there was no blood.

Sayer took the dead man under his arms and manoeuvred him through the hole in the shed that he had made earlier. He dragged him down to the waters-edge. Each step was agony but he finally managed to roll the body over and into the river. He used an oar he found nearby to push it further out into the stream where it was soon carried away by the current. He left the empty brandy flask by the bank.

If and when the man was eventually found it would look as if he had fallen into the river by accident or because he was drunk. His bruises could be explained by his body having hit underwater obstacles as it drifted away downstream.

Sayer's coat was covered in dirt from the fight in the yard. Sayer crouched by the water's edge and cleaned it as best he could. He covered the hole he had made in the back of the shed with a pile of old nets before climbing back over the yard's fence.

He limped away from the river's edge and took a different route back to Windsor. If anyone remarked on his appearance, he would say that he had fallen over a hidden branch during his walk. He went slowly through Oakley Green via the *Braywood Inn* favoured by the foresters and the *Nag's Head* where the bargees came off the river to quench their thirst in the evenings.

He saw nothing suspicious on his journey and took the night stage back to London. He was back in his office again in Bow Street the next morning where he locked the sketch that he had made of the balloon into his safe. He would inform Hazell and Townsend of all that had happened when they met on Monday morning.

Meanwhile on Saturday morning Edward left his house early to collect Julia for their day out together.

As he rang her bell, expecting a footman to answer, Julia herself opened it, a broad smile on her face. Edward caught his breath; she looked quite stunning. She was wearing a plain white blouse cut low at the bodice which was threaded with yellow ribbon and a skirt of the same colour to the ankle.

The linen skirt showed off her slim figure at its best. She had a pair of white patent leather shoes on her feet and a yellow bow in her hair. She carried a folded parasol, also yellow, to provide shade on the river.

"Good morning Edward. What a perfect day for a picnic", and kissed him on the lips.

"My, you are a picture in yellow and white. Come on, we need to hurry if we are to catch the connection."

They reached the stop in good time and set off for Windsor. Edward carried the picnic that Julia had prepared in a wicker basket. The coach was crowded and Julia and Edward were obliged to sit close together. Julia held Edward's hand tightly in hers as they travelled west.

They reached Windsor and went down to the riverside. The boatman greeted them and showed them to their skiff.

"I hope you will like it, Sir", he said, "It's the best hire we have."

It was a clinker built skiff, varnished to a high shine with a wrought iron-backed seat in the stern for a passenger with a bench set in the middle for the oarsman. The ironwork was painted a light blue reminding Edward of his days on the Cam. Edward handed Julia into the boat and loaded the picnic. He removed his jacket and took up the oars.

He showed Julia how to steer the boat and they set off upstream round Upper and Lower Hope.

The lock keeper helped them through Boveney Lock. It was by now almost one o'clock and Edward decided to land for lunch on Queen's Eyot island half a mile upstream.

The island was closer to the Berkshire bank and the main stream flowed on its far side. Willows grew at its edges. Edward rowed towards an overhanging tree and tied the boat up. He helped Julia step out and found a shady spot on the bank to spread their picnic on the rug that he had brought with him. They sat down companionably side by side. There were salmon and beef sandwiches, strawberries with cream, iced lemon water for Julia and a bottle of beer for Edward.

After they had eaten their lunch Julia lay back on her elbows. "Oh, Edward this is heaven. Can we stay here forever?" and, as she spoke, she stretched out her arm and reached around Edward's neck pulling him towards her before pressing her lips to his.

They kissed long and deeply mouth to mouth as they had the last time they had been together on the steps of Julia's house. This time, however, Edward did not break their kiss as Julia stroked the back of his neck with both her hands before pulling up his shirt and stroking his bare shoulders beneath.

She took her mouth from Edward's lips and nibbled his ear as she whispered; "Dearest, I do love you, you know. What should we do about it?"

Edward responded by moving over her. First he placed his right hand over Julia's breast before taking hold of her at the waist. She sighed as she moved her hands from his back to his shoulders again and looked deeply into his eyes.

Edward felt her kick off her shoes before lifting her skirt and opening her legs. He moved his hand down again and began to stroke the soft skin at the back of her bare knees. Julia shivered with pleasure. He moved his hand again. Under her shift Julia was wearing nothing except a pair of loosely divided drawers. Edward reached up them and began to stroke her bare buttocks. He was excited by the touch of Julia's smooth skin and her urgent response. She raised her legs and crossed them over him as they pressed themselves into each other.

Edward was suddenly taken back to Townsend's fetid office at Bow Street and saw again the moll with her bare legs and red ribbons lying exposed on Townsend's desk.

He went quite still and pulled away from Julia.

"What's the matter, darling?"

"Nothing. Julia, but we must press on if we are to reach Maidenhead in time to return to London by dark."

"Oh, don't be a silly. This is much more fun. Why don't we spend the night here and return home tomorrow?"

"Alas, we can't. I'm on duty at the Office at ten. And anyway, your parents will think I have kidnapped you."

"Your Office! It's all you ever think of. What about us?"

"There is an us and it matters to me as much as to you but duty must come first."

"You and your duty. I'm sick of it. When are we going to settle down?"

"Soon, I promise you".

Edward disentangled himself from Julia and began to pack up their picnic things. Julia stood up and straightened her clothes. He tried to take her by the hand as they moved back to the skiff but she pulled away from him; obviously furious.

He helped her back into the boat and resumed his place at the oars. He needed to make progress upstream now. Julia held the rudder strings tightly and half closed her eyes.

It was very quiet on the river with no other boats in sight except for one or two bargees who had made their camp on its banks for the weekend, their horses tethered out to grass.

As they rounded a slight bend in the steam, Edward saw the tower of Bray church for the first time and shortly afterwards a boatyard appeared on the bank. He would have a discreet look at it as they passed. A slipway reached down to the water's edge and a raft was pushed out into the river. Edward rowed towards the raft.

There did not seem to be anyone around and he decided to land. A sign above the door of the boathouse read *Messum's Boatyard Est. 1782.*

He shipped his oars, tied up to a ring and was about to step out of the skiff when a man appeared from up the yard. He came down the slipway fast and stepped onto the raft. He was heavily built, wore a checked shirt, cord breeches and heavy boots. He looked aggressive.

"You can't stop here", the man shouted. "This is private property, this is. Begging your pardon, Ma'am", as he noticed Julia in the stern and touched his cap.

Before Julia could speak Edward replied. "I am sorry to trouble you but there's something wrong with my left oar and I need to have a look at it. Perhaps you could help?"

Edward stepped out of the boat and stretched his arms. As he moved towards the bank the man came in close.

"I'll have a look at it for you, Sir, but you are to stay where you are. There's no one allowed to land here" and pushed Edward hard in the chest. "My master will have no one trespassing on his property 'specially on a Saturday when the yard's closed and I'm the only one here."

If Edward had been alone he would have forced the man backwards but he had Julia to consider. Neither should he do anything that might raise the man's suspicion about his real purpose in landing.

He moved back to the skiff; knelt down and fiddled with the rollocks before glancing at Julia and saying: "I think I've fixed it."

He got back into the boat without a word, pushed off from the raft and began to row again.

"What on earth was that all about?", Julia said. "I thought you were going to assault that wretched man. What were you thinking of?"

"He was being obstructive", Edward replied, "I only asked for some help."

"Well, you made it look as if he was an enemy of the State. You're not on duty now. Why don't you relax?"

They were three hundred yards upstream and losing sight of Bray village when a boat pulled out of the near bank and began to follow them. At first Edward paid no attention to the craft but, after ten minutes pulling on his oars, he began to think that it was keeping station with him.

When he slowed so did the two oarsmen behind. Either it was pure chance, which he thought was unlikely, or it had been stationed on the bank to keep interlopers away from the yard and, if necessary, warn them off from landing. There was a more sinister explanation which was that he had been expected.

He ran through in his mind anyone who had known about his plans for the day, including Nicholson. Julia herself had to be on the list. It was a dreadful idea. Edward was deeply ashamed of it as soon as the thought came to his mind.

There was nothing he could do about it on the river but the inevitable suspicions of a spy's mind added a horrible dimension to his relationship with Julia. This had not been helped by his erratic behaviour either on the island or at the boatyard.

They paddled on towards Maidenhead which they reached at around five in the evening before leaving the skiff in the care of a local man at the bridge. They took the six o'clock stage back to town.

Edward knew that the day had not been as perfect as the one that he had planned or that Julia had expected. Now she was angry with him and he had his suspicions about her. It was not a good ending to the day.

"I don't know who you are", Julia said. "One moment I'm the most important thing in your life. The next you ignore me and behave like a bully. When are you goiung to make up your mind about us? If it's not soon I shall take my step-father's advice and look elsewhere."

Julia was right, Edward had mixed business with pleasure and had behaved badly. He had been as aroused as Julia when they had been together on the island. He would have liked to have gone further but he had wrecked it by his selfish behaviour.

When they reached Julia's house later in the evening he tried to make amends by taking her in his arms but Julia said goodbye to him coldly. She did not invite him inside, unlike on the previous occasion.

"I suppose I may see you again when you are in a better mood and less busy?" she said, and closed the door behind her.

181

As he turned away from the house, Edward was dismayed that he had not only put his relationship with Julia at risk but also that she might have placed him in danger by breaking his cover. Now he was faced with two choices. He either had to end the relationship and give Julia his reasons or he had to trust her completely and let her fully into his life. Whichever of the two, it was an added complication that he did not need at present.

He spent Sunday at home brooding on Saturday's events and travelled down to Bow Street first thing on Monday morning to meet with Townsend and Sayer.

Sayer spoke first and gave a full report of all that he had seen on his trip up the towpath and at Messum's yard on Friday. He handed over the sketch that he had made to Edward. They pored over it together. Hazell could now recognise the object for what it was - some kind of waterborne craft that might be the object for which they had been looking or might be some completely innocent river project. It appeared to him to be a very flimsy prospect for use at sea.

Nevertheless, here was the first evidence that they had of the construction of a vessel that could be used to mount a rescue operation that was designed to bring Napoleon off St Helena.

Edward told the two men of his experience on Saturday when he had met the water guard. Sayer's account of his experience the previous night could well explain the additional security that he had encountered on the dock.

"What do you think we should do next?"

Sayer spoke first.

"I propose that we should put an agent into the *Hinds Head* Inn at Bray who will also keep an eye on the yard. They can also watch for any suspicious comings and goings at the hostelry or in the village.

It's owned by a friend of mine, a retired comrade from the First Guards at Windsor. I know that he would be willing to take on one of our Runners disguised as a kitchen boy if I ask him. I will place another agent in the village to pass on any messages from my man at the inn to Bow Street."

"Good idea, get onto it at once", Edward responded.

"And I will place a twenty-four hour watch on Blane and Price", Townsend said, "with a rota of watchers stationed at the *Lamb & Flag*.

Are you aware, Mr. Hazell, that there have long been rumours of a secret tunnel between Drury Lane and the inn? Before your time it had a reputation as the place where Jacobite sympathisers used to meet. They were cleared out in '45 and those who weren't executed were sent to the colonies.

Now the pub is still sometimes used to smuggle goods and people out of the city and onto the river. We will need to watch the theatre as well as the Lamb in Westminster and the yard in Bray. This is going to take up most of our manpower. It will cost a lot more money"

It was no surprise to Edward that Townsend thought of his wallet before the safety of the realm.

"Yes, I am aware of that and I will speak to my master about allocating more resources but now that we have some evidence it will be easier to convince him of the threat", Edward replied.

"At least our suspicions have been confirmed. There is a craft under construction and we know who might be involved. Now we will need to destroy the craft and round up the conspirators."

The three men agreed to meet again as soon as there was more news.

12 *The Lamb & Flag*

OVER THE FOLLOWING two weeks, Sayer received regular reports from his man at the *Hinds Head*. As far as the agent could tell, the object was still in Messum's yard. However, on the Tuesday of the third week, Sayer was advised by the front desk at Bow Street that a man wished to speak with him urgently.

It was the runner stationed in the village who had an urgent message from the 'kitchen boy' at the *Hinds Head* at Bray. Sayer ushered the man through Cell No. 7 and into his office, before locking the door behind him.

Sayer asked the runner for his report.

"Well, Sir, this is what your man at the inn has instructed me to report. Last night a party of three arrived off the last stage of the day. They appeared to be gentlemen. One of them spoke with a distinct Scottish accent. When Mr. Saunders, the landlord, asked them if they wished to dine they said that they had already eaten. Mr S. asked them at what hour they wished for their breakfast. One of the men replied that they would not take breakfast and would settle up now.

They said that all they needed were directions to Messum's yard where they had hired a river cruiser to go upstream early the next morning. They said that had a meeting at midday with the manager of the East India Company's timber yard at Reading."

The agent continued. "The visitors left at dawn this morning and my agent followed them at a safe distance. The three men entered the yard and old man Messum arrived shortly afterwards; unlocked the boatshed and they all went inside. Ten minutes later a strange round object shaped like an orange was pushed out of the shed on a wheeled trolley; moved down the slipway and lowered into the water.

A barge loaded with timber was tied up to the yard's rafts and your agent saw a man emerge from its cabin and shake hands with one of the visitors. He attached three ropes to the object which he then tied onto the stern of his barge.

Afterwards, Old Man Messum helped the three visitors into a cruiser moored at the bank. They set off upstream and sailed off in the direction of Maidenhead and Reading.

Your man did not see the barge leave its moorings although he stayed under cover observing the yard. Perhaps the bargee was waiting for darkness before beginning his journey downstream to London. He wanted to report back to you, Sir, as soon as he could."

It looked as if an operation was now underway. Sayer must inform Hazell and Townsend at once.

The three men met at Bow Street later in the day.

At the end of Sayer's report Edward said: "You, Townsend will increase your surveillance of the Holland House set and, in particular their Scotch friends. I want to know every move they make. You, Sayer, will place agents at all the locks, bridges and Thames crossing points between Bray and London Bridge. I will co-ordinate our activities here in the city and give instructions for a party of the river police to come up from Greenwich. They will be ready for a boarding operation at or around the Tower.

We have the name of the barge - the *Mary Rose* - and an accurate description. The barge left the boatyard at Bray towing the object. We can now alert the watchers on each bank. I have no doubt we will get a report very soon. I estimate that it will take up to three days for the barge to reach London Bridge.

All we can do now is to wait until we have a confirmed sighting from the river. It must be significant that the conspirators at the inn spoke about the Company's yard at Reading and that the barge is carrying Company timber."

Edward set up a temporary HQ managed by Nicholson in a government office close to the Embankment. He soon received a series of negative reports from his watchers on the river. He began to think they were on a wild goose chase until a report came in early on the second morning from the ferry crossing at Staines.

It was reported that a barge had come past very late the previous night when the darkness had made navigation almost impossible. The barge had come into the bank to tie up but appeared to be dragging something behind it. When challenged the bargee said that he had been delayed by a broken mast earlier in the day that had become entangled with his rudder.

He had had to make a temporary repair and this accounted for the foam that could be seen churning the water at the stern. He would only remain on his mooring for a short time because he was pressed to catch a vessel sailing from the docks. His cargo of replacement planking was bound for an East Indiaman sailing on the following evening's tide.

This was the intelligence that Edward had been waiting for.

If there was going to be a transfer to a seagoing vessel it would happen tonight or in the early hours of tomorrow morning. The object would be loaded on board and the ship would set sail down the coast of West Africa. or to a port on the American coast.

"Francis, send a man down to our office at the docks at once. Ask them for a list of all Company sailings in the next forty-eight hours whatever their destination", Edward instructed. "Also, I need a list of their officers. If Price is on the list, we will know he is involved."

The three men met on the Embankment in the late afternoon.

Townsend had obtained information from the box office that the Hollands and a party of their friends had tickets for the theatre at Drury Lane that evening.

"I have arranged to be in the theatre for the performance and I will keep a close watch on them throughout. If any of them disappear during the performance I will know about it. I have also alerted my team of watchers at the *Lamb & Flag* who will observe all of those entering or leaving the pub."

Sayer would be responsible for watching the barge traffic on the river. At five o'clock Sayer reported:

"The *Mary Rose* can be identified by its plimsoll line which is painted red, white and blue. The object can be seen trailing in its wake. It looks like a dinghy. The barge has reached Chelsea and is reckoned to reach London Bridge by around eleven this evening. The wind is getting up on the river. I think we may be in for a storm."

Edward looked out of the window of his temporary office. He could see that black clouds were rolling in from the southwest on the other side of the river. A strong cross-wind was beginning to blow. It was not yet raining but it soon would be. It was going to be a foul night.

They separated but agreed to meet again at eight that evening. If and when the barge approached they would move outside onto the river bank some two hundred yards upstream from London Bridge. This is where the interception would take place.

Edward returned to his office. He needed to advise his master of the latest situation. He would also speak with Sir Henry about the issue of arrest warrants for the conspirators. This would be a highly delicate matter, involving the highest in the land in Government and Opposition.

"Well, I'll be damned.", Crauford remarked when Edward told him the full story, "I never thought that wet Holland had it in him. It's good news for us. With any luck he will be impeached for treason at the Bar of the House. He could well hang. At the very least it will put an end to all this dangerous nonsense about one man, one vote. Well done Hazell. What do you want me to do?"

"Two things, Sir. The first is highly sensitive and very personal to the individual. I think that it would be prudent not to advise the Home Secretary, Lord Wellington, about the situation. Although he is entirely on our side politically, I have received an unconfirmed report that he has recently entered into a liaison with a lady whose views are of, one might say, the liberal persuasion. I would not want our plans to leak.

Second, and as an alternative to consulting the Duke, I am going to propose to Sir Henry Bunbury that as this is a matter of state security, he should issue the necessary arrest warrants under Section 7 of the Aliens Act. The section stipulates that the authorisation of a Minister of the Crown is not required and is designed precisely to avoid this kind of embarrassment to ministers. However, I will need a formal note from you as head of the Alien Office to legitimise this procedure."

"Very well", Crauford replied, "I understand and I won't ask you for the name of the lady; I expect my wife will know. Bring me the Section 7 docket for me to sign for Sir Henry. I wish you luck with him and the operation. Report back to me when it is over."

Edward left Crauford's office to draw up the paperwork for Sir Henry.

"Come in, come in, young Hazell. What trouble have you caused now? I was dining out last week and your name came up in conversation. It would have made your ears burn. I was with your paramour Julia's aunt and uncle, the Armstrongs. They have strong views about you and your honourable intentions, or more likely, knowing you, your dishonourable ones.

The lady in question had obviously told her aunt about her day on the river with you last Saturday. That you got into a rage and almost killed someone."

This was not good. It looked as if Julia was sharing her grudge about their time on the river with other members of her family.

"It wasn't quite as bad as that, Sir Henry, I thought the man was about to attack us."

"Well that's as maybe but you would be a fool to let that one get away from you. I have met the girl. She is not only a good-looker but smart as well. Although she's one of these new-fangled women, she does not let her views stand in the way of her being good company. The Goode family are well known and respected in Northumberland. You could do a lot worse than marry her although with your reputation I would strongly advise her to reject you. Both you and that brother of hers in the Secret Office are a thoroughly bad lot."

"I'm grateful for your advice, Sir Henry. I have a great affection for Julia but find that my intentions are continually frustrated by my duties."

"Now, what is it you want?"

"I have some Section 7 Warrants here that require your signature. As you know, Sir, we only use them on very rare occasions. It's so that ministers can deny our activities. General Crauford believes that it is necessary in this case.

We have uncovered a plot to free Napoleon from St Helena using an underwater craft built here in Great Britain. Its construction has been sponsored by a number of his supporters in London. The craft is due to be loaded onto an East Indiaman leaving for the South Atlantic some time tomorrow.

Unfortunately, in addition to some minor figures who include a Scotch doctor and a Company captain, the conspirators include members of the so-called Holland House set including Lord Holland himself.

A theatre party will be at Drury Lane this evening", Edward continued, "and in the event that Lord Holland is amongst them, which we believe he will be, he will have implicated himself sufficiently in the conspiracy to warrant his arrest.

We think that when the performance ends the theatre party intends to move down to the riverside to witness the barge that is carrying the craft pass by on its way downstream. We will arrest them on the riverbank as they watch. I do not see how we can avoid catching Lord Holland in our net."

"This is monstrous! You can't arrest a peer of the realm."

"In normal circumstances you are quite correct, Sir Henry, but these are not normal times. Great Britain was given the necessary powers by the Allies in Vienna. His Majesty's Government took responsibility for the security of the prisoner on St Helena. Lord Wellington was a signatory to the Treaty on behalf of Britain and I doubt if he would wish to renege on our obligations.

I am well aware of the political storm that this will cause but my duty is to the State. My master has the authority under the Act to issue these arrest warrants. He has instructed me to carry them out.

May I suggest the following: that you sign them off but that I will not arrest His Lordship unless he is actually present on the river? We can take the others into custody for interrogation at Bow Street. Depending on what I find out, I will return tomorrow and discuss with you how we deal with Lord Holland. This will give us time to assess the details of the plot and Holland's role, if any, in it."

"I don't like the smell of this", Sir Henry replied. "It could well backfire and cause the country to rise up if it is felt that it is a plot designed to discredit the Opposition. We have already had reports from all over the country of civil unrest caused by these infernal Luddites. This could be the spark that sets more than hayricks alight."

"I understand, Sir Henry. I will take the greatest care not to let things get out of hand this evening,"

Edward passed over the warrants for signature and with a deep sigh Sir Henry signed them off. Edward had made concessions but had achieved what he wanted. Confinement at Bow Street was uncomfortable at the best of times but interrogation by Sayer was a dreadful prospect. They would get to the truth quickly and Edward was confident that the minor characters would be willing to implicate the Hollands if pressed hard enough.

The next news came from a runner of Townsend's at six-thirty in the evening: "The party have left Holland House in Kensington. It is twelve strong and includes Lord and Lady Holland, Blane and Price.

They have travelled up Pall Mall and into Covent Garden and will be taking their seats in the front row of the circle at eight o'clock. The performance is expected to end at around ten-thirty tonight."

The runner also had a private note from Townsend addressed to Edward.

"Mr Hazell. In addition to the ladies and gentlemen with whom we are familiar, there are others in the box that include Sir Thomas Goode, his lady and his step-daughter with whom, I believe, you are acquainted."

"Dammit." This was a complication Edward did not need. He would have to put it out of his head whilst this operation was in progress but it added to his suspicions about where Julia's sympathies might lie. He would have to deal with it afterwards. It could be sheer coincidence or something more sinister.

Sayer's next report came in at nine o'clock in the evening. "The barge has just passed Putney landing but it looks as if it has problems. A strong wind has begun to blow across the river which is whipping up the water of the outgoing tide into three foot waves. The barge is having difficulty holding onto its station in the centre of the stream. The barge might well have to beach itself on the riverbank if it does not sink first."

Townsend now reported that "A number of the gentlemen of the Holland party left their box at the interval and have not reappeared for the second half of the play."

Thirty minutes later Townsend, now hidden in the *Lamb & Flag*, reported again: "Blane, among others, is sitting in the saloon without apparently having entered via Rose Street, where the front entrance is situated. It looks as if they used the secret tunnel from Drury Lane."

Next, Sayer's man reported: "The barge is now moving crab-like down river. It may be taking in water. It is leaning badly to port and the *object* is weaving to and fro across its stern making it almost impossible for the bargee to steer it."

By midnight, with the outward tide at its highest and the wind at its strongest – it had also now started to lash with rain – the barge appeared to be only half a mile upstream of London Bridge.

Townsend reported: "The male members of the theatre party have now left the *Lamb* by its public entrance and, in spite of the weather, are proceeding down Bedford Street towards the Embankment."

Edward reckoned that they were intending to observe the passage of the barge as it passed by the ferry crossing above the bridge. They might even be intending to take a ride on it downstream to see its illicit cargo safely loaded onto the merchantman.

Edward briefed the squad of Runners who would be responsible for apprehending the conspirators as they walked on foot towards the riverside. He also instructed the river police party on the bank to stand by to board the barge; arrest the bargee and confiscate the object.

Sayer, hidden among the trees with Edward, Townsend and the two assault parties five yards up from the river bank, was the first to see the outline of the barge.

"There she is, *there!*" as Sayer pointed out into the stream. Through the gloom they could now see that the steersman was desperately trying to keep the barge on a straight heading as it hurtled through the broiling water towards the middle of one of the three central spans of London Bridge.

Suddenly a particularly strong gust of wind blew the barge sideways. They watched in horror as it struck the bridge with a horrible crack and began to break up.

At the same time the object on its tow swung violently into midstream before being blown to smithereens against one of the bridge supports.

On Edward's signal Townsend pointed towards five men who stood in a huddle by the steps that led down to the river. Townsend recognised Dr. Blane and Captain Price amongst them. He instructed the Runners team to move in and arrest the party from the *Lamb & Flag*. Whilst there was no direct evidence to connect them with Bray, Edward was confident that they had their conspirators.

As they were taken to Bow Street for questioning he was somewhat relieved to note that Lord Holland was not amongst them. Let alone Julia. His Lordship's involvement in the plot could be dealt with later.

Next morning, Edward joined the river party that scoured the river bank looking for any parts of the barge or *object* that could be recovered. They found wreckage that included some leather material which they collected as evidence and took to Bow Street.

Edward doubted if the bargee could have survived but search parties were deployed on both banks of the river to find him. He was found two days later in the *Boot & Flogger* a pub on Borough High Street in Southwark. The landlord said that he had been blind drunk for all of that time. He had been shouting his mouth off to anyone who would listen to him that he was owed money.

He had also been telling a lurid story. Apparently he had been hired by a gentleman he had never met before on the riverside at Kingston. The stranger had told him that after he had secured his contract at Reading he should sail his barge downstream to Bray. Here he would load a special cargo which he would tow down to East India docks. He was to arrange it so that he reached London in darkness. He was to stop the barge just above London Bridge on the north bank where the same gentleman and a number of others would join him on board for the final part of the journey into the dock.

He would be paid handsomely – with half his fees paid in advance on agreeing to the job - and the remainder to be paid on completion.

It had all gone well at first until the wind had got up on the river and his barge had struck the bridge and been destyroyed. Now both his barge and his livelihood were gone.

The man was half carried into Bow Street where, after he had sobered up, Edward heard his story again. Edward thought him to be innocent of any conspiracy. When he had sobered up he would make a good witness if it came to identifying the conspirators.

Edward joined Sayer and Townsend to interview the prisoners. He had already sent down to the docks to order the *Hotspur's* sailing to be stopped.

Blane and Price were the two key conspirators and obtaining their confessions would be Edward's first objective.

Edward found them in a gloomy holding cell below Bow Street. The passages outside the cells were dimly lit by candlelight. They stank of rat urine and prisoners' vomit. The prisoners looked dishevelled after their night below ground but the Scotchman, Blane, was full of bluster. He appeared unaware that Lord Holland's association with the plot was known and threatened Edward with the dire consequences of keeping him in custody.

"His Lordship will hear of this directly. I demand to be released. Fetch me a runner so that I can send Lord Holland a note. Don't you realise that I am known at Court? The King will hear about this."

"You and your friends are facing a charge of treason so there can be no question of any communication with anyone outside", Edward responded curtly.

"I am a distinguished child physician. I have treated the King's own children. I'll see you lose your position at least and be damned to hell at worst."

"That's as maybe, Dr. Blane", Edward said, "however, my powers under the Aliens Act are unlimited. I have the authority of the Home Secretary, the Duke of Wellington himself, to arrest and hold your person. Your home at Foliejon Park outside Windsor is being searched as we speak; so is the boatyard at Bray. Old Man Messum has been placed under arrest. I have teams searching the river bank. I am confident that they will find debris that links the boatyard at Bray with the submersible that you helped to launch there.

I have no doubt that we shall find evidence of your involvement in the conspiracy with or without your confession. Meanwhile you will be taken before the magistrate here before being removed to the Tower to await trial. You could improve your situation if you tell me the whole story before you go in front of Mr. Fielding."

"I demand my rights as a citizen of both England and Scotland", Blane spat.

"You are not a citizen, you are a subject of His Majesty the King and, if you had any rights, they have been suspended by order of the Government. Now, please sit down. Here is pen, ink and paper. You have one hour to write down all you know, before you are taken up."

Edward left Blane's cell and joined Sayer in Price's.

Price was going to be a much tougher nut to crack. Sayer had fitted him into a straightjacket with his arms pinned behind his back.

"I'll have you bastards. I'll find out where you live. I'll make your lives hell. I'll take your children."

"Let's see what we have", said Edward. "You were with Blane and the rest on the riverbank. You were seen in the *Lamb &Flag* with Lord Holland's party after the theatre. You have been identified as having stayed at the *Hinds Head* in Bray with a group of men who visited the boatyard before setting off towards Reading. Your vessel, the *Hotspur* was due to sail on this evening's tide for the South Atlantic. I have no doubt we shall find evidence that the 'object' that was destroyed on London Bridge last night was going to be stowed away on board your ship."

"All lies. I have no idea what you are talking about,"

Townsend took over the interrogation. "You are acquainted with a Mr. Thomas Johnson, shipwright."

"I've never heard of the man."

"Well. He's heard of you. You were an investor in a project of his that went badly wrong. You ended up suing him for damages."

"I know nothing about it"

Edward tried a different tack.

"I don't think you understand the trouble you're in. Quite apart from your dismissal from the Company you also face the seizure of all your possessions, goods, bank assets and the confiscation and sale of your house in Rotherhithe. I wonder how Mrs. Price will feel about being thrown out onto the street?"

"Never, you couldn't do that."

Edward took a document from his satchel and showed it to Price.

"On the contrary, see here is an order signed by Mr. Fielding, within whose power it lies, to do just that."

Edward turned to Townsend and said,

"You've done this many times before, haven't you, John? Get a team of Runners together, take them down to Rotherhithe and discharge this Distraint Warrant. I am not interested what you get for the assets. You can tell Mrs. Price she must be out of the house by midday tomorrow. I suggest that you arrange a lane sale as soon as you are able. Meanwhile, find out where the prisoner does his banking and place a stop on his accounts. His money now belongs to the State."

"What do you want to know?"

By late that afternoon Blane had been removed to the Tower still protesting his innocence and claiming his connections. The piece of paper that was intended for his confession remained blank. He obviously thought that he could rely on his powerful friends.

What he did not know was that he would be tried and sentenced in secret before being transported to Botany Bay. He would not be heard of again in London and any knowledge of his whereabouts would be denied.

Price made a full confession of his part in the plot.

"We paid that old rogue Johnson for the plans of the submarine and I, along with Blane and the others, supervised its building in Messum's yard at Bray. We arranged for it to be brought down river where I would load it onto the *Hotspur*.

The plan was to put in for emergency repairs at Bahia on the South American coast from where another group would have escorted the craft down the coast to Buenos Aires. From there, I assume, it would have been taken across to St Helena for the actual escape attempt."

Edward was pleased with these details but they raised another question: who were the members of this group that Price had spoken of who would take over the project and mount the actual escape attempt to free Napoleon?

Price claimed that he had no idea of their names. Edward said that he would be kept where he was until he could remember.

From Edward's point of view the immediate threat to security had been removed. However, Lord Holland and others who had been involved, remained at large. There was also a question mark over Julia's part, if any, in the affair.

Edward needed to inform Crauford and Bunbury of what had passed and seek their advice about his next move. A home-based plot had been uncovered; but was it the only one or would there now be others? What about the situation in South America and on St Helena?

13   *Mr. Fulton's submarine*

JOHN SKINNER SAT in his office holding in his hand a sealed envelope that Clay, his clerk, had passed to him. It was from one of his senior staff at the Post Office on Baltimore's Main Street.

By this time, his house on Chesapeake Bay at St Leonard's had been rebuilt and his wife, Elizabeth, his two children and his widowed mother in law were back in residence.

At the end of the war, when his services as a prisoner exchange agent had been required no longer, Skinner had returned to his legal practice. He was now in partnership with his wartime friend Francis Scott-Key.

Scott-Key maintained close relations with President Madison and his Cabinet. In 1814 Madison had asked Key if he would be interested in the position of Postmaster General of Baltimore. Whilst the position paid a generous salary, Key was not interested in government service but had asked the President if his partner John Skinner might be an acceptable alternative. Madison replied: "Isn't Skinner the man who had his house on the Chesapeake burned down by the British three years ago?"

"Yes, Mr President, the very same."

"Well, he may be just the man I am looking for. Are you aware that the Post Office in Baltimore deals with more than just the Mail? It also acts as our principal centre for the de-coding of enciphered letters, particularly from abroad. The Post Office also manages our counter-espionage operations."

"I am aware that more goes on there than the sorting and delivering of letters", Scott Key said, "but I was not aware of just how important it is to our national security."

"Since the end of the war and the signing of the Peace Treaty", Madison went on, "whilst the British may have decided that further attempts at invasion would not go well for them, they still want to take over our trade. They will strangle our economy if they can. The Emperor Napoleon may be their prisoner at present but he could well escape. If he succeeds it will bring trouble down on us again.

We need to maintain extreme vigilance. Skinner could be just the man to ensure that we know what they are up to. He's got good reason to hate the British. Ask him to come and see me."

Scott Key had returned to his Calvert Street offices and reported his conversation with Madison to Skinner.

A few days later the President arranged to meet with Skinner and, after a short discussion, Skinner agreed to help. Madison gave him his instructions.

"You are to ensure that we have advance warning of any plans for invasion that the British may have and for any way they may try to restrict our trade contrary to the terms of the Treaty. This applies in territories that they consider their bailiwick, for example the Mediterranean Sea, and in the Far East. They think that they have a monopoly on trade - they do not.

You are also to frustrate any attempt by the British to prevent us from making trading arrangements with foreign governments or to interfere in our domestic affairs", he went on.

"It's a wide remit and you have extensive powers.

I understand that you are conversant with the role of the Post Office in our security arrangements. Congress has voted an annual sum for its activities in addition to a generous salary for yourself. You will report to me directly as and when required. In an emergency you may request an immediate appointment."

"Very good, Mr. President, I will do my utmost to keep us safe."

It was now over four years since his appointment as Postmaster and Skinner had led a number of operations against the British.

Recently, one of these had successfully identified a British spy on the Baltimore waterfront who had been passing information to London about American shipping movements.

It seemed that the South Atlantic had once again become an area of strategic interest to the British. Skinner was anxious that this might lead to another round of hostilities at a time when US merchants were dramatically increasing their share of international trade. These were precisely the circumstances of which Madison had warned him.

Skinner now broke the seal on the envelope that Clay had handed him and removed its contents. It contained a note from his senior man at the Post Office that explained that he thought that Skinner would wish to see the enclosed original encoded letter - which was unreadable - as well as its de-coded counterpart, that wasn't.

He added that Skinner might understand its contents. The de-coded note read:

URGENT

From: Sharrow

You are to ascertain whether there exists in the US any means whatsoever for the underwater propulsion of ships that would enable an individual or object to move under the sea without detection.

from

Sharrow

Skinner had no idea of what was being written about but he did have contacts in the Navy Yard from whom he could make enquiries. As important, would be knowing who the writer was and to whom the letter had been addressed.

On the following morning he called into the Post Office on Main Street on his way to his office in Calvert Street.

"What do you think we have here, Taylor?", he asked his chief agent.

"Well, I'll start with how we come to have it, Mr. Skinner", Taylor replied. "You know that we have been watching the movement of British shipping down on the quays since their level of interest in us increased.

One of my men saw a sailor coming off an in-bound schooner. She was the *Charlotte* from out of Vigo in Portugal and carrying wine. The man seemed a little too tidy for your usual Portuguese deck hand and so our man followed him ashore.

On his first evening in port he took rooms at Ma Bailey's on George Street and then repaired to the *Stars & Stripes*. You know her place, a little tidier than some. He seemed to be expecting company and kept asking other drinkers if they knew of any other vessels that had docked that day. By closing time, he had taken in much drink and as he staggered back to his lodgings our man distinctly heard him whistling *Lilli Burlero*. He wasn't Portuguese; he was British."

So, thought Skinner, why had he arrived into Baltimore from Portugal?

"As you know, we have good relations with Ma Bailey", Taylor went on. "We don't look at her books too closely and in return she does us small favours from time to time.

The following morning the sailor left his rooms and went back out into the port again. He spent most of the time looking out to sea or accosting sailors he met and asking them for the name of the ship that they had come off.

Whilst he was out, one of my men entered his room and searched it. The copy letter you have there was well hidden in the sole of a spare pair of sea boots. He brought it straight to me. I knew at once that it was important. Do you remember during the war we intercepted coded messages from an agent *Sharrow* who we identified as a man named Edward Hazell. We learned later that Hazell is a senior official at the Alien Office in London.

During the war Hazell put spies into Baltimore to watch for shipping that might be out-bound for the English Channel. We caught a number of his agents from whom he did not hear of again after we had sent them to Fort McHenry.

I copied this letter and returned the original to its hiding place in his boot. It's taken us over four hours to crack the code which has similarities to the ones Hazell used during the war. It's another reason that we think Hazell is involved now", Taylor finished.

"I agree, Hazell's at it again, but I'm damned if I know why."

"To finish the story - and bring you up to date, Mr. Skinner - the sailor returned to his rooms and he has not yet re -joined his ship although she is preparing to sail on tomorrow's tide."

"We obviously need to confirm from whom the message originated", Skinner said. "If it is Hazell then something is afoot. The man is now a senior official in Whitehall. His spy is obviously on the look-out for incoming ships either to receive new instructions; to send his report to London, or to return to Britain. We should put a watch on all vessels that come into port and see if he leaves his lodgings to meet any of them."

Three days later Skinner had a second message from the Post Office: could he drop by on his way home?

The sailor had not re-joined the *Charlotte* before she sailed but a British merchantman had put into harbour that afternoon. She was the *Marjorie* out of Liverpool. The British spy had left his rooms and was sharing a drink with the vessel's captain in the *Stars & Stripes*.

Skinner snatched up an old cap and, pulling it down over his eyes, walked as fast as he could to the *Stars*. He entered the pub and looked around but couldn't see anyone he knew. He sat down and ordered a pint. As his eyes adjusted to the semi-darkness, he noticed two men seated in a corner in deep conversation. He thought he had seen one of the men before but he couldn't remember when and where: Who was he?

He had developed a method for recalling faces and events from his past. He would think back to his earliest memories of boyhood and recall the faces of his family and friends. More recently one of his most enduring memories were the terrible events that had followed the burning of his house; the rescue of his wife and his prisoner exchange work at Fort McHenry.

Suddenly, he could see the man. He was starving, haggard and in rags. The seafarer in the corner was Skinner's former captive from the Fort: Captain Wild, previously of the *Butterfly* He now appeared fully restored to health and was engaging in the Atlantic trades once again. Wild must also be connected with Hazell somehow.

Skinner now grasped what was going on here: the British spy staying at the *Stars* had received his original instructions from Hazell in London; sailed to the USA from a neutral port in Europe to cover his tracks and was now giving an interim report via Wild to his paymaster back in London.

The meeting broke up; the captain returning to his ship and the spy to his lodgings. Whatever information that he had been looking for had clearly not yet been found or he would have accompanied Wild back on board and sailed for England and safety.

Skinner instructed that the spy should be left in place and kept under observation whilst he found out all he could about the existence –

204

or otherwise - of this underwater craft. Whatever was going on, Skinner would see to it that one way or another Hazell's new spying operation would be obstructed.

The visit to the Navy Yard opened his eyes.

The Dockyard Superintendent reported that there had indeed been a project during the Napoleonic wars to build a craft that could attack shipping from underwater. At the time the American government had rejected the idea as unworkable but Skinner could meet the craft's inventor if he wished.

"Robert Fulton is a chancer with a chequered career", the superintendant went on. "He left America and trained originally as a landscape painter in England before studying engineering under James Watt. He was in our Navy for a short time but was discharged for the theft and resale of Dockyard property.

He is without doubt a brilliant and innovative engineer but his obsession with his underwater chariot drove the naval establishments of Britain, France and our own to distraction.

He insisted that whilst his invention would make a significant contribution to national defence, it should also be a major source of income for himself. As a result, he made impossible demands on our naval budget.

At a time of extreme danger for the Nation he insisted that we should not only repay all his development costs - and a lump sum for his finished product which was completely unproven at that stage in the war - but also a percentage of the value of all enemy naval and commercial shipping and their cargoes that we either captured or sunk using the submarine.

If successful, Fulton claimed, his invention would change the course of the war against the British. He omitted to mention that it would also make him a millionaire. However, the funds he demanded for the initial investment were enormous and our government turned him down.

Undeterred, Fulton took his invention across the Atlantic and made similar offers to both the British and French governments. Neither side wanted to see the other develop such a destructive weapon. Nor were either willing to agree a contract with Fulton that would make him rich at their expense. His proposed contract with the British would have provided him with a royalty of £4,000 for each captured or sunk French cannon."

"What an extraordinary idea! I've never heard of such a thing. That the British would pay him per French cannon sunk to the bottom", exclaimed Skinner.

"Fulton was turned down by Prime Minister Lord Liverpool; by the Admiralty in London and by the French", the superintendant continued. "Fulton has deep Republican feelings and he crossed the Channel to negotiate with Napoleon himself in Paris. A prototype of his submarine was built at Rouen and demonstrated in front of the Emperor on the Seine. In the end Napoleon decided that he was a money-grabbing American and refused to back him. Napoleon also thought that it would not be playing the game to attack the enemy from underwater."

Skinner laughed. "I don't blame Napoleon for not agreeing to Fulton's terms. He would have emptied the French Treasury."

"However", the spuerintendant ended, "Fulton has never given up on his idea of attacking ships from underwater and the third and latest version of his submarine the *Nautilus* - as the vessel is named - incorporates a number of advanced ideas that include ways to attach limpet mines to the hulls of ships."

"Do you know what the vessel looks like?"

"I've seen the plans of his current version, the *Nautilus III*", the superindent said. "It has a cigar-shaped design surmounted by a conning tower, behind which is a collapsible mast and sails. When not under sail, the vessel is driven by an internal wheel and pin four-bladed propeller shaft. A flooding compartment at the bow can pump water in and out of a ballast tank and vertical and horizontal rudders are used to steer the vessel."

"It sounds thoroughly unstable", Skinner observed.

"The standard crew of the *Nautilus* is three, but this can be increased to five if needed. It can stay under water for up to one and a half hours."

"I am going to need to meet him."

"I understand he's in New York at present", the superindent said, "but I expect that he would leap at the chance to impress a US official. Do you want me to invite him down here? You would be welcome to return to the Yard to speak to him in person."

Skinner thanked the Superintendent and returned to his office.

What was Hazell's interest in the *Nautilus?* Was the British Government going to change its mind about underwater warfare and invest in a submarine fleet? Were the British going to buy out Fulton and his plans to prevent other nations using them? Was this part of a larger plan to use submarines to attack American vessels on the Atlantic coastline or from British bases in the West Indies or Far East?

Two weeks later Skinner received a message from the Yard that Fulton was expected the following day. He had agreed to make himself available for interview.

Skinner entered the Superintendent's office as a man rose from his chair and held out his hand. He was a scruffy individual, careless in his dress and with a withered left hand.

"Delighted to meet you, Sir. I am pleased that the American Government is seeing sense at last and is going to invest in my craft."

"I fear you are under a misapprehension, Mr. Fulton. My interest is a purely commercial one."

Skinner had to think fast. He certainly could not reveal his real purpose and would have to make up a convincing story.

"As you know I am responsible for the Post Office in the city. We are interested in the commercial potential of your machine to carry the Mail into areas that are inaccessible by road, for example, the Florida swamplands."

Fulton brightened and unrolled a set of drawings. He clearly knew his business and explained every detail of the design of the *Nautilus*.

"The vessel has an eight-inch draft and would be ideal for carrying the Mail. She can operate with a minimum crew of two leaving maximum space for cargo. She can be away from her mother ship for periods of up to three days and travel at up to four knots an hour. It would be a world first for the US to adopt such an idea."

Skinner hid his impatience. His interest was not technical but he had to show Fulton that he was serious before he could ask him about his current contacts and his hopes for future sales now that the war had ended.

Fulton's attitude changed dramatically from one of openness to one of suspicion at this point.

"I have no idea what you mean by future sales. I offered myself and my machine to the US Government during the war against the British but I was rejected. I am currently in discussion with a number of foreign governments who are showing an interest. I shall be sailing the *Nautilus* down the East Coast from New York this summer if you wish to see a demonstration of its potential for your General Post"

It was clear to Skinner that Fulton was suspicious of officialdom. He was not going to find out more at this meeting. After thanking Fulton for his time, Skinner returned to Baltimore.

The following morning Skinner instructed his staff at the Post Office to place a watch on both Fulton and the *Nautilus* and to report to him any suspicious activity. In particular, they should bring to Skinner's attention anything that might be associated with British interests. Skinner was clear that Fulton was in the market and would be willing to sell to the highest bidder. The British could well be in that market.

Meanwhile, the British agent in the docks had not been idle.

Taylor, Skinner's chief clerk at the Post Office, asked to meet with him again at Calvert Street.

"Good morning Alan, what can I do for you?"

"We think that Hazell's man is on the move", Taylor replied. "Yesterday he moved into town. First he went to a barber's shop. He had his beard shaved off and his hair cut. He then visited a gentleman's clothing store. He bought himself a complete outfit of shirt, suit and tie in which he appeared back on the street. He was almost completely unrecognisable. He then checked into the *Continental,* a moderately priced travellers' hotel and paid for a single room for two weeks.

My man followed him to a hackney hire company where he hired a carriage and pair for a week starting tomorrow morning. He is obviously intending to travel beyond the city."

"Well done", Skinner said, "he's clearly on the move and if our suspicions are correct he is going on a hunt along the coastline searching for this underwater vessel of Fulton's. You had better organise a team to follow him that will report back to you each day. I want to know exactly where he goes, what he sees and who he speaks to."

Over the following days Skinner received regular reports of the spy's progress. He could have taken the route directly overland from Principio towards Wilmington but instead took the much longer coastal route along the north Chesapeake via Pocomoke, Ocean and Dover before reaching Philadelphia. He stopped at every creek and walked around or into every boatyard. He spoke with dock workers and anyone he found in the locality of ports, docks, ships or warehouses. He was very thorough and missed nothing. He found nothing.

Skinner met with Taylor, his chief agent, to review progress.

"He's not found anything yet", Taylor said, "or he would have returned to Baltimore. He's obviously a professional. I went out with one of our men on Tuesday and we watched him engage with a shipbuilding worker up at Dundalk. He has an easy manner.

When he had moved on we questioned the worker who reported that the spy had asked him about the project he was working on at present. The spy asked the man directly if he had ever heard of a craft that could travel underwater. The man said that he had not.

He is staying at small lodgings on the coast as he moves about. He eats in the dining room and then moves to its snug after supper each night. He is posing as the sales director of a sail-making firm. He questions fellow guests about the local yards and their current contracts."

"Keep up the good work, Alan. The crunch will come when he reaches New York and if he identifies Fulton's workshop and yard. If and when that happens we will strike. The information that he could obtain there must never reach Hazell in London."

Skinner received regular reports from the Post Office as Hazell's spy got nearer and nearer to New York. Finally, he decided that he should take direct control of the operation and told Elizabeth that he was going to be away for a few days on business in the north.

He met Taylor at Post Office headquarters in New York city.

"What's he been up to today?"

"We've had trouble following him. He's started taking evasive action. He may suspect he's being followed. My team lost him for a time as he moved from one dockside pub to another. He must feel comfortable in those surroundings as we picked him up again this afternoon in another drinking den. He is now only half a mile from Fulton's place so, depending on what happens tomorrow, we may need to take him."

"Very well", Skinner said. "I will meet you outside his hotel and join the watchers team. What time do you want me to be there?"

"At dawn because we do not know when he will appear."

The following morning Skinner joined Taylor at half-light some fifty yards from the entrance to a seaman's lodging. A light drizzle was falling. At six in the morning the spy stepped out of the front door. He turned to his left and, keeping close to the walls of the warehouses that lined the cobbled street, moved towards a dockyard entrance above which was hung a wrought iron sign that read *R. Fulton – Engineers*. On the double doors were written the words *Strictly Private – No Admittance*.

The spy reached into a pocket of his coat and took out a miniature saw. Skinner watched as he sawed a link in the chain and, opening the gate, slipped inside closing it silently behind him.

"Should we follow him in and see what he gets up to or wait until he leaves and then nab him?", Taylor asked.

"If we follow him in there is a risk that he sees us and gets away. If we wait out here, so long as he uses the same route to leave the place, we will catch him. I vote we stay here", Skinner replied.

Skinner, Taylor and two of Taylor's men spent an anxious hour standing outside the yard's doors imagining the different ways that the spy might leave the dockyard and how they could lose him as a result. An hour later they heard footsteps from inside the dock. The yard's doors opened a crack.

As the spy emerged ino the street Taylor and his men grabbed his arms and slipped a pair of handcuffs on his wrists.

"Good morning, Sir, and who might you be?", Skinner asked.

The spy said nothing and stared defiantly at Skinner. Skinner ordered one of Taylor's men to search his pockets. The man passed a folded paper to Skinner who saw that the spy had drawn a diagram of a vessel which was almost identical to that which he had seen in the Superintendent's office at the Naval yard in Baltimore.

"And what's this?"

The spy remained silent.

"Have you a name? No matter. I have a carriage waiting in the next street. These men will take you to it and escort you back to Baltimore. You will be lodged in the cells at Fort McHenry. We will meet there in due course."

Skinner was pleased with their morning's work; now he had to decide how he would play the situation.

He returned from New York to his office in Baltimore. Three days later he instructed his clerk to make an appointment for him to visit the Fort the following morning.

Skinner knew the conditions at the Fort from his wartime duties. Although there were no longer POWs held up there, it was still a very grim place to be incarcerated. The spy faced the prospect of undergoing a secret trial followed by execution.

He took Taylor with him to the interrogation.

"First, I need to know your name. We know you came off the *Charlotte* out of Vigo but you did not sail home with her. Instead you waited for another vessel the *Marjorie*, out of Liverpool, Captain Wild commanding. Now, it so happens we know about the captain, He was a prisoner in this very place during the war. I personally oversaw his repatriation to Canada. That is why I recognised the two of you at the *Stars & Stripes* when you met him there. So we know all about you and your mission. I just need confirmation by you of who you are working for."

The man still said nothing.

"Very well. I regret that I am obliged to instruct the Governor to put you in chains and to provide you with a reduced diet until you recover your speech. These are matters of state security and I will have answers to my questions. You may ask your jailors to attend on you at any time if you decide to speak."

With that, the prisoner was handed over to the Fort's authorities and Skinner left McHenry.

It took ten days before Skinner received a message that the prisoner wished to see him. Skinner waited two days before he and Taylor went out to the Fort.

He met with a sorry sight. The spy was in wrist and leg irons. He lay on a dirty straw palisse in a stinking cell below ground.

"What is it you wish to tell me?"

"I want a guarantee of safety before I tell you anything. A new name, documents and a passage to the Argentine."

"You are in no position whatsoever to make any demands", Skinner responded. "You are a British spy who has been caught red-handed stealing national secrets. The penalty for spying is execution and you have the choice of a reasonable death or a very nasty one. I suggest that you tell us all you know."

"Only if I have the guarantees I have asked for."

"I will make that decision when I have heard your story."

"I work for the Alien Office in London. I met with Mr. Hazell and received his instruction to come across the Atlantic. I was to check the ports and docks for the existence of a vessel that can travel and fight underwater. Mr. Hazell is aware that an engineer called Fulton made some prototypes but needs to know if any of these are still in use or could be used."

"By what means were these orders given to you?"

"In coded correspondence."

"Right", Skinner went on. "I am going to dictate a letter to you which you will encode and which you will forward to Hazell to London. It will say that you have been up and down the eastern seaboard over the past three weeks and have found no evidence whatsoever of any kind of underwater vessel and that in your professional opinion no such vessel exists in America. In return for this, I am prepared to consider your release."

A day later Taylor arrived in Skinner's office with a coded letter.

"I have checked the code, Sir and it is correct in every particular. I cannot detect any deviation that might alert London that it has been written under duress."

"Good. We will now await Captain Wild's next visit to Baltimore which I doubt will be long in coming. When it does, you will send one of your men on board with the letter and an explanation that the spy has not been able to deliver it in person as he has had to go out of town on urgent business.

If things go as we plan, Hazell will believe that his spy remains free and that the British have nothing to fear from this side of the Atlantic. Meanwhile, we will keep an eye on Fulton and his submarine and check that he is not up to any mischief that we should know about."

14   *The Liberators*

It had been some weeks since Hazell and Bow Street had prevented the object or submarine if that is what it was - from being taken down to the South Atlantic. Rumours continued to circulate in London of an escape attempt to be organised on behalf of Napoleon imprisoned on St Helena.

In spite of being implicated in the London Bridge escape conspiracy, Lord Holland was not himself arrested - his connections were too powerful for that. He was now getting up a petition that he planned to present to Parliament in which he would urge the Government to facilitate the great man's return to Europe.

His wife, Lady Holland, was behaving no better. Because of her own independent social position she felt free to continue to send the prisoner newspapers and books delivered to St Helena by passing visitors.

None of these reached Napoleon directly because Governor Lowe had imposed a ban on all reading materials reaching him. Nevertheless, secret communication with his supporters continued via numerous intermediaries on and off the island.

It was even suspected that conspirators were using the Daily Courier to print coded messages for Longwood's attention in the advertisments it published on its front pages.

As an additional precaution, Edward ordered that all out-going and in-coming passenger lists to and from St Helena should be delivered to his office. If sympathisers were planning direct action, he would know about it.

Extra staff would be needed at the Office to check up on any suspicious names which would then be passed to either Townsend or Sayer depending on their status. Bow Street would place them under surveillance.

One evening on his way back from the theatre Edward became aware that he was being followed. It was a moonless night and the street lamps had been extinguished. Each time he quickened his pace he could hear his follower's footsteps doing the same. He tried crossing the road several times but the individual behind him did the same. Instead of the direct route back to his apartment, he started zig-zagging left and right down the narrow streets but his follower hung onto him.

Finally, he reached the front door of his apartment. He was about to enter its vestibule but, as he placed his key in the lock, he felt a violent blow to the back of his head. He sank half-conscious to the pavement. The man who had been following him came up beside him and was joined by a second man, his attacker, who had obviously been lying in wait by his door.

The two men began to kick him viciously first in the groin and then all over his body. Edward was groaning as the blows rained down on him but at that moment a man came running towards the building shouting and brandishing what looked like a cane.

When the man got close Edward could see from a half closed and bloody eye that it was a sword stick. The man began to cut about Edward's attackers. After a minute they turned and ran. The man - a neighbour of Edward's who lived in the same building - helped him to his feet. Together they staggered upstairs to his apartment.

"Damned vagrants. London's full of them. A man can't go out at night."

His neighbour helped Eward through his door and sat him down in a chair. "You saved my life", Edward said, "and I can't thank you enough. I'll be alright now."

Edward was in agony. He suspected that he had at least two broken ribs and could feel a lump swelling on his head. His rescuer found a bottle of brandy and a glass and helped Edward to pour it down his throat.

"These damned footpads, they are like rats and attack anyone they choose. The city is becoming lawless after dark. I'm glad to have been of help."

Edward thanked his neithbour for rescuing him from greater injury and, after seeing him out, put himself to bed. He would need to see a surgeon in the morning.

What worried him more was that it could not have been a random attack because his second assailant had already been at his door before he had been joined by the man who had been following him.

This implied that someone not only knew about him and his work but had also found out where he lived. This attempt on his life showed either, that his opponents were becoming stronger - and believed that could operate against the government with impunity - or that they were becoming more desperate which showed that he and the Runners were getting closer to them.

Two days later when both his black eyes were turning from deep purple into yellow and blood was no longer seeping out from under the bandage around his head, Edward went to the Office to inform Crauford about what had happened. He looked a sorry sight. He could hardly sit up straight, his ribs were so painful.

Crauford had seen much worse in battle but even he was shocked at the audacity of Edward's attackers. He was also furious that a senior member of his staff had been almost killed.

"You had better get yourself some security in case they try and have another go at you. The same for Nicholson. It shows that we are closing in on them. I want a full list of all your contacts and anyone you have met or spoken to for the past three months. That includes your family. Have it on my desk in an hour and we will try to work out who are the most likely individuals to have been involved.

Holland may have got away with it on the river but if I see his hand in this outrage - a direct attack on a government servant - he won't get away from me again. I'll destroy him and his cronies."

In addition to his contacts at work, Edward would also have to share his social contacts with Crauford, including Julia's name.

Later that day Edward went down to Bow Sreet and met with Sayer. He told Sayer what had happended and that Crauford had authorised around the clock protection for him and Nicholson.

"Leave it to me, Sir. I have friends who did this kind of work in Spain. You won't see them but they will be guarding your backs day and night.

Next day Edward received a letter from Lombard Street bearing the seal of the *Secret Office*. It was from his friend James Longdon, Julia's brother.

James wrote: "I think that you will want to read this as soon as possible."

The decoded message read:

> "I made a series of shop to shop enquiries in the
> town. There are more than nine that deal in carvings
> and special gifts. Under duress, and with a generous
> bribe, my seventh try was successful and the
> shopkeeper revealed that he had sold a chess set six
> months ago. He had been instructed by the purchaser
> to hollow out the Queen. I asked the shopkeeper

to describe the purchaser and he said that the man smelled of the sea; had an English accent and wore the buttons of the HEIC on his frock coat."

The timing was right - it was Captain Dance of the Company.

Here was more evidence of a plot. The only question was the extent of Amherst's involvement and if it would be possible to tie him directly to Holland. They had certainly been seen together on many occasions since Amherst had returned to London but could Edward be justified in taking his evidence to the ministerial meeting and seeking their adjudication on his treachery?

In addition to Amherst's activities on St Helena when he had visited Napoleon, he had also been in the party at Drury Lane on the night of the sinking of the submersible at London Bridge but, like Holland, he had not been arrested at the river's edge.

Ministers would have to draw their own conclusions when presented with the evidence. At the very least, Edward thought, Amherst should lose his job in government.

Another cause for concern was the increasing number of officers of Britain's army and navy who were causing trouble after being placed on half pay or compulsorily retired when the war had ended. Many of these had enjoyed rich pickings from prize money and booty during the conflict but were now living beyond their means and experiencing severe financial difficulty.

It was even rumoured that a number of them had taken to highway robbery and that others were looking to offer themselves as mercenaries in foreign armies. Many had joined the Company's forces in India to fight against its Mogul rulers and some had even joined the Maharajahs themselves to fight *against* the British.

A fresh worry for Hazell was that such contacts might extend into the South Atlantic and might well include ideas of a seaborne assault on St Helena.

He decided to take his latest suspicions to Crauford who had spent time in almost every profession in his varied career - except as a mercenary - and would certainly know something about the activity of those who might be involved.

When Edward had explained his interest, Crauford sat back in his chair.

"I think you are exaggerating the threat but I know a man who can tell us. Thomas, Lord Cochrane is the hero of the burning of the French fleet in the Aix Roads. However, as you will find out when you read his file, he was dismissed the Service for stealing prize money from the Navy. He has also served time in prison for a stock exchange fraud while an MP. He ended up tied up in the stocks for a day on Parliament Square under some ancient city law.

Cochrane is a man of extremes in both his opinions and in his friendships. He is either loved or hated. He is permanently short of money - his wife is a spendthrift - and he has limitless confidence in his own abilities. He is mad and bad enough for anything. The noble Lord St Vincent described him as 'romantic, money getting and not truth-telling'. If anyone could be making mischief, it will be him.

I am told he is currently on the look-out for any employment that will restore his fortunes whether at home or abroad. The Government has made it quite clear that he can expect no Commission from them. I will make some enquiries for you."

Edward wondered if there might be a connection between Cochrane and Holland House and instructed Townsend to place ex-Admiral Lord Cochrane under immediate surveillance.

The intelligence that Townsend uncovered was highly disturbing.

"Lord and Lady Cochrane are regular visitors to Holland House. Their talk is all of the liberation of the Americas, Brazil, Chile and so on and how this can be achieved. Lord Cochrane has said that the greatest obstacle to success is the Spanish Navy but that it is also the revolutionaries' greatest opportunity.

If the annual gold fleet can be taken on its homeward journey to Cadiz, as we took it when we invaded twelve years ago, there would be more than sufficient treasure to purchase ships and crew. The Spanish navy could then be attacked on equal terms in the Pacific and driven from the South Atlantic."

"As you know, Sir", Townsend continued, "we are selling off our warships as fast as we can to recoup our wartime financial costs and reduce the cost of the Navy. The number of flagged vessels has already been reduced from over seven hundred craft of all types to less than one hundred and thirty.

It is even rumoured that Lord Cochrane has been approached by the Junta in Chile to create a navy by buying up our ships; recruiting crews in Britian and appointing himself its first commanding admiral. He has enough friends and ex-brother officers to do it.

I have also heard that he has been raising the capital to build an ocean-going ship of his own design powered by steam that will be built in London and sailed to the Americas. Apparently he has already named it the *Rising Star.*"

This looked like another demand on Edward's operations. He would need to place a spy in the shipyard whilst the vessel was under construction. Would it really be able to cross the Atlantic under steam alone and be used in an escape attempt?

Edward was kept busy managing his secret work and trying to fit a number of pieces of an increasingly disturbing jigsaw into place. These included reports from St Helena, Baltimore and Bow Street.

He received the first of a series of reports from St Helena written by his friend Goldie of the 66th who wrote:

'Another row has broken out between the Governor and the Regiment that has led to the removal of an officer from the island. Like the O'Meara affair, it had to do with a charge of over-fraternisation between certain individuals of the British Garrison and Napoleon's household. However, this time it included William Balcombe who is charged with conveying messages to Longwood without going through the required censorship process. It is even rumoured that it will lead to Balcombe's dismissal from his position and removal to England.

The cause celebre was a letter from Napoleon to Lady Holland in London that criticized the Governors regime as being unduly harsh and called him Un Ane - a donkey. The Duty Officer at Longwood our Captain Nicholls of the 66th had been handed the letter at Longwood and had failed to pass its contents to the Governor. Instead, he handed it directly to Balcombe who sent it with his private dispatches to London where I understand Lady Holland forwarded its contents to the Daily Courier. I am told that Sir Hudson Lowe has received a severe reprimand from Lord Bathhurst, the Secretary of State, whose own position is now threatened, at a time when Holland is pressing him hard with his petition to the House of Lords. I am sure that you know all of this already but the timing of the episode could not have been worse for the Government and will not have made your task any easier.

Both civil and military society on the island is becoming increasingly fractious and divided. The new naval commander Admiral Robert Plampin has caused a scandal by arriving with a lady who it has turned out is not his wife and who is to be removed from the island at once on Lowe's orders. In the meantime, it is becoming very obvious that the officers of the Naval Squadron are almost universally of a liberal persuasion and favour the release of Napoleon whereas their counterparts in our garrison are mainly of the opposite opinion.

I am becoming particularly concerned about the residents of Mr. Porteous's Boarding House. As you know the French Commissioner, Montchenu, lives there and is sound but a Captain Marryat holds court most evenings and apparently expresses strong views about the iniquity of the conditions up at Longwood. You will be aware that Marryat is no ordinary captain but a well-known cartoonist and popular writer whose father is a wealthy shareholder of the HEIC with connections in both the Company's Court and in the City of London.

Marryat has gathered a clique around him and whilst they discuss only current affairs openly, I think there may be more going on. I intend to keep as close an eye as possible on them.

It has also been reported to me that a small group of the younger army and navy officers have been meeting out of their barracks at a small house that overlooks Longwood's boundary called Mason's Stock House. I am told the group's ostensible reason for meeting is for regular prayer – one of its members is dying of consumption– but I am suspicious because a Captain Reardon, with whom you are already familiar from a previous report of mine about an incident at Deadwood, lives up there permanently with them. I understand that he has also been seen at Porteous's place in Jamestown in the company of Marryat.

I will communicate further when I have more news and trust that the information above will be of use to you.

Yours, Dandy

PS
I have met a rather jolly girl known on the island as the 'Nymph'. She is ravishing!

Goldie's letter gave Edward much to think about. The first thing he did was ask Nicholson to check if the Office had anything about Frederick Marryat in its files.

What Nicholson found was highly disturbing.

"Marryat has form. He was a Midshipman under Cochrane in the Mediterranean for seven years. They were like two peas in a pod. They were both reckless, ambitious and quick-thinking. They came out smelling of roses although Cochrane sailed very close to the wind and was often within a hair's breath of court-martial. Their speciality was cutting out enemy ships, almost always smaller than their own, and sending them back to Portsmouth as prizes.

When the war ended, Marryat went on half pay like the rest of them but he put his experience of war to good use. He drew a series of pen and ink sketches depicting shipboard life that his father had printed up for him. They were purchased by Naval officers and the like. I am told that even the King has acquired a set.

Marryat has also written a series of novels about adventures at sea. One of these, *Mr. Midshipman Easy*, about his exploits in the Mediterranean with Cochrane, has made Marryat famous.

Six months ago his father petitioned the Navy Board to give Marryat a full-time command and he was sent to join the Squadron on St Helena. He and his father are both well known for their liberal views. I would not be at all surprised if he was making trouble on the island."

Edward was aware that a man could rise from the Navy's gun decks to the ship's bridge in a way that it was almost impossible for a private soldier to become colonel of his regiment. However, such differences between the two services should not have become a potentially treasonable matter.

He had a cousin, James King, a Lieutenant in the Navy, who was currently posted to Greenwich. Edward would arrange to meet with King and hope to find out more about both Cochrane and Marryat.

Meanwhile, he would write to Goldie at once with this new information. He would ask him to keep a close eye on Marryat and any others lodging at the boarding house in Jamestown.

Edward was forcefully reminded of trouble on St Helena two days later when his clerk knocked on the door of his office.

"Come in".

"Excuse me for disturbing you, Sir, but I think that you ought to see this."

"What is it?"

"I was following your instructions and carrying out my usual check of passengers on the *Inwards List* disembarking from ships returning from India via either the Cape or St Helena. I noticed this."

The clerk pointed with his finger to a name.

"It's a Lieutenant Birmingham returning from St Helena. Isn't that the name of the officer Mr. Goldie told us about who was removed from the island by Governor Lowe two months ago for insubordination?"

"So it is. We had better ask Sayer to put a tail on him to see where he goes and who he meets. I bet you a pound to an orange he will end up in Kensington."

Edward would also ask Nicholson to check if there was any record of a Lieutenant - formerly Sgt. - Birmingham in the Alien Office's files.

A glance at the day's *Outwards List* also showed a Major James Dunne, who Edward remembered meeting at his club. Dunne was leaving London for St Helena with a company of the 44th.

The Governor was certainly taking no chances if he was reinforcing the island's garrison like this.

The next day Edward received a visit from his old friend Captain Wild formerly of the *Butterfly* now commanding the *Marjorie*. Edward was hoping for some useful information from him.

Fortunately, the Americans had never discovered Wild's spying activities on Edward's behalf. He had been held by the Americans as a civilan only until he had been returned to England via Canada in a prisoner exchange. Edward had visited Wild while he was recovering in the naval hospital at Portsea and had kept in touch with him after the war had ended.

"Come in, come in Gilbert. Sit yourself down. Good to see you. When did you return?

"We docked yesterday afternoon and I have left the crew to unload the cargo. I came into the City as soon as I could this morning. I knew you would want news as quickly as possible."

"Yes, indeed, I hope your trip was productive."

"Unfortunately not. I met your man at the agreed place but he reported that he has not yet uncovered any evidence of a vessel that moves under water except, of course, what we already know about the *Nautilus* which is that it capsized in a storm off Cape Cod two years ago with the loss of its whole crew. Its inventor, Fulton, has not been seen or heard of since and is, I believe, completely discredited."

"I know nothing has turned up yet", Edward said, "but I am still suspicious about the potential involvement of the United States in any kind of trouble-making. How did you leave it with my agent on the waterfront at Baltimore?"

"I left it with him that he will continue to keep his ear to the ground particularly around the Naval shipyard", Wild replied, "but he is fearful that the Americans are onto him. He says that he will not be able to stay much longer in the area."

"That damned John Skinner", Edward responded, "he's always poking his nose in where it doesn't belong. Wasn't he involved in your exchange?"

"Indeed he was and he made it very clear that he had no love for the British."

"When will you be returning?"

"I am bound for Philadephia with a load of coal out of Whitehaven. It will be a couple of weeks before I sail, then another ten days to cross. I should be in Baltimore by the end of next month."

"I will let our agent know by another source of your estimated date of arrival. It will be the *Marjorie* again I presume? Let's hope he can stay alive until then. Now, can I offer you a glass of Madeira?"

Later that afternoon, Edward composed a message to his agent in Baltimore advising him that the *Marjorie* would be back in port in six weeks and he should watch out for her. Meanwhile, the threat of a seaborne rescue of Napoleon had increased and he should do his utmost to locate any submarine, should one exist.

Finally, Edward warned his agent that it was very likely that either the Americans or subversive elements in Britain would attempt to stop him and that he should be on his guard. He sent the message to the Secret Office for encoding and dispatch by the next fast pacquet across the Atlantic.

Just as Edward was about to go home Crauford came to his office.

"The Government has just agreed that Lucien Napoleon, who, as you know, is under house arrest with his family in Ludlow, is to be allowed to cross the Atlantic. He intends to make a new life for himself and his family in the United States. We don't want him here. It costs us to look after him and he is a potential source of trouble. He will be leaving within the next two months."

"That's all very well", Edward replied, "but at least we have him where we can see him. There's no knowing what support Lucien might generate on behalf of his brother in the United States. The danger is that he could provide the focus and funds for an escape attempt mounted by the Americans."

"There is nothing I can do about it. It's a political decision at the highest level. The Cabinet wants him out of Europe."

"I have a man in Baltimore keeping an eye on the eastern seaboard", Edward continued, "but I have no one in Washington and, since you and your *green jackets* burned down the capital, it's been impossible to place anyone there. There is great suspicion of any individuals with British accents, actual or supposed. This makes gathering information very difficult."

Crauford ignored the implied criticism and changed the subject by remarking: "You seem to be getting through our budget at a phenomenal rate. Are we any closer to finding out if there is an active and credible plan being laid here in London for Bonaparte's escape?"

Edward replied: "I cannot yet say if there is an actual plan or even if it is credible. What I can say is that we have enough evidence to take the idea seriously - look at the arrests we made at London Bridge. My teams and I are working flat out to uncover more hard facts so that the Government can take the actions it deems necessary both here in London and on St Helena."

"Speaking of which", Crauford replied, "I think that you should draw up a report of the current intelligence that you do have to hand and be ready to present it to the Cabinet's Colonies sub-committee. They are responsible for the prisoner's safe-keeping. It meets once a month in Downing Street. The Prime Minister chairs it. Shall we say next month's meeting? I think it's on the 22nd. August. Let me have a draft by the end of next week."

"Very well, General."

Whilst the idea of a presentation made Edward anxious because of the danger of leaks, it would provide the opportunity for him to review all of the material that he had to date and to make a full assessment of the overall risk.

He calculated that there were now at least four strands to his investigation. These included Lord and Lady Holland and their network of sympathisers in London; Cochrane and his liberators along with any other disaffected British officers in London heading for South America; Skinner in Baltimore and the threat of an escape attempt organised from St Helena itself.

Edward wondered which of these strands would provide the break that he needed. Hopefully, this would emerge before he had to make his presentation to Ministers.

He called Nicholson to his office and instructed him to draw up a first draft of his report for discussion.

Meanwhile Edward had some private business to attend to. Ever since he had been attacked he had been trying to work out in his mind if Julia could have been involved in it.

True, her step-father was associated with the Holland set, but Edward had nothing that implicated Sir Thomas Goode directly.

However, he continued to be suspicious and in particular he could not get out of his mind the family's attendance at the theatre performance at Drury Lane that had preceeded the affair on the river. Had they been invited to make up the numbers on the night or had they been a part of the conspiracy? Edward needed to know.

Enclosed in the decoded message from his agent at the Cape, his friend James Longdon at the Secret Office had included a private note.

Dear friend, I saw Julia on Tuesday and she said that she has not seen you for these past few weeks and that you parted on bad terms. I know that you are very busy at present but I urge you to contact her and put things right between you. I know how fond you are of each other.

J.

Edward sighed. James was correct; it was an unsatisfactory situation. He would send Julia a note asking to meet with her.

When he reached home the following evening he found a note from Julia that had been delivered in respone to his own that invited him to come around at eight that evening. Her parents would be out.

Bunbury's words now rang in Edward's ears.

He took a carriage to Hans Place in Knightsbridge and knocked on Julia's door. As before, it was not a footman who answered it, but Julia herself.

She gasped in horror when she saw him.

"Oh! My dear. What have you been up to? You look as if you have been in a fight. Come in. I have given the servants the evening off, so we can be quite alone,"

"Hello Julia, it is good to see you."

"Let's go upstairs to the drawing room."

Edward followed her up to the first floor.

"I am sorry that I have not been in touch. I have been fearfully busy at work. I apologise for my churlish behaviour on the river the other week, I can't think what came over me."

He stood awkwardly in front of her.

"No apology needed. Sit down and tell me what's been going on."

They sat at opposite ends of the large sofa.

"My uncle Matthew had news of you via Sir Henry Bunbury who said that you were involved in some operation associated with state security. I don't understand, you've always told me that you did immigration work at the Home Office. And what's happened to your face?"

"Well, yes. My work is mainly about that but from time to time I have to follow up specific cases. Then I get involved in more active work."

"What do you mean 'more active work'?", Julia said.

"I work with John Fielding and his Runners at Bow Street. Sometimes they help me to arrest individuals who are in the country illegally. This can include our own citizens."

"What are you, a snooper?"

"Not exactly, no."

"Well, what are you then?"

It was now or never, Edward thought. He had to decide here and now whether he could trust Julia with his secrets or walk out of the door and never see her again.

"At the beginning of the war the Government set up an office that would keep watch on the Channel ports for undesirables entering the

232

country who might foment trouble - revolutionaries and so on. By the time I joined the war had almost ended but then we had trouble with the Americans. We had to fight them; this time mostly at sea. That's when I had my first experience of secret work.

My job was to watch American shipping and prevent their privateers raiding our sea lanes. You remember when I sent you a message via your brother that I would be away for a few weeks on government business. I was actually in the South Atlantic carrying out an operation.

Since that war ended I have been involved in internal security but at present my main responsibility is for the prisoner on St Helena. The Government is absolutely determined that Bonaparte should not return from exile in the South Atlantic.

Unfortunately, there are those both in this country and elsewhere who want him back. My job is to make certain it doesn't ever happen."

Now Edward was at the point when he would need to place his career in Julia's hands.

"Sometimes this can lead to difficult situations like, for example, an incident on London Bridge a few weeks ago when we had to arrest some conspirators.

I have to ask you if you were involved in any way whatsoever in any of the events of that night. I know that you and your parents were at the theatre with some of those who were arrested later. Did you know what was going on?"

Edward held his breath.

Julia remained silent.

"Now that you know what I do, what I have told you will always have to remain a secret. You will never be able to tell another soul about my work. You must understand that my position depends on the absolute trust that my employers have placed in me. If I am compromised in any way I cannot continue in my role and particularly with the work in which I am currently involved. I will never be able to tell you about its details and you can never be involved in it in any way. I shall be very sorry if this means the end for us", Edward ended.

At this point Julia jumped up from the other end of the sofa and leapt straight into Edward's lap.

"Oh, Edward darling, don't be such a silly. I have had my suspicions for ages but Papa said that I should never ever question you about your work. There was nothing odd about our attendance at the theatre that night and I know nothing of any river. We went home afterwards and the following morning Papa made growling noises as he read the *Courier* at breakfast. He is no traitor and I have never heard him speak sympathetically of Napoleon. Don't forget my darling mother was made a widow in Spain by that unspeakable man. I hate the monster.

I knew there was something odd about your work but I would never have guessed what it was. Now there is nothing that we don't know about each other. I will love and support whatever you do. I am so, so happy."

And with that, Julia began to kiss Edward passionately first on his lips and then all over his face.

Edward responded and a long, passionate clinch followed that was only broken by the sound of the front door opening. Julia's step-father's voice boomed: "Julia, we're back."

Julia and Edward tidied themselves up before the door to the drawing room opened and Julia's step-father Sir Thomas stepped inside: "Good evening Hazell, I see you two have made it up."

After an exchange of pleasantries, Edward took his leave and he and Julia went downstairs.

Edward had his hand on the door as they kissed passionately again. Julia took Edward's face in her hands. "Darling, I hope that this horrible business will end soon. I don't want you to look like this on our wedding day."

"It's not over yet, I'm afraid. We may have foiled one plot but there could well be others being planned. We are looking at another group at present that includes a bunch of ex-Navy types led by Lord Thomas Cochrane."

"You mean that MP who was put in the stocks after escaping from prison?"

"Yes, that's the one. A thoroughly nasty piece of work."

"From what I hear he's all mouth. Anyway, remember that I love you and take care."

Edward left shortly afterwards but not before another long embrace on the doorstep.

"I'll come around after work tomorrow and I will speak with your father. I am going to seek his permission for your hand. I hope he will approve"

"Goodnight, darling."

The following morning Nicholson brought Edward a dossier containing all that they had on the St Helena situation.

Edward would have more work to do on it before the meeting of the Committee but the broad lines of their intelligence was clear. He knew what he would say:

"There is an active cell in London headed by the Holland set that includes East India Company officials and their supporters. An underwater craft has already been destroyed on the Thames and searches are continuing in the Docks.

A group of disaffected ex-officers is about to leave London and sail to South America. They are led by Lord Cochrane, with whose career you are all familiar. Their main aim is to turn the Spanish out of their continental provinces and seize their wealth. These so-called *liberators* also include a number of individuals who have been dismissed from St Helena by Governor Lowe for insubordination. It is suspected that one of them has very detailed knowledge of the island and its topography. It is the Alien Office's opinion that a rescue attempt made by this group is highly likely.

Our old enemies in the United States of America, led by their President Madison, are busy making trouble again. We have evidence that their man Skinner, who is my opposite number in Baltimore, and who has reason to hate us, is preparing to support any rescue attempt that will be made. We think that Skinner will join forces with the liberators.

We also believe that the most likely launching-off place for any escape attempt will be from Buenos Aires. It has a sympathetic revolutionary population and leadership; includes a number of British deserters who stayed on after our failed invasions and is the closest place to St Helena with the level of support required.

Finally, the situation on St Helena itself is increasingly unstable. The views of the civil and military establishments are split. We now have intelligence that an active plan of escape may involve both military and naval officers in the garrison."

15 *The Damned Yankee*

IT CAME AS little surprise to Edward when, five weeks later, he learned that the party to be led by Lord Cochrane would be leaving London shortly. It would include one A.W. Birmingham Esq., late of the 66th Foot.

Edward's man in the shipyard at Deptford had been reporting regularly on the progress of the construction of the steamship *The Rising Star* but it was becoming clear that the vessel would not be ready to sail in time. *Kitty* Lady Cochrane would stay behind and bring the ship over to South America later whilst her husband and his mercernaries sailed ahead in the *Rose,* an ex-East Indiaman of 1200 tons. The passenger list Edward held in his hand made disturbing reading.

"Have a look at this, Francis. In addition to Cochrane himself and his private household, a motley collection of ex-military officers are sailing with him some of whom have most unsavoury reputations.

James Paroissien is an adventurer. He trained originally as a doctor before joining the Army. He served with Popham at La Plata in 1807 where he was captured. He later took part in the attack on Washington and the burning of the White House under Ross in 1812. He returned to South America to set up a gunpowder factory in Cordoba for the Revolutionary forces of Peru. He's a thoroughly nasty piece of work.

And here's another one: William Miller. He joined the Royal Artillery aged 15 and fought in the Peninsular. He was also with Ross in Washington before moving to Buenos Aires and commanding the *Cabildo's* guns during the wars of liberation.

Stephen Goldsack is another bad egg. I met him in Portugal when I was doing secret work. He was quartermaster to William Congreve inventor of the *Congreve Rocket* and was dismissed for the theft and resale of military stores. It looks as if Cochrane has recruited him to set up a local rocket factory in Chile.

I wonder what other tricks Cochrane's liberators have up their sleeves.

I don't know how we are going to keep track of this lot as they may well split up when they get to the other side of the Atlantic. A number will sail around the Horn at once where they are expected in Peru. Others may remain on the Atlantic coast to await the arrival of more ships before they form the fleet that will attack the Spanish in the Pacific. We know that their first port of call will be New York but after that who knows what their movements will be.

I've had no word from our man over there who is hunting for the submarine; it will be at least eight weeks until the *Marjorie* gets back over here. Even then Captain Wild may have no news for us. We will be working completely in the dark."

Edward had never spotted the men who had been appointed by Sayer for his personal protection but one morning as Edward prepared to leave his apartment, the porter knocked on his door and gave him a message. A Miss Jamieson had called and left a bunch of violets for him which the porter now pressed into his hand. Edward remembered that it was the code that he had agreed with Sayer for an emergency meeting. He took a carriage to the Embankment and caught the ferry to the South Bank. Ten minutes later he could see Sayer pacing up and down the landing stage at Lambeth.

"Good morning, Sayer, what's so urgent?"

Sayer beckoned to Edward to join him a short distance away from the landing so that they could not be overheard before turning to Edward.

"I'm afraid I have some bad news, Mr Hazell. Last night one of my men disobeyed his orders for some reason. You had a visitor last night, didn't you? After she left, instead of staying at his post outside your apartment he took it into his head to follow her. I simply don't know if it was from boredom at the long night on watch ahead or that something had made him suspicious.

He says that the lady gave an address to the cabby that he did not recognise. Instead of going straight home, she stopped the hansom at an address in Mayfair and went inside. She was there for around half an hour and then came out. She arrived back at her home thirty minutes later.

I have identified the owner of the house", Sayer went on, "as a Captain Northey. A dockyard contact of mine tells me that he fought with Admiral Cochrane in the Channel. I am very sorry, Sir, but it looks as if your fiancée has been playing for the other side. It may account for that attack on you outside your apartment a month ago."

Edward ceased breathing. His heart stopped. Julia had betrayed him. The words she had used and the promises she had made to him were worthless.

Sayer was speaking again: "You will have to cut her out, Mr Hazell, or she will give our operation away. Can you think of anything specific that you have said or done that might have given her any clue about who and what we are after?"

Edward thought back to the evening of their engagement and his conversation with Julia before he had left. He had mentioned Cochrane's possible involvement in plans to rescue Bonaparte. This slip, made in a moment of euphoria, had now destroyed his prospects, both romantic and professional. He was devastated. This gross breach of security would take some explaining when he told Crauford. He would be fortunate to keep his job. Crauford would be furious.

"Thank you, John. This is most unpleasant news. I will take the necessary steps to deal with the situation. As you know I am very fond of Miss Longdon. I should like you to commend your man for his work. This could have become even more ugly."

As the *The Needles* disappeared over the horizon Alan Birmingham went below. He found himself in mixed company but on the whole he preferred the naval party.

He had made contact with Holland House to offer his services as soon as he had reached London. His dismissal from St Helena had been grossly unfair. He intended to fight for his rights but when they met he found that he did not need to explain his situation to Lord Holland; his Lordship knew all about him already.

"I intend to make full use of the information you have about the situation on the island", Holland said. "Come around again on Thursday evening – I want you to meet someone with whom I think you'll have much in common."

Birmingham had done as he was instructed and later that week had been introduced to the charismatic Lord Cochrane and his glamorous wife for the first time.

Later the three men sat around a table in Lord Holland's study.

"I wanted you two to meet at once. Thomas, this is Mr. Birmingham late of the 66th from St Helena. He has vital information about the conditions on the island including the disposition of the Garrison; the guards around Longwood House, Napoleon's residence, and the routes into and and out of the island's harbours and beaches. I propose that you, Birmingham, should accompany His Lordship on the rescue mission that he and I are planning. I don't have to tell you that what we are discussing is treasonable. If any of this get's out we are dead men.

I have already had one brush with the security services and only narrowly avoided being detained when a submersible that I had commissioned to be constructed on the Thames was discovered and destroyed. A number of my colleagues were arrested. We cannot risk any more breaches. Do I have your word?"

"Of course, My Lord, willingly", Birmingham replied. "I would like nothing better than to be involved in Napoleon's rescue. I conversed with him on a number of occasions and I am clear in my mind that he means no harm to Great Britain. His main focus is on America and rejoining his family there. How can I be of service?"

"Lord Cochrane will be sailing shortly for the United States and you will be going with him", Holland continued. "He is on his way to Chile via Buenos Aires but has offered to assist me in freeing Napoleon on his way. I have made contact with a man called Robert Fulton in New York. He has invented a machine called the *Nautilus* which Lord Cochrane tells me can move underwater. It is suitable for taking Napoleon off St Helena and bringing him on board a rescue ship. She is *The Damned Yankee* an American schooner which I have hired for the purpose. I am assured she is the fastest ship afloat and can outrun any warship of the Navy's Island Squadron.

On the island itself, there are individuals who will help us. One of them is, I understand, a comrade of yours, a Captain Reardon of the 66th. He will be leading the landward party. The other is a naval officer, one of Lord Cochrane's most trusted lieutenants and an old comrade, Frederick Marryat, who will be organising the seaward side.

Lord Cochrane will be in overall command of the rescue and you, Birmingham, will take your instructions from him. You will be well rewarded. In the event that you cannot return to Great Britain afterwards, you will be settled in a country of your choice in South

America. I hear that there are great opportunites on that continent. Any questions?", Holland ended.

"None, Sir, I am pleased to be of assistance. I was held prisoner in the Argentine and know the place well."

"Excellent! We shall not be meeting again, it's too risky, but I wish you the best of luck." With that Lord Holland shook Birmingham's hand and left the room leaving Birmingham alone with Cochrane.

"I don't know you. Sir, so I don't trust you", Cochrane said. "But if you prove yourself useful I'm sure that we will come to an accommodation. We sail in a week's time. Keep your head down until then and stay out of trouble. We think that we are being watched so keep a sharp eye out. The authorities cannot prevent my party leaving England but they may well try to uncover our plans. As a precaution, I will tell you nothing more of them at this stage. You will be fully briefed when we have put to sea. We sail from Falmouth on the fourth of next month. Make sure you are there in good time."

With that Cochrane too left the room leaving Birmingham alone. He remained seated for a few minutes thinking about how he had committed himself before fetching his cloak from the hall and leaving Holland House.

That had been four weeks ago. Now they were sailing west across the North Atlantic. A hard easterly filled the *Rose's* sails. At this rate landfall would be reached in eight day's time.

Their first port of call would be New York where they were expected to rendezvous with *The Damned Yankee* and her crew. Here they would leave the *Rose* and transfer to the American vessel for their journey further south to Baltimore where it was expected they would load up the underwater craft.

They arrived into New York without incident where they met Captain Henry Deacon commanding the American schooner the

Yankee. Deacon cut a formidable figure. He was by now in his late fifties with more than thirty years of experience behind him in the sea-lanes of the world.

He had worked the North African shore during the French revolutionary wars and taken merchantmen and their cargos of all nationalities. In the war of 1812 he had loitered in English waters and taken ships from as far apart as Bristol and Glasgow. With the coming of the peace he had transferred his interests to the East. He was now attacking British shipping at sea as far away as China.

It appeared that he and Cochrane were aquainted from some previous escapade. They were as thick as thieves as they went off into the city together.

The liberators transferred from the *Rose* to the *Yankee* and three days later Cochrane's party arrived in Baltimore and went ashore.

"Holland has given me an influential contact here", Cochrane told Birmingham next morning. "He's called John Skinner. He's a well known lawyer and also head of the Post Office in the city but he's a lot more than that. Baltimore is the principal trading centre of the USA and, in addition to being involved in commerce, Skinner runs the American secret service. He has contacts at the highest levels in government. He also has information about Robert Fulton, the inventor and owner of the submersible that we want to use for Napoleon's escape from St Helena. We are expected in his office."

That afternoon Cochrane took Birmingham with him to the meeting. As they entered the lawyer's offices a younger man came into the room. Skinner introduced him as Patrick Kennedy, his junior partner.

The Irish Rebellion of 1798 remained a dreadful memory for Patrick and all of those who survived that terrible time. Ballymullen was the most westerly town in County Mayo and its inhabitants claimed that there was nothing between its harbour light and the North American shore three thousand miles away.

At first, the rumours of an uprising against the Dublin government were dismissed as being wishful thinking. Patrick knew well enough the hardships of surviving the West Coast weather and the unrelenting drudgery of daily life. He had watched his parents agonising over the births and almost routine deaths of younger brothers and sisters in a family already trying to keep eight children from starvation.

Patrick was also familiar with the incessant rain that spoiled harvests. Most bitterly of all, he routinely witnessed the behaviour of the agents of absentee and unsympathetic landlords, both English and Irish, who gave short shrift to anyone who could not pay their rent when it became due.

When the United Irishmen recruiters finally reached the town calling for volunteers to join its resistance wing, the *Defenders*, there was no shortage of men willing to fight. The news of a republic having been declared in County Wexford, the centre of the rebellion, fanned the flames of revolution.

A local chapter was formed in Ballymullen and plans were made to obtain arms by attacking the residence of their nearest landlord. This would be followed by the taking of the barracks at Castlebar ten miles away. Then, the local men would join up with other rebel troops who would include, so his father told Patrick, military support from France and the United States of America. His father had even heard a rumour that a French invasion force had aready landed.

Two weeks later, Patrick watched his father prepare to leave home armed with a long stave to which he had bound a curved hand scythe to make a crude weapon of war. The rebel party would leave at night and join with others in the planned attack on Sir John Scott's estate. They would assault the house, take the arms and ammunition they knew were kept there and then burn the place to the ground.

According to later accounts from survivors, the first part of the plan was carried out successfully but the attack on the barracks at Castlebar went disastrously wrong.

Warnings must have been given to the garrison who appeared to be fully prepared to resist the assault. As the rebels tried to break down the barracks gate and gain entry to the armoury, a murderous fire swept the area. Many of the attackers were left killed or mortally wounded on the street outside. The remainder fled, Patrick's father amongst them.

Retribution was not long in coming to Ballymullen.

A company of red-coated Highlanders led by an officer reached the village two days later. Patrick's father was arrested and taken into the square in front of Ballymullen's Catholic church. Every road and track in and out of the town was blocked. Every dwelling was searched.

Patrick was at home after spending the morning cutting peat with his brother when the raids were carried out.

It was no routine search.

Patrick and his Ma watched as the soldiers turned over every piece of furniture before breaking it up.

The glass in every window was smashed and their curtains torn off. The carpets were taken up before being dragged outside. Mattresses were slashed open and taken downstairs. Finally, three of the soldiers climbed up onto the roof's thatch and dug holes in it with their bayonets, searching for hidden weapons.

When the cottage had been comprehensively ransacked and emptied of all its contents, all of the family's possessions were piled up outside and set on fire.

Patrick followed the soldiers from a good distance before entering the square. What happened next would be burned on his memory for the rest of his life.

The prisoners, including his father, stood in a ragged line with their backs to the church porch. A file of Highlanders stood some ten paces away and, at an order from their sergeant, raised their muskets.

Their officer, holding a paper in his hand, came out of the church accompanied by the parish priest, Father Connolly and stood in front of the soldiers before addressing the rebels.

"You have dared to rebel against the lawful government of King George rightful King of Great Britain and Ireland. I will now read the sentence:

> *'I, George, King of England, Scotland and Ireland, Supreme Governor of the Church of England and Ireland and of all the Dominions, Colonies and Settlements in my domain and under my jurisdiction as authorised by my Parliaments at Dublin and Westminster, do lawfully and rightfully condemn you to suffer death in the prescribed manner for rebelling against my Sovereign power as invested by me in the loyal armed forces of the Crown.*
>
> *Issued at Westminster this Tenth day of May 1798'"*

Father Connolly moved forward and raised his right arm to give a final blessing before moving out of the line of fire:

> "O, Most gracious & most merciful God, we earnestly beseech thee to have pity & compassion upon our unhappy brethren who now lie under sentence of death…….."

The officer moved to stand at the side of his men before giving the order "Fire." At first, smoke from the soldier's muskets partly obscured Patrick's view. As it cleared, he could see his father lying slumped on the ground amongst the other men.

Patrick turned away and crept home to give his mother the dreadful news. She sent him back to the square in the evening to find out what had happened to her husband's body. There was a soft glow at the entrance to the church that came from the lit candles inside. As Patrick came closer he could see that a row of bodies had been laid out in the nave. He jumped back when Father Connolly came out of the church into the square.

"Don't be fearful, boy. Lieutenant Reardon here says you can come in and pay your last respects before the soldiers bury your father at daylight. It will be a communal grave; not on sacred ground"

The officer, still in his feathered bonnet, but now wearing a dark grey cloak that covered his scarlet uniform, appeared at the priest's side. He confirmed the priest's words with a quick nod of his head.

"I am sorry that it had to end like this and I regret the loss of life you have suffered but the King's Peace will prevail. I hope that you have a learned your lesson. Please convey my sympathy to your family."

With that he saluted, turned smartly on his heel and went back into the Church.

Patrick placed the family crucifix, retrieved from the ruins of the house, on his father's body inside and returned to what had been his home.

Over the following months the rebellion was supressed with unrelenting brutality on both sides - a total of thirty-one thousand rebels were to die like Patrick's father. Patrick himself never forgot the dreadful scenes that he had witnessed that day or, as darkness fell, the mournful sound of the pipes of the 71st's that could be heard all over Ballymullen.

'Hey, Jonny Cope are ye waking yet…'

Patrick did his best to comfort his widowed mother and the younger children. He helped to repair the cottage and took responsibility

247

for the smallholding on which the family relied. It was harsh and up-hill work. He had to supplement their meagre living by working in the nearby flax mill. After the rebellion had been crushed conditions in Ireland were almost unbearable. Starvation and death stalked the land.

As the family sat at table one evening six months later Patrick's younger brother Shaun spoke first: "What prospect do we have here, Ma? We have become strangers in our own land. The rebellion has set the English against us and our religion once again. I don't see that changing soon. Yesterday there was more trouble down at the mill. They propose cutting our wages for the second time this month. Patrick and I were part of a protest outside the office. It became violent and some hot-heads threw some stones that broke one of Mr. Carney's windows. He called in the Militia. Now we have been locked out. There's bound to be more trouble before long."

"I agree", said Patrick, "there is nothing left for us here. I've a good mind to join 'The Secrets'. By this he meant the Roman Catholic secret societies that had gone underground since the end of the troubles but remained a potent threat to English rule.

Their mother sighed. "I can understand your frustration, boys, but where would you go and what would you do? It would be out of the frying pan and into the fire for both of you."

"Jim McCarthy is planning to move to England and get a job in Manchester", Shaun said. "He says that there is plenty of work in the northern mills. He's leaving next month."

"What, leave Ireland?", said their mother, "we would never see you again. How would I manage without you."

"Oh Ma, of course you would. Jim and Gerry are old enough to work the land. We would only be a ferry's ride away. There are crossings every day to and from Belfast and, don't forget, we would be able to send you money each month"

"That heathen city.", she replied. "Don't do anything rash." On that note the discussion ended.

However, two weeks later the boys packed their bags and left home like thousands of others. They crossed to Liverpool and found lodgings at a hostel for Irish boys that had been recommended to them by a neighbour. Their next task was to find work. Asking around they learned that Ashton's Mill at Hyde in Manchester was recruiting machinists. They left their rooms and, travelling by water up the newly built ship canal, arrived at the centre of the world's cotton manufactory.

As they had been told, Ashton's was hiring men and they both found work at the mill.

Whilst Shaun seemed content to work at the looms, Patrick was determined to better himself. One day he saw a notice outside the office advertising a clerk's job. He applied for it and was accepted.

At first he missed the company of his fellow workers and the repartee of the shop floor but he soon began to enjoy the work. Patrick was good at the job and he liked it when his boss, Mr McFarlane, complimented his work with; "Well done, lad!"

McFarlane, had come down to Manchester from Biggar on the Scottish borders. He had learned his trade in wool before appreciating the opportunities in cotton and coming South. He was a natural-born trader and liked nothing better than haggling prices with wholesalers and merchants. He had also worked in shipping and forwarding at the Port of Leith and knew all about Bills of Lading and the difference between FOB and CIF.

After two years in the general office, McFarlane took Patrick into his private den and he began his training as a sales assistant. As the empire expanded so did Ashton's and his first order was a dispatch of cotton to the Rio de La Plata.

Patrick had to ask Mr. McFarlane what and where La Plata was. "Get yourself a map of the Atlantic, lad, and I will give you a sixpence if you can find the place on it."

On Saturday afternoon when work had finished for the day, Patrick went into the city and bought his first map of the Atlantic Ocean at a shop in Corporation Street. He took it back to his lodgings in Hyde that evening and after supper he spread it out on the floor of his room.

The map showed the principal trade routes across the ocean with thick lines going from east to west between Liverpool and Halifax, New York and Baltimore that continued all the way down the coast to the Caribbean islands. Other routes could be seen between Bristol, Lisbon, Cadiz, the Azores and West Africa as well as across the Atlantic to Bahia, Rio de Janeiro and, further south, the gulf of La Plata and Buenos Aires.

"Ah, there is the Rio de La Plata. I have my sixpence".

There was very little to see in the vast mid-Atlantic, Patrick thought, except for a few islands marked Cape Verde, Ascension and St Helena. At the southern-most tip of Africa Patrick read the words *Cape of Good Hope* and opposite at the tip of the Americas, *Cape Horn*.

He underlined the principal ports on both sides of the Atlantic with a pencil – north, south, east and west - and pinned the map on the wall opposite his bed. Over the following months, as Mr. McFarlane continued Patrick's education, he memorised the outlines of the continents, their principal shipping routes and port cities.

Mr. McFarlane wouldn't catch him out again.

Patrick began to read the Manchester Guardian, a Liberal supporting daily newspaper. He paid particular attention to its business news and Lloyds List of shipping movements in and out of Liverpool. As he completed the documentation in the sales office that would take Ashton's goods across the world, Patrick made a note of their destination on a scrap of paper which he took home with him at night. He entered them onto the map in his room with a set of pins that he had bought for the purpose.

Two years later – it was on a Thursday afternoon of sweltering heat with all the office windows thrown open and Mr. McFarlane giving permission for the clerks to remove their jackets and work in their shirt sleeves – that Patrick was summoned into McFarlane's office where he and another man sat at his table.

"This is the lad I was telling you about, Sir. He has been with us now for four years and I have been training him up in sales for the past two."

Turning to Patrick he said: "Sit down, lad. This is Mr. Thomas Ashton, one of our directors. He has a proposition to put to you."

Ashton took Patrick's hand and gave it a firm shake.

"Nothing to be concerned about. McFarlane, here, has been telling me of your work and that you are reliable and ambitious. As you know, our export business has been expanding, particularly in South America. We already have agents in Halifax and Philadelphia and we think that an agent in South America can now be justified. How would you feel about going out to Buenos Aires and setting up an office for us there?"

Patrick held his breath. This was what he had been dreaming of these few past years as he had stared at his map night after night.

"I should be honoured Sir, but I should need the blessing of my mother to the plan before I leave."

"Quite so. You may have three day's holiday from the office. Make certain that you're back here with your answer by the end of next week. In anticipation of your response, your passage has already been booked out of Liverpool via *The Southern Star* bound for La Plata on the 15th of next month.

Mr. McFarlane will provide you with Bills of Exchange from Rathbone's here in Manchester that will enable you to draw on our funds when you arrive in South America. You will be able to use them to find lodgings and set up an office in the Port area.

We already have a correspondence arrangement with a leading Buenos Aires merchant, Don Manuel de Melo, who we have advised of your impending arrival. His firm has agreed to take care of your immediate needs"

Mr. Ashton rose from his chair and took Patrick's hand in his.

"We are placing our confidence in you, young man. Don't let us down. Serve the Company well" and with that he left the office.

McFarlane placed his hand on Patrick's shoulder. "Well done. lad. You will do fine, I know. Now be off with you and come back here by Thursday morning when I will brief you on the duties of a company agent."

Patrick reached home two days later and advised his mother of his plan. His mother tut-tutted but local employment prospects had become even worse. More trouble was expected. Whilst sad to leave his family and local friends, Patrick was excited by what lay ahead. He left with his family's blessing. He told his brothers that if things went well and he found good prospects in South America, they could join him later.

Patrick had confidence in himself and knew that he had shown initiative since starting at Ashton's. He got on well with other people; liked a challenge and had no fear of change. He had decided when he left Ballymullen that staying in the village would condemn him to a life of back-breaking work and penury. He believed that he had a good chance of avoiding that in South America.

He returned to Manchester and after receiving his final instructions from Mr. McFarlane, left for Liverpool where he boarded the ship that would take him away from England into the Atlantic World.

He had never travelled further than across the Irish Sea and as *The Southern Star* sailed south, he marvelled at what he saw. The ship put in at a number of ports including Lisbon and the Canary Islands at which passengers and cargo were exchanged before the ship sailed on down the coast of Africa. They called in at Freetown before crossing the Gulf of Guinea to Ascension, recently taken by the British from the Spanish.

The ship then turned westwards and for the next three weeks no land was to be seen as they sailed on towards South America. They reached the coast at Bahia before moving on to Rio de Janeiro where more cargo was unloaded.

Patrick was never bored during the voyage. He had brought with him his bedroom map and now marked up again the places where the ship called in. He also studied his fellow passengers and, although his cabin was well below decks, found congenial company amongst his fellows. Some of them were appointed, like himself, to companies trading with La Plata. One, James O'Fallon, an Irishman, from Cork, became a particular friend.

O'Fallon was going to work for Lockett & Co., ship owners and merchants of Liverpool, who were developing an Iguana mine at Potosi, a city situated five hundred miles up-country from Buenos Aires.

On a chilly morning in November after eighty-five days at sea the rumour of their final landfall ran around the ship and Patrick crowded the rail along with all the other passengers.

It was past midday when he first sighted the estuary, a long low, grey wall of sea and land; the great waters of La Plata flowing from it. The entrance was reputedly dangerous with underwater sand banks that were impossible to navigate safely so that the ship had to anchor far outside the city. The passengers and cargo were transferred into lighters before being conveyed across the mud flats in high-wheeled carts from which they stepped out onto the quays.

It was not until the following morning that it was Patrick's turn to disembark the ship and board a sailing barque that would take him ashore. Ashton's had sent some cargo along with their new representative and Patrick watched anxiously as the bales of cotton were loaded into the barque moored alongside him.

Soon they were moving away from the ship. After an hour of tacking backwards and forwards across the estuary he could see a long line of low buildings emerging from the horizon: a church spire and the arched entry of the port and quay-front warehouses. The narrow streets were packed with townhouses.

Patrick's bales were unloaded and Patrick stood beside them on the dock with his personal luggage, a somewhat forlorn figure. Twenty minutes later a carriage drew up and a man lent out of its window and shouted: "Do you play cricket?"

It was Don de Melo, partly educated in England and a fanatical cricketer. The Don dismounted and shook Patrick's hand. "I am looking for a spin bowler and I am told that you play." Patrick looked dismayed; he had never played cricket in his life but he realised he needed to make a good impression.

"Delighted to meet you, Sir. I bring greetings from Mr. Ashton and Mr. McFarlane in Manchester." That would have to do for now.

"Hand up your luggage into the carriage. I have arranged for you to lodge in my house until you have found a place of your own", and, pointing to a mule-cart that had drawn up behind them, Don Melo instructed his men to transport Ashton's cotton to his warehouse in the city.

Three months later Mr. McFarlane received the following letter posted to him a week after he estimated that Patrick had arrived in South America:

December 1801
43, Cordoba
Buenos Aires

Sir,

I have the honour to advise you that I reached this city on the 5ᵗʰ last and was greeted most warmly by Senor Don Manuel de Melo. He not only took delivery of the sample merchandise but most generously invited me to lodge with him at his home (which also serves as his offices) until I can find my own place. He has also given me the use of his business facilities so that I can commence making contact with potential customers.

Those merchants that I have already met have spoken of the opportunity for an expansion of the business and I attach for your information a list of prospects one of whom has placed an order with me.

I have taken the liberty of accepting the order FOB, Liverpool via Lockett's (whose agent here is an acquaintance of mine) and have arranged for payment to be made via Rathbone's to the Company's account in Manchester.

I am beginning to find my way about and to understand some words of the language.

I expect to find suitable lodgings soon.

With my highest regards to you, Sir, and Mrs McFarlane and with best wishes for the Christmas season,

I remain, yours, etc.,

P. Kennedy

Patrick was painstaking in his duties and over the next four years he built up a successful import business for his employer who appreciated his efforts and rewarded him well.

As for his social life, he and his Irish friend O'Fallon, set up together in a rented house in the city close to the church of St Catarina with a good view of the port and the estuary. O'Fallon was a flashier character than Patrick and liked the ladies. There was plenty of company to be had and the two young men were not short of amusement.

They gravitated towards the small Irish community in the city and joined its Irish Club where they spent many a long night complaining about the English and fantasising about a free Ireland. Patrick told and re-told the story of his father's death at the hands of the Highland soldiers and swore that if he ever had occasion he would have his revenge and kill every Englisman he met.

De Melo had an only daughter, Maria, who used to come into the office to see her father from time to time. She had been a pretty girl of fourteen when Patrick had first arrived in the city but now, three years later, she had turned into a real beauty. With long dark hair shaped into ringlets; beautifully smooth olive skin and a long back, Maria had a teasing nature and often remarked to her father at the way that Patrick turned back to his papers whenever she tried to make conversation with him.

Patrick fell for her at once but knew that he would never be able to make her his own. De Melo must have other ideas about his daughter's future that did not include her marriage to one of the clerks in his office. But as time went on Patrick became less shy and they made firm friends. It was only much later that they both realised that their relationship had turned into mutual love and that they would have to tackle Maria's father together.

When they told him that they wanted to get married he said: "Do you take me for a fool. I am not blind. I have known for ages that you two are in love. We'll have to see what we can do about it." Six months later they were married.

In due course Patrick extended his sales activities further into the Viceroyalty and even visited Montevideo in Portugal's Banda Oriental on the opposite side of the estuary.

Although Patrick stayed clear of the complicated politics of the country it was impossible to ignore the growing tension between those who were Iberian-born and held all the important administrative and government positions and those who were native born and preferred to owe their allegiance to La Plata rather than the distant King of Spain on the other side of the Atlantic.

When war finally broke out between Great Britain and France, the situation became acute with Spain taking France's side.

Patrick found it increasingly difficult carrying on his business as local Spanish officials demanded higher import taxes for British goods. Customers cancelled their orders on receiving rumours that British vessels were being attacked by Spanish ships and their precious goods were being either re-sold or thrown overboard.

One afternoon in June 1806, Patrick sat at his desk in his office, pen poised to write a letter to Mr. McFarlane advising him that it was no longer possible to continue and that Ashton's should close the agency.

It was a stifling day and Patrick had his office windows opened wide to catch the passing breeze.

He could hear the usual sounds and bustle of the street outside: voices calling, carts creaking on their axles and pots and pans being burnished. Then he heard a noise, quite unlike any other he had heard since he had arrived on the South American continent.

It was a high pitched, squealing kind of sound. At first he thought it must be a funeral procession leaving St Catherine's church, but it appeared to be getting louder and coming closer.

Then, Patrick recognised a tune emerging. He had heard it once before being played on the pipes of the 71st as they had settled down for the night in their bivouacs after the killing of his father in Ireland.

> 'Hey, Johnnie Cope, are ye waking yet,
> Or are your drums beating yet,
> If you were waking I would wait,
> To gang your coals in the morning............'

He rose from his desk and leaned out of the window. A minute later around the corner and into the street marched twelve pipers dressed in full highland uniform, followed by a column of kilted soldiers, their bayonets glinting in the sun led by their officers with drawn swords.

It was impossible! How had these skirted demons from Patrick's past re-appeared and what on earth were they doing here?

During the time of the two British invasions Patrick kept a low profile but his hatred of the interlopers increased. He witnessed the first defeat of the City's volunteers when many of them were ruthlessly hunted down. It gave him immense satisfaction when the second British invasion failed and their whole force was taken captive before being deported back to England.

However, although Patrick remained optimistic, the occupation had had a devastating effect on trade, When the British had finally left, Patrick wrote a long letter to Mr. McFarlane at Ashton's Mill.

August 1807
43, Cordoba
Buenos Aires

Sir,
You will have heard of the recent troubl?s that we have been through out here. Trade has been completely disrupted. I fear that the peoples struggle for freedom will be long and hard as there are many competing factions amongst this herd of mechanics – as one returning British officer has described the inhabitants of this city. Factions include those born in-country and those born in the Peninsular; those who favour independence and a democratic future and those who wish for the security blanket of imperial rule; those of one race and class and those of many including Mesquites and Gauchos. However, I believe that the people of La Plata will achieve their independence before very long. There is already talk of the declaration of a Republic ruled by an elected Junta.

In spite of this I am expecting trade to recover quickly and that the citys main export staples of hides, live donkeys and dried beef will grow fast. Our Nation with its command of the high seas will soon have the largest share of imports and I think that our business -with your support in Manchester – can quickly recover and expand beyond cotton goods into general merchandise that will include fertilizer, ironware and machinery. I shall send you my detailed plans for expansion next month.

259

Meanwhile, I have news of a personal nature. I asked Mr. De Melo for the hand of his only daughter Maria, who graciously accepted to become my wife and we shall be married at Christmas after what has been a most traumatic time for us all out here. My future father in law continues to insist that Ashton's should share his offices and this gives us advantages over our competitors.

I remain, Sir, etc.'

However, Patrick's father-in-law had other plans. "Well, Patrick", De Melo said one morning, "You are now a full member of the family and its trading empire. It's time for you to spread your wings. I propose that you take charge of our business with the United States in addition to your work here for Ashton's. I have written to Mr. Thomas and he has agreed that the two roles go well together: my network of agents throughout South America and Ashton's access to capital and trade goods. This continent is going to become a place where fortunes are made.

I have a good friend in Baltimore", De Melo went on, "a lawyer by the name of John Skinner, who has been our corresponding agent for some years now. I want you to meet him. One of our vessels is leaving next week and you and Maria will be on board. I have written to Skinner and he will be expecting you in his office when you land. Baltimore is the centre of US trade and he will make the necessary introductions for you. Bring me back some good agency contracts and Maria and you will have the house you have both dreamed of."

A week later the couple left for Baltimore.

Patrick's career in John Skinner's office had flourished and he and his wife Maria had not gone back to Buenos Aires. He had trained in the law in his spare time and was now the commercial partner in the practice with responsibility for a number of highly profitable agencies. He had also become a man of property owning a fine house on Beaufort Avenue in the city.

"Patrick looks after our commercial work", Skinner said, turning to Cochrane. "His dislike of the British equals my own. We both hate you and your race and the last thing we want here are British uniforms in Baltimore.

We had quite enough of that during the war, so don't expect a warm welcome from us or any special favours. I respect Lord Holland as a democrat but that's as far as it goes. What on earth you are doing sailing on the *Yankee* I can't imagine. Deacon loathes the British as much as I do."

"I am very well aware of your feelings against us", Cochrane replied. "Perhaps it would help if I make plain that my first loyalty is to my native Scotland, the place of my birth. I have ordered my men to stay on board and only come ashore for essential supplies. They are not in uniform and we do not serve the Crown. I don't want any trouble. However, before I left England Lord Holland advised me that he has been in communication with you and that you are aware of our reason for being here.

What I have to say is, of course, highly confidential and if anything of what I am about to tell you gets out, we are finished. I believe that your opposite number in London, Edward Hazell, has placed spies on this side of the Atlantic and will do his utmost to frustrate our plans.

I understand that Lord Holland has given you the broad outline of what we intend", Cochrane went on, "and I am here to provide the detail. We plan to rescue Napoleon from St Helena and bring him to the Americas. As you will be aware, his brother Lucien is already on his way across the Atlantic and the emperor can join him if he wishes. Alternatively, there are those in South America who wish him to be appointed the leader of their newly liberated territories. His final destination can be decided when he is a free man again.

I have studied the conditions on St Helena; they are amongt the most hostile in the world. Fierce and continual winds blow from all directions; the coastline is rugged with very few accessible beaches from which a rescue can be made and all of which are overlooked by steep cliffs. No ship can get close inshore.

I have decided that the only possible way to bring Napoleon off will be by submarine. The craft will be launched from the *The Damned Yankee* which will be standing well out to sea. The submarine will proceed inshore and get as close to the beach as possible. The emperor will be rowed out to it.

A landward party will be responsible for snatching the emperor from the house where he is imprisoned and bringing him to the coast. The submarine's landing party will meet him at the beach and remove him from the island. Both of these groups have an intimate knowledge of the island and all the circumstances of the emperor's conditions.

Mr. Birmingham, here, has only lately left the island and has the most up to date information about the emperor's guards and their movements. I have an ex- comrade who served with me for many years who is now in command of one of the Navy's ships guarding the island. He will divert the attention of the squadron whilst the escape is taking place.

Our main purpose in being here in Baltimore is to seek your support in negotiating with the engineer Robert Fulton for the use of his submarine the *Nautilus*. I understand that you are in contact with him and that he will listen to you. He has resisted direct communications with us. I understand that he fell out with the British Government over the value of his invention", Cochrane ended.

"Not so fast", Skinner said. "I tried to do business with him six months ago but he rejected my efforts. He is an impossible man who has a grossly inflated idea of what his invention is worth which he believes is a great deal more than anyone is ever likely to pay. However, you may have deeper pockets than the rest of us. Do you wish me to contact him on your behalf and invite him to join us down here?"

"We would appreciate that very much, thank you."

"Very well. Kennedy will draft a letter which I will dispatch to Fulton. What sum should I mention for his co-operation?"

"Lord Holland has made substantial funds available. How do you think he would respond to an opening offer of £25,000 for the hire of his submarine?", Cochrane said.

"We can try, but I should warn you that Fulton is not reasonable and has defeated greater men than you. He turned down £150,000 in Paris from the Emperor himself. Meanwhile, whilst we wait for his response, you and your team should keep a low profile. In order to impress Fulton, I will send Kennedy up to New York to deliver your offer in person. He has an Irishman's way with words."

That evening a copy of Skinner's letter to Fulton in New York was sent to Cochrane on board the *Yankee*.

Two days later a clerk from Skinner's office delivered a note that confirmed that Fulton had agreed to come to Baltimore in three day's time.

After Fulton had left Skinner's offices, Patrick Kennedy and Alan Birmingham sat in Kennedy's office reviewing its outcome. They both agreed that Cochrane had played a superb hand.

"I never thought to see it", Patrick said. "An American embracing a Britisher. The way the His Lordship ignored the jibes and just leaned over the map table and started a very detailed discussion about the

Nautilus; its construction and capabilities. He had Fulton eating out of his hand. And at the end when he said to Fulton 'this is the most advanced piece of nautical engineering I have ever seen', I knew he had won Fulton over completely. Shaking hands on the price was just a formality.

Mr. Skinner has instructed me to draw up a contract for the hire of the *Nautilus* that will include the training of a crew off the *Yankee* and the use of the submarine at sea. 50% of the fees will be due when the submarine is loaded onto the American schooner back in New York and the balance when the operation has been completed successfully.

A bond for the full value of the vessel in the event of its loss is to be lodged with the First Pennsylvania Bank in Pittsburgh that includes a payment to Fulton which will make him a very rich man for the rest of is life. I understand that Lord Holland has already remitted the sums required. He must have some very wealthy backers.

Mr. Skinner has instructed me to come with you on the expedition, first to see that the contract is discharged under its terms - our good name is involved here - and second, because I have lived in Buenos Airies and know the region well. This will be helpful to his Lordship and he has agreed to having me on board."

Cochrane was impatient to be off and twenty-four hours later the *Yankee* left Baltimore's harbour and set off back up the coast again. They reached Fulton's yard in New York where the *Nautilus* was loaded onto *The Damned Yankee* and lashed to the deck at dead of night disguised as cargo. Then they sailed south again into the Chesapeake. Here Deacon found a deserted stretch of coast with a beach that Birmingham confirmed was similar to St Helena's shoreline and practice landings began.

They started with simple exercises by raising the *Nautilus* from the deck and lowering it over the ship's side into the water below. Then its crew practiced scrambling down nets and entering and leaving the submarine. Next the crew worked the craft around the schooner over and over again until they were expert at driving and steering it.

A party that included Birmingham and Kennedy went ashore and the submarine set in as close as possible before a canvas dinghy was erected on its deck and a member of the crew rowed it ashore. Birmingham acted as Napoleon and was rowed back out to the submarine and climbed inside through the hatch before it returned to the schooner's side.

When Cochrane and Deacon were satisfied with these basic manoeuvres, the *Yankee* left the shoreline and went further out to sea. At first the landing process was practised by day as the ship moved further and further away from the beach. Then they practised their first night landing.

Birmingham and Kennedy were left ashore before nightfall and as the daylight faded watched the *Yankee* disappear over the horizon. It was a still night and they felt very alone.

Two hours later when it was quite dark except for the dim light of the distant stars, they first heard the sound of the dipping of the oars of the small canvas boat as it approached the beach. They ran down to the sea's edge and helped to haul it in. A sailor stepped out onto the beach and shook hands.

"Come aboard and I'll row the first of you back to the submarine." A few minutes later Birmingham could see the outline of the *Nautilus*'s cigar shape. When they were alongside he clambered onto its deck and through its hatch. Another crew member had stayed inside and instructed Birmingham how to sit on the seat amidships and turn the handle that would drive the propeller on the outside. Kennedy came next. It took forty minutes of hard effort to get back to the *Yankee*.

As Birmingham came back on deck he was met by Lord Cochrane. "Debriefing in my cabin in five minutes."

When Birmingham and Kennedy entered the cabin Cochrane and Deacon were standing side by side looking at charts.

Cochrane turned around. "Tell us what it was like." Birmingham replied: "It was fine but it was not realistic. The conditions at sea and on the beach on St Helena are very different. The weather comes in continuously; the sea is choppy and it would be almost impossible to land, let alone re-embark."

"We know that. It has just got to be done", Cochrane responded. "We are going to wait here until the weather changes for the worse - the glass is lowering - and then we will be able to practise under much harsher conditions."

The weather did indeed change for the worse; the wind blew a gale that whipped up the waves into white horses. Even launching the *Nautilus* became hazardous as she swung to and fro on her davits whilst being lowered into the water and there was a danger that she would be smashed against the sides of the *Yankee*.

However, both Cochrane and Deacon were adamant that the practice landings should continue and after a day and a night of inactivity, launchings were resumed. Birmingham took his turn again in the submarine and it was agreed that he would be a member of the crew who would land on the beach when the actual rescue was made.

The next night's landing was the most terrifying to date.

It was a dark night and the sea was still rough. The *Nautilus* was launched at eleven o'clock and Birmingham, Kennedy with two other crew went over the side and scrambled down the ship's nets.

As Birmingham reached the deck of the submarine a wave came over its side and he would have lost his footing if he had not grabbed a sheet attached to its mast. He steadied himself and crawled towards the conning tower before lowering himself into the cabin. Kennedy followed him on board.

The submarine moved away from the mother ship but the crew found it almost impossible to steer as the wind drove *Nautilus* away from the direction of the shore. Eventually, they managed to turn her into the wind and they set off again towards the beach.

As they approached they could hear the rollers breaking on the shore fifty yards away from inside the submarine. They were anxious that they would be driven sideways onto the beach by the wind before they had a chance to step up out of the conning tower and launch its canvas dinghy over the side.

Once they were outside on deck, the two crewmen held the *Nautilus* at right angles to the beach whilst Birmingham knelt unsteadily to erect the dinghy. The wind was stiffening and he could hardly see the shore. He and Kennedy took up the two oars and began to row towards the beach. The wind kept pulling them to port but they hung on and with great effort drove the fragile dinghy onto the sand.

They pulled it up the beach and looked around for a piece of rock that would represent Napoleon's weight in the dinghy in addition to their own. The rock would also prove to Cochrane that they had actually landed. They hauled the dinghy back down to the water's edge before putting to sea; rowing back out to the *Nautilus* and setting off again to the schooner.

The two men clambered up the *Yankee's* netting and hauled themselves onto the deck. The first thing they saw above them were Cochrane's seaboots.

"You took your time, where have you been?"

Birmingham straightened before replying: "The sea conditions are very bad in-shore. You can't tell from here just how rough it is in the breaking waves. We almost turned over and I had great difficulty beaching the dinghy. We are going to need a lot of luck for the whole thing to be remotely possible."

"Don't talk like a woman, Of course, it's possible. We just have to keep our nerve. I want you in the *Nautilus* on the night of the rescue. Napoleon knows you and you will be able to reassure him that we are his rescuers. Going in there will be you two and two crew. Coming off there will be five of you. Will you all be able to fit in?"

"I think so although it will be a tight squeeze", Birmingham replied.

"You had both better go below and dry off. We will do another couple of nights landing practice and then that will have to do. We need to move South again now to make our rendezvous at La Plata which will our jumping off point for St Helena."

Birmingham and Kennedy took part in two more night landings both of which were carried out in poor sea conditions but by this time they had become more confident sailors and more efficient at managing the *Nautilus*.

They sailed south again and made their first landfall in South America at Bahia on the Brazilian coast where they picked up fresh supplies. They would not put in to either Montevideo or Buenos Aires for security reasons but would wait at the mouth of the estuary until a message that the rescue operation should commence was received from St Helena.

This would be done by fast packet out of Jamestown using a pre-arranged code supplied to Cochrane by Marryat. British spies had been reported in both cities and it was too risky for them to be seen tied up in either port.

"How long are we likely to be here?", Birmingham remarked one morning two weeks later.

"I have no idea whatsoever," Cochrane replied. "We are entirely in Marryat's hands now. He will have to judge when the conditions on the island and at sea are most suitable. We need reasonable conditions at sea and and at least a quarter moon rising above the island to get onto the beach. But more important, the security situation on the island and around Longwood needs to be right.

I understand that there will be a change to the duties of the guard parties sometime in September and that your friend Reardon will alert Marryat to their revised schedule. We will be ready to strike then. Meanwhile, we will need to be patient."

16 *Captain Piontkowski's room*

THE SECURITY SITUATION on the island had worsened significantly.

Goldie noticed that he was doing less and less barracks work and was becoming increasingly involved in internal security duties.

Patrols had been stepped up on Governor Lowe's orders. Random sweeps of the island were now a regular occurrence day and night. Reardon dropped into the 66th's operations room almost every day. He took a keen interest in what was going on that included volunteering for extra duties whenever these were on offer. Goldie thought that this was admirable. Perhaps it was Reardon's way of dealing with the extreme boredom of their circumstances unless there was a more sinister reason.

Goldie also noticed that the guard parties were being changed on a more frequent basis than before and wondered at the reason.

"The Governor is concerned that there should be no fraternisation whatsoever on the fenceline at Longwood", his friend Baird, the Adjutant, reported. "The exchanges are becoming intolerable as the men purchase small items of snuff and liquor from the servants at Longwood. At the same time the men are becoming rebellious because their free time is being continuously interrupted. They can't plan their leisure.

The word from the Governor's office is that he is becoming more erratic and domineering as the opposition to Napoleon's captivity increases both on and off the island.

By the way, Reade spoke to me the other day about your friend Reardon. He thinks there is something funny going on up at Mason's Stock House with those new-born Christians and, as you know, he hates the Navy. Reade thinks they're a bunch of revolutionaries. He believes it's the influence of the lower-deck. You had better get up there and find out what's going on. And, while you're there, take a good look around the perimeter.

The 44th are on duty this week. It's their first time on the fence. They only arrived into Jamestown two weeks ago and they are new to this game. We don't want any incidents between our men and theirs. I have met their commander, Major Dunne. He has campaign experience but seems a little naive about what we are up against here. His men look solid enough. They have come via Washington and the Peninsular."

A visit to Mason's Stock House and Longwood would be a good opportunity for Goldie to carry out some discreet reconnaissance on Edward's behalf. He was due to make his next report to London.

There was another reason for him to visit up there. For some time now he had been pursuing Robinson's daughter Elizabeth, the Nymph, who was without doubt the prettiest female on the island. She had first come to his notice at a race day on Deadwood Plain. The Regiment had constructed a rough course outside the barracks and now held regular meetings. As a keen rider Goldie had quickly become one of the foremost competitors at the races. He had won a number of events riding Dolly and Regent, two hacks brought over from the Cape. He had met Elizabeth at one of these and was smitten at once. She was tall, fair and had a mysterious air about her. She was housekeeper to her widowed father. It was rumoured that Napoleon himself had taken a shine to her. She was certainly attractive enough to warrant his attention. When Goldie heard about Napoleon's interest he was determined to compete for her.

Since their first meeting Goldie had taken any and every opportunity to impress her. They had danced together at a number of the soirees held at The Briars which were usually attended by Napoleon and his suite. After one of these, Elizabeth had finally agreed that Goldie could call upon her up at Hutt's Gate, her father's farm. Since then he had been a regular visitor.

Although the nightly curfew forbade anyone to be out of barracks without a lesse-pass, Major Lascelles and the 66th were both pleased and envious of the young beau's success. Goldie was able to obtain special permission to be out at night on a regular basis.

The Nymph welcomed his attention, but whilst there was no more good looking officer on the island than Goldie, there were many of more senior rank. As a result, she continued to hold out from his advances and still enjoyed flirting with the other officers of the garrison. Goldie believed himself to be in love and expressed only honourable intentions when he and the girl were alone together.

The path from Deadwood Camp to Elizabeth's home ran directly past Mason's so he could combine business with pleasure.

Goldie borrowed a charger and set off for Mason's. It was a chilly day with a strong wind blowing from the Antarctic that was whipping the sea into white horses to the horizon. He did not envy the sailors out on the guard vessels. He reached the house and knocked on the front door. A few minutes later it was half-opened by a somewhat dishevelled looking Theo Reardon.

"Good to see you Goldie", Reardon greeted him, frowning. "What are you doing up here? I thought you were deskbound."

"I needed a breath of air", replied Goldie, "and Baird wanted me to have a look at how the 44th are getting on. It's some time since I was up at Longwood. Are you well? Is anything the matter? And, by the way, how is poor Grant? I know you said that you don't expect him to live for much longer. This weather can't be helping him much."

Reardon didn't just look surprised to see him, there was something more about his reaction that Goldie felt was strange. He appeared evasive. Goldie wondered if there was anything else going on up here.

"Why don't you come across to Longwood with me? We can look around together", Goldie said, as he edged his way inside the house. Grant was lying on a chaise-longue in the parlour covered in a thick rug. "How are you, Old Man?", Goldie asked. The young man looked pale and could hardly raise his head. "Oh, as well as can be expected", Grant replied, as a fit of coughing wracked his body. "Reardon and I are going to take a look at Longwood, any messages for Boney?", Goldie asked. "None at present", the Midshipman replied, "but you can tell him I'd rather be with him in the sunshine on Elba."

Reardon, now fully dressed and armed with a pistol tucked into his belt, came and stood at Goldie's side. "What do you want with that?", Grant asked him. "You're not going to shoot Napoleon are you? Up here we pray for his release."

"We had better get moving", Goldie said to Reardon, "or we will miss the changing of the guard. Good to see you Grant. I hope you are feeling better the next time we meet."

Goldie and Reardon left the house together, Reardon leading the way. It took around fifteen minutes walking over rough ground to reach the perimeter at Longwood. Reardon had brought his spy glass. He would try and fulfil his daily duty to Govenor Lowe by having sight of Napoleon.

"Look", he said, a few minutes later, "there he is", and handed the instrument to Goldie.

Goldie took the glass, and raising it to his eyes, quickly found Napoleon at its centre. He was standing in the garden looking, it seemed, directly at them. He was not on his own, however, but was leaning heavily on the arm of a huge man whom Goldie knew to be

Piontkowski, his personal ADC, bodyguard and general factotum at Longwood House.

The Polish Lancer had been by Napoleon's side for at least eight years. He had insisted on accompanying Napoleon into exile on the *Northumberland* – in spite of his recent marriage - attaching himself limpet-like to Napoleon from the first day of their arrival on St Helena. He was known for his utter devotion to his master and for his vile temper - he reacted violently to any implied slight to his hero's honour. He had recently got into a fight in Jamestown over a remark some soldiers had made as they passed him by.

It was now rumoured that Lowe wanted Piontkowski removed from St Helena. Blakeny, the Orderly Officer at Longwood, found him quite impossible to deal with and often complained that he could not fulfil his duties at Longwood because of Piontkowski's antics.

Napoleon now appeared to raise his arm in a gesture of acknowledgement of the two officers before turning to go inside the house, leaning heavily on Piontkowski.

Goldie had been told that the Pole, in addition to his personal duties, was one of a number of Napoleon's household who were helping him to write his memoires. Piontkowski spoke several languages and Napoleon used him as a writer. He also had an excellent memory for facts and could recall some of the key events in Napoleon's career. Napoleon was fond of him and valued him for his simple-mindedness and romantic character.

Blakeny reported that five desks had been set up in the billiard room and that the household staff had each been allocated a part of the emperor's story which he dictated to them each day.

It was well known that justifying his actions had always been an absolute priority for Napoleon since being made prisoner. Now it occupied all of his waking hours, that is when he was not in his bath or in bed. He believed that this record would be his gift to posterity and an enduring legacy to his greatness.

The record started in the days of his first Consulship in 1800 but its main sections were concentrated with the military triumphs that made him the master of the Continent of Europe: the battles of Austerlitz, Jena and Marengo. Piontowski had been given the final part of the story, the years 1810 to 1815, when Napoleon's distrastrous campaign in Russia had cost him his empire and his position after the annihilation of the Grande Armee on the retreat from Moscow.

Piontowski was a good choice for this section as he had been a member of Napoleon's personal bodyguard throughout the Russian campaign. The Pole had intimate knowledge of all that had happened there. The invasion of Russia had been the lancer's realisation of a long-held dream for a free and independent Poland guaranteed by France. This would be realised after the defeat of Czar Alexander's vast and ramshackle empire.

"Piontowski, where did we get to yesterday?"

"You had just described your triumph at Smolensk, Sire, after we had crossed the Niemen into Russia. Kutozov's First Army had retreated along the Borowski road in complete disorder towards Moscow before we met them again at Borodino."

"Ah yes, Smolensk. I should have realised what the Russians would do next. As they retreated they burned the city to the ground and left behind them on the road east a ruined and smoking land. They burned all of their crops, windmills, bridges, fodder and grain stores and killed all their livestock as they went.

My army had enough rations for twenty-four days when we crossed the Nieman into Russia as my plan was that our troops would be able to live off the land. I aimed to take Moscow within weeks. Instead our men suffered from typhus fever and began to die in the heat and dust. They had to drink their own urine and a thousand horses died each day.

I couldn't believe that the Russians would deliberately set out to destroy their own land and its people but the burning of Smolensk should have been a warning to me. Of course, I could have had no idea that they would do the same in their precious capital, Moscow.

Then there was Borodino", Naploeon went on. "It was a dreadful business. The bloodiest battle in which I was ever involved. That Kutosov was often an old fool but he played a good hand that day. Those stone redoubts that he built in the centre of the battlefield were a damned nuisance and cost us over 28,0000 casualties. Some say that it was all my fault for not releasing the Imperial Guard into the assault when I should have done, but I wanted them in reserve until I was sure that our flanks could not be turned.

As you know, Piontkowski, I was not feeling myself at the time. I gave my marshalls far too much discretion. Two days later, and after we had cleared the battlefield, I first saw on the horizon the glow of the fires started in Moscow. That madman Alexander had set his capital on fire."

Napoleon paused. "I think we will stop now, I don't feel quite myself this morning."

Perhaps Napoleon had been reminded that he had been struck down by an attack of dysentery on the morning of Borodino. He had spent most of the day sitting on a stool in his tent shitting into a bucket.

"Very well, Sire. Shall I prepare a hot bath?"

"Thank you, Piontowski."

This was happening more and more frequently. Although the ex-emperor claimed that he was only suffering from the inevitable aches and pains of a life-time of campaigning, Piontowski was increasingly worried that his master was not at all well.

Since O'Meara's departure a series of garrison doctors were appointed by Lowe to be responsible for Napoleon's health. The Governor believed that the prisoner's ailments were imaginary and that Napoleon was deliberately exaggerating them as a way to attract the sympathy which would lead to his repatriation to Europe.

The British doctors reported that Napoleon was suffering from no more than occasional bouts of indigestion, but there were other opinions about what might be wrong. These included that Napoleon was suffering from gall stones, hepatitis, gout, scurvy or haemorrhoids.

When Napoleon was not giving dictation he was in his bath where it seemed he was most comfortable. It was Piontkowski's job to keep him supplied with hot water for hours at a time. The ship's carpenter of the *Northumberland*, Mr. Cooper, had made Napoleon a book rest during the voyage to St Helena so that he could read comfortably in his cabin. This was now positioned across the bath to hold his books and papers. As Piontowski entered with a fresh can of water, Napoleon covered his extended stomach with a wash cloth. The Pole noticed that Napoleon's ankles were swollen and that he was holding his right side as if in pain.

"Bring your notebook in here, I want to go on."

"As we approached Moscow the Grande Armee's condition deteriorated further", Napoleon continued. "The weather remained unseasonable. Baking sun was followed by heavy rain. Men and horses continued to die in their hundreds. We had to get to Moscow quickly before the Russians destroyed the whole city and all of its supplies.

It was inevitable, I suppose, that when we arrived the men would go wild and take their revenge for their troubles. For a week, the army behaved like a pack of wild animals as they raced around looting the city. Officers' chargers became pack horses and their carriages became vehicles for transporting plunder. The men raided the wardrobes of every fine house in Moscow and roamed the streets dressed in a motley assortment of civilian clothing. They abandoned their arms and ammunition and filled their knapsacks with valuables instead.

Discipline broke down completely. My abiding memory is of the appalling stench in the air from a combination of burning timbers and cooked horsemeat as the army ate its only way home.

In October the weather changed dramatically for the worse with day after day of feezing rain and, with no hope of defeating the Russians or of surviving a winter in Moscow, I had to give the order to retreat. We would cross back over the Niemen and spend the winter in Dresden before attacking again in the spring.

Now, have you got all that down? Read it back to me."

"Yes, Sire, I have it but could I suggest a slight change?"

"What is it?"

"I think that Your Highness would perhaps like to include something about the bravery and endurance of your men on the retreat?"

"Of course, of course, Piontkowski, what do you suggest?"

"Well, something along these lines.

"The road to the west was blocked by dead men and horses", Piontowski began, "as the Grand Armee began its retreat and all about us were broken tree stumps, dead bodies, discarded weapons, swords, saddles, chests and empty suitcases: the detritus of a retreating army. The men were soon starving and left the line of march to hack pieces of meat from the dead. When horseflesh was no longer available, they took to cannibalism.

They used anything they could find for firewood and tore down the beams of the few remaining barns left standing to build their cooking fires. This meant there was soon no shelter to be found anywhere along the route and men died each night under open skies at temperatures of -30c.

In the morning they dragged themselves awake and stepped over the faces, arms and legs of both the living and the dead, many of whom bore the signs of torture and mutilation. The weather was atrocious with bitter and violent storms and winds, icy rain and snow so thick they could not see in front of their eyes.

Meanwhile small bands of Cossacks harassed the retreating army continually and, as men fell behind, the Cossacks would surround the stragglers and cut them off before slashing them to death from the saddle. Anyone left alive dragged themselves painfully after the retreating columns staining the snow with their blood and crying out for help.

We lancers formed small groups of cavalry and did our best to head off the enemy attacks but for each man we saved, thirty more were slaughtered. The men left alive began to look like ghouls; their feet wrapped in rags; their uniforms torn beyond recognition and their greatcoats tied with string.

Typically, a man's head was wrapped in a filthy cloth; his nose was almost frozen off; his ears covered in wounds and a number of his fingers and thumbs missing. But through all this, they never lost the love of their leader and emperor so that whenever he appeared beside them, they still shouted Vive l'Emperor!"

Pionykowski paused for a moment as he recalled the ghastly scenes that he had witnessed day after day. By the time the retreating army had reached the Berezina, the last obstacle before the frontier, the Grand Armee and its allies whose army had originally numbered over 450,000 men had now been reduced to fewer than 40,000.

"Enough, enough, Piontkowski. I never saw anthing as bad as that but we escaped, after all."

"We did indeed, Sire, but only thanks to those brave Swiss engineers who, up to their necks in the half frozen river, built the pontoons over the Berezina across which we could reach safety. Even so, many of the men who had reached that far were drowned in the crossing when sections of the pontoons collapsed. As you will recall, Sire, you left for Dresden soon afterwards in your carriage and we were back in the city by the end of December."

Piontowski was reminded of Napoleon's escape escorted only by a small party of Polish Lancers which had been attacked by Cossack bands again and again. One night during the flight, Naploeon had shown him a phial of poison hung on a ribbon around his neck.

"I shall never be taken alive.", he had told Piontowski.

Since first setting foot on St Helena, Napoleon had maintained a strict policy that he would never contemplate escape and that he would only ever leave the island on his release from imprisonment by the Allies and in the full dress uniform of a marshall of the Grande Armee.

Whenever Piontowski, or any other member of the suite, had raised the subject, they had been sharply rebuked by Napoleon and Piontowski appreciated just how sensitive a subject the idea was to his master. Napoleon remained very uncomfortable when he recalled the humiliation of his escape from Russia. His reputation in France had never recovered from the defeat. Worse than that, his soldiers, who he called *Mes enfants* and who he had led to victory on so many glorious occasions, never fully trusted him again.

As a way to remind Napoleon that escape nevertheless remained an option, Piontowski decided to ask Napoleon to tell the story of his escape from Elba and his triumphant return to power in early 1815.

"Oh, that.

I would never have been sent to Elba if it had not been for that traitor Marmont who betrayed me when he transferred his allegiance and the men of my, *my*, army to Blucher and the Allies.

I was left with no option but to agree to become the monarch of that tin-pot island. They made me Elba's sovereign for life - damned insult after the continents that I had conquered. Who did they think I was?

It became clear that I would not be their prisoner for long. Once my people had experienced those awful Bourbons for a few months I began to receive emissaries begging me to return to France and take up my role once more. When it became clear that support was growing daily I set about organising my departure.

You were with me then, weren't you, Piontowski?"

"Yes, Sire, I was and privileged to be so. There were over one hundred of your faithful Lancers on the island and we all followed you to the boats when they arrived. I shall never forget our little flotilla setting out from Ajaccio. It was a stroke of luck that the island's Governor was away on private business. They say it was a romantic assignment. More fool him."

"Yes, well, it all worked out for us", Napoleon said. "We escaped and when we reached Frejus, my old comrades soon gathered around me once more. France awaited me and my soldiers acclaimed me and shouted 'Paris or die!'. That was a glorious time."

Now, with no permanent improvement in Napoleon's health, perhaps the time was right for Piontowski to broach the subject of escape again.

"You know, Sire, that we could do the same thing here. Your supporters on this island and in Europe are increasing every day. I know that you have spoken with some English officers who are sympathetic to your cause and that the message from London that you received in the chessman can be acted upon as soon as you give the signal."

Napoleon sighed.

"You have reminded me, Piontowski, of my past good fortune which seems to have deserted me. You have used the word 'escape'

281

which I have forbidden in my hearing but, if I am not to die in this God-forsaken place, we will now have to trust Lord Holland to get us out of here.

We had better speak to that British officer who I met at that picnic up at Mason's and who used the code word for eacape. I saw him with another officer on the fence-line the other day. The next time we see him to speak to, we will tell him that we will make ourselves ready."

"Very well, Sire, we will find a reason to meet with him and see what he has to say. It will need to be done as soon as possible and you will wish to prepare yourself. There will be some physical exertion required to cross the island as rescue can only be made by ship at the coast."

Napoleon called for another jug of hot water which Piontowski fetched before going to his own room and, sitting on the side of his bed, thought about how those officers would organise the escape itself. It would be very risky indeed for all of those involved. Governor Lowe would be ruthless in his pursuit. He would take no prisoners.

Piontowski took Napoleon into the garden twice a day for the next four days before he spotted the English officer that he knew as Captain Reardon from the picnic at Mason's.

"You are using me as bait", Napoleon said to Piontkowksi after three days.

"I know, Sire, but we have to lure him out to make contact with us and the circumstances have to be exactly right. He needs to be alone or only that Irish sergeant of his with him. We can't trust anyone else. There is a new regiment on duty and they know nothing of the way that we have developed our connections with the guard parties of the 66th. We certainly can't rely on the new men to keep their mouths shut. Timing will be critical. It will have to look completely co-incidental."

Piontowski walked Napoleon up, down and around the garden each morning as close to the fence as they could get and on the fourth day saw Reardon approaching. The 66th. were doing duty so there was less risk of exposure. The officer was accompanied by a party of Pioneers. They were carrying posts and rails and began to repair a short length of the fence that had been slightly damaged.

Piontowski watched Reardon and the working party from out of the corner of his eye. After fifteen minutes he noticed that Reardon was now standing on his own and a little apart from his men. He led Napoleon over to where the officer stood. Napoleon spoke first.

"Good morning, Sir. We have not seen you up here for a few days. I trust that you have been well."

Reardon bowed from the waist and replied: "Very well, your Excellency, and you?"

"Oh, well enough, thank you. I have been thinking about what you spoke of on the last occasion that we met. I have been thinking of *Angouleme* and where you might have stayed in the city."

"If I remember correctly, your Excellency, we stayed at the *Lion D'Or*. But we spent as little time as possible there and *escaped* into the country as soon as we were able."

"How sensible. I wish I could do the same but I see no way out of here", Napoleon replied.

"I am sure that if this is what you desire there are those who can help you", Reardon responded. "If you will trust me and my fellow sympathisers, we can arrange for your escape. We have had word from our colleagues in England and in the Argentine. They are ready to set off as soon we give the signal.

It will not be without risk but our plans are well advanced both on the island and out at sea. The less you know at Longwood the better for all of us as if any word of this reaches Governor Lowe's ears we will hang."

"I quite understand. I will be alone with Piontowski here. No other member of my suite will be with me. They will organise some diversionary tactics inside the house to delay the English finding out for as long as possible that I have escaped."

"Excellent, Sire. I will now confer with my friends on the island. We will speak again together when our plans are fully prepared. It will be an escape by night across the island by foot so you will need to be ready for that."

Napoleon bobbed his head and said; "Thank you Captain. We will await your next contact. In the meantime, I wish you well." With these words he turned on his heel and, helped by Piontowski, resumed his walk.

"What was all that about, Sir", Reardon's sergeant asked as he came up beside his officer.

"What we spoke about is now going to happen. He has agreed at last that he is willing to escape and we are going to help him. It will take a few weeks to organise but the rescue party in Buenos Airies is ready to leave. It's up to us now to arrange the actual break-out. I take it that you are still for the attempt?"

17 *The Corporal's Tunic*

THE CONSPIRATORS MET later in the week. The loathsome Monchenu was out dining with the Governor at Plantation House so they had the snug in the boarding house to themselves.

Reardon spoke first. "I met with Napoleon on Tuesday. He was taking a stroll in the garden. Piontkowski was with him. It looked as if our encounter was deliberate. We only spoke for a few minutes but for the first time Napoleon made it clear that he would be agreeable to an escape. I used the code word *Angouleme* in our discussion again, so there can be no mistaking our intention. I said that we would now alert our friends in London and South America and that I would be in touch with him again as soon as our preparations were completed."

"Excellent", Marryat said. "We now have a lot to do. Our first step will be to alert Lord Cochrane in Buenos Aires and advise him that *The Damned Yankee* should set sail towards St Helena. With decent weather it should take them no more than ten days. I shall give him a rendezvous approximately five miles SSW of Sandy Bay and instruct him to stay just below the horizon until I give him the signal to approach.

From my survey of the coastline, Porteous, and your reports about the security situation on the island's landward side, I judge Sandy Bay to be the most suitable place for the rescue. It is the furthest point on the island from Jamestown and the garrsion stationed there. I know that it means an arduous journey across the island from Longwood to the coast for you Reardon, but at least it will be away from the usual tracks taken by the guard parties. My first step will be to get a message on board a vessel sailing from here to La Plata which can be passed to Cochrane via a merchant in the city who is sympathetic. The message will tell him that we are ready.

I have had word from our friends in London that Cochrane is already anchored offshore in the estuary and awaiting our instructions. When he has confirmed that he is on his way I will find a good reason that my ship should be stationed in the south east sector at the time.

When the *Yankee* approaches the coast, I will send her a signal and then make myself scarce. I can't have my crew implicated. I will invent some reason that we were off-station and failed to spot the schooner as she neared the island. It can be an outbreak of sickness or a broken spar. I will think of something."

"That sounds sensible to me", Reardon replied, "but the main risks are going to be on land as Napoleon leaves Longwood and we take him across the island. We don't dare use horses at night, so the whole journey will have to be made on foot. When I met him in the garden, I thought that Napoleon looked quite ill just as Porteous here has reported. I don't see us being able to move very fast and the hours between darkness falling and dawn breaking will be limited.

Like Marryat, I too have to ensure that my men and I are on duty on the night of the escape. As you know I have been volunteering for extra duties for the past month or two but I don't want to raise further suspicion. My pioneers and I are already being watched by Baird and Goldie."

"That damnned Goldie", Porteous broke in. "He is spending more and more time romancing the Nymph up at Farmer Robinson's at night. Hutts Gate is in a direct line between Longwood and Sandy Bay. We are either going to have to cause a diversion so that he is nowhere near the girl on the night of the escape or eliminate him if he tries to interfere. We can't risk him running into the escape party in the dark.

Another concern is that the path we will be taking up Diana's Peak is very narrow in places with little room for a single person to pass. There will be even less if we have to carry Napoleon which sounds as if we might. It's a real hazard."

"I know, I've been up there to inspect the ground", Reardon said, "and I think we will manage. My sergeant is the strongest man we've got."

"Good", replied Porteous, "It is not going to be easy to co-ordinate the timing of the escape from Longwood with the landing of the submarine off the *Yankee* onto the beach. We will have to allow ourselves some flexibility in our plans. Reardon, I will rendezvous with you at a point to be agreed.

I suggest that it would be best if I do not come onto the fenceline with you; the fewer of us the better at that point. What about I join the escape party at the end of the garden at Mason's Stock House and we can go on from there?"

"That will suit well.", Reardon replied. "As you say, the fewer of us the better but you know the island as well as any of us. I am expecting Napoleon to be alone and that Piontkowski will stay behind to organise some diversionary tactics. He's played that game before and can disguise himself as the emperor again. It won't work for long, but he could win us some valuable time if we get delayed.

My plan is that the guard that night will be drawn from amongst the Pioneers of the 66th. My sergeant is fully briefed. He will be accompanying Napoleon to the rendezvous at Sandy Bay. He has no fears about making a new life abroad. The remainder will feign ignorance and say that the sergeant and I threatened to shoot them.

Napoleon will put on the uniform of a corporal of the 66th which will disguise him a little. I don't expect that patrols will be out during the night on that part of the island. If anything goes wrong, and the alarm is raised, the disguise should pass superficial inspection. Especially if it looks as if the sergeant is helping a drunken comrade home. A lot can go wrong but this is the best plan that I can think of. The main risk is that the piquets of the 44th positioned on either side of us get wind of what is going on and raise the alarm. That's just a chance we have to take."

"Very well", replied Marryat, "I think that's enough for now. I need to send that message to Cochrane. As soon as I hear from him we will meet again to discuss the precise date of the escape and any other last minute arrangements. We are going to need a fair wind behind us for this to work."

With that the meeting broke up and the three men retired to their rooms.

Crauford was as angry about Julia Longdon's treachery as Edward. "You will have to cut her out and at once. I will have no more of this poodling about. Miss Longdon will not see or hear from you again. Do I make myself clear?"

"Yes, Sir, and I am very sorry for what has happenend. What do we do about her brother at the Post Office? Do you think that he may also be involved?"

"I think it is unlikely. The security around Lombard Street is very tight but you had better put him under surveillance and he should not be involved any further in this operation; no more coding of messages and so on."

"Very well, Sir, I will instruct Bow Street and I apologise again for my error of judgement."

Edward left Crauford's office and returned, chastened, to his own. It had been a gross error of judgment and he would be fortunate to keep his job. He could forget any hopes of marriage. He would write a note to Julia's step-father ending their connection. He did not trust himself to write to her directly. That would be the end of it.

It was now clear that the conspiracy reached much further into society than he had imagined. He would have to suspend all of his social relationships until this affair was over.

In the mean time there was much to do. His first task was to respond to Goldie's last dispatch and make certain that his friend was on his guard and alert to the variety of rescue attempts that were likely. Edward would write to Goldie at once.

Six weeks later Goldie received a dispatch from Hazell in London. In the letter, Edward described the events at the theatre and on the Thames; the departure of Cochrane and his liberators from London in *The Rose* and his suspicion that whilst he had no direct news from America, a rescue by sea remained the most likely scenario.

Edward was still trying to obtain more up to date information from his spy in Baltimore but had heard nothing from him in the past three months. It seemed likely that he had been taken by Skinner.

Goldie was to be on his guard and, in particular, should keep Marryat at Mr. Porteous's boarding house and Reardon at Mason's Stock House under as close observation as possible. If he found any evidence of conspiracy between them he was to take his suspicions at once to Sir Thomas Reade at Plantation House who would know what to do with them.

James King, Edward's friend stationed at Greenwich, had put Edward in touch with his counterpart at the Admiralty from whom he had learned that Reade was in secret communication with their Lordships as an alternative conduit to Governor Lowe's reports. This could explain the reason that all the governor's actions were known in London, often before he had communicated them to Bathhurst.

Goldie now spent most of his time at the 66th's headquarters at Deadwood as he and Baird struggled to organise guard duties both around Longwood and right across the island. Lowe demanded more and more of the Regiment's time and the men were becoming exhausted with a number being charged for sleeping at their posts. The Adjutant had pointed this out to Lascelles on several occaions. He had received short shrift. "If any man is found asleep at his post he will be punished most severely. I have advised the governor that the 66th will not be found wanting in this matter. The Regiment will do its duty and I will come down heavily on any officer who fails me."

Goldie was finding it as difficult to keep awake as his men. By day he was in barracks and at night he visited Elizabeth Robinson, the Nymph. He discovered that he was not without rivals for her affection on the island and it was rumoured that a number of more senior officers had also been visiting her.

Goldie spent as much of his off-duty time up at the farm as he could. He and the Nymph spent many a happy hour in each other's arms in front of Farmer Robinson's living room fire. From time to time on his way he would come across a night patrol but usually he saw no one on his way to and from Deadwood Camp.

Goldie had good reason for passing Mason's Stock House regularly and was able to observe Reardon as he checked the guard on the fencelines at Longwood House. It was more difficult to find an excuse to go down into Jamestown to check up on Marryat and Porteous. The port area was the responsibility of the Navy and the Army's garrison kept away. However, he managed to have himself appointed a garrison victualling officer. This enabled him to visit the food depot on the docks.

Goldie went down once a week and asked the warehouse staff about Porteous's movements. They reported that Porteous was seldom in his office and was out riding across the island most of the week. Porteous had told them that he was carrying out a survey of all the Company's holdings on the island as part of an audit ordered by Bombay.

Goldie was also able to keep a closer check on Reardon who appeared in the Adjutant's office every day. He always seemed interested in the guard rota up at Longwood and, in addition to offering his Pioneers for extra duty - to keep them out of mischief, so he said - he was also keen to help the 44th to become familiar with their role. It appeared that he had befriended Major Dunne, the 44th's commanding officer, and that they were sharing out their duties on an informal basis.

Marryat was often out at sea on the *Beaver* and Goldie had less reason to know of her movements around the island. All he could do was to keep a sharp lookout for Marryat when his ship was in Jamestown and keep his ears open for gossip or strange behaviour.

The wind from the South Atlantic was erratic. Sometimes it blew hard and cooled *The Damned Yankee* above and below decks. More often a stiflingly hot breeze blew off the land that stank of the slaughterhouses on the docks in Buenos Aires.

Patrick had forgotten quite what a stench they made.

Cochrane allowed small parties to go ashore while the schooner remained at anchor off the coast. It had been arranged that when the word came to set off, Marryat would send word to De Melo's offices in the city and Patrick, who was able to land without suspicion, would bring the news back to Cochrane. The crew, trapped on board, were becoming increasingly fractious and Cochrane was not finding it easy to maintain discipline in spite of the rewards that had been promised for their effort.

Patrick had messages for his family and was pleased to go ashore and visit old friends, but there was no news yet from St Helena.

On his third visit to the agency, his father in law met him at the door with a letter in his hand. "This arrived from St Helena yesterday. I trust it is the news that you have been wairting for." Patrick did not open it as it was addressed to Lord Cochrane, but he knew what it would contain, "Thank you, father. Now I must be off. You will not see me for a week or two but when I return I hope that I will have good news for you."

With that, Patrick returned to the port and took the schooner's dinghy back out to the *The Damned Yankee*. He entered Cochrane's cabin and handed him the letter. Cochrane opened it and exclaimed: "Now we have him. Well done, Kennedy. Tell Birmingham, I want to see him at once."

Patrick found Birmingham in the focastle trying to keep cool. They went below together. Cochrane said: "We shall leave on the next tide and sail towards St Helena. It should take no more than ten days. We are to keep below the horizon south-south-west of the island and wait for Marryat's signal. Although the glass is set fair, make certain the *Nautilus* is secure and do some more dry drills on deck. We will need to get in and out fast."

They sailed east for a week and on the eighth day the lookout cried: "Land ahoy" and they could see a smudge of land on the horizon. Cochrane ordered the schooner to turn about and they began to sail up and down on their station.

On the third day they saw a sail about three miles off. When Cochrane looked through his glass he recognised a British man of war. Marryat's instructions now required him to exchange the Stars and Stripes with a red ensign so that the warship's crew would think that they were a merchantman tacking towards Jamestown. He was also to raise a green pennant at his masthead so that Marryat would recognise the schooner as Cochrane's.

Marryat was out at sea for the first of four days' duty and observed the schooner. "They will be in the Roads before us", he told his First Lieutenant, "Lucky devils" and entered the schooner's details into the log.

However, they were back in port earlier than Marryat expected. A sailor complained of severe pain in his abdomen and Marryat used this as his excuse to put the man ashore at once. Late that night the *Beaver* anchored back in Jamestown and Marryat was rowed into port with the sick man. He went up to the boarding house hoping that Porteous would be at home. Mrs Porteous came to the door. "Good evening, Captain. I'm afraid my husband is out. He said that he would be back by ten this evening but there's no sign of him yet. Your room is ready as usual. Have you had supper?"

Marryat went straight to his room and sat down to wait for the sound of Porteous' return. At eleven he heard the front door opening and left his room quietly to go downstairs. Porteous looked surprised. "I thought that you were at sea this week." "I was, but as luck would have it, one of my crew was sick and I had to come back in. I have news. I have sighted the American schooner off shore. She is keeping below the horiozon at present but is disguised as a British merchantman. She's flying the signal pennant that tells us she is ready to carry out the rescue. She won't remain undetected for long so we need to inform Reardon that Cochrane is ready."

"I'll do it in the morning. I need to go to Mason's anyway to look at the gardens up there. I'll tell him then."

After receiving Porteous' news, Reardon went down from Mason's to the barracks at Deadwood. It had become almost routine now that he joined Goldie and Baird each day for their morning tiffin. "Morning James, morning Dandy, all well today?"

Goldie turned towards Reardon and noticed that his eyes were fastened on the operations map. "Actually, old boy, we are running out of troops. The Governor's insistence on extra patrols has exhausted the supply and we have over one hundred men on furlough this week as well as the sick."

"Perhaps I can help you. The Pioneers are always willing to swap leave with duty when offered the right incentive. I'll speak with Porteous at the stores down in Jamestown and ask him to release some fresh beef. That will rouse the men. Even better, we'll offer them a barbecue before they go on watch. I assume you want them for night duty? Dandy, you're the victualling officer at present, aren't you? If you give me a chit I can draw the stores. I'll throw in a few bottles of beer as well.

"Thanks, Theo", Goldie replied, "but make sure they are not found drunk on duty later on. You will have the fence between the cow sheds and the pavilion on the south side of Longwood. You will need at least ten men. On the other side of you will be Dunne's men from the 44th. I know your old soaks don't get on with Dunne's lot so stay well clear of them.

Reardon finished his char and went to find his sergeant.

He found sergeant Flynn in the Armoury. "We are for duty tomorrow night. I will need ten men."

"They will not do it, Sir. We've been on duty non-stop for theee weeks now and the men need a break."

"I know, but this will be the night that we spoke of. Tell no-one but bring a haversack with your essentials. I also want you to pack a corporal's tunic which we will be using for the escape."

"How am I supposed to do that? It's a court martial offence for a man to mislay his uniform."

"You'll have to make something up. Tell your corporal that I have ordered his uniform to be repaired. Say that you will take it down to the tailor's shop for him. Bring it with you tomorrow night. As an incentive I'm offering a beef supper with beer up at Mason's before the men go on duty. That should stop them moaning. Come at six for the food and we'll go up to the line just before eight when the guard changes. Is that clear?"

"Yes, Sir, it is, but if anything goes wrong, my men will be for the firing squad. You know that."

294

"I realise that. You will tell them to say that we threatened to shoot them. Only you and I will accompany Napoleon. Mr Porteous is going to meet us up at Hutts and help to guide us across the island. He knows it better than anyone. Until tomorrow night then."

The same evening Marryat, Porteous and Reardon met back at the boarding house. Marryat explained that he would be going back out to sea on the *Beaver* at first light. He would sail into sight of *The Damned Yankee* and fire a shot ascross her bows, which meant that the vessel should proceeed at once towards Jamestown. This would let Cochrane know that the escape was planned that night and that the schooner should come closer inshore whilst still sailing under a friendly flag. Afterwards, Marryat would head off in another direction on some pretext or another.

Porteous would meet up with the escape party from Longwood at Hutts and then escort Napoleon to the top of the cliffs at Sandy Bay. It would take about an hour and a half. They might need to carry Napoleon on the most hazardous parts of the route.

Marryat took two flares from his coat-tails. "When you arrive on top of the cliffs, light these flares pointing out to sea. They will be the signal for Cochrane to launch the submarine and bring it onto the beach. How do intend to get Napoleon down the cliffs, Reardon?"

"My sergeant will have the tackle with him to make a bosun's chair", Reardon replied. "We will be attaching it around a boulder at the top of the cliffs and dropping him onto the beach. I will go down first, followed by Napoleon and my sergeant."

"Very well. We have done our best. Now it is down to a strong dose of good luck and a dark night."

The three men drank a final toast to the endeavour and went to their rooms.

The following morning Reardon did not go down to Deadwood but instead stayed at Mason's Stock House until eleven o'clock. It was a grey morning with clouds scudding across the island but no rain had fallen yet. He had been watching the routine at Longwood for some time now and knew that it was Napoleon's habit to take his stroll in the garden with Piontkowski at eleven every day.

Reardon left Mason's and went down to the fenceline. Dunne and a party from the 44th were on duty. "Good morning, Major. I trust all is quiet?"

"Indeed it is, Captain Reardon. We have had no sight of Bonaparte this morning. I understand that you will be taking over the guard tonight."

"Yes, we will be arriving at eight this evening from Mason's. I have arranged to give the men their supper before coming on guard. It will be a long night."

Dunne turned away but Reardon stayed where he was and after half and hour he saw the doors of the pavilion swing open and Napoleon stepped out on Piontkowski's arm. Reardon stayed where he was. Five minutes later Napoleon was standing opposite him.

"Good morning, Sire, and how are you today?"

"I am comfortable, thank you. And you?"

"I have heard from my friends in *Angouleme* and they are keen for news of you."

"My news is as before. I should not be here."

"No, Sire, you should not. My men and I will be on duty at this spot tonight and I wish to meet with you then if you would be agreeable. I suggest that you wrap up well; wear a stout pair of boots and be here at ten tonight."

"Do you mean that the time has come to visit my old friends in France? What about Piontkowski here?"

"We are relying on him to create a diversion at the house for as long as he is able. I have no doubt he will manage to rejoin you in due course wherever you may find yourself."

With that Reardon saluted and turned back towards Mason's.

He went down to Jamestown; met with Porteous at his stores where he drew a side of beef and advised him that Napoleon was ready for the escape before returning to Mason's.

At six in the evening the pioneers arrived in the garden. Grant and his friends joined in. By eight it was getting dark. Reardon called his men together to go down to the fenceline at Longwood. None of them were drunk but they had consumed three of four bottles of stout each so their reactions had lost their edge.

The men went in single file and took up their positions around Longwood. Each man was ten paces from his neighbour. Reardon and Sergeant Flynn stood at either end of the file so there was a gap of twenty paces between themselves and the 44th's night duty men on either side of them. The distance should be enough to obscure what would be going on. The lights in the house were lit and they could see the shadows of movement inside. At ten all the lights went out except in the billiard room and Napoleon's bedroom. It grew darker and a light drizzle began to fall. At ten, two shadows appeared at the appointed spot in front of Reardon. It was Napoleon and Piontowski.

There was a shallow ditch beyond the fence and Flynn climbed down into it and made a gap sufficient for Napoleon to squeeze through. Napoleon turned to shake Piontkowski's hand and, bending low, came through. Reardon handed him the corporal's tunic. Napoleon took off his topcoat and threw it back over the fence to Piontowski. The lancer could use the coat as part of his deception back at the house.

There did not seem to be any reaction from the guards on either side and the three men crept away.

18 *Napoleon's Drop*

IT BECAME CLEAR at once that Napoleon was not going to manage on his own. He was unsteady on his feet and his shoes were quite unsuitable for a journey over rough ground.

Reardon and Flynn walked each side of him but very soon had to support him under the shoulders. They moved as silently as they could and headed towards the furthest of Farmer Robinson's fields where Porteous had arranged to be waiting for them.

He emerged from the dark as they came up to the field post and whispered a greeting. "Your Grace," Napoleon did not respond. They set off again.

A few minutes later as they went up the track back towards Mason's Stock House, there was a sudden sound behind them. Before they could move off the path a horse and rider was upon them. The horse took fright in the dark and reared up as the rider drew his sword. It was Goldie who shouted: "Whoa, halt, what have we here," and, when he recognised Reardon, "Theo, what the hell are you doing up here. You're supposed to be on duty at Longwood tonight."

Porteous and Flynn did not stop and hurried on with Napoleon but Reardon turned and, grabbing the horse by its bridle, drew a pistol from his belt. The horse was plunging wildly as he fired and his shot entered Goldie's shoulder. Goldie fell to the ground. The horse ran loose.

They were some way from Longwood and the shot might not have been heard by the men on duty but if the horse ran back towards its stables at the barracks, the alarm would be raised. Reardon looked at Goldie lying on the ground in agony. If he stopped to tend to him, they would be lost. He turned and ran into the dark after the others.

They had now reached higher ground on the slopes of Diana's Peak. The going was becoming increasingly difficult. They were having to carry Napoleon's full weight now. It would take all of Sergeant Flynn's strength to get him as far as Sandy Bay.

There was a faint crack far behind them and, looking back, Reardon could see a blue flare go up from the direction of Longwood. It was the first sign that the alarm had been raised. Goldie's horse must have reached the fenceline. Minutes later Reardon heard the first bugle call. Soon it was joined by others sounding the call to arms as more flares went up from the direction of Jamestown.

Now they were in real trouble. It would take a little time to work out who was the owner of the horse but when it was realised that it was Goldie's, and that he had been up at Hutts Gate visiting the Nymph, the search parties would know the general direction to take.

They had been criss-crossing the island paths towards Sandy Bay for more than an hour now and had come down off the mountain. They were entirely dependent on Porteous's intimate knowledge of their route. The two men took it in turns to help Flynn support Napoleon who was suffering badly. He was very unfit; his breathing was shallow and laboured. His feet were dragging behind him. They would be lucky to make the top of the cliffs.

As they rounded a corner, they saw lights in the distance and heard faint voices. They stopped and crouched in a storm culvert off the path. Napoleon sat heavily on the ground with his head between his knees. Reardon and Porteous spoke in whispers. "It's probably the guard from Castle Rock Point", Reardon said, "they are the nearest troops between here and Longwood and so are likely to be the first in the area. They are gunners manning the battery on the beach. My experience of them is that they are not at all soldierly, especially at night and in the open. What do you think we should do?"

"I think that we should stay off the track and lie low whilst we see in what direction they are heading,", Porteous replied. "If we can get behind them and they go back towards Longwood over the next half hour, we will stand a better chance of reaching our destination. But we haven't got all night. It will be dawn in three hours' time. Napoleon has to be off the beach long before then.

"You're the military man, Reardon, so we'll do as you say but we can't stay here for long."

They watched as the torches pointed aimlessly across the ground to their right. There did not seem to be any sense of urgency from their pursuers. After ten minutes the sound of voices faded away. They rose from their hiding place and moved on. It would be at least an hour before fresh troops could reach this part of the island. The Navy's patrols offshore would be blind until daylight.

Napoleon, strung between them, started coughing violently and it was clear that he would not be able to keep going for much longer. They would need to take a break. They stopped for ten minutes before struggling on.

Half an hour later they saw on the horizon the faintest line of lighter colour and minutes later realised that they were nearing the sea. They would be at the top of the cliffs at Sandy Cove in ten minutes.

There was no sign of any troops nearby but flares and bugles continued to be seen and heard. They would have to work fast when they reached the sea.

When they reached the edge of the cliffs, Porteous took out the flares that Marryat had given him and fired them towards the sea. They were the same blue colour as the Governor's warning flares so should not raise suspicion.

Porteous had brought climbing equipment to the rendezvous at Hutts Gate which the sergeant had carried across the island. He looked more like a Spanish guerrilla fighter than a British soldier. Flynn had a coil of rope off one shoulder and a rope and tackle off the other. The bosun's chair was slung across his back. He looked for a secure object to which he could attach the apparatus. He decided on a boulder and tied a double loop of rope around it.

Flynn took the other end and fitted it in a knot around Reardon's chest and under his arms.

"We'll need to test this before it is used by Napoleon. Are you going to do it, Sir?"

"Yes", Reardon replied. "I've got to help the submarine's crew ashore so it should be me. You and Porteous stay on the top here and help Napoleon down. Then you, Flynn, will come down last. I assume you, Porteous, will make your way back to Jamestown and will be found tucked up in bed beside Mrs. Porteous in the morning if anyone comes looking."

Just as Reardon was about to start his descent, there was a tremendous explosion from the direction of Jamestwon which lit up the night sky to their north east. They didn't know how he had managed it, but Marryat had obviously been as good as his word and had set off a magazine or something similar. It would certainly help to put their pursuers off the scent.

Reardon let himself over the cliff edge and started gingerly down the cliff face. At one point he lost his footing and caught his breath as he swung out over the beach below before bouncing against the cliff face again.

After five minutes scrambling down he reached the beach and stood unsteadily on a small strip of sand. He could hear the sound of the waves washing onto the beach ten feet away. There was nothing to see beyond the water's edge.

Reardon looked back up the cliff and could see Flynn's face peering down at him. Somehow they now had to drop Napoleon onto the beach. He was not going to manage it on his own. They would need to use the block and tackle so that Reardon could take some of Napoleon's weight from below and Porteous and Flynn from above.

Flynn tried to make himself heard above the sound of the wind.

"I'm going to tie him into the chair before we start lowering him, Sir. He'll fall straight out otherwise. You will need to control his rate of descent with this", as Flynn threw a rope down to Reardon on the beach.

"I'll tell you when we are ready so you can take the strain when I say."

Reardon looked up and could see Napoleon being slung out over the cliff top by Porteous but still held firmly by Flynn.

"Begin to let go now."

Reardon began to pay the rope out from the crook of his elbow as he saw Napoleon's body beginning its descent in the chair.

The emperor was not just out of condition, he was feeble and could hardly use his legs to push himself off the cliff face and keep the rope and tackle tight. If it slackened there was a risk that he would drop several feet and be dashed against the cliff face or plunge down all the way onto the beach.

Reardon could see that Napoleon was somehow hanging onto the two ropes above his head and stopping them twisting. The chair was still horizontal.

He was now more than half way down the cliff when Reardon felt a sudden jerk on the rope he was holding. Looking up, he saw that Napoleon had become snagged on an outcrop of rock. He could neither go back up or move safely down.

When Flynn saw what had was happened he started climbing down the cliff. Napoleon was now suspended and immobilised above the beach. At any moment the submarine could appear on shore or fresh troops reach the top of the cliffs.

Reardon watched as Sergeant Flynn lowered himself carefully down until he was face to face with Napoleon.

The sergeant pushed himself away from the cliff and used his hands to pull Napoleon's chair towards him and free Napoleon from whatever had snagged the apparatus.

The rest of the descent was without incident and finally Napoleon, Flynn and Reardon stood side by side on the sand. Napoleon looked shaken and shrunken. Reardon looked up at the cliff top one last time. He raised his arm in salute as Porteous turned and disappeared. They were now quite alone. Reardon turned around to face the sea. There was still no sign of any submarine. Reardon reckoned that they had no more than fifteen minutes before the nearest troops would arrive.

All three men now looked out to sea.

"There, there", whispered Flynn, pointing into the dark.

"There, I saw a light." Reardon followed the direction of Flynn's finger but could still see nothing. Then he saw it, a faint light bobbing on the surface of the sea some thirty yards out.

The light had now risen just above the surface of the sea and was swinging to and fro. The light that was cast shone down onto a black shape that was darker than the surrounding sea. It looked like a whale that had surfaced from the deep after becoming tangled up in a fishing net. A piece of flotation glass must have attached itself to the monster and was giving off the glint they had seen.

But as Reardon watched, the shape took on a more boat-like appearance and he could now see a mast and rigging above the waves.

"It's the submarine, Sir", Flynn whispered and Napoleon turned towards the sergeant and gave a weak smile. "So it is, gentlemen!"

The submarine now moved a little further in towards the beach and Reardon saw the hatch open and a man step onto its narrow deck. The man knelt down and appeared to be fiddling with some rods before Reardon could see that he had erected a small dinghy which he now let down into the sea. The man got into it, took up two oars and started rowing towards the beach.

Reardon and Flynn ran into the water and hauled the dinghy ashore. The oarsman turned around. It was Alan Birmingham who Reardon had last seen on the quay at Jamestowen months ago.

"Hello, old boy. How are you", Reardon said.

"Never mind me", Birmingham replied. "We have very little time. It will be dawn soon and we have to get Napoleon out to the submarine and then transfer him to the schooner. She's waiting two miles off but she can't stay long. The Navy's patrols will be out at first light and then we will be in trouble. Lord Cochrane wants us back on board at once."

"How many can the submarine take?", Reardon asked.

"A maximum of five. There's two crew on board already to keep her steady in the swell. A man called Kennedy is acting as one of the crew. Then there's me plus you three. That's six. We are going to have make two journeys out to *The Damned Yankee* and that's if we're lucky. It's going to depend on how easy it is going to be to get Napoleon aboard. Anyway, we need to move fast now. There is only room for one at a time in the dinghy. I'll take Napoleon first."

It was not clear if Napoleon had followed the whole of this conversation but now Reardon and Flynn took him by the arms and heaved him into the dinghy before pushing it back into the surf while Birmingham took up the oars again.

They watched the dinghy reach the side of the submarine and one of the crew came out through the hatch and held the dinghy steady while Napoleon got out of it. There was a nasty moment when it looked as if it might capsize but Napoleon hung onto a stay. Then they could see him being helped down the hatch and disappearing inside. Reardon and Flynn would be next.

Birmingham turned the dinghy around and came back in towards the beach. At the same time there was a sudden shout from the top of the cliffs. The first of the patrols had arrived.

There was a lot of noise as the soldiers shouted to each and rushed backwards and forwards above them. Flares were lit which cartwheeled down onto the beach illuminating the dinghy which was now completely exposed.

Birmingham kept on going and came onto the beach again. Reardon and Flynn had found shelter under the cliffs where they were out of sight of the marksmen now shooting down at them.

Birmingham shouted and the two men dashed to the water's edge as the fire from above them intensified. Reardon dived into the dinghy as shots spurted into the sand around him. Flynn followed but, as the dinghy began to pull away, Reardon saw that Flynn had been hit. He lay just short of the boat and was bleeding from three wounds in his back. He was dying.

Reardon made to jump back out of the dinghy and haul Flynn into it but Birmingham pulled him back.

"It's no good, Theo, he's done for. We will all be lost if we stay now. Come, help me row us back out to the *Nautilus*.

After a few strokes they were out of the immediate range of the muskets at the top of the cliffs but some rounds were still being fired in their direction churning up the water around them. The submarine was now in full sight and one or two rounds were pinging off its sides.

The two men jumped out of the dinghy onto the deck of the *Nautilus* and a few strides later they literally threw themselves down the hatch to join Napoleon and the rest of the crew below.

It was very cramped inside the submarine. Napoleon half lay on a cushion forward. The two crew and Birmingham sat amidships and began to turn the paddles and Reardon sat in the stern hanging onto the steering column. They still had some way to go before they would reach the safety of the schooner.

The *Nautilus* travelled best on the surface and they made good progress in a south-south easterly direction. One of the crew went on deck to hoist the small sail and remained at the hatch to keep watch. All the men except Napoleon took turns at the paddles. They were now well out of sight of the cliffs.

Suddenly there was a shout from above.

"Ship ahoy!"

Dawn was beginning to break and a three masted ship could be seen on the horizon. It was impossible to know if it was friend or foe but they could not afford to take any chances.

They took down the sail and secured the hatch before blowing the ballast as the *Nautilus* shifted underwater. Birmingham raised the periscope and kept a close watch on the vessel as it passed half a mile off. It looked as if it might be Marryat's *HMS Beaver* sent back out on station from Jamestown but he could not be sure. There was still no sign of *The Damned Yankee*.

After half an hour, the submarine surfaced and they could move faster again. The lookout went back up the hatch and ten minutes later they heard him shout "There's the *Yankee*."

Twenty minutes later they came alongside the schooner and tied up. Napoleon squeezed himself back up through the hatch and onto the deck followed by Birmingham and Reardon.

Peering upwards the they could see the whole of the ship's company leaning over the side to have their first glimpse of Napoleon. The emperor mounted the gangway steps and was met on deck by Lord Cochrane.

"Welcome to freedom, Sire. I trust that you had a satisfactory journey in our secret weapon?"

Napoleon rubbed his hand across his forehead. "I saw that contraption years ago in Paris and it's been a long time coming, your Lordship."

Cochrane introduced Napoleon to his officers and the two men went below together.

Eight days later Reardon and Birmingham stood side by side at the rail of *The Damned Yankee*. Patrick Kennedy joined them. They could smell the heat off the land two miles away on either side of the river. It was very humid. The schooner came to anchor and when the three men turned they saw Napoleon had come up from below and was leaning on the rail looking towards the shore.

"Good morning, Sire, I trust that you have had a comfortable voyage", Reardon said.

"Ah!, it's my good friend *Angouleme*. Well, anything's better than that godforsaken island. I hope Governor Lowe rots there still."

"Indeed, Sire. We shall soon be ashore and you will be able to taste real freedom again."

Soon one of the Buenos Aires lighters approached the side of the ship and Cochrane, Napoleon and the rest of their party stepped into it.

Reardon and Birmingham followed in a second lighter.

Whilst they were still far out in the bay, the two men could hear the noise of the crowd and, as they got closer to the shore, it became louder and louder. Word must have reached the city that Napoleon was amongst the passengers. By the time they had reached the flats and transfered to a cart to be carried across the mud into the docks, the sound was deafening and they could now see and hear its origin.

The last time Reardon had been here it had been during the ignominious evacuation of the Soutie invaders in 1807. Now the two miles of docks and wharves were lined with thousands upon

307

thousands of cheering inhabitants. They made a thick ribbon of colour and noise. There were bands playing impromptu; fanfares sounding and the troops of the Cabildo were drawn up in ceremonial order on the quays.

Napoleon landed at the bottom of the steps opposite the Customs House and, as he reached the top, a huge cheer went up from the crowd as a series of loud booms marked a 21-gun ceremonial salute and fireworks exploded across the city's skyline. The Emperor had returned.

Edward Hazell resigned from his position at the Alien Office and returned to live at his father's estate on Ullswater in Cumberland.

Sir Hudson Lowe was appointed to the deputy-governorship of Ceylon before retiring to England.

Theo Reardon remained in Buenos Aires and went to work for Don Manuel De Melo's import-export agency.

Napoleon was elected the first President of the Republic of the Argentine and two years later visited his brother Lucien Bonaparte at Point Breeze, Philadephia.

Frederick Marryat returned to England and went of half-pay from the Navy. He purchased a farm in Norfok where he wrote stories including his best known novel *The Children of the New Forest*.

Lord Thomas Cochrane led the Chilean Navy to victory over the Spanish Empire.

Dandy Goldie returned to England with the Regiment where he sold out his commission and lived at Stanlake Park serving on the Wokingham Bench for thirty-eight years.

The corporal of the 66th who mislaid his tunic was executed by firing squad at the barracks in Jamestown on May 18th 1819.

The End

Acknowledgements

My INTEREST IN telling this story was quickened when I carried out research for a biography about my father whose first regiment, The Royal Berkshire Regiment (Princess Charlotte of Wales's), formerly the 66th Foot, served as the guard regiment whilst Napoleon was imprisoned on St Helena.

This historical novel is a work of fiction but Robert Fulton *was* the inventor of the world's first submarine; an Alien Office *was* established in London during the Napoleonic Wars and there *was* a boatyard on the Thames at Bray called Messum's.

Emilio Ocampo's book *The Emperor's Last Campaign,* opened my eyes to telling the story of Napoleon's final years in an alternative way and Brian Unwin's *Terrible Exile,* which described Napoleon's imprisonment on St Helena, alerted me to the idea of his escape from the island by submarine.

I should like to thank Tim Rose Price, my beloved cousin and writer; Robin Boon, my delightful pub lunch companion, and his wife Olivia, and Ged Watts, a fellow academic. Each of these has helped me to improve the narrative - as far as they have been able.

I have also appreciated that my family and friends have endured prolonged discussion of this story with me on many occasions over several years.

I should like to record my debt of gratitude to all those who have inspired my love of history throughout my life. They include:

- My maternal grandfather Henry Verey, a classicist, who often discussed my school history projects with me.

- The producers of the BBC Children's Hour radio progamme *Pretty Polly Oliver* to which I listened devotedly each Thursday afternoon as a child in the 1950s. It told the story of a little orphan girl who falls in love with a Sergeant's son, a drummer boy, who she follows to the Peninsular in soldier's disguise. The boy was serving in the 88th of Foot, the Connaught Rangers, one of the most illustrious (and infamous) of Wellington's army.

- The late Brian Rees, Assistant Master, who introduced me to the joys of history as a sixteen-year-old specialist at school and my Headmaster, Sir Robert Birley, who preached history on many occasions from the pulpit of the school's chapel. I have never forgotten his sermon about Lanfranc, Abbott of Bec, who became Duke William's first Archbishop of Canturbury. Sir Robert believed that history is made as much by personality and coincidence as by the sweep of great events.

Finally, as always, I owe a great debt of gratitude to my darling wife, Iola Mary Ashton, who has lent her unfailing support to this project, as for so many others, throughout our long life together.

www.napoleon-on-st-helena.co.uk